Age of Asango
Book I

Matt Russell

Dragon Tooth Press LLC.
PO Box 1353
Claremont, CA
91711
www.DragonToothPress.com
ISBN – 978-1-7328192-4-5

For my wife, Angelique

Chapter 1: The Boy in the Woods

I have heard many refer to Cassian Asango as 'the Heretic,' and claim he is the greatest evil our world has ever seen. This troubles me a great deal. When we first met, I was just a savage in the wilderness while Cassian was a wealthy young lord, yet he still treated me with respect. He could be ruthless and conceited, yet beneath that was a profound sense of compassion. Cassian was the most remarkable person I have ever known, and I shall always call him my friend.

—Kota of the Forest

Kota crouched in silence upon the wet grass as the cool evening air gusted against his skin and the fur on his ears. His silver eyes were fixed upon a large stag forty paces ahead. *His prey.* Slowly, Kota's left hand curled around the grip of his bow while he rolled the shaft of an arrow between the thumb and forefinger of his opposite limb. If he delivered a perfect shot just above the creature's front legs, it would rupture the heart and lungs, and the stag would die quickly, with very little suffering.

Kota had tracked this creature for a full afternoon, catching its scent far back in the forest and following it

as the sun set until it reached the tiny stream from which it now drank. He would savor its flesh, for he had not had meat for days, and he was hungry.

Ever so slowly, Kota set the notch of his arrow against the cord of his bow and aimed, drawing the feather-tipped end back. It was then that his ears twitched. Kota held his breath. Far behind him, a faint clopping noise echoed through the trees. He knew instantly what the sound meant. It was the steady hoof beat of a horse being ridden in his direction, and horses carried the dangerous creatures known as humans.

Kota glanced back over his shoulder, his heart accelerating in his chest. The sound grew louder as brush and dead twigs snapped under the weight of a horse. He looked back at the stag, which pricked its head up and looked around. After a brief instant of hesitation, it darted away. Kota clenched his fangs together in frustration, but he did not dare make a sound. Humans were known to sometimes hunt his kind, and he was alone and only a boy. His eyes scanned about for a place to hide and quickly fixed on a large tree with branches thick with leaves.

Kota returned his arrow to the quiver draped across his left shoulder and slid his right arm through his bow. Without hesitation, he dashed across the wet ground to the tree and called upon his blood. The yellowish, pointed nails on his fingers and toes extended instantaneously into thick, hooked claws as Kota leaped up the trunk. He dug them into the bark to keep his momentum going through quick, agile movements until he was safely up within the canopy. He found his footing on a thick branch and perched, drawing his bow once more and notching an arrow. There he sat silent, invisible, and deadly—as a shamalak should be.

The clopping grew louder and louder until a white horse emerged from the brush carrying what seemed to be a young human male. Kota peered at the boy through the

shroud of leaves and guessed from the smooth, pale features that this stranger was perhaps fifteen or sixteen winters old—two or three winters older than Kota himself. He wore what appeared to be leather tanned to a dark brown and sewn intricately together to fit his form, as well as a white cape that hung off his back and shoulders. Judging by the absence of any other sound behind him, the finely dressed young man was alone.

Kota aimed his arrow at the boy's chest, remaining silent. He had no wish to harm a human, but he would defend himself if necessary. Kota watched as the young man rode his animal in a slow trot closer and closer, gazing around as if looking for something. After a moment, his dark, human eyes shifted upward, seeming to lock upon Kota through the shroud of leaves. The muscles in Kota's shoulders tightened as the boy drew his horse up to the base of the tree and called out: "Hello!"

Kota blinked. He could scarcely believe it was possible that the boy could see him, shrouded as he was in the blackness behind the branches. Humans were said to have far weaker eyes than the shamalak, and it was after dusk no less, yet the young man continued to stare right at him, waiting.

"I no enemy," Kota called out uneasily. His grandfather had been captured and spent many years as a slave to humans and had taught him a great deal of their language, though it felt strange to be attempting to speak it to an actual human.

"I know," said the boy, and there was the slightest touch of humor in his thin face. He held up gloved hands, palms raised and said: "I have no weapons. I am not seeking a fight. I only want to speak with you. Will you come down?"

"I...not..." Kota stuttered, looking around the forest floor and flicking his ears in all directions to listen for danger, "I no trust you."

"I swear to you on the grave of my mother that I mean you no harm."

Kota hesitated. His grandfather had warned him many times that humans were treacherous, yet… the young man had invoked the name of his departed mother. To a shamalak, there could be no stronger oath. Was it the same with humans? There seemed to be no deception in the boy's voice nor his eyes but in fact quite the opposite. Kota could see no weapons on the human except a small, silver-handled dagger sheathed at the belt. As he peered closer at the boy's friendly expression, he decided to take a chance.

Kota slowly climbed down the trunk, letting his hands and feet feel the right places to sink his claws while keeping his eyes on the human. When he got to the bottom, he dropped into a slight crouch and moved one hand to the hilt of the knife sheathed at his waist on his back. Then he stared up at the visitor on the horse.

"My name is Cassian," said the boy, seeming entirely unthreatened by the defensive stance.

Kota studied this new acquaintance in silence. He had never seen a human up close before, and he was startled by how similar in form this boy was to himself. The young man's build and the angles of his smooth face might have belonged to a shamalak youth. There were remarkably strange differences though. The young man had rounded, hairless ears and his eyes had rings of a brilliant green instead of silver. Finally, he smiled with rows of teeth that had neither a pair of fangs at the top nor the bottom.

Finding his voice, Kota said: "I Kota, of Nakawa Tribe."

Slowly and deliberately, Cassian climbed down from his horse and stepped forward, saying: "I have always wanted to meet a shamalak." His green eyes traveled up and down Kota's form, and the side of his mouth tilted up a bit as he added: "You are not quite what I expected."

"What you expect?" said Kota.

"Honestly? A stupid, drooling, hairy brute, barely capable of standing upright," said Cassian.

The frankness of the words surprised Kota. He frowned at the young human. "You think I stupid?"

"Not at all," said Cassian, looking Kota over. His voice was sharp and decisive. "In fact, I find you quite fascinating." He held out a gloved hand. "I am very pleased to make your acquaintance."

Kota peered at the outstretched appendage. It took him a moment to remember about the human custom of 'shaking hands.' The gesture made little sense to him, but he knew well the importance of manners when dealing with strangers. He gave the silent mental command to the claws on his right hand to retract, and they vanished back into his fingertips, leaving yellowish, vaguely pointed nails in their stead. Then, nervously, he reached out and gripped the human's appendage.

"Incredible," Cassian exhaled, turning Kota's hand in his and staring down at the fingertips with a fascinated look in his eyes. He muttered, as if to himself: "primal magic...so beautiful." Then Cassian let go of Kota's fingers and said: "You can let go of the blade you have back there. I have no more desire to attack you than you me."

"How I know I can trust you?" said Kota.

"I never lie," the boy said in a serious tone, "Not ever." His green, human eyes did not blink. So close, Kota could hear the beat of his heart, and it was slow and steady.

Kota paused, then said, "I believe you," and slowly lowered his hand from his weapon.

"Thank you," Cassian said, flashing a grim smile of perfect, white teeth. He cast a slow look around. "Tell me, Kota, are you alone out here?"

"Yes, my tribe four nights walk away," Kota answered, inadvertently gazing back through the trees in the general direction of his village.

"What brings you so far from them?"

"I on . . ." Kota hesitated. His command of the human tongue provided no simple translation for what he wanted to say. He thought carefully and then said: "I on *spirit walk*."

The human's eyebrows rose. "Spirit walk?"

Kota pursed his lips, again struggling with the human tongue. "In Nakawa tribe, boys sometimes sent out to world to . . . find spirit. My father send me. It is important test to live in wild, without help of tribe."

Cassian frowned. "All by yourself? How old are you?"

"I thirteen winters," said Kota. When he saw the surprised look on the human's face, he thought he understood. "Shamalak is different than human. We know how to live in forest, which plants to eat, how to track and hunt and set traps, how to make shelter." With a touch of pride, he held up his finger and let the yellow claw extend fully. "We *made* for forest."

"I suppose you are. How long have you been out here?"

"Two moons," said Kota.

"Two months," said Cassian, gazing outward, as if speaking to himself. "You must miss your family."

"Yes," said Kota, "but I must honor them. My father walked the wild for twenty moons before he return, and his father walk for more than two winters. I not come home 'till I see my spirit, else I shame them."

"What happens when you see your spirit?" Cassian asked. He seemed amused.

Again, Kota frowned, feeling his command of the human language was too weak to explain what he wished. Finally, he said: "Spirit very important to Shamalak people. When I meet my spirit, I will change inside—I become man."

"I see. It must be incredibly lonely."

Kota sighed. "It not so bad. Sometimes Nakawa hunters or shamalak from other tribes come to these grounds to hunt deer or boars. I talk to them, sometimes eat with them or share campfire. The rest of time, forest is my friend. I scared of her at first, but now I like the quiet she give me."

Cassian eyed at him for a moment. "You are one of the most interesting people I have ever met, *Kota of the Nakawa tribe*." He spoke the title with a touch of reverence.

Kota found himself smiling, almost forgetting the danger he was still possibly facing. Even though he had grown used to it, his life was still very lonely, and it was a thrill to speak to a human, especially one that seemed so intelligent and worldly. Kota had long been fascinated with human culture, with their concepts of reading and writing words on paper, their legendary great cities, the enormous structures they were said to erect, and all the magnificent things they built out of wood and metal.

"Why you out here alone?" he asked Cassian.

Cassian's face became soberer. "I am searching for one of your kind. I understand your people are the finest trackers in the world." He frowned. "I was hoping for someone a bit older. Do you happen to know if any of the hunters from the other tribes you mentioned are out tonight?" He glanced around in the darkness.

"I no think so," Kota said. "This not normal hunting ground for any of our tribes. I only see a few in all the time I out here." He took a nervous breath. "Maybe I can help you."

"The help I need is quite dangerous," Cassian said. "I am...hunting a man."

"Hunting?" Kota swallowed. "You going to kill him?"

Cassian hesitated before answering in a somber voice: "Perhaps."

"Why you hunt him?"

"He has done... unspeakable things. He will do far worse if he is not stopped." Cassian took a sharp breath as if breaking from a troubling thought and then looked at Kota. "Can you track a man by scent if his trail is a few days old?"

Kota frowned. "Sometimes. It depends."

The young man blinked at him, seeming hesitant. "If you agree to help me, I would not ask you to do any fighting. I only wish you to help my comrades and I find this man. We shall take care of the rest."

"What is *comrades*?"

"The others I am working with."

"Other humans?" Kota's heart quickened. He might trust one of them, but a group was far more dangerous.

"You would come as my guest and be treated with respect. I give you my word." Again, the intense honesty flashed in the young man's eyes. "I will pay you for your trouble. Feel free to name your price. I expect the task to take a few days."

Kota blinked. He had heard of the human concept of money, but his people had no use for such things. He had everything he needed. His spirit walk had taught him that more than anything else. "No price," he said. "If you go to stop human from doing bad things, I help you because it *right,* and also for friendship."

Cassian peered at Kota for a long moment, and from his expression, Kota felt that he had said something foolish. Then the young man said slowly, "All right, for friendship then. It shall be my honor."

Honor. Kota knew the human word well, and his instincts told him as he looked into the green eyes of his new friend that he was right to trust Cassian. "When do you need me?" he asked.

"Do you mind leaving now?"

"No," Kota said. With his prey long gone he had nothing of importance to do.

"Thank you," Cassian said with a nod. "First we need to get back to my camp. Do you wish to ride with me, or go on foot?"

"Nakawa no ride animals," said Kota.

"As you wish," said Cassian. "Come." Wasting no further time with words, he turned his horse and set it to a brisk trot.

Kota, finding himself compelled to follow, dashed forward, his strong legs propelling him quickly over the dark, uneven ground. He was glad to be moving. The animal skin pants and vest he wore provided minimal protection against the damp chill as night set in. In only a few moments his blood was flowing hot in his veins. Kota had been known for his stamina among the boys of his tribe. He could run for long distances in silent, liquid motion, never breaking, never slowing.

Many questions flooded Kota's mind as they moved through the trees, but he dared not add to the noise the human and his horse were making. The forest was a dangerous place at night. Shamalak knew to move in silence under the moon. He wanted to admonish his new friend, and yet no enemies were attacking them, and Kota had a strange sense that Cassian knew exactly what he was doing, so he said nothing.

They had traveled for perhaps half an hour when Kota detected the light of torches through the trees. He stared anxiously in their direction as three shadowy figures holding long metallic blades emerged from a thick cluster of brush. One of them dashed toward Cassian and said in a stern voice: "I told you not to ride off."

"And if I were one of your soldiers, I might have obeyed you," said Cassian, drawing his horse toward the figure and halting it as they met. He stepped down from the saddle and stared into the eyes of a human much taller than him. "I found us a tracker."

The man turned to look at Kota. Under the black hood, Kota saw a set of deep blue, intricately patterned tattoos. His heart leaped in his chest as he thought of what this might mean, and Cassian turned to him and said: "Yes, Kota, these men are Onkai."

It did not strike Kota at first that Cassian had somehow gleaned precisely what he was thinking without even looking in his direction. His mind was far too focused on the tattooed man. Kota's people told many legends of the Onkai—warriors whose bodies were marked with blessed runes from their goddess so that they could match the terrible strength of the demons they dedicated their lives to fighting. It was said that an Onkai could cave in an enemy's skull with a single blow or run down a wild horse in full gallop without breaking a sweat.

The Onkai peered at Kota for a brief moment, and then back to Cassian. "Does he even *understand* you?"

"This is my friend Kota," said Cassian. "He is quite intelligent and well mannered. I expect you and your men to treat him with every respect you would treat me."

"I see," said the soldier, peering at Kota again.

"Kota, this is Darius. He is the commanding officer of this group."

"H-hello," said Kota, feeling nervous at meeting an Onkai in the flesh.

"Hello," the man said, his dark eyes peering into Kota's as if trying to figure out what he was. After a moment, the commander gestured toward a large bonfire a few dozen paces behind him where many young soldiers sat. "We have plenty of food and drink if you are hungry."

"Yes, Kota, I did frighten away your stag," Cassian said. "That debt must be repaid. Come along." Cassian took his horse by the reigns and walked toward the glowing fire in the distance.

Kota, still feeling overwhelmed, obeyed and followed, distantly registering the smell of cooked meat and the sound of laughter. Cassian led him into the heart of a soldier's camp where some fifteen Onkai, all looking to be seventeen or eighteen winters were sitting around a roaring campfire. The men all looked at him as he came in. Their hoods were drawn back, and Kota could see the deep blue markings traveling from their foreheads down their faces and along the sinew of their necks into what he could only guess to be more magnificent patterns under their black leather armor.

"As I just told Darius, this is my guest and my new friend, Kota," said Cassian aloud to the onlookers. "He is going to help us finally put an end to all this ugly business." Cassian walked over to a large metal pan to the side of the fire and drew the dagger from his belt to skewer a large piece of meat. He turned to Kota and held out the beautiful silver weapon, handle first.

Kota took the food in his hand and then nervously sat on the ground by the fire, eager to converse with the legendary warriors. He smiled at the closest one and said: "It great honor to meet you."

"Heh!" the Onkai chuckled, looking into Kota's eyes. "You can talk!" He was eyeing Kota with great curiosity, a friendly smile on his face.

"Yes, I talk," said Kota, returning the smile. "I no understand you language well, but I try."

The young soldier's grin widened. "You're doing quite well." He held out a gloved hand. "My name is Tovin."

"N-nice to meet you," Kota said, shaking Tovin's hand with nervous excitement.

"Kota's people tell legends of the Onkai," Cassian said. Several of the soldiers cast new glances at Kota, and as they did it registered quite solidly this time that Cassian seemed to know things from his mind. He turned and looked at the young man, and Cassian's eyes met his. "Try not to let it trouble you," he said.

"Is he in your head?" Tovin said. "Gods, that is unnerving, isn't it?"

Kota swallowed. He had never imagined that anyone could know his thoughts but himself. He recoiled a little away from Cassian, and the young man continued to stare at Kota, a calm expression on his face.

"It is not something I can help," Cassian said, and from the quiet pain in his voice, Kota had the sense that he was used to his strange power unnerving people. "Yes, nearly everyone," Cassian said.

"Are you sorcerer?" Kota asked, edging still a little further back. It felt at that moment as though Cassian were staring directly into the most private places of his mind.

"You didn't tell him who you are?" Tovin said, staring at Cassian.

Without breaking his gaze at Kota, Cassian said: "I told him my name. He did not recognize it."

"That must have been quite novel for you." Tovin sighed. The Onkai soldier put a hand on Kota's shoulder and said: "It takes a little getting used to – being around psychics – and Cassian's one of the most powerful psychics in the entire world." A smile played across Tovin's face as he added: "I mean...he's one of the *five points of the star!*"

"He does not know what that is," Cassian said with a sigh. He looked into the fire and said: "I promise you, Kota, I am no threat to you. You asked for my friendship and I shall treat you as a friend. I *never* break my word."

The man called Darius stepped into the circle suddenly and said in a loud voice: "I trust everyone has eaten?"

"Yes, sir," the Onkai soldiers around the campfire all said in varying pitches and volumes.

"Evening prayer!" Darius shouted. Instantly, the men around the campfire set down their plates and utensils and rose. They moved into a straight line in front of Darius, and many other young soldiers followed, appearing from tents and hiding places in the trees that Kota had failed to detect. Within a few heartbeats of Darius's command, around twenty-five Onkai stood shoulder to shoulder in stiff, disciplined poses.

Kota watched in wonder as Darius closed his right hand into a fist and pressed it into the palm of his left hand at the center of his chest. He began to speak words in a language of sharp syllables that Kota did not recognize at all, and after a moment the men proceeded to speak perfect unison with him.

"They are praying in Dhavic," Cassian said in a soft whisper. "It is the language of the holy scriptures of their church. They are asking the Goddess to protect them and help them to defeat their enemies, and to speak for their souls if they die in battle."

Kota looked at Cassian, and he tried to make sense of what he had just learned of the young human. "You sense when I no understand something."

"Yes," Cassian said. He then cocked his head rather suddenly at Darius, who had begun speaking apart from the others again in the ancient language. Cassian was staring at the Onkai captain with an irritated expression, and Kota noted that for a brief moment Darius and all his men cast glances at the young man.

"They are praying for *me,*" Cassian said, rolling his eyes.

"You no want them to?" Kota said.

“I do not see the gods the way they do," said Cassian. There was faint touch of contempt in his voice. "It is a source of tension between them and myself." He sighed and looked up at the stars. "Their hearts are in the right place. They want to *bring me to the light* so that I will not have to be executed by the church, or at least that is their fear."

It took Kota a moment to remember what 'executed' meant, and when he did his heart quickened. "Onkai going to kill you?"

"No," Cassian whispered. "Onkai do not kill their fellow man. Their order dedicates itself entirely to protecting human beings from the dark creatures in this world." Cassian's gaze lowered to the campfire, and his expression grew more severe as he said: "There is another order that also makes use of runes on their skin." Kota heard Cassian's heart quicken as he spoke, and his tone took on an edge of hatred. "They do not protect anyone. These men see themselves as the acolytes of divine justice. They find people they determine to be *sinners* and take them prisoner. Most of the time these poor souls are tortured into confessing to whatever they are accused, but other times... *they are simply killed*." Cassian stared unblinking into the heart of the campfire, as if he were lost in his own words. "That Holy Order is known as the *Nemesai*." The muscles around his right eye twitched as he spoke the name, and, at the same instant, a log in the fire burst with a furious CRACK, sending embers spraying out in all directions.

Kota flinched back as several blazing orange chunks shot at him, but Cassian's right hand whipped up, and the embers stopped dead in the air. "My apologies, Kota," he said in an even voice. He made a subtle motion with his fingers and the burning debris whipped back into the campfire.

Cassian turned to the Onkai. They had stopped praying and were all staring in his direction. "We are fine," he said. His tone seemed to communicate that he had no intention of explaining further. After a brief moment, the Onkai somewhat uneasily returned to their prayers.

Kota swallowed, staring at Cassian. He had never seen magic used before. This young human seemed quite powerful, and that should have been terrifying, but instead the display of anger had somehow made Cassian more like a person and less like a strange, unknowable godling. A thought occurred to Kota amidst his sense of wonder, and he said: "The... *Ne-me-sai* hurt someone you love, no?"

Cassian stared at him for a long moment in silence, and then a bitter smile played across his face. "I do not wish to speak of such things just now. All the same, I am glad you feel more comfortable with me."

Kota hesitated, then blurted: "I no understand what you are. How you see what I think?"

"I do not *see it,*" said Cassian. He seemed relieved at the change of subject and said in a wistful voice: "Have you ever had a dream where you shifted perspective?"

Kota did not understand the question and Cassian, seeming to sense this, said: "A dream where you were one person and then another, changing all the time, sometimes even removing yourself and looking at all the characters in your dream as something outside of them?"

"Ah.... sometime I think," said Kota, straining his memory, "I not always remember dream, but I think I know what you talk of."

"My mind is like that when I am awake," said Cassian. "Pieces of it stretch outward and sink into the consciousness of others. When the connection is weak, all I can sense are emotions, but when I am focused on someone, perhaps someone who interests me, and that person has a thought, I have it too, like it came from my own mind."

"It must be strange," Kota said.

Cassian shrugged. "I suppose it was when it began. Now I cannot imagine perceiving the world in any other way."

"I no understand such things," said Kota. He stared at the Onkai, who were still chanting in Dhavic and said: "I not know as much as a human."

Cassian smirked "I know you do not understand all the words I use, but you are remarkably quick and clever at guessing meaning," he said. "And, for all your ignorance, I very much enjoy talking to you. It is *relaxing*. Most of the people I meet either want something from me or are afraid of me."

"I afraid of you," said Kota with a smile.

"Not really – not the way most people are," Cassian said, and he looked into Kota's eyes and said: "I can trust you. I knew that before I called out to you in the forest, and I swear on the souls of my parents that you can trust me."

"I trust you," Kota said, deciding this as he said it.

"Thank you," Cassian said.

Neither one of them spoke for a time. They sat by the fire and listened to the Onkai pray in their strange language. As Darius spoke the final alien words and the men broke apart, Cassian said: "The one we are hunting... we believe he is a nathret. Do you know what that is?" Before Kota could answer that he did not, Cassian spoke again: "It is a sorcerer who has consumed the blood of a demon."

Kota swallowed. His people rarely spoke of demons, though the stories they did tell were fantastic and terrible.

"I thought you should know," the young human whispered.

"Is... *nathret* very strong?" Kota said.

"Stronger than a normal sorcerer," Cassian said with an absent shrug. "His name is Grodus." He looked up at Kota, a troubled half grin on his human face. "He was one of my teachers."

Kota considered this information for a moment, then said: "Why he drink demon blood?"

"Because of me," Cassian said in a low voice, "at least to some degree. Grodus was a very arrogant man, and... my talents with magic made him very jealous." He put a hand on Kota's shoulder and said: "I need to rest now, and I think you should too, after you eat. You can sleep in that tent when you are ready." He gestured to the farthest right in a line of strange animal skin tents. "I will tell them to set up bedding for you. Goodnight, Kota, *my friend.*" The worry was gone from his face.

Kota smiled. "Goodnight, Cassian."

The young sorcerer stood and walked toward one of the middle tents along the rim of the fire pit. As Kota watched him go, his mind raced through everything he had just witnessed. No shamalak he had ever heard of had helped the legendary Onkai on one of their hunts, let alone befriended someone like Cassian. This was the most thrilling night of his life. He could hardly imagine sleeping. Instead, he gazed up at the stars as his imagination began to run wild at all that the next day might bring.

CHAPTER 2: THE SLAVE MARKET

My father lived in a time when ethereal gods and demons were waging a great war. He was caught between both sides, and in this, he was not alone. The invisible threads of destiny over many were being manipulated as each force moved and concealed its pieces from one another in an elaborate game of strategy to decide the fate of the world. It is perhaps for this reason that some of the most important people in our history were found in the most unexpected places.

—Lilliana Asango

Iona stood near the center of the slave cage, her bare toes clutching at the dirty straw beneath her feet. She was frightened, and yet utterly fascinated by the cacophony of sounds in the marketplace around her. People with differing shades of skin were speaking in different languages to one another. The wonderful smells of freshly baked bread and freshly cooked meats of an enormous variety made her stomach churn with hunger. Iona had never been to a large city before. There were people and buildings and market stands in every direction. Some stopped to look at her and the other slaves through the bars, while others passed by without even a glance.

Iona's heart was fluttering in wonder about who in this great city might buy her. Most likely, she would be sold to a well-to-do family, and she would need to learn to speak, dress, and act like a city slave. The slave-master had told her she was an excellent age for such things. Iona did not know her exact age, of course. Few slaves did. For the purposes of sale, she had been determined to be eleven, and this seemed a reasonably safe estimate based on what she remembered.

"Don't smile, girl," a thin, wrinkled man in stained, tattered, ash-colored rags said from her left. Iona turned and looked into his nervous eyes. "If you smile, they'll think you have too much... *personality*. Gaze down and look obedient."

"Yes," said short man to her right who was also dressed in rags. "You aren't going to be somebody's *daughter*. Don't look anyone in the eyes unless told to do so."

"I-it's just that I've never seen a big city before," Iona said nervously. She took a few slow, clinking steps toward the cage bars. Walking was extremely difficult at the moment, as her legs had been shackled together.

"Gods, get away from the bars!" the first slave said. "The buyers are already starting to look at us."

Iona saw a tall, broad-shouldered man in black robes with thick, golden rings on his fingers looking her over from head to foot. "Hey, girl," he said, his dark, serious eyes gazing into hers, "have you been trained as a cook?"

Iona started to answer, but the slave master—an enormously fat man with a thick black mustache and chin beard—moved from around the cage and said: "This girl is a trained cook and she can do laundry as well. You will never find another wrinkle in your clothes again if you buy her!" He reached out and pinched the man's tunic and pulled at a large crease between his thumb and forefinger and grunted: "I think you could use a good laundry slave." He let out a deep-throated laugh.

The thin slave to Iona's right hunched forward on his knees. "If it please you, master, I was considered to be one of the finest chefs in Aloria." He spoke with enthusiasm, though his eyes remained downcast.

"They have slaves in Aloria?" the tall man said, casting a suspicious frown.

"Not as you do here, master. A man can only be a slave for ten years at a time in Aloria, and then he is granted his freedom by law." The thin fellow smiled down at the cage floor. "I was taken as a slave when my city was conquered, and I was but five. I gained my freedom at fifteen and sold myself for another ten years to serve as a cook in the palace."

"Hmm," the tall man grunted. "What city or tribe did you hail from?"

"Donkest, master."

"Huh," the tall man grunted. "Can you read and write at all?"

The slave grinned. "I know the full Denigoth alphabet, and I can read and write most words you can name. I also learned quite a bit of what is called *geometry*. I managed to pick up a wide breadth of history, my lord, though much of it is focused on Aloria's past."

"Might be useful in the education of my children," the tall man said, looking thoughtful. He turned to the slave master. "What price do you ask, understanding that this man is at least forty?"

"Thirty-three at the oldest," the slave master said with a chuckle.

The tall man's eyes grew irritated. "This slave is well over forty. I will buy him for three hundred desseks."

"I beg your pardon, sir," the slave master said, his smile stiffening. "This man is worth seven at the very least. He can *read and write*! I could sell him to a senator as a secretary for close to a thousand."

The tall man stroked his chin, his eyes moving up and down the slender man's frame. "Five hundred," he said.

"Six hundred else I suggest you look elsewhere."

"Five-fifty."

The two men faced each other for a moment with dark and severe expressions. Then the slave master said: "Five-eighty is my final offer, and you must do the deal right now."

"Agreed," the tall man said, and he reached down and retrieved a small leather pouch from his belt that clinked as he gripped it.

The slave-master gestured to the small wooden shack to the left that functioned as his office. "Go count the money and we will make the contract." As the tall man walked away, the slave master turned to Iona. "You! Do *not* meet the eyes of the buyers, *idiot girl,* if you wish to continue to *keep* your eyes!"

Iona took a deep breath and lowered her gaze to the filthy straw floor of the cage, muttering: "S-sorry, master." She knew that he would not do anything to her eyes. A crippled slave was an extremely difficult thing to sell. Still, she was afraid of him.

"That's better!" the man grunted, his tone softening. "Just like that."

"Yes, I understand, sir," she said in a small voice.

After the master walked away the thin slave patted her on the back and said: "Try as hard as you can to get in as a house slave for a rich family. You don't want to be in a laundry-house." He cringed suddenly and looked around, then leaned in very close to her ear and whispered, "And be very careful you don't get snatched up by a brothel master or mistress."

Confused, Iona whispered back: "What's a *brothel*?"

"Oh gods," the thin man said, dropping back into a seated position on the straw. He seemed to think for a moment, then said: "If someone asks you if you have any diseases in...your *nether region,* whisper that you have dozens of sores filled with pus."

"Why would I say that?" she said, more confused than ever and a little alarmed.

"Please just trust me. I have been a slave a very long time, girl."

"A-alright," she said.

"Girl, turn around," a deep, feminine voice boomed very suddenly from behind.

Iona spun around so quickly that her tangled brown hair spread and whipped in the air. Perhaps the most massive woman she had ever seen was staring at her with an appraising frown. Her bust spilled out from the white linen dress over which she wore a richly embroidered deep blue coat, though Iona immediately spotted several places where the stitching in her clothes was wearing out. Her hair, which was dyed to an almost overwhelming red, was done up in thick, tightly wound curls. This woman glared at Iona with eyes caked in dark paint and said in a very commanding voice: "Come here. Let me see you."

Iona obediently walked to the edge of the cage. The woman reached out with a puffy hand and gripped her rather abruptly by the jaw and turned her head from side to side. "Show me your teeth," she said.

Iona drew back her lips, and the woman peered for a moment and muttered: "Good, I cannot *stand* a disgusting mouth!" She released Iona and then said: "Hervin, come here."

A round man somewhat shorter than the woman walked over from a meat stand and stood next to her. He had a bald scalp with flowing brown hair from the sides of his head that draped over his shoulders. Iona's eyes lingered on his for a moment, despite the slave master's warning. *They were kind eyes.*

Between this pair stepped a slender girl perhaps three or four years older than Iona. The girl glanced up with an inscrutable expression, and Iona was taken aback by how pretty she was. She had beautiful golden hair that was tied back in a long braid behind her back. She had alert, intelligent blue eyes, and Iona might have thought her an aristocrat except that she wore a simple, tattered gray dress. It took a moment before Iona spotted the blue line tattooed onto the graceful neck and realized that this girl, like herself, was a slave.

"I told you I wanted a young girl," the massive woman said.

"Can she cook?" the man called Hervin asked. When the thick woman did not answer, he turned to Iona. "Do you know how to cook anything, child?"

Remembering to keep her eyes lowered, Iona replied: "I know how to bake bread, master. I can make apple pie if you can get apples. I know how to boil eggs. I can pluck and cook a chicken. I—"

"Do you know how to make cakes or other sweets?" the large woman said, interrupting.

"I have made marzipan. I did not taste it myself, but my mistress was very pleased."

"*Marzipan!*" the enormous woman said, a wide grin playing across her thick, red-painted lips, her large fists banging together in front of her chest. "I haven't had marzipan in years!"

"Where did you come from, child?" Hervin said.

"From North Cranton, master. I belonged to Countess Aldaisha."

The large woman bounced on her feet. "And she has experience serving nobility!" She reached out and cupped Iona's chin again and tilted her face up so that their eyes met. "I, myself, am of extremely noble birth."

Feeling unsure of what to say, Iona muttered: "I... it is my honor to stand before you."

"There!" the thick woman said, drawing her hand away and looking at Hervin. "*That* is how a proper slave behaves." She glanced down at the pretty blond girl, her face filling with disgust. "It will be nice to have a slave who knows her place—especially one who can actually SPEAK!" She gave her slave a sharp open-handed slap to the back of the head. The lovely girl jerked forward, and her hands shot out and gripped the bars of the cage to steady herself. Her eyes went wide with a rage that almost made Iona gasp. She took several deep breaths through her thin nose, and then stood up, her face locked in sullen, silent anger.

Hervin, who seemed somewhat troubled by the slap, looked at Iona. "Why did the countess sell you, child?"

"She died, master," Iona said, and for a moment her throat swelled with sadness. "Her son decided to sell her estate. Most of us—um, her servants that is—were sold to slave traders."

"This girl knows how to run a fine house, Hervin," the fat woman said. "*I want her*." The statement seemed somehow to be a command.

"Yes," Hervin muttered with a nod, and Iona's felt a tingle of excitement. This was to be her new family—*so much as slaves had families*. Hervin walked over to the slave master, who looked to be finishing the contract with the first buyer.

"You are going to make my life so-o-o-o much easier, child," the large woman said. She looked Iona up and down and said: "What is your name, girl?"

"Iona, mistress."

The woman stroked her puffy chin. "No family name?"

"No, mistress. I don't know who my parents were."

"Well, no matter," she said with a shrug. "My name, since you should know it, is Merith Sondal. You may address me as mistress, as you have correctly been doing, or Lady Sondal. Is that clear?"

"Yes, Lady Sondal," Iona said.

The large woman grinned. "Yes, you say it beautifully. You have no idea how frustrating it has been dealing with a slave who can't even speak." She glared at the blond girl, whose eyes narrowed in anger in return. The two stared at each other for a brief instant, and then the pretty slave turned from her mistress and walked over to Hervin, who was already deep into negotiations with the slave master.

Lady Sondal's eyes angrily followed the girl. "*That* poor excuse for a servant is named *Livia*. You will be replacing her in many household duties, Gods be praised. Perhaps I'll even be able to be rid of her once you are trained."

Hervin returned a moment later with a grim look on his face. "Well, we have her," he said with a sigh. "Eight hundred desseks!" He gave a frustrated shrug.

"Well, she's young," Lady Sondal said with a dismissive sweep of her hand. "She will serve us until we die."

The cage opened from behind, and the slave master walked with his large iron key over to the thin slave who had been purchased before Iona. He removed the shackles. "Go to your new master." The slave stood up and nodded with a smile and walked down the steps to his new master who stood waiting at the bottom. Then the slave master walked to Iona and looked at Hervin and Lady Sondal through the bars, saying: "I forgot to ask. Do you want the chains off?"

Hervin looked at Iona through the bars and gave her a kindly smile. "You will not run away on us, will you?"

"No, master," Iona said, shaking her head.

"Take them off," said Hervin.

The slave master removed Iona's shackles, and she took a few seconds to rub her sore ankles before standing. Then she moved over the old straw and down the steps onto the stone tile street. There was a little wave of nerves as she walked around the cage and presented herself to her new owners. Just like that, in the span of a few moments, her fate had been decided. Feeling compelled to remain in the good graces of this couple, Iona approached the family and made a low bow, saying: "I thank you for buying me. I will try very hard to please you."

"Hmm!" Lady Sondal grunted in a tone that sounded approving.

"This way, dear," Hervin said. Iona walked with this strange family out of the town square, to a long row of stables where dozens of tied up horses were being cared for. Hervin moved to a large green wagon attached to two black horses that looked a bit old and weather-worn compared to some of the other animals. He held out his hand and Lady Sondal—with no small difficulty—climbed up into the front of the cart. He hoisted himself up and took a seat next to her and took the reins, then said: "Alright girls, take your seats in the back."

Livia immediately walked to the rear of the cart and sat down. Iona followed behind her, suddenly feeling a little intimidated by the older, taller girl. She climbed up into the wooden bed of the cart and took a seat opposite Livia with her back against the sidewall. Hervin cast a quick look over his shoulder at the two of them and then snapped the reins.

The cart began to move somewhat shakily over the ground, and Iona's small body bounced with it. As they rode along, she smiled at the Livia and said: "I hope you and I will become good friends."

Livia stared at her. Her blue eyes were cold and hard. She just looked at Iona for a long time as they bumped and bounced along the road together, never seeming to blink. Iona felt a little frightened of this strange girl who did not seem to speak. After a few moments, she said: "I... I'll be happy to follow your lead in the household."

Livia's eyes narrowed. She reached suddenly into a small pocket on the side of her skirt and drew out a square slip of papyrus paper that seemed to have several things written on it that had been scribbled out. She drew a crude, charcoal pencil from the same pocket and then she flattened the paper against the floor of the cart and found an empty space on the paper and wrote three words in beautiful handwriting:

Can you read?

"Oh! Yes!" Iona whispered excitedly. "I mean I can *a little*. One of the slaves in my old house was the countess's secretary. He taught me in the evenings."

Something in the sullen girl's expression softened at this. She scribbled out what she had written and then found another empty space and wrote:

You seem very nice. Be careful of
the fat cow. She likes her whip.

"*Fat cow,*" Iona whispered, and her eyes traveled to the back of her heavy new mistress's head. Lady Sondal was barely more than an arm's length away.

Livia snatched back her paper, methodically scribbled out what she had just written, and then found an empty space on the paper, in which she wrote:

Don't worry, she can't read.

Livia hesitated, staring at Iona, and then she gave the slightest hint of a smile. Then she put her paper on the floor of the cart and delicately wrote in tiny letters in the last empty space on the page:

I am pleased you can understand me.

Iona smiled at the fascinating silent girl. Livia seemed far too beautiful to be anyone's slave. She looked the way Iona imagined a princess might look. There was perhaps a little ray of hope in the life that lay at the other end of this wagon ride. Whatever was there, Iona thought perhaps she might have a friend.

CHAPTER 3: THE FORGOTTEN CITY

We call the starborn 'Living Miracles,' and for many purposes they are. Generation after generation, they have bettered the human world. They have furthered knowledge, cured disease, and more than once they have pulled the human race back from the brink of extinction. Their command over magic and nigh-omniscient telepathic gifts make them seem as gods, so much so that we sometimes forget that beneath it all they are merely human, and thus subject to human failings.

—Bishop Cromlic of the Nemesai Order

Kota clung to the horn of his saddle as the black mare beneath him galloped wildly over the uneven ground. He had never imagined he would actually ride a horse, but Cassian had convinced him that he needed to save his strength for the coming hunt. The sun had just been rising when they had set out over the winding mountain terrain, and now it was in the middle of the sky, beating down hot summer heat on Kota's back. In those hours, Kota had made almost no progress as a rider other than a clumsy understanding that the strange leather "reins" as the humans called them, could be pulled to make the horse turn and stop, or snapped to make it run. But Kota did not desire to make a horse do anything. He was hesitant, and the beast seemed to sense this and was in turn reluctant to obey him.

Riding a horse just felt wrong. Kota loved the feel of stone and dirt and roots beneath the thick pads of his feet.

He thought on this as he watched the Onkai soldiers dart and weave about on their mounts. They were so at ease that they played games with one another on the road, tossing and catching spinning blunted daggers in the air back and forth. Their reflexes, Kota had noted, were far quicker than those of the finest warrior in his tribe.

Cassian rode nearby with his eyes held closed and his hands hanging loosely at his sides, yet Kota had the sense that the young man was still guiding his horse. Kota could not remember if his friend had so much as looked around since they had set out. The strange young man that the men seemed to refer to mostly as 'the starborn' had said very little to Kota throughout the day. "*I need to concentrate,*" had been the last words he had spoken, and that had been early in the morning. Still, the Onkai had been wonderfully friendly. Kota had barely even minded when Udan, a tall soldier with a very neat chin beard, had asked him if some of his ancestors had mated with wild animals. "We ancient people," he had answered.

The sun was on its descent when they approached a cliff. "All signs of dark magic lead here," said Cassian. He rode his horse up to the edge and gave a loud chuckle. "I see. It looks as though they did not wish outsiders to find this place." Kota caught up to him and stared down into a deep basin within the mountain of jagged rocks and ghastly looking thorn bushes. The cliff on which they stood was incredibly steep, with no visible stepping-stones or other means by which to descend, but there was only lethal danger. Kota's eyes traveled all over the valley, scanning for anything that might have caught Cassian's attention, but he saw nothing but a vast pit of rough stone and ghastly thorns.

"He went down *there*?" Darius exclaimed as he caught up to the two of them.

"You as well?" Cassian said with a sigh.

"What?" Darius said.

"Tell me, what do you see? Snakes? Thorns? I had understood that Onkai soldiers received training to overcome mental magic."

"Mental—" Darius paused, gazing at the enormous pit of thorns. Several of his men joined him when he suddenly exclaimed: "Gods, are you saying this is a veil?"

"The largest one I have ever seen," Cassian said, sounding amused. "The elvin people can produce truly staggering enchantments."

"This *isn't* a valley of thorns?" Tovin said, sounding at least as confused as Kota felt.

"No, it is a constructed illusion that still stands centuries after everything else here was destroyed," Cassian said. "Let me help you see through it."

Cassian closed his eyes and pressed two of the gloved fingers on his right hand against his forehead, just above his eye. Several breaths later, the image of the thorn valley shimmered all about as if it were a reflection upon the face of a swishing lake. Then it seemed to tear in many different places at once, revealing a completely different image. Kota was suddenly staring down at a crumbling stone stairway into overgrown ruins of hundreds of buildings. Some of them were very small, but others stretched as high as mountains. There were strangely angled structures ending in intricate patterns of what Kota would later learn were '*domes*.'

"These are the ruins of the legendary elvin city of Ilnethice—at least that would be my best guess," Cassian said, his eyes traveling all over the valley.

There was silence all around for a moment as Kota and the men gaped at structures and marveled at the astonishing magic that could conceal an entire city. Kota's people had few legends of the immortal elvin people, but they were whispered of as beings with incredible power.

"You're sure he came here?" Darius finally said.

Cassian's eyes narrowed at the city below them. "I can feel traces of the putrid demonic magic he threw around this place." In a lower voice, he added: "He must have known I could follow the tracks he laid."

Darius drew in a nervous breath. "Why would he come here?"

"Grodus was obsessed with elvin talismans," Cassian said. "He mentioned this city to me several times, though he said he could never find it." Cassian sighed and headed his horse down the hillside toward the forgotten city. "I cannot feel him, but that does not mean he isn't here. Either way, Kota should be able to find his scent."

The group made it down the grassy hill at the edge of the ancient ruins and Kota was relieved to leap from the horse's back. As soon as the pads of his feet touched the ground, he felt like himself again.

"Tie the mounts," Darius said as he dismounted. "We are all going down."

The men tied their horses to a small cluster of trees and then gathered their gear. When everyone was ready, they began walking down the broken steps. After a little way, Cassian said: "The Obsidian Guild is going to be quite excited that we found this place. I suspect they will spend the next decade excavating it."

Kota looked around. The city was in a vast valley surrounded on all sides by mountain ridges. It must have been profoundly beautiful when it had been whole. Far below, he could see richly detailed statues he suspected were made of metal, as they appeared to be rusting in places. He felt a deep reverence for what he was looking at as he asked: "What happen to this city?"

"According to legend, Daibok and his army slaughtered everyone here roughly four hundred years ago," Cassian said.

"Who Daibok?" Kota said.

"The Demon King," Darius said in a grim voice.

"Daibok must have told Grodus where to find this place," Cassian muttered.

"Can you sense anything?" Darius said to Cassian.

"I still do not sense *him*. I can tell that extremely dark spellcraft was conducted here recently, but it... confuses my perceptions." They went a little farther and came to an intersection of stairs. Kota saw that the steps spider-webbed in many directions going up but travelling down there were fewer and fewer paths. "This is a good place to begin," Cassian said. "Kota, hopefully your senses are not as clouded as mine. See if you can detect any recent scents on these steps."

"Yes," Kota said. He bent down and sniffed at the white stone. His nose caught many distinct smells upon it, some seeming to have come from small animals, yet others coming from much larger creatures. He slowly dissected and categorized each scent, and several began to stand out. "I think I smell leather boots like all you have. There also smell of sweat from something not human." He turned and looked at his comrades, feeling more than a little frightened. "I think...ogres walk these steps. I no tell how many, but more than one."

"Grodus has ogres at his command?" Darius growled.

"Kota, does the scent seem to grow fresher going up or down?" Cassian said.

Kota sniffed around, moving several paces in each direction and inhaling at the stairway. After a few moments, he said: "I... I think stronger going down."

"Weapons out," Darius said in a sharp voice.

There was a quick flurry of metal scraping against metal, and some twenty-five swords snapped out of scabbards. Kota stared into the tattooed faces of the young soldiers. They bore the expressions of seasoned warriors, grim and focused.

"He should not be able to hide such simple-minded beings as ogres from me, but then gods know what powers Daibok granted him," Cassian said. He looked at Kota. "I want you to follow the scent into the city but be ready to run when I tell you. And if I do, run to the horses, take one, and go back to the forest. Do *not* look back. Is that clear?"

"Yes," Kota said.

"One other thing." Cassian reached behind his back under his cape and drew the strangest knife Kota had ever seen. It was not made of metal, but rather a strange bluish crystal. The blade was a little longer than a dagger but not quite so long as a sword. Cassian held the weapon out to Kota, handle first, and Kota noted that the hilt seemed to be carved bone, though the bone of what he could not say. "Take this, Kota, and be extremely careful with it. It will cut into more or less *anything*." Kota nervously reached out and took the weapon. It seemed to hum just a little in his hand when he touched it. Cassian undid the fastenings of his belt and then slid off a beautifully carved bone sheath that matched the handle. "Tuck this into your pants."

"T-this too great a weapon for me," Kota said, holding a hand up in protest.

"I do not have time to argue with you," Cassian said, frowning. "Take it. Use it only if you need to." He spoke with such authority in his voice that Kota could only nod and obey.

Cassian turned back to the men. "If the old texts are to be believed, elvin cities are constructed with great underground vaults. There could be hiding places anywhere."

Darius glanced at his men and commanded: "When we get to the bottom form double rank, with Cassian, Kota, and myself at the center." The soldiers nodded, and Kota led them down the stairway. As soon as they were on the floor of the city, the Onkai darted into tight formation.

Kota continued to track. The city floor beneath his feet was made of large, smooth slabs of cream-colored stone. Plants had grown up between the squares and through small cracks everywhere, but even with that Kota had the feeling that he was not in the wild. The enormous structures with all of their sharp, precise angles and the lovely engravings in the stone everywhere of symbols he did not understand filled him with a sense of endless awe. Were he not in such danger, he would have stood and gaped for hours or even days at the incredible city.

The further he went, the stronger the scents grew, and the trails began to separate and cross one another. The city was enormous, which made Kota wonder about the thousands upon thousands of smooth flat stones that had been carved to make its streets. How many hundreds of years had it taken to create this magnificent place? How terrible then was its destruction? He felt some inner part of himself sicken as he ventured on.

"Many ogres stand right here," Kota finally said, gesturing around a large open square between the buildings. "I think not too long ago."

Cassian took in a very sharp breath suddenly, and Kota turned to see his friend's eyes close. The boy stood perfectly still for a few seconds and then whispered: "Kota, it is time for you to go. Run! *Now!*"

Kota cast a quick look around, but he neither saw nor heard anything. Still, he had learned enough of Cassian to obey, and he shot instantly into a hard run back the way he had come. Behind him, he heard Darius say in a sharp voice: "Be ready!"

Kota was fifty paces or so away when he caught Cassian's voice in the distance saying: "We are surrounded." Kota froze. His warrior's heart began to thunder in his chest. He turned slowly and looked back at his new friends, and as he did, he heard movement in many corners of the city—what sounded like the footfalls of enormous creatures.

It was not right to leave them! In that incredibly brief moment, Kota understood something of himself he had never known, and he knew he had to stay near because these brave and noble men were going into battle, and a moment might come where he could help them. *That was worth risking his life.*

He looked around and saw a large building with an open window on a second floor that overlooked Cassian and the others. Without a second thought, he turned and bounded through the open door and up the vine-covered steps to the open window where he crouched and looked out at his friends.

Cassian stood close to the Onkai, his eyes closed. He spoke in a tense, quiet voice that Kota's ears strained to hear: "He has managed to enthrall an entire tribe of ogres. This was a trap, and I failed to see it!" He glared around and said aloud: "I can feel you watching me! Show yourself!"

A tall man in a black cloak appeared from nothingness before Cassian. Kota felt an immediate revulsion as he looked at the figure. His skin had a sickly, unnatural brownish-yellow color to it, and as Kota peered, he saw thick purple veins on the man's bald head. His eyes had gone completely white, and yet somehow, they still conveyed hatred. He was an elderly human from the look of his long, gray beard and the wrinkles in his unnatural skin. The man, *or creature,* gritted his teeth nervously at Cassian, and from the way he breathed in loud, deep hisses, he seemed utterly crazed. Kota thought that he had never seen anything so horrible in all his life.

"You should choose your words very carefully, Asango," the figure said in a voice that sounded something like metal scraping against metal.

Darius leaped forward and swung his sword faster than Kota had ever seen anything move, but his blade passed through the man as if he were not there.

"I find it very strange the company you have brought here," the image said, not even looking at Darius. "I would never have expected *you* to ally with the church. Do you not hate them for what their brothers did to your family?"

"You actually *consumed* Daibok's blood," Cassian said. There was a terrible fury in his tone.

"Indeed, I did, and it has transformed me beyond anything I ever dreamed." A vicious smile crossed his horrid face. "I have been waiting for you. There are many things I wish to show you once I slaughter these imbeciles."

"Why couldn't I cut him?" Darius said.

"He is not actually there," Cassian said. He raised his hand, and the old man's form shimmered and then disappeared for an instant, the way the image of the city had done. "An illusion of this degree could only be the result of elvin enchantment," Cassian said, turning to Darius, and then he gazed back at the phantom and added: "You found an Elokien."

Grodus nodded and reached into his cloak, drawing out something small and golden attached to a thin chain. "I have spent most of my life searching for one of these marvelous little things," he hissed as he gave the necklace a small tap, and his image vanished and reappeared an arm's length from Cassian. "You are *completely* at my mercy."

The demonic figure raised his free hand, and the sound of many heavy feet pattering on the stone floor came echoing against the walls from all around. Between the buildings, gray figures began to appear. Kota trembled in his hiding place. These ogres were more massive than any he had ever seen. They stood almost twice as tall as the tallest man in the Onkai troop and more than twice as broad. Some held crude, tremendous swords in their meaty hands, while others brandished great wooden clubs with ghastly iron spikes sticking out at odd angles.

Shamalak did not fight ogres unless they outnumbered them ten to one, and even then, there were often casualties. Their thick skin was like armor. They were cruel, immensely powerful killers. Kota watched in terror as more and more of them appeared. He counted fifty, then sixty, then seventy.

"I would like you to come and speak with me while my army cuts your associates to pieces," the phantom said. He gestured to his left, and two dark metal doors in the ground swung open, revealing a stairway that led downward into some dark, hidden place that seemed to be distantly lit by the red glow of fire.

Cassian took in a slow breath. "I have to go."

Darius grabbed him sharply by the shoulder. "What are you talking about? You cannot let him divide us!"

"He has six children down there, all younger than Kota. He is going to slit their throats if I do not do as he says. It will be blood magic and human sacrifice."

"It's a gods-damned trap!" Darius snapped.

"Yes, it is," Cassian said in a tense voice, "but I still have to walk into it. With the blood of six innocents, Grodus can unlock... *terrible magic*—more than I can protect all of you from. He waited to kill them until we arrived." Cassian lowered his gaze to the city floor and said: "I am sorry, Darius. This was planned—all of it was a trap to lure me here and then separate me from you. Grodus wants to take me back to his new master."

"And you are just going to step into his hands?"

"No choice."

Through gritted teeth, Darius said: "No one's seen a demon sorcerer in nearly *fifty years!* There is no telling what he is capable of—not to mention whatever gods-damned elf relics he's found!" Darius looked around at the ogre army. They were glaring at him with their dark, empty eyes.

Cassian grabbed the captain's shoulder. "I can overcome whatever he has waiting for me in that vault, and when I do, I should be able to break his hold over these brutes. You need to stay alive until that happens." He hesitated, then said in an especially tense voice: "Darius, there is a kothla demon here. I can feel it lurking around. I am sorry, but if I do not come back out of that chamber, you are all going to die."

Kota thought he could see the skin on Darius's tattooed face go pale. For a brief moment, he did not speak but just stood there blinking. Then the captain stiffened. "Nothing to do but fight then," he said.

"Nothing at all," Cassian said. He held out his hand and said: "Good luck."

"Good luck, starborn," Darius said. He grasped Cassian's hand and gave it a firm shake. Then Cassian turned and walked down the stairway, a cold, focused look on his face. Kota watched in wonder at his courage. When he disappeared, the phantom vanished.

"Are you ready to die for your people, men?" Darius shouted.

"YES, SIR!" the soldiers shouted in unison. Kota had never witnessed such heroism, and it moved him. He would remember this moment for all his life... *if he lived.*

A lone ogre charged first, raising its enormous blade over its head and letting out a guttural cry. Kota watched, transfixed as the first swords clanged. To their credit, the Onkai soldiers held in tight formation as the first giant came. One jumped up and blocked the massive sword with his shield while another steadied him, for the force of the blade was enormous. As metal clanged against metal, two more Onkai leaped up, one thrusting a sword into the ogre's chest while the other swiped at its throat. The monster's body and head dropped to the ground as separate pieces, and, before its dying body had even begun to twitch, the Onkai were back in their original stances, ready for the next attack.

There was a brief moment of silence. The superb teamwork had stupefied the ogres. Eight of the Onkai soldiers took advantage of this pause and dropped to their knees. In the blink of an eye, they loaded their enormous crossbows, then stood and fired. As eight black arrows found their marks in the throats and faces of their victims, the soldiers were already reloading their next shot.

A deep-throated cry erupted from all around then, and the ogres charged at once. Their movements were bounding and clumsy. More than a handful tripped on one another, their great bodies crashing to the ground. Still, many closed in on the circle of Onkai, and the battle truly began. The humans stayed close together as the brutes came in. Shoulder to shoulder they stood, working as a team of steel and death against the impossible onslaught, and, to Kota's amazement, this circle did not crumble. He watched as six more hulking bodies dropped. *All the legends of the Onkai were true!*

It was then that Kota saw a shadow pass over the city floor below him. It was in the shape such as a bat might make, only larger. He turned his head, and his whole body went rigid as he saw the dark brown form drop from the sky. It perched on the edge of a broken roof, looking down at the battle. Kota gaped at the thick muscles and the enormous wings. It was a creature of nightmares, human-like in form, but with black horns like those of a goat, slick, oily dark skin, and glossy fur on the sections of its legs not encased in thick bronze armor.

The demon turned and looked at him, or at least seemed to look at him. Its eyes were entirely black. Kota felt terror as he had never felt in his life. Then the creature turned its attention back to the battle. It rose up, a mass of unholy power, and slowly drew a curved sword from its belt. Then it leaped into the air and dove downward, soaring straight toward the circle of Onkai.

It was Darius who saw the attack at the last instant, and though he raised his shield with inhuman quickness, the demon had built up incredible momentum, all of which was focused into one colossal strike. Metal struck metal, and Darius cried in pain. The edge of the creature's weapon had cut through his shield, and he leaped back and recoiled his arm, which seemed to go limp. His shield dropped away, and he began to breathe very hard. Kota saw blood spurting out from the Onkai commander's wrist. The ogres around this collision looked up, and Kota thought he could see terror even in their faces. They backed away as the demon landed on the ground.

It charged then as Darius, with his still-functioning arm, raised his sword and parried its attack. The two blades clashed so hard that Kota could feel the impact in his skin. Darius gasped, stepping back. *The demon was stronger than he was!* The blood continued to spurt from his limp appendage, and he seemed already exhausted. The captain glanced over at his men, but they were fighting yet another wave of enemies and, from the look of their stances, their strength was beginning to falter as well.

The demon charged again, and Darius desperately parried several more blows. As the two fought, a small gust of wind whisked through the air, carrying the scents of the battlefield to Kota. He knew the distinctive odors of blood, of sweat, of ogres, and even of death, but the smell of the demon eclipsed all of these. It was putrid, like rotting meat and sulfur, and as he breathed it in, he began to feel dizzy. His skin suddenly felt very hot. He gasped as the fangs in his mouth extended, the claws on his fingers and toes grew longer and thicker, and his body, as if of its own accord, readied for a fight. Kota's heart began to pump very fast, his thoughts fading away. He forgot why he was at the window—forgot what was happening below. Everything slipped from his mind but the scent, and he stared down at the demon, knowing that he *must* kill it!

Kota leaped from the window, scraping his claws along the vines on the wall to slow his fall just enough so that his legs would not shatter. The impact still hurt, only he did not care. *Pain meant nothing.* Only killing the demon mattered. He watched the creature battle the human for a few precious seconds as the fury in his blood grew, and then, with every muscle in his body poised, he whipped across the battlefield.

As Kota darted between the lumbering ogres, some part of him remembered the dagger Cassian had given him, and his hand snapped back to unsheathe it just as he came upon his enemy. He leaped on the demon's back from behind and plunged the gleaming blade into the side of the thick, oily neck. There was more resistance than he had expected, but Kota's muscles were working harder than they ever had, and he managed to force the dagger in all the way to the hilt. The demon let out a metallic scream of rage, and the great bat-wings flapped hard, knocking Kota backward. The monster tore the dagger from its neck in a spray of syrupy black blood and whirled around.

Kota was not afraid. The sight of the demon's blood—*the smell of it* spurred him on even harder. He snarled at his enemy as it turned and raised its blade. Kota might have died in that instant had Darius not renewed his attack from behind. The demon was forced to turn at the last instant and defend itself from the greater threat. The Onkai's sword clashed with the dark blade, and Kota used the opportunity, rising and springing onto the demon's back again. This time, with no weapon, he reached around the sides of its head and tore at where he judged the eyes would be with his claws. The monster roared even louder than before, and a monstrously strong hand reached back and clamped down on Kota's left arm. He felt his body being wrenched over the oily shoulders and then he was slammed down on the ground. There was a snap in the lower part of his right leg followed by a wave of pain, yet as he experienced this, he looked up and saw that the demon was blinded in one eye, and he felt himself smile.

The human warrior, who looked half dead from all the blood he had lost, attacked again in a clumsy attempt to slash at the hellish creature's throat. The demon parried the blow away almost effortlessly, but the motion left another opening for Kota. With his remaining good leg, he rose and leaped up, thrusting two of the claws on his right hand directly into the demon's remaining eye. His fingers penetrated into gooey flesh, and the creature let out a shriek that shook Kota's bones. It shoved him, thrusting one of its arms out in a blind rage. Kota sailed through the air and slammed into one of the stone walls. He bounced and rolled to the ground, but he kept his gaze on his enemy. Blinded, the demon swung its sword about and shouted in a horrible, guttural voice: "*Where are you?! I'll KILL you!*"

Wheezing, Darius managed a burst of sudden speed as he darted in and struck. The demon's head fell from its shoulders, and the strange battle fury that had overtaken Kota melted away within a few desperate breaths. He lay there, severely beaten, his leg broken, blood dripping from wounds he did not even remember receiving. He became himself again, and he could not make sense of what had just happened.

Darius moved to him then, dropping down next to him and wheezing: "Are you still alive, Kota? Please don't die!"

Kota could not talk. The impact of the wall had taken all the wind out of him. He was only a sweating, gasping mass on the ground, but he *was* still alive. Darius put a hand on his shoulder and shouted: "Soldiers, rally to me!"

The Onkai moved around the two of them, carrying four limp and bleeding soldiers with them and setting them next to Kota. They formed another circle around their wounded. Darius rose to his feet and took his place among the men, holding up his weapon with his still functioning sword hand. Even after all that fighting, there were so many ogres left. Kota could see them through the legs of his protectors. For some reason though, they seemed to be hesitating.

Kota heard a single pair of feet walking softly toward his group. He rolled onto his stomach to get a better view and saw Cassian walking toward them. The dead or unconscious body of the demon sorcerer was sliding and scraping along the city floor next to him, seeming to be dragged forward by some invisible power. The young sorcerer moved between the Onkai and the rest of the ogre army and then turned to face the enemy.

An ogre nearby lunged very suddenly at Cassian, letting out a furious battle cry and swinging a spiked club downward at his skull. Just before the weapon could connect, it burst into splinters and metal nails, all of which flew away from Cassian, and the massive ogre was hurled backward at least ten paces, skidding and rolling on the city floor. It let out a horrible scream as Cassian took a few steps toward it, and it scurried away on its hands and feet.

Cassian's voice came like thunder from every direction: "I AM CASSIAN ASANGO, STARBORN OF THE NINE-TEENTH GENERATION! LEAVE THIS PLACE OR YOU WILL ALL DIE!" Every ogre still standing in the lost city turned and fled in terror.

After the last of them had disappeared, Cassian turned to the men and the group parted. Without a word, he walked over to the first wounded soldier whom Kota suddenly recognized as Tovin. The Onkai's face was pale, and he was leaking blood all over the ground from his chest. Cassian rolled Tovin over onto his back, put his hands on the soldier's chest, and whispered: "*Aridria nes vasulen andas.*" Tovin winced in pain, but the flow of blood out of him seemed to slow and then stop. Immediately, Cassian turned to the next injured soldier, bent over him and whispered more words that Kota could not begin to comprehend. He repeated this twice more and then turned to Kota. A glare came over his face, and then he looked down at Kota's lower half. Kota followed his gaze and noticed for the first time that the shape of his leg changed direction between his knee and ankle.

"Well, you were very stupid today," Cassian said in a sharp voice, and then added quietly: "but I suppose no more than the rest of us." He reached down and put his hands on the wound and began to whisper, and Kota felt his flesh almost seem to burn. "Dammit!" Cassian hissed, his hands snapping back. "These wounds were inflicted by the demon, weren't they?"

"It was one of the bravest acts I've ever seen," Darius said. Kota thought he saw tears mixing with the sweat dripping down his tattooed face. "He... even with a broken leg he fought..." The captain's eyes moved to meet Kota's, and he wheezed: "You saved my life!"

Cassian muttered through his teeth: "I cannot fix this!" His eyes lifted to Kota's, and he answered the question forming in Kota's mind before it could be spoken: "Demons leave a kind psychic residue when they attack mortals. Your entire form is covered in the stuff. " He stared down at Kota's leg and said in a sharp tone: "All this corruptive energy makes it impossible for anything as delicate as a healing spell to work." He shook his head. "I am sorry, but this is going to hurt like utter hell."

Before Kota could ask what that meant, he felt his injured leg lift slowly in the air and then the broken half began to straighten. He let out a scream as Cassian's invisible magic guided the two sections of his bone back together inside his skin. Then, as his leg hung suspended in the air, Cassian's open hand reached out in the direction of a crossbow that hung from one of the Onkai's belt. The weapon immediately unhooked itself and floated forward, and as it did it began to split apart. Chunks fell away until there were only two straight sections of wood in the air, and these moved over to Kota's leg and pressed snuggly against the two sides of his shin.

"I cannot stand being this *sloppy,*" Cassian muttered as he pulled off his cloak. He waved his fingers at it, and five long strips tore away from the fabric. They whisked through the air and wrapped themselves around Kota's leg and the splints. Kota winced in pain and dug his claws into the stone beneath his hands as the cloth tightened. The ends of the fabric tied themselves into knots, and Cassian peered at his work, muttering: "I set the bone and fused it as well as I could, but you will not be able to walk for weeks."

"But he *will* walk again?" Darius said with tremendous worry in his voice.

"So long as someone keeps him alive. He cannot survive alone in the forest like this."

"I will take care of him—whatever he needs," Darius said.

Cassian turned and looked at the captain for a moment, then turned back to Kota. "It seems your foolishness comes with a reward. I suspect you will be the first shamalak ever to visit an Onkai temple —that is if you can spare a little more time from your spirit walk to remain among humans."

Kota grinned, despite the horrible pain he was still in. "I... I no think I was brave...I no remember fight much...but I be very honored to go to temple if you will take me."

"Oh Gods," Tovin grunted suddenly. He sat up, his hand pressed against the place on his chest where he had been leaking blood.

"That reminds me," Cassian said. He stood and grabbed Darius's limp, bleeding arm, causing the captain to wince. "I see these were inflicted by the kothla as well. This will *also* hurt like hell." Darius let out an agonized grunt as Cassian moved his hand slowly up and down his arm, and Kota vaguely detected the scent of burnt hair and roasting skin. "Put vulanthic leaves on this when you get back to your temple," Cassian said as he released the limb. "They should have some in their apothecary. Try not to move this arm for a few weeks."

"I...understand," Darius said, still trembling from the pain.

Cassian looked around at the men and said: "I suppose I am finished with this campaign then." He gestured toward the steel doorway that led underground, and his face became more serious as he said: "There are six children in there fast asleep. I thought it best to take their memories of this whole event. You will see to their safety, I trust. Two of the boys were orphaned by Grodus. They are roughly the correct age for induction into the Onkai Order. I will leave adequate gold on your saddle for their tuition if that is what they wish. If not...use it to see that they are cared for and not snatched up by slavers." Cassian walked over to the body of the cloaked figure and gave it a little kick. "I did not kill Grodus. He has information your order needs. I tore away all of his magic. You can hand him over to your vicious Nemesai brothers for interrogation."

"Did you recover the elvin talisman he was using?" asked Darius.

"Yes," said Cassian, he reached into the collar of his shirt and pulled out the beautiful golden object Kota had seen on the demon sorcerer. "A truly fascinating little object."

"I must take it to the temple," said Darius.

"I think not," said Cassian, tucking it back into his shirt.

The Onkai captain frowned. "We have a very express treaty with the elves—"

"Which has nothing to do with me," Cassian interjected. "I am not a member of your order. I am a Lord of the Denigoth Empire, and I defeated a non-human enemy attacking my people. His possessions *legally* fall to my hands. Only the Emperor may command me to surrender them."

"You play an extremely dangerous game," said Darius. "These are the *elves* we speak of."

Cassian gave a soft laugh. "You know something of my life, Darius. My whole existence is an incredibly dangerous game. I cannot afford to throw away such an advantage." He turned to walk away, then stopped. His left hand rose, and the magnificent crystal dagger Kota had used to stab the demon floated up. It halted before it reached his palm, and Cassian seemed to hesitate for a moment. Then he made a small gesture, and the weapon floated back to Kota, handle first.

"You fought well, Kota," he said, glancing back. "Take this as a reward."

Kota gazed at the hovering weapon and said: "I...I can no accept such great thing."

"I can make another one," Cassian said with a shrug. "Try not to lose it though. It is worth as much as a small village." He turned and started walking away, then called back: "Enjoy your time at the temple and come and visit me someday at my castle if you would. I should like to learn what becomes of you."

CHAPTER 4: THE LITTLE BROKEN BOTTLE

Slavery is the most obvious and obscene embodiment of our antiquated 'caste system.' It is unmistakably an evil that we allow intelligent, feeling human beings to be subject to the irresponsible power of other humans. In some parts of the empire, a man can be fined less than fifty desseks for killing one of his slaves, and only then if it is done on public property. How can anything so primitive and callous be allowed to continue? The reason is obvious, of course. The wealthy senators who write our laws and their aristocratic families own more than eighty percent of the empire's slaves.

—Excerpt from "A Modern Empire," by Cassian Asango

Iona fanned away smoke as she used her woolen glove to pull the pan of smoking bread from the Sondal family's wood-burning oven and set it on the kitchen table as a feeling of frustration washed over her. The bottom was a charred black mass. At least the top was a beautiful golden brown that could be separated and served to her masters, but that left only the burned section for her and Livia for the day. The dimensions of the oven in this home were significantly smaller than the one she had been trained on at her previous estate. The fire burned closer to the bread, which threw off the slow cooking technique she had mastered. This was but one of the changes with which she was trying to cope.

"How goes the work, child?" Lady Sondal bellowed from the next room.

Iona turned toward the clay doorway into the kitchen. "I-it seems to be going f-fine so far," she said, unable to disguise her nervousness. This was only her second week in the home, and she had already assumed all of Livia's cooking duties.

"I am pleased to hear it," the lady said.

"I need to fetch a bucket of water to wash the cookware," Iona said. "Would you like a cup, mistress?"

"How wonderfully attentive you are," the voice bellowed back through the walls. "Yes, fetch me water, but first go see my husband and get some money and buy a duck from the marketplace for my dinner. You *do* know how to roast a duck, don't you?"

"Um, I have never cooked one before, but I think I can do it."

"Of course you can, child. I can already tell you're a *far* better cook than Livia ever was."

"T-thank you, mistress," Iona said, picking up the home's water pail and stepping toward the door. "I'll go and do as you say and be back soon."

"See that you are," Lady Sondal exhaled as Iona slipped outside to the city streets. Her bare feet immediately delighted in the touch of the warm, flat stones, which had just begun to absorb heat from the sun. The Sondal home was a single story structure in the middle of a large section of homes that, so far as Iona could tell, were taken up by local merchants and professionals. It was only a few hundred paces from her new master's storehouse.

Iona walked along the street keeping her gaze cast down. She had only been out a few times and was not sure if it was safe to meet the eyes of the people going about their business. She had heard that the guards in large cities were extremely harsh with slaves who stepped out of their place. There were tales of public whippings and even the removal of a hand in grave cases. As Iona passed men and women here and there though, no one seemed to take much notice of her one way or the other.

When she came to the entrance to Master Sondal's storehouse, the door was open. She spotted him and Livia standing next to one another gazing down at the top sheet of a stack of yellow papers, Livia's thin finger tapping the page's center. They both looked up at her at the same time, and both of them greeted her with warm smiles.

"Good morning, Iona!" Master Hervin said.

"G-good morning, Master," Iona said, feeling strange at receiving such a warm greeting from one who owned her.

"Livia was just pointing out a few errors I made in the bookkeeping," he said with a soft laugh that seemed directed at himself. "Would you like a pastry?" He reached under the counter and retrieved a clay plate with several strange squares of bread. "I have a client who brings me these every so often – more than Livia and I can eat."

"Oh, that is incredibly kind of you, master," she said. Timidly she walked over and looked down at the bread squares. White cream puffed out of their center. Iona picked one up and took a small bite. Immediately she let out a little giggle through her nose. It was the sweetest thing she had ever tasted.

"Have as much as you like, dear," he said.

Iona swallowed and then said: "You are very generous, sir."

"Oh, it's no bother," he said with such a kind smile that it made Iona blush a little. He let her eat a few more bites and then said: "Now why did my wife send you? I assume she wants something."

"S-she asks if you would give me some money to buy a duck, sir."

"Hmmm, she *would* ask for duck this time of year," Hervin said quietly. He turned to Livia. "Would you go to the strongbox and get a few coppers for Iona?" He paused, then said: "Actually why don't you go with her to the marketplace? Timon always gives you the best deals anyway."

Livia nodded and disappeared through a doorway going back into the storehouse. When she was gone, Master Sondal said: "Look around. You might as well learn about the family business."

Iona smiled at this kindly man and then glanced around his shop. The room was quite large. There were shelves along the walls as well as several tables throughout, displaying the various goods her master traded in. One wall was covered with containers of wine, most of which were clay urns, but a few were fine glass bottles. There was a table of assorted spices, another with sheets of silk in different colors, and then several tables of variously sized pottery pieces with images of gods and storms and animals intricately sculpted and painted between perfectly symmetrical patterns.

"Do you like the vases?" he said.

"Yes!" Iona said. "They're beautiful, sir."

Livia returned, and she gazed down, a soft exhalation escaping through her thin nose that sounded almost like a laugh.

"Shall I tell you a secret?" Master Sondal said, lowering his voice and leaning over the counter a little. "We have a kiln on the roof. Livia makes nearly *all of this stuff*." He chuckled. "If anyone found out, there would be even more people hounding me to buy her than I have already."

Iona stared at the lovely ceramic works again. They were so skillful!

Livia walked over to her and slipped an arm through hers and gestured toward the door. Iona fell into step with her and they strode out through the doorway. When they were out in the streets away from the shop, Iona said: "Where did you learn to sculpt like that?"

Livia gave a little shrug. Then she walked over to the wall of a large building and put her paper against it and once again wrote with her charcoal pencil:

How is the she-bull treating you?

Iona frowned. She had been used to other slaves whispering disrespectful things about their mistress. Iona had never informed on any of them, but nor had she engaged in such talk. She disliked speaking ill of anyone. Instead, she said: "Lady Sondal seems to like my cooking. Nothing has been too difficult."

Livia nodded, and they walked for a time in silence. Iona was feeling more and more comfortable with the older slave, and so she finally decided to bridge the subject that had been on her mind since she had met the fascinating silent girl: "Livia, um, do you... w-was your tongue cut out?"

Livia looked at her and opened her mouth, sticking out a pink, healthy tongue. Then she reached into her pocket and pulled out a neatly folded square of paper. Iona took it, unfolded the thing, and read:

I've been waiting for you to ask about my silence. I don't know why I cannot speak. I cannot whisper or even mouth words. Whenever I try, my head begins to throb with terrible pain. I have never known the reason. I just cannot do it.

Iona swallowed. It did not seem right that anyone should be unable to talk. She wanted to ask more questions, but just then they turned into a long row of market stands.

Merchants were shouting about their wares to the pedestrians that were moving up and down the street. Similar to when Iona had been in the cage a few weeks before, she was suddenly amidst a living sea of human beings. She saw roasted frogs on spits and stands selling various fruits. There were street performers working small, intricate marionettes with sticks and strings. Livia led her through this cacophony with graceful, darting speed.

They came suddenly to a large stand of freshly butchered meat. Iona's eyes swept a sizable wooden display with headless chicken corpses and sections of slaughtered cow and pig, yet she scarcely glanced at any of these things before her gaze shifted to the keeper of the stand. Wearing an apron spattered with blood stood a creature she only knew from stories. *A Dwarf*! It could not be anything else. He was scarcely taller than she was, yet he was muscled like an ox, his stocky, rippled arms bare to the world. His nose was as thick as a man's elbow, and it rested above a dense black mustache and beard that were tucked into his apron.

The dwarf grinned at them both, bearing thick, yellow teeth, and shouted: "Livia, my love!" He moved around the counter and reached out with the meatiest pair of hands Iona had ever seen and gripped Livia by the hips. He lifted her and spun her around as if she weighed no more than a baby.

Livia gave a tense smile as she was spun about. When the dwarf set her down, she straightened her skirt. The dwarf chuckled and then his bulging blue eyes shifted to Iona. "And who is *this* young beauty?" he said.

Iona looked at Livia, and for an instant she expected the older girl to introduce her. Livia stared back and gestured toward the dwarf with her eyebrows, her expression seeming to say: *Introduce yourself.* Iona looked at him then and said: "M-my name is Iona, sir. I belong to the Sondal home."

"Yer new assistant, eh?" The dwarf laughed, his eyes going to Livia's and then returning to Iona's. "Well, it is my pleasure to meet you, Iona. My name is Timon." He held out his enormous hand and gripped Iona's arm. His strange face bore such an infectious smile that Iona felt herself grinning back, despite her bewilderment. He seemed satisfied by this and returned his attention to Livia. "What can I get you, my dear?"

Livia pointed to one of the freshly plucked ducks that hung from the canopy and then held up one finger. "One duck," he said, and his tone indicated he took a little amusement in interpreting Livia's signs. He thumbed his enormous nose and glanced up at the sky for a moment, then said: "Five coppers." Livia tilted her head and raised an eyebrow, her eyes seeming to say: *that's ridiculous.* The dwarf blinked and said: "Ducks are harder to come by this time of year." Livia sighed and held up three fingers. "Oh, come now, dear, they were only slaughtered a few minutes ago. I just got finished washing my hands when you got here. Four coppers." Livia bent down so that their eyes were level, her expression becoming extremely serious. Again, she held up three fingers. "Fine," the dwarf said, seeming to sulk a little. Livia retrieved three small copper coins from her pocket and set them down on the dwarf's table.

Timon pulled the duck from its hook and held it out. Livia turned to Iona and pinched her apron and gave it a tiny tug. Iona immediately understood and lifted up the front of her apron. The dwarf dropped the bird into it and Iona rolled it up. The transaction completed, the dwarf said: "You girls have a wonderful day. Don't tell anyone I gave you such a fine deal."

"We won't!" Iona said as she and Livia turned and strode back into the marketplace. When they were through the crowd, Iona said: "You were so confident. How did you know he would go down to three?" Once again Livia gave a little shrug. The two girls traveled back toward Master Sondal's store without another word, and they were within ten paces of the entrance when a familiar deep feminine voice shouted: "There you are!"

Mistress Sondal's puffy hand came from behind and gripped Livia's golden ponytail and gave it a hard yank. Iona turned and saw that her mistress was standing in the middle of the street in her nightgown, her round face contorted in an expression of rage that was terrifying. The woman had a wicker rug beater in her right hand, and she swung it hard at Livia's face without the slightest hesitation. Livia's forearms came up just in time to block the blow. The rug beater whipped several more times on Livia's arms, and then Mistress Sondal shoved her forward and whipped her across the back.

"You shattered my perfume vial on the floor!" the great woman hissed. "It was from Elucia! Do you know how much it cost?" She whipped Livia across the back again. "I know it was you! You put it on so you could attract some filthy sailor, you little *whore*!"

Livia spun around, her deep blue eyes wide with such hatred that they looked murderous. She clenched her hands into fists and they trembled at her sides. When Lady Sondal saw this, she actually flinched a little, but then she hissed: "Don't you look at *me* like that, you little slave bitch!" She raised the rug beater again.

In a panic, Iona fell to her knees at Lady Sondal's feet and shouted: "I knocked over your perfume! I'm sorry! It was an accident! I was afraid to tell you! Please forgive me!"

"Huh!" Lady Sondal grunted. There was a pause and then Iona felt the wicker rug beater come down across her back and she screamed as the hot pain coursed through her body. "Be more careful of my *expensive things*!" Lady Sondal shouted at her. The woman turned and walked away, hissing over her shoulder: "I expect you back with the duck and the water within ten minutes. My feet still need rubbing."

Livia bent knelt down and clutched Iona to her as Lady Sondal disappeared around the bend in the street. Livia held on for a long moment as Iona sobbed from the pain and the terror coursing through her. When she had calmed down, Livia gently lifted her head so that they were facing one another. Livia's eyes, which were also wet with tears, stared into Iona's with strange and visceral intensity. For a moment, Iona felt as though the silent girl were looking into her very soul. Then Livia's face contorted in anger. She stood abruptly and turned to the wall and yanked her paper and pencil from her dress pocket. With a trembling hand, she scribbled onto the paper and then held it up to Iona. Two words were written:

You lied!

Iona began to shake, but then Livia knelt down and hugged her once more and gave her several kisses on the forehead and stroked her hair. Then Livia stood and put her paper against the wall again, crossed out what she had written, and wrote for a long time, tears streaking down her face as she did. When she showed Iona the paper it read:

Don't ever protect me from that cow! I can take care of myself. She probably drank too much wine and knocked it over herself. She's a petty, stupid child!

"I... I'm sorry," was all Iona could think to say.

Livia took several slow breaths, seeming to calm herself. Then she scribbled out what she had written and wrote a new message:

Don't tell Hervin what happened. I'm coming home with you. I won't let her whip you again. Hurry and finish crying.

Iona swallowed after reading the words and then reached up and wiped her eyes with her sleeve. She gathered the duck up - which had rolled out of her apron during the beating - and rose. "I'm ready," she said.

Livia gave her a nod and they both walked toward the entrance to the storehouse. Just before they stepped through, Livia paused, put her arm around Iona and tilted her neck so that their heads rested against one another. It was more affection than Iona had received from anyone in a long time. She felt so happy that the pain in her back did not seem to matter as much.

CHAPTER 5: THE OLD MAN

Here and there, attempts have been made to understand the mind of the Heretic, and one often stands out above all others. Cassian Asango might never have become the devious, calculating creature he was without the tutelage of the infamous General Somar Dojinko. From this man, he learned to be ruthless, efficient, and resourceful. Dojinko taught the boy the art of war, and for that, he must be condemned to the darkest pits of hell.

—Bishop Arodias of the Anti-Cassonian Church

"We're just about on it, my lord," the voice of the driver rasped through the hiss of the storm.

"Thank you," Somar Dojinko said, absently nodding to the wooden barrier between himself and the driver of the carriage. He rolled his eyes and hugged his thick cloak to his body as the cold rain pattered down onto the thin wooden ceiling above him. He could hear the two horses braying as the driver cracked a whip to keep them moving through the downpour. The small carriage, elegantly made as it was, was a clumsy thing on the thoroughly soaked, uneven country road. For nearly a week, Somar had ridden in this carriage through the better part of each day. If he had been any less a soldier, he might have complained of the pain his aged body experienced under such forced indolence in a tight space, but groaning about discomfort had been beaten out of him long ago.

Cold and wet as he was, Somar found himself drawing back the cloth curtain of the carriage's side window and leaning out into the rain to take his first look at the estate. This was where the incredible young man resided—the one who might be emperor if the church did not manage to kill him. As soon as Somar glanced outward, he saw the towering spires of stone, the massive walls, and he could almost feel the raw mystical power of the boy who was so impossibly gifted.

"Announce my arrival when we arrive at the gate," Somar said aloud. Excitement was beginning to overpower his exhaustion.

"Yes, my lord," the driver's voice replied.

Somar leaned back in his seat. As he did, though, he noticed a very sizable crowd of peasants and armed guards gathered together around a nearby windmill. Many of these people stood unsheltered despite the rain, talking to one another, and coming and going from the inside of the mill. This struck Somar's curiosity.

"Excuse me," he said, rapping against the inside of his carriage. "Can you find out what's going on over there?"

Over there evidently did not need to be explained, for the driver responded immediately: "Right away, sir."

The carriage slowed and then came to a halt. Somar peered through the rain as his portly driver climbed down and moved over to a group of men who were walking together away from the mill. He spoke to them for a moment or so and then returned.

"Apparently some boy got his arm torn to shreds in the mill, sir," said the driver. "The starborn lord is putting it back together—has been since the wee hours of the morning."

"Take me there immediately," said Somar.

"Right away, sir," the driver said with a quick nod. He climbed back up, and the carriage quickly changed direction and moved over the wet grass to the mill. A few moments later they were next to the crowd. Somar exited his carriage without another word to his driver and moved out into this group of peasants, which numbered somewhere in the sixties. The ones on the outer edge were talking to one another, and they politely made way for Somar as soon as they saw him coming. As he drew nearer to the door, he saw peasants and a handful of guards standing on their tiptoes and craning their necks to see over the people in front of them.

Somar approached one of the armed men—a tall, broad-shouldered fellow in chainmail—and tapped him on the shoulder from behind. As soon as the guard turned, Somar boomed in the tone of his old military commander's voice: "I am Senator Dojinko, from the Imperium, sent here to meet with Lord Asango."

"Oh," said the guard, stiffening into a soldier's posture. "He's in there." The man gestured with an armored limb to the open door of the mill. "Would you like me to escort you through this crowd, my lord?"

"Yes, but first explain the situation to me."

"Yes, sir," the soldier said with a nod. "The mill owner's son—Alden I think is his name—was helping his father in the early morning. His sleeve got caught in the machinery of the mill, and he was pulled in. It tore his arm up something fierce, and some of the wood snapped as well and got him in the eye. He kept screaming: 'I'm blind' until Lord Cassian calmed him down with magic. Then he put his eye back together and got him seeing again, and then—"

"Put his *eye* back together?" said Somar, incredulous at the words. His many years in the army had left him with a deep understanding of healing magic. Sorcerers could cast spells to close wounds, but tissue as delicate as the eye could not be repaired by magic to the point that sight was restored if someone was blinded.

"Yes, my lord. It took him hours, but Cassian—I mean Lord Asango—got the eye working again—even put the skin back together nice and neat around it before he moved on to the arm. Last I checked he's near done with*that* part."

"Lead me to the front please, but do not create a disturbance," said Somar.

"Yes, sir," said the soldier. He moved in front of Somar, tapping shoulders and motioning people to part ways. They obediently moved aside. Soon, Somar was inside the mill, where he saw a thin young man in elegant if unornamented clothing, who looked to be perhaps sixteen years old, hunched over a scruffy unconscious boy of perhaps ten or eleven years. Across from this pair were a man and a woman, leaning against each other on wooden chairs. From the looks on their faces, Somar guessed they were the boy's parents.

"Who is this?" said the noble young man without looking up from his patient. He was clutching the boy's limp hand in his own, inspecting it. There was dried blood all over both of them, but no apparent wounds existed in the younger boy's flesh.

"He says he's a senator here to see you, Lord Asango," said the guard.

"Oh yes, Dojinko," said Cassian, still not looking up. "You may go to the castle if you like. I am nearly done here. Just a few more nerve endings to take care of."

"I do not mind waiting," said Somar.

"Suit yourself, but you will need to keep quiet. Is that understood?"

Somar nearly smiled at these terse words. Usually, his presence was at least somewhat intimidating, particularly to young men. He might sometimes be spoken to rudely by a particularly arrogant aristocratic youth, but that did not seem to be the case here. The boy's voice had been far too serious to be pompous. Somar felt an instant respect for this young Cassian.

"Understood," he answered.

Asango turned the boy's hand in his own. Somar marveled that this young man could ignore his presence for the sake of a young peasant. Many other senators of the Imperium would simper with indignation, but Somar found the young man's actions both admirable and fascinating.

He studied young starborn, watching the brilliant green eyes stare in concentration at the child's limb. Somar had no gift of telepathy, but he possessed a capacity for reading people nonetheless, and what he saw in Cassian at that moment was fierce determination.

Perhaps an hour passed where the starborn did little more than hold the child's hand in his and gaze at it, but here and there Somar saw tiny shifts underneath the child's skin, and he guessed that remarkably focused magic was occurring.

Finally, Cassian laid the child's hand down and stood up. Turning to the parents first, he said: "He will awaken in a few minutes."

The mother, a thin woman with thick red hair, said in a nervous voice: "Is he—"

"His arm will function normally," said Cassian.

The father, a massive man with a thick black mustache, stood from his chair and said in a deep voice: "My lord, I can never repay this debt to you. I will provide your estate with free bread for a year."

"You will do no such thing," Cassian said. "I did what I did because I wanted to."

"I must repay you in some way," said the Miller.

Cassian sighed, looking almost annoyed. "I can afford to pay for bread. If you provide your merchandise for free to an estate the size of mine, then you will soon lose the ability to care for the boy I just spent the last sixteen hours healing."

Before the miller could respond, Cassian turned abruptly to Somar and said: "It is good to finally meet you, General Dojinko."

Somar responded quickly, sensing that Asango was rather uncomfortable with the gratitude these people were showing him. "It is good to meet you as well, though you address me with too much respect. I am a general no longer." Somar turned to the man and woman and said: "Please forgive me, but I have come on urgent business from the Imperial Senate. I have waited for your child to be healed, but now I must speak with Lord Asango immediately."

"O-of course," said the miller with a nod.

A small smile of relief flashed across Cassian's face. The light had grown very dim in the last hour, and in the shadows and firelight, Somar could see how tired the young man was after the prolonged expenditure of magic. They turned and walked out of the mill together, and Asango's guards quickly started clearing a path among the townspeople. Somar was pleased to find that the rain had finally ceased.

"How was your journey?" said Cassian as they stepped away from the crowd, his voice dry.

"Quite long, but I have enjoyed taking in the countryside." Somar took a slow look around. "You rule over quite a lovely body of land."

"I am fortunate in that respect," said Cassian. He glanced at Somar's carriage. "I see you have a horse and cart. If you prefer to take them to the castle, I would be happy to meet you there. I have been hunched over all day, and I prefer to walk."

"I should enjoy a walk as well, if you would permit the company," said Somar.

"As you wish." Cassian turned toward one of his guards. "Take the men back. I will return on foot and speak with the senator."

"As you command," the man said with a quick, sharp salute. He turned to his men and started issuing orders. Somar made eye contact with his driver in the crowd and gave him a wave toward the castle, indicating he was to proceed on ahead. The driver nodded in understanding.

Somar began to walk alongside the young lord toward the castle, eventually saying: "You appear to run your administration well for one so young, if you do not mind an observation."

"That depends on your definition of *well*," said Cassian. "I run it how I like."

"It was very kind of you to save that poor boy," said Somar.

"Was it kind?" Cassian eyed him sideways. "I could help him, so I did. It would have been horribly cruel to do otherwise. Besides, it was an interesting challenge. I had never repaired optic nerves before."

"You enjoy challenges, don't you?"

The side of the boy's mouth twisted up. "I sensed you watching me back at the mill, yet I could not see your thoughts. I assumed it was because I was distracted, but I find them unperceivable now as well."

Somar smiled at the young lord. "I spent years training in the art of occlusion."

"It is extremely impressive. I cannot catch even an echo of thought."

"Surely you can see the importance of blocking telepathic intrusion for a man of military command."

"Yes, but still I never thought a non-sorcerer could block *my* telepathy. That presents a bit of a problem for our relationship."

"How so?"

"I find verbal instruction to be cumbersome and slow. In most cases, I simply take what I want from the minds of my tutors. It is much easier that way."

"That hardly seems respectful to the tutor," said Somar.

Cassian gave a single dark chuckle. "Not all of them are willing subjects." He stared out into the darkening horizon and said: "My enemies send such wonderfully skilled individuals to kill me. I make good use of them."

Somar raised an eyebrow. "Your enemies? Do you mean the Bishop of the Nemesai Order?"

"Most of the time, yes," Cassian sighed. "It is a game we play. He cannot officially execute a living miracle, so he unofficially sends assassins from all over the world, and I stop them from killing me."

"Those are exceedingly dangerous accusations to level. I find it interesting that you speak so openly."

"I despise dancing around the truth."

"That is an admirable attitude, but perhaps not the best one for a politician to hold."

This drew a sardonic smile from the boy. "Will that be your first lesson then?" He turned his head as they walked. "Tell me, now that you have met me, do you wish to become my tutor in the art of warfare?"

Somar did not speak for a moment. He had expected they would both tiptoe around this question for quite a time before he made any sort of decision. Was this Cassian Asango an impatient child? No, that did seem to be the case. He was just very, very direct. Somar supposed he could be direct as well, and a good soldier is ready for battle at any moment, or so he used to say. He gazed at the young man and asked: "Why did you help that child?"

"Because he was injured."

"So, it was compassion?"

"It was *right*."

"And is it right to kill?" said Somar in a cold voice. "Are you prepared to send men to murder and die for you? Are *you* prepared to take life yourself?"

"It is not something I take lightly, if that is what you ask. Life is exquisitely beautiful to me, and I perceive it in ways you likely cannot imagine."

"Humble, aren't you?" said Somar with a chuckle.

"No, not at all," Cassian said, gazing up at the night sky. "I hope that is not a problem for you."

Somar was silent for a moment, and then he said: "You could have requested any military official in the empire to instruct you. Why did you choose me, an old senator who has not set foot in an army camp in years?"

"Do not speak delicately to me," said Cassian. "Ask the question you really want to ask."

Somar felt a tickle of surprise. Could the boy have really overcome his mental defenses? No, not even a starborn could do that. "All right, of all the great military officers in the empire, why did you pick the only one who is peasant born? You, who could very well be Emperor, should associate yourself with men of greater prestige."

"Prestige grows from accomplishment, in my mind," said Cassian. "You, a peasant, became one of the highest-ranking officers in the world. That is unprecedented—it was *unheard* of before you came along. Even greater, you are the first peasant to achieve the rank of Imperial Senator."

"Yes, and many consider it to be a blight on our great nation's history," Somar said.

"Not I," Cassian replied. "I respect what you have achieved more than I respect any noble-blooded youth who was promoted by his father or his uncle to command. I need a man like you to instruct me because I need to accomplish what you accomplished."

"Which is what?"

"To overcome all the people who think me unworthy—who think I am scum. I intend to be the next emperor of Denigoth. To do that, I need to prove myself as a great military commander. But that will not be enough to put me on the throne by itself."

"No, it certainly will not," said Somar. "The Nemesai Order will stop at nothing to keep you from ruling."

Cassian let out a grim sigh. "They are quite the dangerous enemy to have."

"And you believe I can help you against them?"

"Yes."

"And you believe I *would* – that I would help you fight against the church?"

"I doubt you traveled this far across the empire to tell me you object to tutoring me on moral grounds. A letter would have sufficed."

"If you want an honest answer, I was not certain what I would say or do until I arrived here."

"And here you are," said Cassian.

"And perhaps I require time to think."

"You've had three weeks of sitting in a carriage to *think,*" said Cassian. "I am certain your instincts have already led you to a choice."

"So sure, are you?"

"I know people," Cassian said, and his confident smile intensified as he stared into Somar's eyes. "I suppose, if anything, you want to say yes, but you're afraid."

"Afraid of what?"

"Shame on your name and your legacy—shame on your family by being connected to me, and fear of the church. I have heard the objection before. You have a great deal to lose. However, I do not believe a man like yourself achieves as much as he does by letting his fears rule him."

Somar inadvertently chuckled. "What makes you think I am the right tutor for you? Don't you prefer to go inside your teachers' minds?"

"Sooner or later, I will break your defenses."

"Hah!" Somar laughed. "If I thought you could, do you think that would be an enticement to stay?"

"You strike me as the sort who likes a challenge as well."

More and more, Somar liked the audacity of this young man. Still, Asango was one of the most dangerous people in the world with which to associate. "Tell me, boy, are the Nemesai's fears about you justified?"

"Oh yes, almost entirely," said Cassian without a touch of shame. "I do not actually plan to round them all up and kill them, as many suspect. I *am* a humanist though. I do not pray to the Gods and never will. I plan to add freedom of religion to our citizen compact."

"Freedom to what degree?" Somar asked.

"Freedom unless one's practices infringe on the rights of others guaranteed in our citizen compact."

"And that would be the *only* restriction?"

"It is the only one I could think of worthy of note."

Somar laughed again. "I can see why they despise you so much."

"The Nemesai executed my parents because they dared to think independently," said Cassian, his voice suddenly taking on a sharp edge. "Can you see why *I* despise *them*?"

They stopped walking and turned to face one another on the wet grass. Somar looked into Cassian's deep green eyes and saw ferocity coupled with strength and a powerful intellect. The boy was every bit the threat that many in the empire thought him to be and more, yet this strangely thrilled Somar. "What do you believe your chances are of ascending to the throne over your competitors?"

"I only have one competitor," said Cassian.

Somar raised an eyebrow. "That certainly is not my understanding. Only four of this generation's starborn have been identified. Of you four, I know that Dimitris Singet and Arkas Adronicus – who happens to be the current Emperor's son - are actively pursuing the throne, and Telemachus Vale has yet to declare his intentions."

A dark smile crossed Cassian's face. "First, since you are a man of sufficient rank, I may disclose to you that the fifth starborn is *not* unidentified. I know her well—we have all been able to feel each other and communicate since we were eleven. Her name is Keska Ethedrine, and she lives in the western islands. She would make an extremely formidable opponent, but she cannot compete for the throne because she had the unfortunate luck of being born female. As for Telemachus, he does not want the throne – he never has – and Arkas, *the prince,* is no significant threat to me and never will be."

"Why do you say that?"

Cassian sighed. "Some things are too dangerous even for a senator to know. That is hardly the point though. Dimitris is my rival. He hungers for the throne for very different reasons than I. He is utterly brilliant, focused, powerful, and he has the full backing and all the resources of the church and most of the nobility. The Nemesai have shared ancient arcane knowledge with him that they have kept secret for centuries, and they have hired sorcerers from all over the world to instruct him—all so that he might kill me if we ever duel. On top of that, he is being instructed in politics and warfare by the top ranking members of our government. By and large, the empire's most influential members *assume* he will be the next emperor and have been showering him with gifts and granting him political favors for years—much more so than they do for me."

"You do not exactly make a strong case for yourself thus far," said Somar.

"My case is myself," said Cassian. His sharp, young features appeared very serious now. "I do not parlay with the existing elites in the empire because I am not interested in letting them continue their stranglehold over the lower classes." He leaned forward slightly, as if to emphasize his next words. "Whatever rumors you have heard about me are likely true. I am a radical. I want to teach the common man how to read—give him the tools he needs to decide his own fate rather than work the fields for his noble master. I believe that our empire could be so much more than it is if only its chief purpose were not to allow the wealthy handful of nobles to grow fat off the backbreaking work of their subjects." The boy took a breath and shut his eyes for an instant as if searching his mind. "I want to *destroy* that system."

"You're an *idealist,*" said Somar, speaking the word delicately. "Idealists are wonderful people, except that they often lack an understanding of pacing and compromise. The game you wish to play requires immense cunning and subtlety—not just *strength.*"

The starborn nodded at this and moved closer to Somar. They were more or less of a height with one another, their eyes level. "May I attempt to read your mind?" he said.

Somar blinked at Cassian in surprise and said: "Why?"

"I wish to test your defenses against my will. May I?"

Again, the boy evoked a little thrill in Somar. The challenge felt irresistible. "All right, starborn, show me what you can do."

Cassian's eyes narrowed, and Somar felt a tickle in his mind at first—something like a scratching against the barrier he had learned to construct so many years ago when he began studying the art of occlusion. He had been trained by a starborn of the previous generation—a fascinating older man named Neophis who had taken an interest in a young officer of peasant blood who had a natural aptitude in strategy and logistics. Neophis had taught Somar to shut his mind from anything and everything, encasing it in a sphere of focused will.

The tickle increased rather abruptly as Somar perceived a fierce knocking sensation against his mental barrier. It pounded with a force he could scarcely believe, and his head rang with pain. The boy's will was staggering. Cassian slammed relentlessly, as if dozens of tireless men were thrusting a great battering ram against the wall in Somar's mind.

"Impressive," Cassian whispered, and he reached out and touched Somar's hand.

The instant their flesh connected, the strength of the attack more than doubled, and then suddenly there were two battering rams coming at Somar's mind from opposite directions, and then five, and then ten, and then there seemed a hundred. Cassian struck on all sides, and doing so did not seem to divide the intensity of any one single avenue of attack, but instead his strength only seemed to increase. Somar's skull throbbed with pain. Neophis had never been so focused – *so powerful!*

"Gods!" Somar heard himself hiss. The boy's attacks increased again. Ten thousand battering rams were colliding with what seemed now to be his mind's meager defenses. Somar wanted to scream out. He wanted to die rather than let this battle continue. Still, he held on, however painfully, for this had always been his nature. He was a soldier. He remembered that now as he had not for many years.

The battle went on for what seemed like an eternity, then Cassian finally took his hand away, and the attack ceased as abruptly as it had begun. The part of Somar's mind that was still able to focus on the world heard the boy laughing.

"You are amazing, sir!" said Cassian.

Somar stared in disbelief at the young man. Once, years ago, Somar had been captured by the Iligren army, and more than twenty of the kingdom's most powerful sorcerers had spent several weeks attempting to bore into his mind. Somar had resisted them, as well as the physical torture the army had inflicted on him. None of it had been able to break him. Yet this boy, over the course of a few seconds, had surpassed everything they had done.

"You have my deepest respect, you stubborn bastard," said Cassian, still laughing slightly.

The compliment seemed ridiculous. Defense was infinitely easier than offense. Neophis had taught Somar that. "Why did you stop?" Somar whispered. He felt out of breath, though nothing physical had happened.

"I could not keep going without killing you," said Cassian. "I have never taken the life of another human. I should hate to have you as my first."

Somar stared at the boy. "Why did you make the attempt?"

"You said that strength alone is not enough. Personally, I have very often found that it is. I suppose you proved your own point. Pure force can sometimes result only in destruction. I can agree with you that subtlety is necessary, but I will ultimately not compromise— not on any of the things I know are *wrong* in this empire. That is why I need someone like you. You could help me—teach me to be clever in all the ways that I am not—teach me the arts of war as only you know them."

Somar took in a slow breath as he appraised the boy once again. There was something so magnificently honest about him. Somar had spent the last twelve years of his life among cunning politicians and had come to understand the system quite well: the elite of the empire enacted laws to maintain and increase their own wealth. The Emperor technically had the authority to overrule the Senate in nearly any matter, but tradition held that his role was to reign and conquer, while the senate handled the administration of ruling. Somar found himself wondering what would happen to the existing system of corruption and self-interest if one like Cassian were to ascend to the throne. The thought was intriguing.

"You would need to build rapport with the common man," said Somar. "If you are fighting for peasants, you have to make sure they know that. Your people here love you almost religiously from what I can tell, but this is only one small pocket of a vast empire. You'll need to play the game in a way it has perhaps never been played before. You have to make the people love you while making the church look antiquated for speaking against you, all without looking like a heretic."

Cassian smirked. "You make it sound so simple. Does that mean you are going to help me? Have you decided that I am worth your time, old man?"

Somar felt a grin cross his face as he said: "I make no promises, but why don't we give one another a try?"

CHAPTER 6: TEMPLE TOWN

Kota was the most amazing warrior I have ever known. Before that though, he was a warm-hearted boy who was seldom treated with the respect that his character merited because he looked a bit like a wild animal. It took me a long time to see past his beastly features myself, and I count this among the largest shortcomings of my life.

—Bishop Otho of the Onkai Order

The sights and sounds of the human city delighted Kota. The shapes of the structures, the warm, vibrant colors painted on so many surfaces, the clothes the humans wore and the way they moved about and interacted with other humans fascinated Kota to no end. He peered over the sides of the wooden cart the Onkai had purchased on the trip for him and the two boys, Nevin and Dorik, whom the Onkai had been unable to return to any parents. The pair of young humans were jumping about the cart behind Kota's back, excited as well by the sights. They seemed remarkably happy for children whose parents had been murdered by a demon, but Kota could not begin to guess what Cassian had done to their minds. When asked, each boy could remember that he had had parents and could describe them with great detail, but the words seemed as of something lost long ago. Kota could not decide if this troubled him or not.

This 'Temple Town,' as Darius called the collection of buildings and people, had grown denser and denser as they traveled eastward. It had begun first with a handful of small, rounded houses spread out over vast fields and gradually became what seemed like a completely foreign world where most of the natural elements had been cleared away or reshaped. Kota gazed what he recognized from his grandfather's numerous descriptions and drawings in the dirt as a 'blacksmith' pounding an orange glowing piece of metal atop an 'anvil.' *Humans were so endlessly inventive!* His silver eyes eagerly drank in every sight.

Many eyes turned to Kota as well along the way, and people whispered to one another—whispers that Kota's shamalak ears could easily decipher:

"Is that one of the forest folk?"

"Did the Onkai capture it?"

"It looks just like a brown boy with wolf ears!"

"Look at its eyes, they're so...*beast-like*! Is it safe to have that thing in the cart with those children?"

A few of the looks he received, which were especially frightened or revolted, troubled him, as did being called 'it.' Still, he felt safe and relaxed with so many Onkai around who had become his friends. He imagined a human walking among his own tribe and all the commotion that would stir, and he forgave the townsfolk their staring.

"These people are good folk, they just aren't used to seeing a boy like you," said Darius, who was walking alongside the cart. Kota detected the slightest note of tension in his voice.

"I *un-der-stand,*" said Kota, straining his tongue to carefully speak just the way his new friends did.

This brought out a small chuckle from Darius. "Aren't you afraid even a little? Doesn't it make you uncomfortable to be stared at?"

Kota took a slow look around, taking in every pair of gawking eyes, seeing the fear, the wonder, and even the contempt. "It no matter," he said, returning his gaze to

Darius's tattooed face and grinning. "No shamalak I know see Onkai temple before." He paused, searching for the right words. "It is honor. I very lucky."

Just then, Dorik's little hand grabbed hold of Kota's fingers, and he said: "Make your claws come out, Kota. You can scare all these people."

"Yeah, growl at them," Nevin said.

Darius frowned down at the two boys and said: "Onkai soldiers don't seek to *frighten* people. You live to protect. Is that understood?"

"Y-yes, sir," Nevin said, gazing down. Dorik followed his friend's example. Both boys were enormously excited to be entering into training to become Onkai soldiers, and of course the thought of losing this prospect terrified them.

"Right then," Darius said. He patted Nevin on the head then said, "Keep your eyes open, all of you. You're about to see the temple."

They began to move up a fairly tall hill, the steepness of which caused the cart to tilt back. The two boys ran to the back of the vehicle and leaned against its wooden rails, but Kota maneuvered himself to the front and grabbed hold. He was dizzy with excitement. When the cart passed over the top of the hill, he saw an enormous wall of deep gray in the distance. Men were walking along the top of it wearing armor like Darius had. On the two ends were great towers of stone reaching up into the sky with flames burning up out of their centers. Several poles rose high above the walls, and they were topped with beautiful dark blue flags decorated with a winged figure floating above a crescent moon. The temple was immense. It was not as large as the elvin city had been, but Kota guessed that many hundreds of people could live within the high walls.

"People come from all over the world to train here, and to worship Anestia, our Holy Goddess of the Moon," Darius said.

Kota gawked at the structure. "How long it take to become Onkai?"

"Usually twelve years," Darius replied. "It is incredibly hard work." The captain glanced back at the two boys and gave a dark chuckle. "I see those smiles, but you two aren't going to be playing with swords all day. Most of the first year is about theology. I don't suppose either of you can read?" Both boys shook their heads. "You will learn that first from Master Bendick. He's mean as hell. You can tell him I said so. He'll have you for four hours a day. You'll also spend an hour a day in silent prayer. There will be physical training as well, but for the first two years that will come mostly in the form of stretching and working with weights. Master Donthal will be in charge of that. He's meaner than Master Bendick—actually, I used to think he was the most horrible bastard alive."

The two boys were looking at each other with nervous expressions. To Kota, Darius's descriptions sounded marvelous. Unlike the boys, he had seen for himself the incredible discipline and skill Onkai soldiers possessed. He thought he would endure anything in the world to achieve such perfection as a warrior and be able to protect people the way the Onkai did. These thoughts rushed through his mind as he looked at Darius and said in a nervous voice: "You think that maybe shamalak could become Onkai... if he work very, very hard?"

Darius's expression became suddenly troubled. He opened his mouth to speak, but then only breathed out, hesitating.

Behind Kota, Nevin spoke up: "You can't be in the Onkai, Kota."

"Yeah, you're not even human," Dorik said. "You're what the priests call... um... what is it? A *lower creature*."

There was nothing cruel in Dorik's tone, but Kota felt his heart sink at the words. He looked at the anguish on Darius's face and knew that his idea was impossible. Kota swallowed, forcing himself to forget the notion. The human world was beyond his reach. He was never meant for it, and it was never meant for him. "You right," he said, managing to smile back at Dorik. "Idea no good."

"You certainly have more than enough courage," Darius said, and he put a gloved hand on Kota's head and ruffled his hair. The captain was smiling, but Kota could see he was still troubled. There was very little speaking in the cart after that as they moved toward the enormous structure. The boys fell into some whispered conversation about swords and Kota returned his attention to the human village. There were more stares from the people around him. Some were curious, some revolted, the eyes of a few children lit up with amazement at him, but he could not help noticing that none of the eyes were *friendly*. No one seemed to be looking at him like he was a person. He began to feel strange and ugly, and he recalled his grandfather's many warnings to keep away from humans.

The cart eventually came to the enormous wooden doors of the Onkai temple. They were beautifully carved masses of dark wood adorned with short metal spikes. Two guards stood flawlessly still on either side holding what looked like gleaming short swords at the end of long staffs in front of them. One of them stepped forward as they approached and said: "Welcome home, Commander Darius." He pressed his right fist into his left palm and bowed.

"Thank you, soldier," Darius said.

The doors opened then, and a mountain of a man also covered in Onkai markings walked out with an excited look on his face. He was perhaps ten years older than Darius based on the wrinkles around his eyes and the gray strands within his long, thick beard. He walked up and grabbed Darius's outstretched hand between both of his and said: "Welcome home, Brother Darius."

"Thank you, sir," Darius said, shaking this man's hand and lifting his own trembling, injured left arm to make a fist, which he pressed into his right palm. In this state, he gave a bow.

The large man nodded and gazed at the two boys in the cart and then at Kota, displaying a broad grin. "Welcome to you as well, Kata is it?"

"Kota," Darius said.

"Yes, *Kota,*" the man repeated. He looked at Darius and said: "Most of the temple has heard about the report you sent ahead. We've all been eager to meet this little hero." He turned at Kota again and said: "Did you really tear a kothla's eyes out?"

"I... I no remember," Kota said, flushing a little. "It happen very fast."

"Well, you saved the life of one of our finest officers. That is no small thing, my boy." The large man came nearer and put a meaty hand on Kota's shoulder and peered at him. "Gods you have fierce eyes," he said with a laugh.

"Thank you, sir," Kota said. This human at least seemed very friendly.

The bearded man laughed louder and patted Kota on the arm and said: "Thank *you* for saving my dear commander's life! You shall be our most honored guest." He frowned suddenly. "Where are my manners? I am Bishop Otho Vegen."

"This is the leader of the Onkai Order, Kota," Darius said.

Kota's eyes went wide, and he bowed his head quickly and said: "It greatest honor of my life to meet you, sir."

"Let's have none of that," the bishop said with another chuckle. "I understand you befriended a starborn. Meeting me can hardly be your greatest honor." He turned to Darius and said: "Your little friend has fine manners." He leaned over the edge of the cart and looked down at Kota's leg, then turned his eyes to Darius's arm, inspecting the deep cut in the armor. The bishop let out a sigh and said: "Here I am, holding you both in conversation when you need to see Lady Gretis. She has already made preparations for the two of you. Go to the infirmary right now. That is an order. But..." he glanced back and forth between the two of them and said quickly: "I do insist that both of you dine with me tonight though."

"Yes, sir," Darius said, again forcing his left fist up for what seemed to be the Onkai gesture of respect. "Thank you, sir."

"Thank you, sir," Kota said, putting his own fist into his palm and bowing his head.

This triggered another toothy smile in the bishop. The man turned to one of the guards and said: "Soldier, help this brave young shamalak to the infirmary."

"Yes, sir," the guard said, and he immediately walked over and scooped Kota up in his arms, seeming to lift him as if he weighed no more than a baby. The man carried Kota in through the doors and Darius walked alongside them both. Behind, Kota heard the bishop's deep voice say: "Well now, I hear you two poor fools wish to enter our academy." Then the doors shut.

"He seems to like you, Kota," Darius said. "You have a talent for earning the affection of great people."

Kota almost did not hear him. He was looking around the enormous hall, gazing at the strange, magnificent suits of armor stood up on small stone squares, and the many different weapons that hung from the wall on carefully placed hooks. There were blades of every size and shape, crossbows made from bone and iron, spiked metal balls attached to chains, and so many more things Kota could not begin to recognize.

"The elvin armor is my favorite—most people's favorite really," Darius said. He pointed to an incredibly intricate suit of golden armor that stood in the center of the left wall. It was a little smaller than some of the others, but the etchings in the metal and the beautiful curves and the sparkling mesh of what Kota would eventually learn was especially fine chainmail around the stomach and at the arms made the suit unquestionably the most skillfully made set in the room. "Our curator had to negotiate for two years to have this thing on display. The elves do not like anything of theirs in the hands of we crude and warlike humans."

They walked down the hall and several others, eventually coming to a wooden doorway, and as they drew near to it, Kota began to detect many strong scents in the air that seemed to belong to plants. When Darius opened the door, the smells grew stronger, and Kota coughed, unable to withstand them.

"There you are," said a tall woman with a thick, wild mane of black hair with a few silver strands. Kota noticed immediately that her deep, olive skin was far closer to his own skin color than the other humans he had met. She was standing behind a large wooden table with bits of different plants upon it and several clay bowls. For a brief moment, she stared at Kota with beautiful hazel eyes that held a strange and serious intensity. Then she shifted her gaze to Darius and smiled. "I understand you both have wounds that not even a starborn could heal." She stepped around the table and wiped her hands on the apron the hung from her slender neck. Kota noted that she looked strong and regal. She was built like the female warriors of his tribe – not massive, but lean and strong, *and she was beautiful...*

"Darius, come over here" Gretis said. “And you, put the boy on one of the cots." She spoke with a calm, confident authority that reminded Kota of Cassian.

Kota noted as the soldier carried him to one of the white, cloth beds that the woman had referred to him as ‘the boy’ rather than ‘the shamalak.’ It was a small thing, but he appreciated it. He watched as the woman walked over to Darius and said: "Armor off."

"Yes, ma'am," Darius said, and he obediently stripped off his leather armor and placed it on a cot behind him. As

Darius revealed the dense mass of muscle that was his upper body, Kota could not help but stare at the intricate tattoos that ran all over his arms, chest, and back.

"Mmh, that is an ugly gash," Lady Gretis said, staring into the wound. "It was a good thing your sorcerer friend cauterized the cut, or you would be here to have me remove this arm. Alright, have a seat." As Darius sat down on the cot, the woman moved over to Kota. "Hello little one," she said, meeting his eyes, and again Kota noticed an unnerving intensity in her expression. It did not seem to be disgust or curiosity about what he was. It was something else altogether.

"Hello, ma'am," Kota said, following Darius's example.

Lady Gretis knelt down and eyed the splint Cassian had made for him, frowning. "Well I suppose this is the best he could achieve in the middle of an abandoned city, but I think we can do better now. You have not put weight on this leg, have you, Kota?"

"No, ma'am."

"Good. Your leg seems to be in remarkably good shape given what you put it through." She tilted her head up then and looked into Kota's eyes, and to his complete astonishment she said in the shamalak tongue: "*When you smelled the demon, you lost control of yourself, did you not?*"

He was too shocked to answer at first. She had spoken the words with effortless precision. "*Yes, that is correct, mother of wisdom,*" he finally said, addressing her as he would one of the honored elders of his tribe.

Gretis blinked, seeming to process his answer. "*You are a true warrior born, little brother. It is my sincerest honor to help you heal.*"

"You can speak shamalak?" Darius said, staring at both of them with a look of shock.

"It is a beautiful language," Gretis said, rising. She walked back to her table and added: "I am nearly finished with your ointment, Darius."

"Cassian said you should use...what was it?"

"Vulanthic leaf," Kota said, remembering Cassian's words.

"Yes-yes, I do know something of what I am doing," Gretis replied. She began to press what looked like a small clay sword handle into a little bowl and mashed it around, carefully sprinkling in other ingredients from little bowls about her table here and there and mashing them together. All the while, Kota watched, wanting to understand the art of what she was doing. With her eyes on her work, the woman said: "You will both need to take things very easy for a time. Darius, you will not return to the field until I approve it. I have already told Otho this. And Kota," she switched to the shamalak tongue: *"You and I must talk more about what happened with the demon and... about a few other important matters. Please come to my home in the morning and let me feed you. We will speak then."*

"I will come, mother of wisdom," he said.

"Lady Gretis will do," she said, returning to human speech. "Now, let me get the two of you wrapped up so that our dear Bishop Otho can have his fun with you."

CHAPTER 7: THALICE

Human beings have unquestionably become the dominant race in the world. Though our bodies are fragile and short-lived compared to some of the older peoples, we can breed and multiply faster than any of them, and we have perfected ways to augment our weaknesses with steel and magic. We cut down vast forests to build our cities, and we have learned to domesticate animals for labor and eating. We have even developed extensive science around growing and harvesting crops. These are the fruits of the glorious human will!
It comes as perhaps no surprise then that several of these older races refer to us as a 'cancer.' They are jealous of all that we have accomplished. They fear us because we dare to be bold, but we will continue to be just that.

—Romulus, Senior General of the Denigoth Imperial Army

Cassian gazed up at the dark sky and watched lightning strike down all around him. He was standing alone atop a hill of black stone. The wind was blowing hard against him, but he could not feel it. *He never felt it.* This dream was about sight and sound. He looked into the many caves and saw hundreds of tiny flowers growing from the rock ceilings. The flowers glowed a fierce blue in the pitch darkness and drooped down like tears.

The dream was coming nearly every night now. There was only one place in the waking world like this. He knew what was calling to him here, and it scared the hell out of him. Still, he called out to the ancient being that lived on this island with the full force of his sleeping telepathic mind: <Let me see you!>

Cassian's eyes flicked open, and he let out a gasp. There was terrible ringing in his skull. He sat up his bed, clutching the sides of his head, digging tense fingers into his scalp. The most powerful creature in the world was summoning him. It had killed all who dared to seek it out... *yet it was calling to him*!

He stared down at his sheets as beads of sweat dripped down his face, and a realization dawned upon him. *Something was wrong.* Nothing ever woke him from the dream. Moreover, the ringing in his skull had not come from the vision, but from somewhere else.

Cassian drew in several slow breaths, willing his mind to clear. When his thoughts quieted, he heard it. He had awoken because some part of his subconscious had sensed another in danger, and now he heard a distinct and terrified voice screaming out. It was coming from a very powerful psychic mind, but one that felt strange and alien.

Cassian called out telepathically. He waited several seconds, but no response came.

Cassian shoved the silk sheets off his body and aligned his senses, and then stared into the murky blackness of his room, calling upon his power. Invisible tendrils of his magic reached out to the metallic sconce on his wall and carried back a mental image of the fibrous wick of the candle. There he focused his energy, accelerating the particles of air into a furious vibration until the candle burst into flame. As warm light brought the details of his enormous room into view, he quickly got to his feet and moved to his cabinet.

The other mind continued to cry out as Cassian almost clumsily slipped on a fresh set of clothing. His heart was beginning to race. Whoever this person was, he or she was running scared from some threat. Cassian could feel this even as he dressed. Through some deep instinct, every fiber of his being cried out that he could not let this person come to harm.

He slipped the chain of the Elokien around his neck. Then with his tunic, pants, boots, and a thick cloak on his body, he dashed to the window nearest his bed and shoved the shutters open. His room was in the Western tower of his estate, overlooking the castle entrance on one side and on the other, where his gaze was locked, the courtyard. Far below, across to the opposite wall were the stables where Sonta, his favorite mare, rested. He reached out to her familiar consciousness, rousing her simple mind and then slipping inside. Within a few seconds, he was seeing the interior of the stable through her dull horse eyes. Stretching his magic field out through the air and downward, he took hold of the latch to her stall and lifted it. Then he willed her to walk out to the small room at the end of the stable where Fomis, the stable boy, slept. He opened this door with his magic as well and guided Sonta to the young man where he willed her to drop her head and nudge his face.

"What?" Cassian heard Fomis mutter through Sonta's ears. The young man gazed up and saw Sonta standing over him. "Oh," he said, staring into the horse's eyes and smiling, "It's you, my lord. I'll have her saddled up for you right away." Cassian returned to himself in the tower and took a brief moment to open the drawer under his bed and snatch out a silver coin to give to Fomis. He was grateful for quick-minded servants who understood their lord and how to serve him, especially at such critical moments, and it was his policy to reward competence.

Cassian hurried from his room and ran down the spiral staircase, down to the main hall where he found one of his soldiers standing guard. "Get the gates open," he said.

"Yes sir!" said the soldier, looking a little confused.

Cassian ran out into the courtyard where the stable boy was already bringing his horse into view, bridled and saddled. Cassian sprinted to the beast and took the reins from Fomis's hand, exchanging the silver coin for them.

"Thank you, sir," said the boy, grinning at his reward.

Cassian mounted his mare and rode up to the front gates. They were already being opened. He came to the pair of guards at the entrance, who stood at attention, and said: "I need twenty men ready to head west. Look for my signal."

"Yes, sir," said the man with a nod. "Is there trouble in the town?"

"I am not certain. Just get the men out." With that, Cassian sent Sonta into a gallop. In the back of his mind, he was ever aware of the telepath calling out to him. He focused, trying to locate the source of those cries. It seemed to resonate from the small forest to the west of his castle, at the cliffs that overlooked the ocean. He made his best guess at the direction and pushed Sonta to the limits of her endurance over dirt and wet grass.

Fear began to creep into his heart as the two of them neared the cluster of trees. Impressions of other minds than the one he was searching for entered his perception that were vicious and bloodthirsty. They belonged to humans, and in contrast, he knew with sudden certainty the one who had cried out to him was *not human.*

The hunters were in a cluster at the south end of the trees, while their prey was somewhere near the north end. Cassian rode Sonta along the edge of the trees, reaching out with his mind, trying to communicate to the strange being that he wanted to help. It would not answer, or perhaps it could not. Its consciousness was so alien that he wondered if it was even possible to communicate with it telepathically.

Cassian and Sonta moved together through the trees to the edge of a sharp cliff when he finally sensed the being was very close by. He climbed down from his mare and walked around, perceiving a strange energy in the air. Again, he tried to reach out with his consciousness, but no answer came. Then he tried merely calling out: "Hello?"

The sound of his voice sent a shock of terror through the being, and from this, he sensed precisely where it was. Cassian moved to the cliff's edge. Below his feet, he saw a small cave in the side of the cliff. Carefully, he climbed down to it. The ocean was crashing hard against the rocks below him, spraying up its horribly cold mist and making his path slippery. His face was dripping when he came to the cave mouth and poked his head in.

A pair of turquoise eyes glowing brilliantly in the pitch black of the cave stared out at him. They illuminated a smooth, thin face that was contorted in fear. Cassian heard nervous, high pitched breathing as the eyes looked him over. They were so utterly beautiful... It took Cassian a moment to see past them to the shape of a small, thin body clothed in a dress. Under folds of golden hair, he saw pointed ears, and he realized with sudden shock that he was looking at an elf.

Cassian swallowed. Irreverent as he was of most things, it was exhilarating to be in the presence of an immortal. His magic reached out to the elf's form, and it sent back strange and impossible impressions. Her body seemed almost not to be physical matter but highly focused energy - an energy that was unlike anything he had ever encountered. It was magnificent! He was in awe, and for a brief moment, all he could do was stare in wonder.

"Hello," he said again, finally composing himself enough to speak.

"*Andraka,*" the elf girl squeaked, pronouncing the word in a strange, beautiful accent. "*Andrak kes venta*!" She sounded terrified.

Cassian took a few steps into the cave. The ceiling was so low that he had to hunch. As he moved closer, the girl let loose a shriek and backed deeper into the shadows. "It is alright," he said, speaking in a gentle tone so that even if she did not understand his words, she might at least comprehend that he was not her enemy.

The elf *was* a telepath—of this, Cassian was certain—possessing psychic powers on par with his own, yet he could not form a connection with her. She was not blocking him. It seemed more a matter that their minds were too radically different from one another to coalesce. He had read of this before. Telepathic connection between an elf and human was believed to be impossible. Each time he sent a piece of his mind to her, it rebounded back into him, yet as he tried over and over, the elf seemed to form some understanding of what he was doing, for, after a moment, the fear of him greatly diminished, and she dared to crawl closer to him.

"Paradai?" she said, tilting her head to the side and staring at him. The word seemed to be a question.

"Can you feel my emotions?" said Cassian, gazing back at her. "I can feel yours. I will not hurt you, I swear it."

"Naj mekan," the elf said, and she edged closer. She was a small thing, looking by her features to be perhaps fourteen or fifteen years old, though Cassian had no idea if elves matured through childhood at the same rate humans did. She stared into his eyes for a long moment, and then timidly reached out her hand toward his face. She hesitated before touching him, looking again into his eyes as if to make sure it was safe. Cassian remained still, anticipating what he guessed she was attempting and readying himself. "Naj mekan," she said again, and then she pressed the tip of her finger against his forehead.

Cassian gasped. He had been readying another attempt to bridge minds with her, but the instant she touched his skin, there was a furious psychic reaction. He could feel a wall between them, alive and electric like solid lightning. It pushed against him with terrible crackling force, blocking him from the girl. Cassian might have drawn back from it, but a stubbornness rippled through him. He could feel the elf's mind just on the other side of the barrier. *Connection between elf and human was possible!* It was only that no one had ever pushed hard enough.

Cassian shut his eyes and drew into himself, gathering all his psychic strength at once. Then he lashed forward with every shred. The barrier between them hissed and snarled, but Cassian pushed still harder.

With a terrible crash, the wall shattered, and suddenly their minds were drawn toward one another uncontrollably. Memories, thoughts, feelings rushed from the girl into Cassian faster than he could comprehend, and just as furiously his own thoughts and memories were spilling out into her.

The elf drew her hand back in terror, but it was too late. The gates had been opened, and their minds continued to flood one another. Every piece of knowledge, every secret of Cassian's, every thought he had ever held was flowing into the elf girl. At the same time, what he gained from her was beyond the scope of any telepathic exchange he had ever imagined—*an entire life*!

Cassian could not say how much time passed in the maelstrom of that exchange, but for at least several minutes after it finally ceased, he sat stupefied, and so did she. The two of them stared at one another, both in awe of the profound connection into which they had blundered.

"Your name is Thalice... you are from the house of Corostine," he finally said.

The elf's gleaming eyes widened. She was panting, but she managed to say: "Naraj Cassian Asango, coro tes sahalek vesladine," and Cassian's mind translated the words as quickly as she spoke them: *"You are Cassian Asango, Starborn of the Nineteenth Generation."*

He was amazed to find he understood the elf language perfectly. His mind had absorbed far too much to sort out in a few moments, but he knew everything Thalice knew. He could see the palace she grew up in, could see the faces of her parents, and could feel the love she had for them. Cassian knew what it was to be an elf: to exist as an immortal, to commune with the life force of every living thing in existence, to neither eat nor drink but draw energy from the sun.

It was unbelievable to know someone so thoroughly, and to be known as well. Cassian could not wrap his mind around it. In a few seconds, this girl had become closer to him than anyone ever had, or probably ever would, and as he stared at her, all he could do was laugh. She laughed as well. They were still connected.

"I do not think there has ever been a pair like us," said Cassian.

"No", Thalice said with a giggle in her beautiful native tongue, *"No one has ever dared to do what you just did."*

"I... barely understood what I was doing," laughed Cassian.

Thalice crawled closer and wrapped her arms around him and whispered: *"I cannot believe how alive you are!"*

No one had hugged him in years—not since his mother had died. It made his heart ache. Thalice was his family, or at least that is how it felt.

"I am sorry about your parents. It is so horrible... the way you had to watch her die... your mother!" Thalice was crying suddenly, and Cassian was gripping her. He had never spoken of his mother's final moments to anyone.

This profound intimacy was abruptly interrupted by the sound of snarling dogs. Cassian breathed deeply and said: "I nearly forgot you were being hunted."

Thalice rose to her feet. *"It was so foolish of me to come out here alone."*

"I will not let them near you," said Cassian.

"I know," said Thalice, gazing into his eyes.

"Stay here," he said. Thalice nodded, and he crawled back out of the cave and climbed up the cliff face. As his head came up over the top of the stone, he found himself face to face with a dark-furred hunting dog that growled and bared its teeth. Cassian glared back. The minds of dogs were simple. He wrestled control of the beast's psyche and quickly bent all of its instincts and loyalties to his will. By the time he made it up the cliff, he was the dog's master. When its original owners came bounding through the brush, it snarled at them, ready to fight and die to protect him.

Cassian stared as a group of swarthy looking men came into view. He counted seven, three with crossbows, three with swords, and an older man holding a torch whom he could feel was a sorcerer of limited talent. Cassian stood still as they approached, his new pet at his feet, growling.

"Hello," he said in a loud voice that did not conceal his irritation.

The word took the men by surprise. One of them, a very tall man with a long orange beard holding a curved sword, stepped forward and said: "Who might you be, my young lad?"

"I am the lord of this land," said Cassian.

The man laughed, and most of his comrades laughed with him. "Are you now?" he said. "You're the *starborn*?"

"Yes," said Cassian. He glared at them, and his eyes fixed on those of the sorcerer. Telepathically, he said: <Tell them who I am.>

The man's wrinkled eyes went wide as he finally sensed Cassian's aura. "H-he's telling the truth," he rasped, immediately beginning to tremble. "H-his power—he could kill all of us right now!"

Cassian sensed fear creep through the cruel minds. He did not bother to tell them to disarm. He looked at the sorcerer, scanning his thoughts for a brief moment. "Your name is Bokin. I understand it takes a sorcerer to track elves. How many have you caught?" The man's thoughts shifted to the subject, and Cassian found his answer. "Three. The last one was a boy. You cut his throat over a barrel to get his blood." Cassian stared into the sorcerer's terrified eyes and suppressed the urge to kill him immediately. Instead, he held up his hands and whispered: "*Estrieka nesagul vedath.*"

The three spectral entities he summoned entered the mortal dimension through his mind, and he allowed them to take hold of pockets of his energy. They combined according to his thoughts, forming into a glowing white construct that mirrored the face of Thalice. Cassian gave a tiny smirk at this. *She had already become ingrained in his subconscious.*

As the men stood gaping at the glowing face, he willed it into the first of them. Intangible, the spell passed into flesh. It took hold of the man's vascular system and drained blood away from his brain. Before the murderer knew what was happening, he lost consciousness. The other killers began to panic, but Cassian moved the spell at the speed of thought from one to the next to the next. The sorcerer might have put up some resistance if he had had any real skill, but he fell victim as readily as the others.

"That was well done," Thalice said from behind. Cassian turned to see her face looking up from behind the rock.

He stepped away from the unconscious men, already forgetting them. "I will never be able to pronounce the words of your language," he said with a chuckle.

"You will. Muscle memory was part of the exchange. Let it flow between your brain and your tongue." She grinned and said in perfect Tethric: "Cassian Asango enjoys eating clams."

"I suppose elves have an easier time sorting so much. Your brain is designed to take in thousands of years of information. Mine can probably handle a century at most."

"Yes, but your mind is so vibrant!" she said, and Cassian noted that she had developed complete fluency in his language in the span of a moment. There was not even a trace of an accent. "If I lived two thousand years on from this minute, I do not believe I would ever feel anything so fierce and beautiful as your short, mortal life. Do you have any idea how beautiful you are?"

"I can hardly believe this is real," Cassian said, gazing into the marvelous turquoise eyes that burned in the night. He had never been so at peace with anyone, not even his mother. He watched her climb up from the stone and dance across the grass to him, perceiving every step as viscerally as if he were taking it himself.

"You are happy," Thalice said. She reached out and touched Cassian's face. "It is alright to be happy, you serious, angry boy. You used to be very happy once. Do you remember?"

"I remember," Cassian whispered. He thought of a moment long ago when he was feeding ducks near a pond with his parents. He kept trying to catch one of the baby ducks, but they could all run on their little feet just a little faster than he could. His parents were both laughing, and so was Cassian. He knew Thalice was seeing this memory with him. She had never once laughed with her own mother and father.

"Your parents," Cassian whispered. He reached into his cloak and drew out the Elokien. "Your father came here to ask me—to demand this. It belongs to your family." Cassian understood every detail of what had happened. Thalice had followed her father without his knowledge. She had wanted to learn more about the humans, especially one that was what the elves refer to as *sahalik,* a starborn. Her father was probably only a short distance away, resting and hiding from human eyes. Elves were at the height of their power during the day, and he likely wanted to face Cassian at his full might. Thalice had called out to him telepathically when trouble had come, but Cassian's mind had interfered with their connection.

"Call your father," Cassian said.

Thalice hesitated, then nodded. He felt her telepathy reach out as if it were his own, and almost immediately he felt her father awaken to it. The elvin warrior moved toward the two of them. Cassian could feel the swell of energy approach. He watched in anticipation as a slender figure stepped silently from around a tree and looked at him with the same burning turquoise eyes as his daughter. The elf wore the full golden armor of an elite warrior, a Zenthrite.

"Hello," Cassian said in the elvin tongue, surprised to find that it flowed easily from him.

The elf tilted his head a little to the side, peering at Cassian. After a moment he said in a cold, even tone: *"You speak our language? No human can speak Naliskish."* He turned and looked at his daughter, and his eyes widened just a little. *"What have you done, my dear?"* He was angry, or at least the elvin approximation of anger, which seemed to Cassian more like mild irritation.

"Can you see it, father?" Thalice said, and she smiled a beautiful smile at him.

"How ghastly," he said, his tone barely changing.

"I am well, father," she replied. She was not afraid of him. He had never punished her, and likely never would.

"I believe you are looking for this," Cassian said. He held up the Elokien.

"Yes, that is my property. I require you to give it to me."

"I refuse," Cassian answered.

The elf stared at him for a very long moment, then reached down and drew out a sword from his belt. The blade glowed a fierce yellow. Cassian understood the enchantments on the thing enough to know he could never achieve infusion of such magic if he lived to be three hundred years old. He also knew it was not enough to kill him. Even at his full power and skill, a Zenthrite could not overcome a starborn.

"A human has no right to refuse an elf his property. You risk conflict between our people. Give me the Elokien." The elf raised the brilliant blade and pointed the tip at Cassian.

"You may have it when I die," Cassian said. *"I will make sure it will be returned to you then."*

"That is unacceptable. A human has no claim to such things. You hold a sacred object that members of my house spent many human lifetimes constructing." Though the tone hardly changed, the elf's blazing eyes narrowed in an expression that nearly approached hostility as he added: *"Keeping such a relic from its rightful owners constitutes an act of war."*

"War?" Cassian said, returning to his native tongue, which he knew this elf understood because *Thalice knew.* "We would crush you."

The turquoise eyes narrowed still further as the elf replied in perfect tethric: "Your arrogance—"

"Is entirely founded," Cassian said. He possessed vast knowledge of the elvin people now, and all of it rushed to the forefront of his mind as he spoke: "Shall we go over the logistics? Your people are extremely potent on the battlefield. Every one of your soldiers is worth at least twenty of our very finest. However," Cassian took a step toward the elf, staring into the blue-green eyes, "you have less than three thousand able-bodied fighters on this continent, while my empire has hundreds upon hundreds of thousands. You know this, and I know this, so do not make impotent threats."

The zenthrite nearly glared now. "You would steal from us?"

"I did not take this from an *elf,*" Cassian said, holding up the amulet. "Your family lost this trinket nearly five centuries ago to Daibok's army. A demon used it against me, but I defeated him. I claim the elokien as my prize for the rest of my human lifespan. Then you may have it back."

"Our treaty with your empire has no provisions for such an arrangement," the Zenthrite said.

"It contains no provisions at all regarding talismans," Cassian replied. "You and I must reach our own agreement."

"And what if I refuse your terms?"

Cassian returned to the elvin tongue as he said: *"Then I invoke Eskathon."* Cassian could feel Thalice's alarm at this, but he whispered in her mind to trust him.

The elvin warrior stared at Cassian, his eyes showing both surprise and fear. He had, of course, not imagined a human would invoke elvin law. *"You would fight me to the death?"* he finally said.

"I would kill you. Easily." Cassian held up his hand and sent a small burst of his power forward to the tip of the elf's weapon. There was a brilliant white flash, and the sword was knocked back so hard the zenthrite nearly lost his grip on it. Cassian sensed great fear in the immortal's mind, and he said: *"Do you accept the challenge, or will you reconsider my original offer?"*

The elf thought on this for a long moment. Then he said: *"I accept your original offer. Swear to your own terms by one of the Gods."*

"I do not worship any gods. I swear it to you on the grave of my mother."

"Acceptable," the elf said after yet another long pause.

<You can be something of a bully,> Thalice whispered in his mind.

<Does that make you detest me?>

<I could never detest you, but I knew you would not kill him.> Thalice put her hand on his chest. <I fear for you.> She drew ever so slightly closer to him and whispered through her lips: "I never knew I could feel so much for anyone or anything."

Her father made a little grunt. They both turned to see him staring at them. *"Thalice, we must return home now,"* he said.

"Go with your father," Cassian sighed. There were countless things they might have said to one another, but none of them could ultimately matter.

"Goodbye, my dear one," Thalice said as she pressed the side of her face against his chest. Then she returned to her father, and the two of them disappeared back into the forest.

Cassian turned back to the men lying unconscious on the ground. What had just happened felt like a dream. It was a beautiful dream, and he would hold it in his heart as long as he lived, but this was his life, cold and harsh, with little room for the warm affections of the heart.

CHAPTER 8: THE BLADE WITCH

Certainly not all the humans I met were friendly to me. I was a brown-skinned 'creature' with strange retractable claws and eyes like a predator. Still, I came to learn that, just like my own people, most human beings are kind and try to do right in their lives. When you travel the world and experience as much as I have, eventually you stop placing so much importance on the differences and instead seek out the virtues that are universal everywhere, such as simple kindness.

—Kota of the Forest

"Hello!" Kota shouted as he came to the hilltop. Gretis was thirty or so paces away sitting at a small table on the grass in front of her beautiful wooden house. A second chair and plate had been set out. Kota detected the scent of roasted meat and the grease that humans used in their cooking.

"My goodness, Kota," Lady Gretis said in a soft voice. Unlike the others in this place, she understood how well he could hear and did not shout. She stood and walked over to him quickly. "I gave instructions for a horse to be given to you."

"I no like riding horse," Kota said.

The woman laughed. "It is quite impressive you would hobble all this way rather than sit on a saddle." She gazed down at the cast. "How does your leg feel?"

"It itch a little, but no hurt."

"Good. I don't claim to understand what the starborn did, but you are healing remarkably quickly for such a wound." Gretis gestured to the table and said: "I hope you like eggs, though perhaps you have never had fried ones before. Please come and take a chair." The two of them walked together back to the table, and Kota sat down in front of a clay plate of eggs, which smelled of butter and salt.

"Did you sleep well in the infirmary?" Lady Gretis asked as she took a delicate sip from a small ceramic cup.

Kota smiled at the lovely woman. "I no like human beds. Too soft. I like sleeping on grass or on a nice tree branch when it curve and split just right. I like to look up at stars."

"I enjoy sleeping under the stars myself," Gretis said, giving him a little wink. She had a strange black paint around her eyes that made her look even more mysterious than she already was. Kota found himself gazing at the silver cuffs around her arms above the elbows, which had intricate carvings of wolves and lions bearing fang and claw.

"Did you have trouble finding your way here?"

"No," Kota said with a shrug. "Darius worry I no find your house, but you easy to track. You work with smelly plants. I follow your scent without needing to bend down."

Gretis chuckled softly at this. "I know you are new to this culture, but you must learn never to tell a human woman she is *smelly,* Kota."

"Oh, I sorry," he said. He lowered his gaze to the small metal knife on the table and an accompanying tool he did not recognize. Kota preferred to eat with his claws, but he thought it polite to eat as humans eat when among them.

"So, tell me about the demon. Did you see it first or smell it?" As Gretis said this, she sliced off a bit of egg with the knife and scooped it with the other utensil.

Kota attempted to follow her example, though the egg slipped out of his spoon. "I see it," he mumbled. "It look right at me. I get very scared. I want to run."

"But you did not run." Lady Gretis leaned forward ever so slightly. "Describe what happened next."

Kota took in a slow breath, forgetting the meal and trying to remember the strange event that seemed so muddled in his memory. To tell it as accurately as possible, he switched to the shamalak tongue: *"I was trying to be brave, but when I saw that horrible creature, I felt terror in my heart. I looked in its eyes, and it was... pure evil. The demon did not seem to care about me though. It leaped toward Darius and started to attack him. Then I smelled it, and suddenly.... my blood began to burn in my veins. I felt my claws, and my teeth change on their own. There was no fear anymore. I...I forgot everything. I only wanted to kill—no, I needed to kill that horrible creature!"*

"Hmm," Gretis muttered, and for a moment she was silent. Then she slowly moved her hands across the table and laid them palm up. "Kota, may I ask you to put your hands in mine for a moment?"

"I . . . if you want," he answered. He reached out and laid his dark, rough hands in Gretis's much smoother ones, and as he did, he became acutely conscious of the dirt beneath his fingernails. The beautiful woman did not seem to notice. Her eyes were closed. She slid her fingers gently around his hands and then leaned her head back.

Kota watched Lady Gretis for a long moment, wondering what was happening. She remained perfectly still, breathing softly. Kota listened to the beat of her heart. It was slow and growing slower. Eventually, he said: "What you do—"

"Silence please," she whispered.

Kota lowered his head, feeling once again embarrassed. He closed his own eyes and tried to make himself still and silent, as if he were stalking prey in the forest. He thought about the hard mixture of bandage and bark around his leg. His skin itched underneath it. He listened to wind blow against the tall grass and the yellow flowers around him.

Slowly, he felt warmth begin to pass through him, and his mind drifted back to the moment he had caught the putrid stink of the demon. The memory flashed in clear brilliance, and... something was coming to the surface inside of him. There seemed to be two separate parts of his mind: the boy and the beast. The beast was alive. He could feel it in his soul, and suddenly that part of was awakening again. It rose up, taking control.

"AHHH!" Gretis screamed.

Kota's eyes flicked open. He looked down at his hands. His claws were fully extended, and they were digging into Lady Gretis's olive skin. He released her hands immediately and said: "I sorry!"

Gretis's eyes were still shut, and she looked dizzy. She wobbled in her chair and then started to slump to her left. Kota shot up and hopped on his uninjured leg around the table to catch her just as she fell toward the grass. "I no mean to hurt you!" he shouted. He looked at the red blood dripping from his fingers, and he felt horribly ashamed.

"Huh?" Gretis grunted, and she grabbed Kota's arm. Slowly, she sat up and then got to her feet, panting. Kota smelled the salty wet scent of sweat in the air and noticed she was dripping. The woman opened her eyes and looked down at him. Her skin had grown pale, and she seemed unable to speak. She just stared at him with wide, incredulous eyes.

"I sorry," Kota said again, his voice cracking. He rose on his good leg. "I no mean to claw your hands."

Gretis lifted her hands and gazed down at the blood. After a long moment, her eyes seemed to soften, and she looked at him. "You have done nothing wrong, Kota," she said in a voice that sounded distant. "This was entirely my doing."

"What you mean your doing?" Kota said.

"I...I need to think. Please give me a few moments. Wait here, I beg you." Without another word, she turned and walked almost clumsily to her house and went inside, slamming the door behind her. Kota stood on the grass feeling very confused.

Gretis stayed in her home for quite some time. Kota sat back down in his chair and waited. Eventually, hunger tugged at his stomach. He resumed his attempt to use the human eating tools, and he got most of the eggs into his mouth, though several pieces dropped onto his lap. When he finished, he sat in silence. The sun climbed slowly up the horizon until it was high over his head and still there was no sign that Gretis was coming back. Kota was quite used to being alone, and he bore the solitude of the chair without self-pity or frustration. When the sun was beginning to dip back down over the treetops though, he began to worry about Lady Gretis. Eventually, he picked up his crutch and moved across the grass to her house.

Standing at her door, Kota said aloud: "Lady Gretis? Is you alright?" No answer came. He tried to work the latch, but the door was stuck firmly in place. He looked over and saw a small window with wooden shutters, and he hobbled on his crutch to it. He found a small crack at the center and leaned up to it. Just inside, Kota saw the woman. She was sitting with her legs folded, and her hands, which had been bandaged, were resting in fists on her knees. Gretis's eyes were closed, and she looked utterly still. Kota could not even hear her breathing.

He sighed and leaned back against the house. Whatever Lady Gretis was doing, it was not his place to confront her. For all he knew, she was a great sorceress, and was working some magic he did not understand. Kota only knew that Gretis had been kind to him, and she had asked him to wait for her. He slumped down and sat on the grass and began counting the trees as he had sometimes done when the forest felt especially lonely.

The daylight was beginning to fade when Kota heard the clopping of a horse's hooves. He turned his head and saw an Onkai soldier far in the distance riding a horse toward Lady Gretis's house. Kota watched the figure draw nearer and nearer until he stopped his horse a few paces in front of the house.

"You're that shamalak everyone is talking about," the soldier said. He peered down, and Kota saw that he was a young man, perhaps sixteen or seventeen winters old. Both his chin and head were cleanly shaven, and Kota noted that his tattoos curved up and around his scalp into strange, intricate patterns.

"Yes, I Kota."

"I'm looking for Lady Gretis."

"She inside. You can try to call her, but she no move most of day."

The door opened very suddenly from behind, and Lady Gretis stepped outside. She was calm and collected as compared to the morning. "Hello, Glavius," she said, smiling at the young man. Kota noticed immediately that the bandages were gone from her hands, and he saw only vaguely purple spots of skin where the gashes had been.

"Lady Gretis," Glavius said, nodding.

Gretis turned to Kota and gazed down at him. "You waited all day for me out here. My apologies, Kota, but I needed to make a very important decision—*you have no idea how difficult.*" Her eyes were grim and serious.

"Should I come back later, ma'am?" Glavius said.

"No, Kota will observe."

Glavius looked a little irritated at this, and he muttered: "An audience. *Wonderful.*" He rode his horse over to a wooden rail along the side of Gretis's house and got down and tied up his mount. Gretis stepped inside her door and came back with a pair of swords. Kota's heart quickened just a little at the sight of the weapons, and he peered at them and noticed almost immediately that they were flat where the sharp-edges should be and rounded at the tips. Gretis tossed one of these dulled swords to Glavius, and he caught it by the handle.

"We're sparring today?" he said.

"Yes. Show me the dashban stance." The soldier immediately stepped forward with his left leg and held his sword up with both hands at a slight tilt to his left shoulder. "Too much weight on your left foot," Gretis said, eyeing his body. "You're also gripping the sword too tightly." Her tone was surprisingly harsh.

"Sorry, ma'am," the soldier said, and Kota noticed the quickening beat of his heart.

Gretis stood in front of the young man, her own weapon pointed toward the ground between her feet. She looked at him for a moment and then commanded: "Attack, soldier!"

Glavius leaped forward and swung his dull blade downward toward Lady Gretis's chest, but her weapon snapped up and knocked it away so quickly that Kota almost could not follow the movement. The power of the blow was sufficient to cause Glavius to stumble to the left, and as he did, Gretis's sword whipped up to his throat where it pressed delicately into the skin. "*Clumsy,*" she said. Kota was in awe.

"What did I do wrong?" the soldier said, his eyes wide.

Gretis pulled her sword back and returned to dangling it between her feet. "Let me see. You overextended, which of course we have talked about several times now. You showed me with your eyes *exactly* where you were going to swing. You are breathing too hard, and, worst of all, there was a slight hesitation just before your strike. Try again."

The soldier resumed the stance he had just held. He locked eyes with Lady Gretis and quieted his breathing. He struck again very suddenly, this time stabbing straight for her heart. Gretis's blade again snapped up, causing his thrust to pass over her shoulder. In the blink of an eye, her left hand separated from her sword and darted out to his wrist as her left leg snaked behind his extended right leg, and she flipped him over her hip. The soldier slammed onto his back without his weapon. His sword was in Lady Gretis's left hand.

"Overextension, *again,*" she said. "You're too used to fighting opponents slower than you. You think that reckless style will keep you alive in a fight with a kobold?"

Glavius picked himself up, and Kota saw the frustration in his tattooed face. "I will try to do better," he said in a tense voice.

Gretis handed him back his sword and once again stood with her blade hovering down. "Again. You will continue to *try* until it is done correctly."

"Yes, ma'am," Glavius hissed. He took his time on the next attack, dancing to the side. He tried a few careful, quick strikes, all of which Gretis knocked away with ease and countered with soft stabs with her blunted sword into his chest. She countered attack after attack and gave Glavius sharp criticisms here and there that Kota tried to follow. The lesson was fascinating, but not nearly so fascinating as the strength, speed, and immense skill Gretis displayed. She bested the Onkai soldier over and over, and she had none of the Onkai markings.

"That is enough for today," Lady Gretis finally said. Both of them were sweating heavily. The poor young man had not landed a single strike. "I do see improvement, Glavius. We train with shields tomorrow."

"Yes, ma'am, and thank you," the Onkai said. He walked slowly back to his horse, untied and mounted it, and rode away.

"Were you able to follow the lesson at all, Kota?" Gretis said.

"I... I try," Kota said. "You very great warrior." His heart fluttered just a little as he asked the question that had been burning on his mind since he had first seen her prowess. "Is you stronger than Onkai?"

"Hmm," Gretis grunted. She seemed amused. "Of course, you wish to understand that part. Actually, the answer is more complicated than you might imagine, but before we discuss such things, I elected to show you my training session with Glavius for a reason. Did you notice the way I spoke to him?"

"Yes, you tell him many things about stance and grip and—"

"I said the *way* I spoke to him. Would you say it was kind?"

Kota fidgeted. In his tribe, it was unspeakable for a young one to criticize an elder. "I think you point out many things he do wrong." Kota looked into her eyes and knew this answer was not sufficient. "You scold at him a lot. I think you make him feel foolish."

"Yes," Gretis said with a nod. "Glavius was the best swordsman in his class, *by far*. When he first came to me a short time ago, he was much too cocksure of himself. He harbored the belief that he would become a legendary warrior in the order and achieve the rank of legate. Perhaps he will when I am done with him, but can you imagine why such overconfidence might prove to be a deadly mistake for an Onkai soldier?

Kota's mind flashed to the battle in the forgotten city. Darius's men had fought as one. "Maybe because Onkai fight together. No one try to...to show he strongest."

"That is a piece of the answer, but try to think harder."

Kota thought of the kothla and how it had descended down at Darius and nearly killed him. "Because some things is stronger than the strongest Onkai."

"Indeed," Gretis said, her lips pursing into a grim smile. "The Onkai are worshiped by the rest of humanity as heroes. They are what young boys pretend to be when they play with wooden swords, but they cannot afford to think of themselves as heroes. The business of the soldier is the business of death, Kota. You saw what a single one of those demons was like. Imagine an army descending from the sky. And there are other dark creatures of terrible power in this world. The Onkai stand between these things and the human race, and, very often, for all their training and power, they die horrible deaths. One of the greatest assets an Onkai can possess is the knowledge that the slightest overestimation of himself can bring about such a death for him or for his brothers." Her face became somber as she added: "There is no room for pride in the Onkai Order."

"I think I understand," Kota said in a solemn voice.

Gretis stared into his eyes for a moment, then said: "Yes, I think you do. That is at least some assurance to me." She walked briskly back to the table where she had set out breakfast and picked up both chairs. She carried them back and set them facing each other a short distance apart. Then she down and gestured for Kota to do the same.

"What do you know about the Onkai tattoos?" Gretis said when he had climbed into his seat.

"I no understand such things," Kota said.

"I must give you a brief lesson in history then. The markings are called 'holy,' but they are actually magical in nature. The magic itself is in the ink. It is made from the petals of small mystical blue flowers called the 'The Dragon's Tears,' which can only be found in one place in the world—an incredibly dangerous place. The design of the tattoos is actually a complex control system for the power the ink continuously generates. Without these runes, the magic would tear a soldier's body apart within seconds. When administered correctly, the power flows evenly through an Onkai, granting him enhanced strength and speed and resistance to injury. It even bestows a fair degree of protection against other magic.

"The process of placing tattoos on soldiers' bodies is called 'apotheosis.' It was invented by a starborn of the eleventh generation named Dracus Mobius. At that time, the human race was on the verge of being wiped out in what we now refer to as the *first* Demon War. Dracus found a way to create an army capable of defending our people, but he thought it wise to keep this force outside the control of any kingdom. Around this period, the different orders of the church were beginning to form. Dracus created the Onkai Order and became its first bishop. He and the army he built are more or less credited with saving the human race from annihilation."

Kota smiled. It was an honor to learn such things, and Gretis spoke them with a soft, clear voice that made the history seem more magnificent.

She went on: "The process of apotheosis is actually remarkably fast. For all the years of training the initiates undergo, the more experienced sorcerers in the order can imbue one of them with runes in two or three days. This is how Dracus was able to form his army as quickly as he did." Gretis's face suddenly became deathly serious. "The power I showed you when I fought Glavius is far more difficult and...*dangerous* to attain. It is drawn from an art many centuries older than the Onkai Order."

Her hands reached out and took his, and she leaned in, a burning intensity in her blue, human eyes. "I offer you a choice, Kota. Your spirit walk has led you to me, and mine... *after so much,* has finally led me to you." Gretis hesitated, then said: "I will teach you this art if you will choose to learn."

Kota sat up in his chair, gaping. He had not even remotely expected such an offer. The shock overwhelmed him. His mind began racing, imagining acquiring such strength and speed as this woman had displayed.

"You must take time to make this decision, Kota. If you choose to become my apprentice, it will be the greatest commitment of your life. You might never return to living among your people. Your training would take at least ten years, and it will be more difficult than you can imagine." Her grip on his hands tightened ever so slightly. "As I said, this power is *dangerous* to acquire, and the danger is even greater for one of your kind. It may kill you, or change you into something...*horrible*." She released his hands and whispered: "I can explain no more than that. This knowledge has been kept secret for thousands of years for good reason."

Kota gazed down at the grass beneath his feet. His mind was alive with thoughts, but all he could think to say was: "Why you choose me?"

"Because of what you are—what I *think* you are."

"What am I?"

Lady Gretis gave a strangely troubled laugh. "You are the last thing in the world I *ever* expected." She stiffened in her chair and said: "We shall say no more tonight. It is time for you to return to the temple." She stood, and Kota obediently grabbed his crutch and stood up as well.

"Give me your decision when your leg is healed," Gretis said. "That will be enough time, I hope. You have much to consider—abandoning your people for one." She looked sharply into his eyes and said: "Tell no one of this. Not even Darius or Otho." Then she turned and walked back into her house.

For a long time, Kota stood, leaning on his crutch. He could scarcely believe what had just happened. The thought of spending ten winters or more away from his family filled him with sickly worry, and all of Lady Gretis' warnings echoed in his mind... *and yet he knew in his heart he had already made his choice.*

CHAPTER 9: ARKAS

The word "starborn" is an archaic term from a less scientific age that has become far too ingrained in our vocabulary to ever lose. The power that we, the chosen ones, wield does not come from a 'star' at all, but from what we now know to be a comet. 'Estrathian,' as the elves long ago named this celestial object, appears twice a century to fill our world with its vast magical energies. Five human children born around the time the comet graces our sky are imbued with a concentration of magic beyond all others. Most know this, but only those who have studied the old Dhavic texts understand that this power was never meant for man...

—Dracus Mobius, Starborn of the 11th Generation, First Bishop of the Onkai Order

Arkas wiped a bit of sweat from his brow as his gray stallion cantered to within a few hundred paces of the massive stone temple of the Norn. The sun was rising, and the people in the fortified mountaintop town were just beginning to go about their dull, pathetic lives. He slowed to a trot and watched them come out of their squalid little homes, sensing their fear and wonder as they noticed him and his companion.

"You didn't say there'd be this many people," Gorlick grumbled in his low, unnatural voice.

Arkas turned and gazed at the enormous head still concealed under the hood of the expansive black cloak. His companion took a perverse delight in showing his horrible features to his victims or to small groups of people he merely wanted to frighten, but in large cities in the light of day, he was disgustingly shy. Arkas had wondered more than once what the half-breed hoped to accomplish by hiding. He was far too large under the dark cloth for anyone to think him human.

"Calm yourself," he said in a terse whisper.

Arkas willed his horse to trot through the streets. He watched the peasants part ways, some darting into doorways to hide. The town of Aramanthia was quite large, considering how secluded it was from the rest of the empire. The small folk before him were likely very used to receiving visitors from all over the world, but he doubted many of them had stood in the presence of a starborn, or a half-breed ogre for that matter.

The stallion veered suddenly as a boy stumbled backward out of an alley, clutching a leathery ball. Arkas peered down in annoyance as the child, who could have been no more than ten, looked up in shock. Across the alley, a second boy was standing stupidly with his mouth agape.

"I... I'm s-sorry, sir," the lad clutching the ball muttered, stumbling nervously to his feet.

Arkas raised his right hand and sent out an invisible tendril of magic, willing it to wrap tight around the boy's neck. It was best to make a show of power when entering a new place. He lifted the boy up, squeezing the throat and watching without pity as the young arms paddled uselessly at the intangible force.

Arkas spoke aloud in an authoritative voice to the fifty or so people staring. "Which of you fools raised this little rat without any respect for his betters?"

He sensed the satisfying cascade of terror running through the crowd. There was anger as well, but no one dared give voice to it. The boy began to hiss desperately for air, and Arkas said: "I suggest someone speak up before I crush his little peasant neck."

"Sir!" a loud voice shouted. Arkas turned to see an old man in light gray robes with a well-trimmed white beard looking at him. From the silver chain around the man's neck, Arkas knew immediately he was a Lucinian Priest, and from his tone and the air of authority emanating from his mind, he was likely the high priest. "Release that boy at *once*!" the man snapped in a nervous, yet angry bellow.

At these words, Gorlick reached behind his back and unhooked his enormous ax and whipped it out in front of him. Arkas watched the old priest's eyes widen in horror. The double-bladed weapon was massive enough to split a horse in half at the waist, and in Gorlick's quick, powerful hands, it could cleave five men in a single swing.

Arkas smirked as the priest shook. That was how it should be—even a high priest was nothing before a living miracle. "My friend does not like it when people shout at me," Arkas said aloud. He turned to the boy and released his hold. The child fell to the ground, gasping for air. "Scamper away, little rat," Arkas said. "If I see you again, I may dash your brains out."

He felt a wave of relief pass through the crowd as the terrified boy stumbled away. Killing a peasant would mean a good deal of trouble with his father. It had not been necessary anyhow. He had made his point quite clearly.

"Who are you?" the priest managed to ask.

"I am Arkas Adronicus, Starborn of the Nineteenth Generation and Prince of Denigoth."

The priest's face paled, and a new fear seeped through his mind. Arkas's reputation had evidently preceded him. He stepped down off his stallion. "You will take me to see the

Norn." He relished the stupefied look on the old man's face for a moment longer before adding: "*Now*!"

The priest flinched, then said through gritted teeth: "Follow me, my lord." Arkas pulled his horse up alongside the old man and they proceeded forward at a slow pace through the city streets. Gorlick moved to the other side of the old fool, still holding his ax in his hand. The thump of the hard, heavy boots Arkas had had made for his friend fell loud as horse's hooves on the stone tile streets, shaking the ground just a little with every heavy step. The priest walked in utter terror between the two of them, not speaking for several minutes. When he finally was able to form words, he said in a dry voice: "My name is Septicus Mars."

"Yes," Arkas muttered in a tone that reflected how little the priest or his name mattered.

The old man swallowed. "We received no word you were making a pilgrimage here, my prince."

"What of it?" Arkas said.

"What I mean to say, my prince, is that the Norn is in one of her deep slumbers. She rests before a journey across the empire."

"Surely she will speak to me. I am one of the points of the star."

The old man hesitated. "Y-yes, my prince, perhaps she will. It is actually a starborn she is going to visit."

Arkas tensed. The Norn had ignored his summons weeks ago. *Now she was leaving her sanctuary to visit one of his siblings?* Forcing his mouth into a smile, he said: "Who, may I ask, has the honor of her visit?"

"I do not know, my prince, but a prophecy has been ordained for one of your generation from on high. Our lady intends to head west, so logically it would be either Telemachus Vale or Cassian Asango."

"I see," Arkas said. The Norn would cross the empire for one of them. "Has she spoken with Dimitris or Keska?"

"She ventured out several months ago to speak with the female starborn. That is all I know."

Every muscle in Arkas's body began to coil in hatred, but he managed to hold on to his smile. "Well then, it is good I arrived when I did."

They came to the magnificent white steps to the temple. Arkas gazed up at the carved path toward the row of stone pillars that continued along the circumference of the famous temple. So many of the prominent kings and bishops and starborn of the past had come here to speak to the ancient one. Now it was his turn.

"I will see her now," Arkas said. "Wake her if you must and get someone to see to my horse." Arkas held the reigns of his mount out to the old man, who gazed at them incredulously for a few seconds before reaching out. *Evidently such a task would normally be beneath him.*

Arkas watched the grotesquely old man walk along the side of the temple to a young man in white robes of perhaps twenty years who stood gaping at Arkas and his enormous companion. The high priest muttered something to his underling, and the younger man's eyes widened, and then, frowning, he accepted the reigns and led Arkas's horse away. Then the elder priest walked with quaking knees up the grand stairway.

"That decrepit wretch had better retire soon, or he'll fall and crack his head open on these steps," Arkas said.

"I'd love to see that," Gorlick's deep, croaking voice answered with a chuckle from under the hood.

"I may well make it happen if he doesn't hurry the hell up," Arkas said, glaring at the quaking figure. "The Norn should keep better servants."

The two of them had to wait perhaps half an hour at the bottom of the steps before the old man emerged from between the two columns again. "The ancient one will see you, Prince Arkas, but your friend must wait outside."

Arkas turned to Gorlick and said with a shrug: "I guess they do not allow hideous half-ogres in the temple. Oh well." Then he spun on his heels and walked up the finely carved steps.

The inside of the temple was beautiful in the morning light. It had human-sized diamond-shaped openings in the wall facing the rising sun so that beams of sunlight passed through and reflected on small pools within. There were fresco paintings of various gods reaching down from the clouds and bestowing gifts on more diminutive mortals with sweeping waves of their great hands. Priests and young scholars walked about reading from scrolls, old men in robes sat in the inner courtyard engaged in discussions of theology. The Norn's temple housed many ancient tomes that had no copy anywhere else in the world. Arkas found all of this vaguely amusing, but he had a destiny far grander than that of any scholar or priest.

"Where is she?" he said, feeling impatient.

"The Ancient One waits below," the old man said. He led Arkas through several hallways to a set of spiral stairs that that led down into a subterranean chamber that had been carved into the rock. Without hesitation, Arkas walked down these steps into the darkness beneath. He realized as he went around the first curve that the path led further than he had first guessed. He reached out with his senses and felt level upon level of winding stairs. Each step had been meticulously carved from the dark stone to be perfectly flat and angled. No human mason was so precise. This chamber beneath the temple had been created with powerful magic.

For several minutes, he walked in near complete blackness as the light from above faded into obscurity, and the warm torchlight from far below just barely crept up. *Was this meant to intimidate visitors?* Arkas chuckled at the notion and heard his voice echo against the smooth walls along with his footsteps. There were far more direct ways to instill fear.

<Hello, young man,> a finely aged feminine voice said in a gentle whisper that was nearly as loud as a shout. There was no echo. The words had come in pristine telepathy communicated into Arkas's mind so clearly that he might have mistaken them for speech.

"Hello," he answered back with his human voice. He could feel the vast, unknowable mind of the being below him. She was thought by many to be the oldest creature in the whole of the world. Arkas doubted his telepathy could resonate in a consciousness so ancient and infinite. There was no need to impress her though. Eternal and wise though she was, she was only a slave.

He stepped into a small chamber lit by candles all around upon shelves and stone tables. The ancient one stood at the center, an incredibly thin figure clad in a cloak like his friend, only far more eerie. She and her clothing were not physically there, or at least that is how it seemed. She was like a *living spell* – a collection of magic standing before him that might disperse or become something entirely different in an instant. The edges of her cloak wisped up and danced like black fire. She stood taller than Arkas by more than a head, though what physical form lay beneath her coat of magic he could not guess. It might be a skeleton from how thin she was, and yet perhaps nothing.

"I have come to hear your prophecy," he said, staring at the strange being. When the Norn said nothing, he continued, "It is my birthright. I am a point of the star."

<Are you?> her telepathic voice hissed in a mocking tone, and suddenly she was directly before him, staring down through what seemed to be an empty hood. He had not seen her move or even vanish and reappear.

Arkas swallowed. This creature could not hurt him. According to every legend about her, she could not touch mortals, nor they her. He found his voice and said: "Y-yes. You will answer my questions. It is my right."

<Questions,> the Norn whispered as if this amused her. She was behind him, whispering in his ear in a way that made his whole body shiver:

Arkas grimaced. "It is still my right to ask three questions, is it not?"

<You may ask, but I give you a warning I have given many times in one form or another: my prophecies have saved kingdoms, but they have also doomed men or driven them to madness. Knowing what lies ahead may alter what lies ahead, and there is nothing I might reveal that you are *meant* to know.>

"Yes," Arkas said impatiently. "Your warnings are well known, and I have read all the stories of men whose lives you destroyed, but I am not some fool. I am *starborn*!"

<As you wish,> she said softly.

Arkas's heart began to race. He had thought carefully for years about this moment. "How am I fated to die?"

<Ah-h-h-h,> the Norn whispered. She was gone entirely then from the room, but he still heard her voice in his mind: <Cassian Asango is your destroyer. He will challenge you to a duel, and you will lose.>

Arkas felt a cold terror seep through him. *He would die at the hands of the heretic?* She had spoken the words so plainly. If it was a duel, would it come soon? What could he do to prevent this? His mind began to run wild, and yet he knew to be careful. The tomes warned that the Norn could not be compelled to give details. As much as he desperately wanted to use his remaining questions to learn more about this duel, he understood the nature of prophecy. She had told him all he needed to know. The rest was up to him.

Arkas breathed slowly for a moment, pushing away his fear. When he was ready, he spoke in an even voice: "Tell me why my father favors Cassian and Dimitris over me. Are they stronger than I am?"

<That is a question of the past, not the future,> the Norn said. She was before him again, standing only a few steps away. <I warn you not to make that mistake again.>

Arkas balled his fists, glaring at the ancient being. *She was so calm.* He hated her. "Fine," he whispered. There was another question he had thought about very carefully: "How can I cause my father to choose me as his successor?"

"You cannot."

The words struck him nearly as hard as the first prophecy. He felt pure fury inside. *Why would the throne be denied to him?* Was his life an absurd joke? Why did his father favor the other two? It was unfair! It was disgusting! Without thinking, he hissed his final question: "How can I kill him? How can I destroy my father, the Great Tacitus?!"

He sensed a psychic gasp from the Norn. All of her haughty arrogance seemed to melt away. *She had not expected him to ask this question.* That gave him some measure of cruel satisfaction. He stared at her and whispered: "Answer me, wretch."

After a moment, the Norn answered in a voice dead of emotion: "On the sixty-eighth day of your twenty-second year, if you sit in front of the sundial in the town of Bendal as the sun sets, a weapon that can destroy your father will fall into your lap."

"Hah!" Arkas grunted, a smile crossing his sweating face. "It will fall *into my lap,*" he repeated. Was this a metaphor? No matter. He could figure it out when the time came. He was sure he could. His terror faded, and confidence returned once more. All he needed to do was stay alive for five more years and he would find a weapon. Whatever it was, if it could kill his father—perhaps the greatest sorcerer in history—then it could kill Cassian Asango, and Dimitris as well. If he were clever, and if he could make the correct alliances and conceal his plans, the throne could still be *his.*

CHAPTER 10: THE SHAMALAK CHILD

Many people think that humanism is a rejection of the gods and religion altogether. On the contrary, our philosophy neither rejects nor embraces theology. Humanism is not focused on exclusion but is a set of ideals about the self and the human race. It is a belief that humanity as a whole is more important than any of its individuals, and yet the greatest service one can render is to achieve his or her own greatness. We reject despair and hopelessness. Whatever made us and why ever we are here, the gift of intelligent life is to be embraced and loved with a fearless heart.

—Cassian Asango

Kota slid his hand up and scratched his ribs under the gray cloth shirt Lady Gretis had given him. It felt unnatural to cover the skin on his back and chest. The cloth smelled like the white substance the humans called 'soap.' Gretis had insisted he wear this human clothing, and she had given him a matching pair of pants, which he liked a little better. They were airy and loose. He thought he could run and climb easily in them when his newly healed leg had regained all of its strength, which was well on its way to happening. She had at least refrained from asking him to wear boots.

The two of them had come to an agreement: Gretis would train him for two moons, or 'months,' as the humans called them, before either of them fully committed to becoming master and apprentice. She had told him she needed to see if her assumptions about him were true, and he needed to decide if he could endure the mental and physical challenges of the training. If all went well, Kota would return to his parents and seek their blessing to continue on for ten or more winters with the fascinating woman. These were her terms, and Kota had readily accepted them.

He sat upon the grass waiting for Gretis to come out of her home, wondering how the lesson would begin. She had instructed him to arrive at sunrise for their first day of training together, and the morning light was just starting to shine through the trees. He grew excited as her wooden door swung open, and she stepped out. Her hair was tied back, and she had a somber look in her eyes. The morning light reflected brilliantly off her silver arm cuffs, giving her a regal glow. Kota's heart quickened even further when he noticed she held the pair of blunted swords under her arm that he had seen the other day. Beneath her other limb was a large wooden box which clinked a great deal as she walked toward Kota.

"Have you eaten?" she said.

"Yes. They give me food in kitchen before I come."

"They *gave* me food in the kitchen before I *came,*" Lady Gretis said in a stern voice. "You will learn to speak Tethric correctly, Kota. Is that understood?"

"Yes, ma'am," he said.

She set the box down and held out one of the swords. Kota took it in his right hand, and his arm dipped immediately. The weapon weighed more than he had guessed. "You will carry that with you all day today," she said. "If I see it out of your hands for even an instant, you will be reprimanded." Kota tightened his grip on the hilt, feeling a little afraid. "No," she snapped, staring at his hand.

"Relax your grip. That weapon in your hands isn't a club. A sword is a precise tool. You must hold it with respect."

Kota relaxed his fingers and tried to imagine wielding the sword with the kind of skill and grace Gretis possessed.

"Yes, good," she said, though there was no warmth in her voice. "Hold it with both hands, right hand on top." Kota obeyed, and Gretis gripped her own sword with both hands and lifted the handle in front of her eyes, angling the blade back over her head. "Raise it up like this," she said.

Kota obeyed, lifting the weapon over his head. It wobbled in his hands.

"Yes, just like that," Gretis commanded. Still holding her own sword, she cocked her head and stared at him, not saying a word. The blade grew slowly heavier in his grip, and it became difficult to keep his balance. Gretis was as still as a statue except for her eyes, which Kota was keenly aware were slowly moving all over him. "Swing downward just like this," she said, and she brought her sword down in a slow, smooth swing until it was level with the ground where it froze again. Kota's muscles were aching, but he tried to follow her movements. He managed to bring the weapon down, but he tipped a little forward when he tried to stop and had to step forward.

"I see," Gretis said, and Kota could read nothing in her tone. "Come this way." She reached down and scooped up her clinking box and then turned and walked across the grass to a tree stump to the left of her house. Kota followed her. She set the box down and opened it, and Kota saw that inside were small red clay cups stacked neatly one on top of the other. Gretis picked one of these cups and placed it upside down in the center of the stump. "You will raise that sword over your head as I showed you and bring it down to touch this cup without breaking it," she said. "You will do this one hundred times in a row without making a mistake. If you break the cup, you will come and ask me for a new one, and the count will start over. Begin." She gestured to the stump.

Kota swallowed and raised the sword and took aim at his target. "No," Gretis said, her voice cutting sharply into his concentration. "Raise your hands higher. Hold it as I *showed* you." She took his hands in hers and lifted them slightly and then angled his hands back further. Then she let go and said: "Strike."

Kota lowered the heavy steel as slowly as he could toward the cup, his arms burning as he did. He managed a tap on his target. It clinked sharply, but to his relief, it did not break.

"Again," Gretis said immediately.

Kota took a slow breath and lifted his weapon. He was careful to hold it the way she had shown him, but once more she said: "No," and gripped his hands and made what seemed like incredibly small corrections. "Strike," she said when she was done. Kota brought his weapon down faster than he had the first time, but he slowed it with his wrists at the last instant. The clink was softer than the first try. He started to smile, but Gretis said: "Again."

Kota successfully struck the tiny object several times more without breaking it, but the sword grew heavier and more cumbersome in his arms. On the eleventh swing, it came down too quickly, and the cup cracked into several pieces. He looked up at Gretis, who did not seem surprised or angry. She calmly bent over and brushed away the broken pieces and then pulled another cup from her box and placed it where the first one had been. "Begin again," she said.

Kota broke the next one on his sixth swing. His arms were beginning to burn. The sun was burning down on his back now, and his sweat was soaking into his cloth shirt. He made it all the way to twenty-three swings on his next try, but on the twenty-fourth, his arms gave out completely, and the dull blade slammed down on the brittle ceramic mass so hard that pieces flew in every direction. Kota knelt down on the grass and panted. The muscles throughout his arms and chest were trembling.

Gretis said nothing to him but walked into her house. She came back a moment later with a large cup of water, which she held out to Kota. He started to drop the sword but then remembered her warnings and gripped it with his left hand while he took the water. He managed to wheeze "Thank you," before gulping the liquid down.

"Are you tired, Kota?"

He looked up at her, blinking sweat out of his eyes. "It no matter if I tired. You tell me to do this. I do it."

For the first time that day, Lady Gretis smiled at him. "All right," she said in a softer voice, and she brushed away the bits of clay and placed a new target in front of him. "You may rest in between strikes if you wish. We have all day. Your goal is one hundred times without error."

"I understand," he said. He raised his weapon and began again.

By the time the sun was at its zenith, Kota had gone through seventeen cups. He had made it all the way to forty-eight strikes once, but then his grip and slipped. Kota's muscles hurt more terribly than he had ever imagined they could, and the skin on his hands was beginning to blister. Gretis had left the box out for him, and he had taken to placing the cups himself. He was just setting up for his eighteenth try when he heard footsteps behind him. He whirled to see the Onkai captain from his adventure, Darius, walking toward him, a curious expression on his heavily marked face.

"You must truly despise cups," Darius said, gazing around at the broken fragments everywhere.

"I am beginning his instruction at a different point than I began yours," Gretis said from behind.

"You are training Kota in swordplay then?" Darius said, turning to face her. His voice sounded troubled.

"Yes, I am."

"Is that *all* you are training him in?"

Gretis gazed into Darius's eyes. "No."

The captain sharply inhaled through his nostrils and moved his hand to his forehead in an expression of exasperation. In a tense voice, he said: "Does Bishop Otho know about this?"

"I do not require Otha's permission to take an apprentice."

Darius looked into her eyes. "Might you and I discuss this somewhere private?"

"There is nothing we need to discuss."

Darius cleared his throat and fidgeted. "You know I hold you in the highest respect—"

"Thank you," Gretis said. She had a serene smile on her face. Kota could not help but listen to her heartbeat, and it was slow and soft as opposed to the flutter he heard from the captain.

Through clenched teeth, Darius said: "*With respect,* after what happened with your *last* apprentice, we all assumed you would never take another."

"So did I, yet here we are." Gretis walked gracefully to the Onkai and put a hand on his shoulder. "I can see you are troubled by this, Darius. So was I, but Kota is already beginning to convince me that I made the correct decision. You may tell Otho, of course, and I shall expect a similar visit from him. But please save us all a bit of time and explain my position to him very clearly: I *am* training Kota. I will do it here if none of you holy men stand in my way. Otherwise, Kota and I shall disappear, and neither you nor anyone in this order will ever see me again. Is that quite clear?"

Darius's jaw clenched, and he muttered: "Yes."

"Lovely," Gretis said, and she patted Darius on the arm. "Now, I believe these simple townsfolk need to start getting used to a shamalak among them." She gestured in the direction of Temple Town. "I would like you to take Kota for a hot meal at the Bear's Claw Inn. I shall pay of course." She reached into a small pocket in her shirt and drew out a metal coin, which she held out to Darius.

"That is why you asked me out here?"

"Quite so." She gripped Darius's thick arm through his shirt and said: "You are a fine, strong captain in the Onkai force. Eat with Kota and let everyone see you eating with him."

Darius took the coin, though his face seemed bitter. "This will stir up a great deal of trouble."

"Yes, I assume so. Please enjoy your meal." She turned to Kota and said: "You may put the sword down until you return."

Relieved by these words, Kota laid the blade flat across the tree stump. Gretis walked over to him and knelt down and drew from her pocket a small clay jar with a neatly shaped cork at the top. She pulled the lid off to reveal a dark brown paste. The thick, oily scent of this substance jumped immediately to Kota's nose, and he hissed.

"Show me your hands," Gretis commanded. Uneasily, Kota lifted his hands and she scooped up a glob of the brown stuff with three fingers and began to delicately rub it into his palms and fingers. It felt warm and made his skin tingle. "This will help with the blisters. Let it soak into your skin on the walk to the town. You may wash your hands when you get there."

"Yes, ma'am," Kota said when she released his hands. Before he turned to go, he lifted his two appendages and looked at them. The stink continued to bother him, but the feeling in his flesh was much stranger. He could not decide if his skin felt hot as fire or cold as the ice from the mountains.

It seemed to be both at once. He bore it in silence and turned and walked to Darius. "It good to see you," he said, smiling up at his Onkai friend.

"You as well, Kota," Darius said, and his serious expression softened. "Let's go eat."

The two of them walked in silence for a time while Kota thought of the conversation Darius and Gretis had just had. When they had gone fifty paces or so, he said: "I no mean to cause trouble for Lady Gretis."

"It isn't your fault," Darius muttered. "That woman does whatever she wants. Not even Otho can control her."

Kota swallowed. "Is trouble because I shamalak?"

Darius turned and looked at him. "I might as well be honest with you. Yes, that is a problem. I like you, Kota." He shrugged. "Everyone in my squad likes you. Even Otho likes you. But... you're..." He hesitated, then said: "Anyhow, that doesn't matter as much as the real problem. Has the Blade-witch mentioned Soulic to you?"

"*Blade witch?*" Kota repeated.

"Oh, that's what most in the order call her—particularly those of us who were her...*special* students." Darius cast a grim smile. "She beat the hell out of me more times than I can count. I understand young Glavius is her current victim. But I ask again: has she mentioned Soulic?"

"No."

Darius let out a slow sigh. "Soulic was her first apprentice. Things...did not go well. Soulic went insane. He became a murderer, and an extremely skilled murderer at that. He's still on the loose right now actually. Not even we can seem to catch him." Darius glanced into Kota's eyes and said: "Perhaps you can guess why the idea of her taking on a new student might be troubling to the order."

"Yes," Kota said.

They arrived the edge of Temple Town. When they stepped between the first two buildings, Kota immediately began to feel human eyes on him as he had before, and the whispers started. He walked with Darius over the flat stones in the street and watched as many people stepped away from the two of them, some with fear in their eyes, some with revulsion. Kota tried not to look at any of them. This was his first time back in the village since he had arrived, and he felt just as strange as he had then.

"Right here," Darius said, gesturing to an open doorway of a large yellow building. Kota gazed up at a hanging wooden sign carved into the likeness of a bear claw upon which were simple white paintings of a bed, bowl and what Kota had learned was a spoon. Inside, he listened to the sound of many voices and caught the thick scent of meat and vegetables cooking. He and Darius walked into a large room with many humans walking about or sitting at wooden tables together. When the two of them stepped past the door, many of the conversations immediately began to drop away. Kota saw many pairs of eyes fix on him.

"Good afternoon," Darius said aloud, gazing around the room as if to meet the stares of everyone. "This is my friend, Kota. He saved my life very recently, and he is the guest of the Onkai Order. I thought I might show him a bit of human hospitality." The captain walked to an empty table and pulled out a chair and gestured with a calm smile for Kota to sit down. Kota trembled just a little as he walked over to it, aware that everyone in the room was looking at him.

"He's going to eat with us?" one voice whispered from a few dozen paces away.

"He saved an Onkai's life. We should show him respect."

"Look at it! It's half-wolf or something!"

"Look at its eyes!"

One man who seemed to be having trouble sitting upright in his chair gave Kota a broad smile and held up a mug full of some foamy liquid.

Darius walked to the left side of the room and spoke to a large man with a thick black beard wearing an apron: "We'll have two beef stews and a loaf of bread please."

The man cleared his throat and leaned in toward Darius. In a low whisper that Kota's ears could easily decipher, he said: "You're Captain Darius, aren't you?" Darius nodded. "Look, I respect the Onkai Order as much as anyone, but you can't bring that creature in here. He's making my customers uneasy." He gestured outward and said: "Just look around."

Darius cocked his head and gazed about the room. Many of the people had resumed talking to one another, though Kota could hear that most of the conversations were about him. "Hmm, you want to throw him out?" Darius asked.

The man with the apron whispered: "I don't mean to be rude, but I run a respectable establishment, and Bishop Otho has been very clear over the years that the town doesn't serve the order. I don't have to have him in here if I don't like it."

Darius let out what sounded like an exasperated breath and then whispered back: "No, I cannot force you to serve him. However, you should know that that *creature* you're about to treat so poorly is a personal friend of Cassian Asango."

The man's eyes widened and shifted to Kota, then back to Darius. "You're serious?" He sounded very nervous suddenly.

"Quite serious. The two of them fought in battle together recently, and Asango gave Kota there a gift worth more than this inn."

The man seemed to shrink a little. He muttered: "I... uh... I didn't know..."

"As I said though, you are free to throw him out," Darius whispered, gesturing toward Kota.

"Uh, n-no!" the man grunted. "I'll...I'll get your food." He disappeared into a doorway.

Darius walked back to the table and sat down across from Kota and peered at him for a moment. "You could hear every word, couldn't you?" he said.

"Yes," Kota said, gazing down at the table.

"I'm sorry, Kota. We can leave if you like."

"No," Kota said, and he forced himself to look up. "Lady Gretis want me to come here. Maybe... maybe I can show these people that shamalak is not *creature*."

"You're a better man than I," Darius said. "At least Cassian's name can be some protection for you. Very few people in this world are willing to risk angering a starborn."

The bearded man came over with two wooden bowls of steaming stew on a slate tray as well as a small loaf of bread. "Here you go," he said, setting the food down along with utensils in front of Kota. He looked nervous.

"I thank you, sir," Kota said with the most precise enunciation he could manage.

"Yeah," the man muttered. He gazed into Kota's eyes for a brief moment and then turned away.

Kota picked up the wooden utensils, and he remembered the ointment on his hands. It had seemed have disappeared into his skin, leaving only a slight stickiness. He also noticed that his hands no longer hurt. There was no sensation of blisters as he gripped the wooden spoon. He might have liked to wash his hands, but he felt too tense with so many eyes still staring at him. Instead, Kota sat and ate the thick warm stew, being careful not to spill a single drop - to show the people that he was not a simplistic animal.

When they had both finished eating, Darius slapped the coin down on the table, and they left together. Darius walked with Kota a little way past the edge of the village into the forest and said: "I hope that experience wasn't quite as uncomfortable as it looked." He put his hand on Kota's shoulder and said: "Listen, most of those people have never been more than half a day's walk from where they were born. They're just...not used to visitors like you. We Onkai have an easier time with you because we're educated and because many of us have traveled all over the world."

"I hear you priests in temple talk about me. They call me the *lower creature*. What that mean?"

Darius gazed down at the ground and muttered: "You know, I'm not really sure, Kota. I have read all the Holy Scriptures in the temple, and, between you and me, I believe less than half of them. I joined the Onkai because my parents were killed by a demon, just like Nevin and Dorik I suppose." Darius gazed into Kota's eyes and added: "The more time I spend with you, the more I see a very fine young man. Cassian didn't think you were a *lower creature,* and he could see far into the depths of your mind." A small smile crossed the captain's face. "I don't think you're a lower creature either. I think you're my friend, and I am yours."

"Thank you, Darius," Kota said. He shook the Onkai's hand, said his goodbyes, and then turned and hurried down the path to Lady Gretis's home. When he arrived, he saw her sitting on the tree stump balancing his training sword on the tip of her finger.

"How did it go?" she said without looking up.

"Human food very tasty," Kota said.

"Human food *is* very tasty," Gretis corrected. She tossed him the sword very suddenly, and he caught it in the air by the handle. The blade-witch stood up and then placed a new cup in the center of the stump. "Are you ready to continue?"

"I am," Kota said.

CHAPTER 11: THE AUDACITY OF THE BOY

We have tried to suppress his writings and burn all copies of the foul books and pamphlets the heretic wrote, but his followers continue printing them and polluting the world with the foul blasphemies of Cassian Asango. They do not see what we know: He could have been a shining, holy star in our history, but he chose to willfully turn his back on the gods, and the human race shall forever suffer for his hubris and his sin.

—Arodias Shian,
First Bishop of the Anti-Cassonian Church

"What is the most important advantage in war?" Somar said, staring at his young pupil.

"Knowledge," Cassian whispered. The young man was sitting upside down on the ceiling of the study. His eyes were shut, and he seemed locked in whatever mental process it took to reverse gravity and keep himself suspended so that not one hair hung down toward the floor. Still, as focused as Cassian seemed to be, the boy was responding quickly to every question with no discernible lapse of intellect, and this was all Somar required. Over the past six weeks, he had grown used to the boy's many eccentricities.

"A force of three thousand is running rampant through your countryside. You have only five hundred men at your immediate disposal—only two hundred of which are skilled veterans. What *knowledge* would be most valuable to you under these circumstances?"

"First, the organizational structure and objectives of my enemy," said Cassian. "I need to know if he is part of a larger army. Three thousand men might pillage my lands, but they are by no means a force capable of conquering Denigoth. Most likely, such a small army would be a displaced tribe or small kingdom from the east, or, worse yet, a horde of Northern Kisken men looking to take from *the arrogant and evil Denigothians.* The former force would be far more likely to negotiate and would work very hard to appear *reasonable.* Strategically, I could delay a confrontation by offering complicated terms while I surreptitiously gather more men and learn my foe's strengths and weaknesses through the use of spies."

"What if he is spying on you at the same time?" said Somar.

"I would sense anyone he sent and either kill them or feed them false information to manipulate my enemy."

"Your enemies may have spies that can block you just like I can."

"Highly unlikely."

Somar thought on this answer for a few seconds, wondering if the confidence in Cassian's tone was justified, and then decided to let the matter pass for the moment. Instead, he said: "Assume you learn your opponents are indeed a displaced army, and that their king intends to raid and pillage your lands and take over your castle in an attempt to strong-arm the empire into granting him land within the empire, with himself as legally named lord."

"I take all the steps I mentioned already. Logically, the shipyards would be the best point of immediate attack for this king, since they would be far easier to take than this castle and would block my most immediate means of receiving supplies and reinforcements, as well as possibly yield him a great many riches."

"Be careful with logic when it comes to kings—or for any military leader for that matter," said Somar. "This man may come directly after you because it suits his pride to do so, or he doesn't understand the consequences of siege warfare, or because he is greedy to have a starborn as a hostage and is idiotic enough to believe that to be a simple thing to acquire. He may simply determine that his numerical advantage is best used before you can send for reinforcements—not an altogether *illogical* line of thought. This, Cassian, is why knowledge of your enemy's mind can sometimes be the greatest advantage of all."

"That would not represent a problem," said the boy, the hint of a smile appearing on his face. "This castle is impossible to take with only three thousand men."

"Why would that be?"

"Because I am here."

Somar raised an eyebrow. "So powerful, are you?"

"Yes," Cassian said softly. "I read your collection of essays and accounts on siege warfare. Arrows and men on ladders—that is what I could expect from such a small army. No one can hit me with an arrow, or really hit anything around me that I do not wish to be harmed, and I can hurl back ladders quite easily." With eyes remaining closed, the young man made a small gesture with his finger, and the table next to Somar went scraping across the floor and slammed into the wall, cracking just a little. "Behind stone walls, I can work my magic without the nuisance of direct combat, and, as Neophis told you long ago, '*defense is a far simpler matter than offense.*'"

A small shiver went through Somar. This phrase was indeed the exact one the starborn Neophis had spoken to him many times during their training together. It was part of a memory locked tightly away in Somar's mind, and one that he had never spoken of to his pupil. Cassian had penetrated his mind! There was no other logical explanation. The boy was taunting him.

"You seek to throw me off balance even as I am testing you," said Somar.

"Warfare is the highest game of the mind, is it not?" Cassian chuckled.

Somar decided not to play any further into the boy's hands. How much Cassian had been able to invade his thoughts was impossible to determine at present, and stopping to question the boy would end Somar's test and severely weaken his position as an authority figure. Instead, he said: "Consider that your opponent has some thirty sorcerers at his disposal."

"Thirty?" Cassian said, sounding amused. "That would be difficult to handle. You propose this number because it would negate enough of my concentration to render me incapable of defending this castle. Your ultimate goal is to see if I can think my way out of this scenario without simply relying on my abilities as a starborn, correct?"

"Yes."

Cassian grinned. "The second I knew the enemy was in my territory, I would gather all available rations into my castle, evacuating the local farmers and leaving only a small number of supplies on the farms between myself and my opponent. These I would surreptitiously poison - a slow-acting toxin such as ackanthosine, of which I happen to keep a supply. Since this hypothetical king is displaced, he will have little to no supply chains and will be forced to feed his army from the countryside and from farms in his path. I won't be able to calculate exactly how much damage this will do, but many of his troops would die within the first few hours of the siege. This would, of course, create enormous discord within his army. They would panic, and many would desert, if not all."

"Interesting tactic, but it would require perfect timing and execution to work, else you would either end up killing your own people or wasting time and resources on something that will be easily discovered. Remember, your enemy may have spies."

"Have you interacted with my men? Perfect execution is not a problem."

This was true. Many of Cassian's soldiers had been assassin's sent to kill him, and rather than execute them, he had used his considerable psychic might to subvert their emotions and turn them into intensely loyal servants. Such men were nearly incapable of mistake and utterly incapable of betrayal. "What about the siege itself?"

"The *thirty* sorcerers," Cassian said, "would all still be in play in your scenario, I assume? Shall I further guess that they have broken off into groups of five, spread out to different angles to my castle, with each group commencing to attack with entirely different schools of magic simultaneously? By my best guess, this would be the best stratagem for thirty sorcerers to overcome me."

"Alright," said Somar.

"I estimate it would take six days for reinforcements to arrive by sea—I would guess between seven and fourteen hundred would be sent from the capital by ship. I suppose you want me to guess at the low end."

"Certainly."

"Alright. Let us say that six hundred able-bodied men arrive—counting on a rampant infection at sea."

Somar chuckled. "I can see you're enjoying this game."

"I am. I must admit though I haven't yet told you how I would *actually* handle this scenario."

"Why not?"

"Because it is far too easy."

"Do tell."

Cassian gave an upside down shrug. "I would simply take control of this king almost as soon as he set foot in my territory."

"And how would you do that?"

Cassian drew a strange amulet of gold and burning blue crystal from underneath his tunic and held it out, letting the object dangle upside-down in front of his chest. "I do not believe I have shown you the properties of my newest trinket." He waved his hand in front of the amulet and, in the blink of an eye, Cassian vanished, and Somar's own image appeared in his place. Somar gazed in wonder at himself sitting calmly on the ceiling of the study, eyes still closed. This phantom spoke in a much deeper voice than Cassian's: "With this elvin device, I can look and sound like anyone." The image melted back into Cassian's and the boy continued: "If an enemy were foolish enough to invade *my* territory, I would apprehend and assume the identity of one of his men. I would rip the information I needed from my victim, of course, before taking his form, and then make my way to my opponent. It might take a bit of cleverness to get so close, but I am clever of course." He gave a little smirk as he said this and Somar himself smiled. "I would overwhelm this king with my telepathy and force him to obey my will long enough to end his campaign and take him into custody. If he somehow possessed psychic defenses such as yours, I would simply kill him, assume his identity, and surrender to myself." Cassian waved his hand, and the image of Somar appeared standing on the floor, separate from him. The illusion looked up at the boy and said: "I humbly surrender my forces to you, Cassian Asango, greatest of all men now living or dead."

Somar blinked. "That is quite a formidable trick."

Somar's phantom vanished, and Cassian dangled the beautiful elvin device and said: "The enchantments folded into this Elokien took more than a thousand years to bring into being. The amulet possesses its own kind of consciousness, and it can cast stable illusions that no twenty starborn in history could replicate with all their powers combined. I would hardly call its power a *trick,*but yes, it is formidable."

"Why did you not simply explain this in the beginning?"

"I like your games, old man. Shall I resume how I would handle the army and the thirty sorcerers?"

Somar sighed and muttered: "Indeed."

"Well, first I would—" Just then the boy's eyes opened, and he hissed in anger: "*No! Dammit!*" He dropped from the ceiling, his body turning in the air and lowering softly onto the floor. Glaring, he exclaimed: "Why would she come here now?"

Incredibly confused, Somar said: "Who is here?"

"*The Norn!*" Cassian spat the word like it was an obscenity.

Somar gasped. "The Norn has come to see you?"

Cassian cast a sharp gaze at the wall of books to his left, but Somar had the sense he was looking through it. "Ugh! My people are *bowing!*"

"Of course they are," Somar said. He put a hand on Cassian's shoulder and said: "I know you have a somewhat strained relationship with the gods, but *the Norn has come to see you!* There is no greater honor."

Cassian's deep green eyes shifted to Somar's and flashed with anger. "I do think you are my favorite of all my tutors, old man, but it seems you do not understand me just yet. That may be about to change."

The boy pulled free of Somar's hand just as one of his servants, a bald man of middling age named Tarmun, burst into the room. Half out of breath, the servant said: "My lord—"

"I know she is here," Cassian said in a sharp voice. "Show her in I suppose." He hesitated, then said: "Bring her straight here. Ask the priests to wait outside."

The servant swallowed, and Somar saw the nerves play out across the poor man's face. Cassian had asked him to go and see to the most ancient creature on the mortal plain. He was to speak to the emissary of the gods as if she were a simple guest and lead her around. The servant visibly started to sweat as he turned and muttered: "Y-yes, my lord."

Somar was feeling quite nervous himself. He had dreamed his whole life of meeting the oracle. She, the mother of prophecy, the ancient one, the bridge between Gods and man, had played a part in every transcendent moment in human history. When Somar had reached the rank of general, he had taken leave to make a pilgrimage to Aramanthia to see if the Norn would speak to him. Her priests had turned him away as they turned away thousands every year. Her words were reserved only for an extraordinary few whose destinies were worthy of the gods' attention.

Somar cast a nervous gaze at his pupil as he thought on all of this. The boy was staring at the doorway, a dark look on his face. "This is a blessing, Cassian. Can you not see that?"

"You do not understand," Cassian whispered back.

After a moment, a very nervous Tarmun returned to the door and gestured in. The Norn appeared in the doorway, a dark and magnificent figure nearly too tall to pass through it. She whisked over the stone in perfect silence, seeming to float. Somar gazed at the shimmer of her liquid-like cloak. It was ever-moving, and it caught and the light, reflecting back soft traces of blue and green. Some believed the cloak was all she was. Out of the corner of his eye, Somar saw Cassian's poor servant disappear and close the door, leaving the three of them alone.

The Norn glided to Cassian, who stared up into the blackness under her hood. <Most of my hosts over the centuries have come and greeted me themselves,> she said in a soft, musical voice. Somar knew instantly it was telepathy, for he felt it pass through the walls he had constructed around his mind as if they were nothing.

Cassian answered in a cold tone: "I am sure most of your hosts actually desired your presence. I do not. *Leave.*"

Somar gasped. Could the boy truly be so reckless? "Cassian—" he started to say, but the Norn cut in.

<You have the right to refuse my help, but it must be offered. Yours is an incredibly precarious and important fate.>

"Your help," Cassian whispered. He drew in a slow, angry breath, and then said: "I understand most come to you with questions."

<Most do, but for some, a specific prophecy is ordained. Yours is such a case.>

"Perhaps as an assurance against my clumsy, human attempts to guess at what to ask," Cassian said with a dark smile. "You must, of course, ensure that I am manipulated with exactly the correct words." He glared up into the dark face, but the Norn said nothing. After a tense moment, the boy went on: "But I do have questions, so long as you have forced your way in here. Tell me, if the gods are pulling at invisible threads in my life—if they had a *plan* for me—then why did they allow my parents to be killed in their name?"

<I cannot answer questions of the past.>

"I am not asking a question of omniscience," the boy snapped. "These are questions of logic. Would it be reasonable for me, a mere mortal who surely cannot understand *the will of the mighty gods,* to suppose that they possessed the power to keep one of their servants from cutting my mother's head from her neck?"

Somar swallowed dryly. The contempt in Cassian's eyes was terrifying. If anyone were to find out he was questioning the will of the gods like this, he would be executed, starborn or not.

<It would be logical,> The Norn answered. She seemed remarkably unconcerned by his words.

"Would it then be logical to assume that either the gods chose *not* to intercede or, worse, the act was part of their design?"

<The interplay of individual free will and the infinitely complicated machinations of divinity are beyond your understanding. Yet I will concede that both the scenarios you mention are possibilities, *logically*.>

Somar blinked. He could not tell if the Norn was condescending to the boy or merely giving an honest answer. He could read nothing in the tone of her telepathic voice.

"Mmh," Cassian grunted, mashing his lips together. "Well then, not being able to comprehend the machinations of divinity, I do not believe I shall bother with them. I refuse to hear your prophecy, Ancient One."

<No one has ever refused a direct prophecy from on high before. I warn you, this choice is far more dangerous than you imagine.>

"I have made it."

"Cassian!" Somar said, and he reached out and grabbed the boy by the arm. "You must not spit in the eyes of the gods! You are not simply risking your life! You risk *damnation*!"

A calm smile played across Cassian's face, and he reached up and gently brushed Somar's hand away. "I risk no such thing," he whispered. He turned and looked at the Norn and said: "That is the great illusion that she and her *gods* use to control us—that when we die our souls will travel to their realm where the five of them sit in some ridiculous council and judge us for our obedience to their laws." His eyes narrowed as he glared into the black hood and said: "I have dared to look upon the truth. The beings we call *gods* have nothing whatsoever to do with what happens to our souls when we die. Deny it, Norn. I dare you."

The words sank into Somar's mind with a terrible weight. He could imagine no greater blasphemy. He turned and looked at the Norn, fearing the rebuke that would come from the ancient one, but as he listened for her telepathic answer, she began to laugh. It was not a dark or angry laugh, but soft and light.

<I see now why all sides have their eyes fixed upon you, Cassian Asango,> she said.

Cassian's eyes lost some of their intensity, and he stared at her. She leaned in over him and whispered: <Your choice has been made, and it will cost you dearly, and yet—> she tilted her head a little to the side and then added: <it changes the rules in a way I did not expect... for *both of us.*>

"What do you mean?" the boy said, frowning.

<I am allowed to help you, it seems.> The Norn straightened up, and her dark cloak whisked and stretched so that she grew perhaps a head taller. In a voice that seemed to echo from all around, the ancient one said: <I shall come to your aid three times, Starborn. The last time you will call out to me, and I will appear, and shortly thereafter, your mortal life will reach its end.>

Cassian stiffened at these words, but before he could answer she was gone from the room. There was no flash of light nor a fading away. She was simply no longer there.

"What the hell just happened?" Somar exclaimed after a moment had passed.

Cassian drew in several deep breaths and then grunted: "Trouble." Through gritted teeth, he said: "Damn that old wretch! She did this to me on purpose! The Lucinian priests keep meticulous records of the Norn's activities. I doubt she will withhold the fact that I refused her prophecy."

"No, I mean that bit about the gods and human souls!" Somar rasped. "Why did you say that?"

"Oh, that." Cassian turned and faced him with a somber expression. "Because I was profoundly connected to someone when she died. I can feel where the gods reside, and she did not go there. I doubt I am even the first starborn to discover this," he rolled his eyes and whispered: "though most of my brethren have been too cowed by the church to look where I dare to look."

Bewildered beyond belief, Somar muttered: "Where did she go?"

Gazing down, Cassian replied in a whisper: "*Somewhere better.*" He looked into Somar's eyes and said: "It is unknowable, my friend, and we have far more tangible and immediate concerns. I estimate word of my *audacity* will reach the Nemesai Bishop within a couple of weeks, and I will have an inquisitional army at my gates in less than a month."

Somar glanced at the place where the Norn had been, his mind still spinning with all the revelations he had witnessed. Cassian moved to him, and the boy's thin hands reached out and grabbed hold of his tunic and gave him a little shake.

"Hey!" Cassian said sharply. His fierce green eyes pulled Somar back from his momentary spiritual crisis. "Are you still with me? I could use your help to figure this out."

"Figure what out?"

"The political crisis I am about to face. I have a contingency plan – a way to keep the Nemesai from prosecuting me—at least I *think* it will work."

Somar forced himself to attention, pushing away all of his concerns of gods and the afterlife. "What is your contingency plan? It will have to be something I cannot possibly think of at this moment, because I see this as the excuse Bishop Cromlic has been waiting for to finally kill you."

Cassian cast him a smile that was almost free of anxiety. "You were correct earlier that I more or less spit in the eyes of the gods, but *gods* are not the only thing the church worships, are they?"

Somar's thoughts accelerated to their normal speed. The boy could only be referring to one thing. "Promethiock," he whispered.

"Yes-s-s-s." Cassian's white teeth flashed in a thrilling grin. "We are going to go visit him—that is, if you wish to come with me."

"Huh!" Somar grunted aloud. "This day...gods above..."

"Dragon below, actually."

Somar laughed, wondering if this was all some absurd dream. *The Great Dragon!* "If I recall, only one person has ever visited Promethiock and lived, and that was a thousand years ago."

"Nine hundred and eighty-nine years by my research, but yes, only one mortal has ever spoken to him: *Kalieus, the first starborn.*" He spoke the words with dramatic reverence.

"Are you sure Promethiock is even still alive?"

"Yes. He has been calling out to me for years in my dreams. I have long been afraid to answer him, but now it seems I no longer have a choice. If I can receive some kind of blessing from him, the Nemesai will not dare touch me." Cassian gripped Somar's arm and said in an excited voice: "What about it, old man? You have met the Norn. Would you now like to go with me to meet the being that stole magic from the gods and gave it to man?"

Somar gazed at the strange and amazing boy. He wondered whether Cassian was a blessing to his life or a curse. Only three months ago, he had been a retired senator living in wealth and comfort on a quiet farm. He could return to that life now and live in peace with all the grand events of his life behind him. Somar had grown very old—perhaps too old for such matters as these. Then again, *only one person had ever spoken to the great dragon.*

"You say Promethiock calls to you?"

"Yes, in my dreams since I was eleven. He never shows me his face, but I know it is him."

Somar narrowed his eyes at the young starborn. "How certain are you the dragon will not kill us both?"

Cassian's face scrunched up and he gazed up at the ceiling for a moment, and then said: "Sixty-eight percent." There was such a fantastic look of daring in his young eyes.

"You gods-damned little bastard!"

"I shall charter us a ship."

CHAPTER 12:
A VERY OLD PROPHECY

I can say now, looking back, that Lady Gretis was the most influential figure in my life. She was a mentor, a friend, and perhaps even a bit of a second mother to me, but she was also a Sansrit master, bound by the doctrines of her shadowy art, and she kept many secrets from me.

—Kota of the Forest

"Thank you for seeing me," Otho said as Lady Gretis took her seat in front of the large oak desk in the bishop's small, private office. It was deep into the night, and the Bishop's face appeared haggard in the warm, shadowy light of the torches on the wall. Gretis sat calmly before him. She had known this confrontation was coming and she was ready.

The burly man gazed at her for a moment before opening his mouth. He was noticeably uncomfortable. "You and I have been partners for a long time—at least that is how I have felt," he said.

Gretis gave him a warm, reassuring smile. He was going to flatter her a bit before telling her she could not train Kota. That was his way.

"I have relied on your strength and your wisdom for many years. More often than not, I have listened to you above all others. It has never bothered me that you are a woman—" he paused as Gretis gave the softest chuckle at this awkward speech he had prepared. He smiled a little himself and continued: "You're as fierce as any man or beast

I've ever met. I still think about our fight every now and then." He reached up absently and touched the scar below his right eye. "I don't think any woman as beautiful as you could work in a temple full of young boys imbued with magical strength unless she was as tough as—"

"You're rambling," Gretis said.

"Yes, I am," Otho said softly. He swallowed and gripped the edges of the table. Otho had been in love with her for many years, she knew, which was of no help to him here. He drummed his gloved fingers on the desk for a moment, then looked up at her and exhaled: "I cannot let you train that shamalak boy."

"No?" she said, remaining relaxed.

"After what happened with Soulic—"

"*My son.* You may say it."

"Yes, your *son* is still running around the continent. He's a damned killer, and no one can catch him."

"I know. I made a terrible mistake with Soulic."

"Yes, and your *terrible mistake* has cost me very dearly. The Nemesai have been screaming for your head for the past six years. You have no idea how many favors I have had to do for Bishop Cromlic just to keep you alive."

"I did not ask you for your help."

"But I gave it because you are incredibly important to—this order."

"You are a good man, Otho," Gretis said. Now it was her turn to flatter him a bit, and to remind him. "In my experience, good men rarely ever rise to power, but *I knew* you would be a great leader, and I did everything in my power to help you become Bishop." Otho swallowed and started to say something, but she cut him off: "I need you to be a good man now, Otho."

He shrugged. "There is only so much I can do. Kota is a nice boy, but he has fangs and claws and eyes like a wild beast. You cannot ask people to be comfortable with you training him to be a *Sansrit master*—certainly not after your last..."

"My last *what*?" Gretis heard the irritation in her own voice. She had not come here to lose her temper, but Otho was repeatedly touching at a deep wound.

"*Disaster!*" he said, slapping his hand on the table. He looked into her eyes, his face slightly reddened. "I am sorry. You ask far too much this time."

Gretis glared at this man who claimed to respect her and slapped her own hand on the desk. "Soulic has only killed one man, and he was a Denigoth general who had a well-known lust for taking *slave wives* of the young girls he captured! My son has assaulted several nobles who were particularly cruel to the peasants who work their lands, and I believe he broke a slave master's arm a few months ago. Soulic is a criminal, but I would hardly call anything he has done a *disaster*. We are not speaking of a plague; we are speaking of an angry young man with a harsh sense of justice and a little too much power. Your Nemesai brothers should be able to identify with that."

Otho's eyes hardened, and Gretis knew she had made a mistake. Defending Soulic was not helping her case with Kota at all. She said quickly: "Anyhow there is no such darkness in Kota as there was in my son. You have met him. Can you imagine any cruelty in that boy?"

"Not really, but then I remember liking Soulic." She heard the bitterness in his tone. Otho's mind was utterly set. Still, she had come prepared for that.

Gretis drew in an uneasy breath, her stomach filling with nerves as she said: "How is your ancient Dhavic?"

"What?" the bishop said, raising an eyebrow in confusion.

"Can you read it?"

"I am a damned bishop of the church, am I not?"

"Can you read it?" she repeated.

Otho sighed. "I'm not the best at it, but I manage."

"Good. Then I will show you why I decided to train Kota." Gretis reached into a pocket and drew out the folded sheet of parchment she had carefully stowed before coming here. As she gently unfolded it in front of Otho, she said in a soft, reverent voice: "This is a prophecy that has been handed down from master to student for over nineteen hundred years among the Sansrit. It was given by the Norn herself to one of my predecessors long ago. For all I know, this is the last copy in existence, so please be exceptionally careful with it."

Otho gazed down at the paper. His eyes fixed on the first brown symbol and then the second, and she saw his lips begin to move as he worked to translate. The cloth was centuries old, but it was still legible enough even in the soft torchlight. Gretis felt some small satisfaction when Otho's eyes widened as he made it about halfway through the text. By the time he reached the end, he was gripping the edges of his desk, and the veins were standing up on his hands.

"You think this is about Kota?" he said, looking up at her with still gaping eyes.

"The evidence is quite strong."

"Goddess," Otho muttered. He sank in his chair and looked down at the ancient parchment again. After a moment, he muttered: "You say this came directly from the Norn—not some fortune telling crone with a cloak and talent for a strange voice?"

"Do you believe a charlatan could fool someone with skills like mine?"

Otho clenched his jaw and waved his hand at the parchment, snapping: "Why the hell did this not come to the church?"

"That prophecy is older than your church."

The Bishop looked over the paper again, carefully inspecting each symbol. After a few moments, he said in a low voice: "This is... Gods..." He shook his head. "What is it you expect me to do with this information?"

"I expect you to help me protect Kota. If I am correct, his life is more important than yours or mine."

"Yes... *if* you are correct." Otho gazed at the bottom right corner of the paper and said: "There seems to be a bit missing from this *prophecy*. Is there another page?"

"Yes, but it has nothing to do with Kota. You have my word on that."

Otho's eyes narrowed. "May I see it?"

"You may not."

The bear of a man stared into her eyes for a long moment. "You are very protective of your secrets, my dear," he said.

"I am. I would never have shown you this if the importance were any less than it is. The secrets of the Sansrit masters are shared with no one, but I am trusting you, Otho. Do not take that lightly."

"Oh, I do not," he grunted, rising from his chair. "If there is one thing you do not have to worry about, it is me taking *any* of this lightly!" The enormous man pressed his gloved hands together in front of him and bowed his head into them. With eyes clenched shut, he exhaled: "You really believe this, don't you? That brown-skinned little boy is destined to—Gods how can it be true?"

"I looked inside of him," Gretis said in a quiet voice. "I've never encountered *anyone* with an animus that strong. I wouldn't have dreamed it was even possible to contain so much in a mortal body."

Otho rested his hands down on his desk and gazed down, a bewildered look on his face. Whatever flaws he had, he was a good man dedicated to the protection of others, and he could not ignore the implications of the prophecy she had shown him. In a quiet voice, he finally murmured: "What would you need from me?"

"I would like Kota to have a proper education here at the temple."

"Bah!" Otho grunted, shaking his head. "You want him to sit at a desk with the initiates?"

"I would, but I shall find it acceptable, however crude and narrow-minded it would be of you, to set one or two of your monks to giving him private tutoring sessions."

"They'll *love* that, I'm sure," Otho hissed. He glared at her and said: "Anything else, *my dear*?"

"Yes," Gretis said, and she leaned around him and snatched up the parchment. "You will tell no one of what I revealed to you, not even the other bishops."

"I cannot keep a prophecy of the Norn from them."

"You must. Daibok has spies in the church even now. If he finds out what Kota is..."

"What you *think he might be*," Otho said, enunciating the last four words with a bitter sharpness. "But...yes, I see the danger. All right, I shall keep the prophecy secret until...I know whether it is about that boy. But, my lady," he put his hand on her shoulder and leaned forward, "if you are wrong – *terribly wrong* about Kota, and he is as strong as you say..."

"I will kill him myself. You have my word."

"Then we have an agreement," Otho said, and he released her shoulder and walked back around to his chair and sat slowly into it. "Let us control this absurd situation as much as we can. The story that you, I, Kota and, because of your foolishly loose tongue, *Darius*, will tell anyone who asks is that you are training the boy to work as a tracker and assistant to Onkai soldiers in the field because of the wonderful job he did on the last mission."

Gretis smiled. "Agreed, and Darius can be trusted. Didn't you tell me a few months ago he was your favorite choice to be your successor?"

"I don't remember," Otho grunted. He was determined to be angry, and Gretis supposed he had some right to be. She was putting him in quite a difficult situation.

"Thank you, Otho," Gretis said. She turned and walked from the office, closing the door behind her. As she moved down the dark hall of the Onkai temple, she considered how fortunate it was that Otho had not pressed her about the other part of the prophecy. If the first half was indeed about Kota, then the second half was unquestionably about the starborn boy who had brought him into the human world, Cassian Asango. Gretis had chosen to bury that ancient, terrifying page. It had been far too dangerous to show to anyone.

CHAPTER 13: LIVIA

Cassian's parents were killed because of the complicated political and religious aftermath of the Second Demon War. Had it been a century before, the Nemesai would not have dared to execute such high-ranking nobles. The order was only a small arm of the church then who mainly advised kings and emperors on religious law and only occasionally held tribunals over heretics. When the Demon King's followers began to appear in every city though, the Nemesai took on the responsibility of hunting these traitors to the gods, and society was happy to give them all the authority they wanted.

—Telemachus Vale, Starborn of the 19th Generation

As Livia dusted the Sondal home's modest collection of vases, she watched the chipper little Iona bounce about the kitchen, leaping up to grab at ingredients that were out of reach to her small body. The cow had come out for her evening meal and was sitting at the table devouring a marzipan confection that Iona had prepared for her. From the sweat dripping down the woman's temples and the acrid stench of wine, Livia deduced that the *lady* of the house was drunk, which meant it was best to be on guard. The she-bull was most prone to fits of violence a few hours into her drinking.

"Did you hear that that arrogant little fool, Cassian Asango, actually *refused* a prophecy from the Norn ordained to him by the gods?" the cow said as lifted a gob of the marzipan to her mouth. Between rasping bites, she wheezed: " To think that *some* people in this empire actually believe the nonsense that heretic is spouting! The youth these days, even among the nobility...such disrespect. I hear Asango actually grabbed the poor old thing by her cloak and threw her into the street and spat on her! I hope the Nemesai do their duty quickly and cut his throat."

"No one can *grab* the Norn," Hervin muttered from his chair across the room, and as he did, Livia gave a little smile. He was reading from an old tome he had gotten hold of that encompassed the early days of the empire, a candle behind him providing dim but usable light. Livia knew he would lend the book to her when he was done. "It is not possible to physically touch her, according to the church."

"Well, Asango *is* a starborn after all," Lady Sondal grunted, "and a particularly arrogant one. Have you heard he wants to *end* slavery if he becomes the next emperor?"

"Perhaps that might not be such a bad idea in the scope of things," Hervin muttered.

"Might not be such a *bad thing?"* Lady Sondal slammed her fist down hard on the table, and Hervin gave a jump, dropping his book. The sweet little Iona hurried over to him and picked it up and placed it in his outstretched hands, and he cast her a smile that lasted only an instant before the cow bellowed on: "You can be such a naïve *fool*, Hervin. Think what would happen to our two girls if there weren't slavery through which they could find a home? They would starve to death!" She gestured to Livia. "Look at this one. Her parents obviously did not *want* her because she is such a freak! Thank the gods that we feed her and tolerate her absurd limitations."

Livia rolled her eyes at the stab and continued to dust. She knew the childish woman was staring at her, watching for any satisfying sign that her words had cut. They had not.

This was an old, petty game that Livia had long since lost interest in, but she had begun to notice that the constant stream of insults upset Iona, and that was troublesome. Livia saw the young eyes peering around the corner at her as if to make sure she was all right. Livia gave her sister slave a little wink and a smile to reassure her and saw instant relief on the young face.

"Bah!" the cow grunted, and she wiped her hands on the cloth in front of her and then lazily held out an empty goblet. "Be a dear, Iona, and get me more wine."

"Yes, mistress," Iona said, and she moved with lithe obedience to the call of her owner. Livia eyed the puffy, waving hand and flush skin. The cow would likely soon start talking about her great, noble family, droning on and on about how much better she was than the rest of them.

Livia moved to Hervin and gave his leg a little tap with hers. He looked up, and she stared straight into his eyes, letting her eyebrows raise and fall quickly. He read her almost immediately and glanced at his wife, saying: "I think it's about time the girls and I headed to temple—that is unless you would like to join us, my dear?"

"Already?" the cow ejaculated. She was so drunk now that she had lost the ability to control the volume of her voice. The woman took a slow sip from her cup and then murmured: "No, I think I should stay home tonight. I feel unwell-l-l-l. Perhaps Iona should stay with me-e-e."

Hervin looked up at Livia, and she gave him a scowl, letting him know he could not leave Iona behind. "My dear," he said, rising with a calm smile. "The Gailand house will be sending at least two of their slaves for service. I don't mind if you keep Iona home, but—"

"NO!" the cow grunted, wobbling in her chair a little. "I won't be outdone by that stringy little peasant!" She wiped sweat from her forehead. "Take Iona and have her work as late as she is needed! I... I will see myself to bed tonight, sick as I am, *for the church*."

Livia shared a surreptitious smile with Hervin. He was not an incredibly clever man, but he knew how to pull the cow's petty strings. She was a jealous creature and sending slaves to serve in the Vestilite temple was a significant show of both wealth and theocratic service, with the number of slaves sent representing a measure of both for a family. Lady Sondal never went herself of course, but Livia had served many hundreds of hours in her name.

The three of them quickly gathered up what they needed, knowing that their freedom from the woman of the house's demands was by no means a definite thing until they were a good hundred paces away. Within a few moments, they were dressed warmly and walking down the street under the stars, and Livia felt a thrill of relaxation. She walked along behind the prancing little Iona, breathing in the fresh night air.

"I cannot wait for you to read the newest tome," Hervin said with a fidgeting smile. "There are some wonderful little anecdotes about Avinos. Apparently, our first emperor had intended to leave the throne to his son rather than one of the starborn from the next generation! The matter was actually settled by—" Hervin shook his head, "well, I'll let you read it."

Livia leaned her head against Hervin's shoulder as they walked. She had not considered how unusual their relationship was for quite a long time until Iona came along. Hervin had never treated her like a slave, even for a moment. Many of the village's fathers were far less kind to their daughters than he was to her. No one had ever really loved her except him, but that was changing now with the chipper little girl who flounced along in front of them. That thought troubled Livia. Already she felt protective of Iona, and she did not want to feel any more ties to her slave home than she already did. That would make leaving all the more difficult.

"Everyone's already here!" Iona shouted as she rounded the corner ahead of them and scampered forward on her bare little feet.

Livia came around the corner a moment later and saw the collection of slaves and townspeople moving about in the temple's courtyard under torchlight. Iona was running toward the group of children, and several of them were dashing to her. Livia watched her little surrogate sister squeal and giggle with her friends. Everyone seemed to love Iona instantly, and she loved everyone in return. Livia herself had never had such ease with people. Much of the town was kind to her, though she knew that more often than not they pitied her because she could not speak. Here and there, a few actually saw and respected her intelligence, but she did not suppose she had ever really made friends with any of them.

She and Hervin approached the crowd together and almost immediately High Mother Alcmene broke away from a conversation and moved to them, her dark, serious eyes fixing on Livia.

"Hello, my dear," she said in a terse voice, reaching out with both hands palm upward. Livia placed her hands in the woman's, and she felt the High Mother's sharp grip on her flesh. "It is fortunate you have come. The Nemesai have sent word that a repentant soul is in need of stitches. They will be bringing him here any moment." The woman spoke the words without inflection. Livia could read the emotions of almost anyone, but the High Mother seldom showed anything of how she felt, especially when she discussed the dealings of her Nemesai brethren. Livia knew that the *'repentant soul'* would be a person who had been tortured and eventually confessed to a sin of some kind. The need for stitches usually meant whipping, though it sometimes involved far worse. Livia was something of a prodigy even among the experienced Vestilite sisters with a needle and catgut. She had been sewing wounds shut for them since she was eight.

Livia gave a nod and let the mother lead her briskly through the crowd. She glanced briefly back at Iona, who happened to look at her at the same moment and gave a happy little wave. Iona would be handing out bread to the city's poor or tending to the temple's garden with her little friends. The sweet girl would enjoy the simple tasks the sisters gave her. That was good, Livia supposed.

Alcmene led the way through the sermon room along the rows of benches where people came to pray for the Goddess Hermia's blessings. Livia had spent many hours in this chamber in silent prayer, asking for the goddess to grant her a voice. The miracle had never come. She thought only briefly upon this as they passed down a long hallway into a small, secluded room in the back reserved for sinners who had met righteous punishment. Lit by only a few candles, the chamber had three empty cots with old bloodstains on them, and a small table. On the table was a clay bowl that smelled of alcohol and several bits of cloth lay next to it, ready to wash fresh wounds. There was also a thin plate with a few needles and a sloppily wound ball of catgut.

Livia tensed when she saw all of this. There were no Vestilite sisters in the room, which meant she was to tend to this victim of inquisition by herself. That was a very troubling thought. What if this man's wounds were severe? What if he died with only her there in the room? She was neither capable of calling for help nor offering words of comfort to a dying soul.

Livia scarcely had time to consider this when there was a sharp knock at the wooden door that led out into the city. High Mother Alcmene moved to answer, slowly unbolting the door and then swinging it open.

Livia stared at an exceptionally tall man standing in the doorway clad in black armor and robes. He had the unmistakable deep blue runes of the Nemesai on his cold, serious face. Livia had read that the Onkai had similar such strength-enhancing markings on their skin, but they were missing the dark spearhead in the center of the forehead, the symbol of the dark god Balthar's spear. Livia did not look at any of the markings though but stared directly into the man's eyes. Her soul seemed to convulse inside as it perceived cruelty and hate in those eyes.

The Nemesai did not seem to notice her at first. He looked at the High Mother and said: "We have a confessed sinner for you." His voice was deep and gritty, with a subtle sneer to it. He had a thin black beard that traced the sharp, lower angles of his gaunt face. The inquisitor stepped aside after he finished speaking, and two more men who bore Nemesai tattoos carried in a limp, rasping man of perhaps twenty years over to the nearest cot where they unceremoniously flung him. Livia heard the poor soul's whimper of pain, and it told her he was conscious. His shirt had been torn away, leaving the work of these holy men plain to see. There were angry red stripes going down his back, some of them large welts, some tears in the skin. His face was obscured under a thick mane of long, auburn hair that was soaked with sweat, but she could hear his slow, hissing breaths.

"What was his sin?" the High Mother asked, again her tone icy and neutral.

"This one lay with another man," the tall Nemesai with the beard said, and he cast an angry glare at the blood-dripping body as he said the words.

"I see," the High Mother said. "We will grant him Hermia's mercy." She turned to Livia and said: "Please see to him, child."

Livia was not looking at her. She was staring again into the eyes of the leader of these men, and he was staring at her. A strange, visceral moment passed between the two of them. Though she could not explain why for the life of her, most of the time Livia could see emotion in people's eyes as clearly as the color of their hair. This was different. She felt a little tingle pass through her head, and suddenly, just for an instant, she saw a young hand bringing a stick down on the face of a dog. In that moment, Livia felt her own hand gripping that stick, and the delightful thrill of hurting something weak and stupid. She blinked, and the image vanished, and she was gazing at the tattooed man again. He looked nervous suddenly. *What had she just seen?* Was it a memory?

The man lunged very suddenly at her. He was inhumanly fast. Before Livia could even flinch, a leather gloved hand was around her throat. It squeezed and lifted, the one arm bringing her up off her feet with unnatural strength. Terror ripped through her mind as the thick fingers cut off her breathing, and she could tell in that instant that the man could snap her neck if he only squeezed a bit harder... *and that he would.*

"I dislike the way this slave was just looking at me," the Nemesai growled, and there seemed to be a bit of fear in his hate-filled voice.

"This girl is a cripple," the High Mother said, sounding almost frightened as she moved next to Livia. "She is a simple-minded mute, but she has a talent with a needle. Pay her no mind. She is harmless."

"Heh," the man laughed, the anxiety leaving his face. "A *cripple*. I should have known." He let go of Livia's throat, and she fell to the floor, coughing. "Still, you should try to teach this imbecile not to glare at holy soldiers like that. Next time I might take an eye." He turned and walked out the door with his men.

"What were you *thinking*?" the High Mother said in a sharp hiss after the door closed. She was crouched next to Livia, holding her by the arm. "You know what those men could do to you! Even I could not stop them!"

Livia drew in a painful swallow and nodded. Her heart was racing, but she had never been allowed to hold back from working because of such things before. With a hand that shook a little, she reached up and touched one side of her throat. The places where the man had just gripped her throbbed with pain. Still, Livia rose to her feet. She drew in a slow breath, trying her best to calm her nerves as she had done after so many of the cow's assaults, blinked out a single pair of tears, and then gestured to the injured man with her eyes.

"Y-you still think you can help him?" the High Mother asked. She sounded surprised. Livia answered with a nod, and the old woman stared at her for a brief moment, then whispered: "Yes, well, please do what you can for him." She cast Livia an extremely uncertain looking nod and then left the room.

Livia turned to the blood-dripping mess of a man. She bent over him, watching the way he trembled. After a moment, she reached out and very slowly, very gently brushed the hair away from his face. Her hands were growing steady once more. This man had suffered far worse than she had, and he needed her help. The poor soul looked into her eyes, and she saw his fear and what seemed to be shame.

"I—I'm very s-s-sorry for my terrible s-sin," he whispered.

He meant the words. Livia imagined he had been repeating them for hours or even days. He had been put through a hell she could not even imagine. She could not speak to him, but there were other ways to communicate. She stroked his head and gave him a warm, gentle smile. He looked at her for a long moment in silence, his eyes wide and searching, and then he pressed his face into the cot and began to weep.

Livia rested her palm on the back of his scalp, letting him cry. He sobbed for several minutes, seeming to let out the horror and the misery of his experience into the dirty fabric of the cot. Finally, his breathing grew quieter, and eventually he lifted his head again and looked at her.

"I-Is it over?" he said. His eyes were wide, like those of a child.

Livia nodded, and she saw a touch of relief illuminate his face. She wanted to let him know more, so she pulled her papyrus paper from her pocket and the little charcoal pencil she had recently finished making and began writing against the table:

Your suffering is over now. I need to clean your wounds. I do not judge you. I am your friend.

She held the paper in front of the man, and he stared at it for a moment, and then looked up at her. "I—I can't read," he said.

Livia sighed. *So often in her life, this was the barrier between herself and others.* She put her paper and pencil back away and then picked up one of the cloths and dipped it in the bowl, then made a little dabbing motion in the air and pointed to his back.

"Oh," the man said. He nodded and said: "Y-yes, please d-do."

Livia nodded and then moved behind him. Very gently, she dabbed the cloth over the first streak of open flesh. The man hissed and went rigid. She withdrew the cloth and waited, and after a moment he unclenched and said: "k-keep going."

He continued to tense as she wiped away the blood, but otherwise made no complaints. His wounds had mostly clotted. Livia hoped whatever alcohol the sisters had mixed with the water in the bowl was potent enough to prevent his injuries from festering. If not, this man would die. She carefully cleaned his wounds for perhaps ten minutes before he turned a little and looked back at her.

"C-can you not speak?" he said. His voice was still nervous, but not quite so much as it had been.

Livia shook her head.

"Did someone...c-cut out your tongue?"

Livia opened her mouth and stuck out her tongue as she often did to answer this question, wiggling it in the air.

"You have no voice then?"

Livia shook her head again.

The man frowned. "Can you not just whisper at least?" He spoke again, his lips and tongue whispering words through only the exhalation of air: "*Like this*?"

Livia shook her head a third time. She had been asked questions like these many times. The cow believed she could speak or at least whisper if she were not so stubborn. In truth, her mouth could work to chew food and to smile and yawn, but never to form words. Whenever she tried, a horrible pain burned in her head, and her mind glazed over into dullness until she let go of the desire.

"I'm s-sorry."

Livia gave a little shrug and then held up the cloth, casting a questioning look. The man nodded and returned his head to the mat. She had just begun to dab at his skin again when she heard a little creak in the door behind her. She turned, hoping that one of the sisters had come to see her, but instead Iona's little face was peering from behind the wood.

Livia shot up and held out her hands, fanning her fingers and shaking them to motion for Iona not to come in. She did not want her little sister to see the bleeding man. The young girl was not looking at her hands though. Iona had already seen past Livia and was indeed looking at the man on the cot. She pushed the door open and stepped into the room, her eyes gaping, and she began to pant.

"W-what happened to him?!"

Livia ran over to her young sister and forcefully spun her around and whisked her out of the room. When they were outside, she shut the door and put her hands on Iona's shoulders. She gazed into the sweet child's eyes and cast her a look that demanded answers.

Iona seemed to understand, and she whispered: "Hervin said you had something really difficult you had to do. I...I wanted to come help you." Livia shook her head and then sharply pointed back down the hall toward the other children. Iona gazed back in the direction Livia was pointing, but said: "No, I...I want to help you."

Livia sighed, frustration seeping into the muscles in her back. Iona was too innocent to see what was in that terrible room. It was a revolting shame that the young girl had even caught a glance of such suffering. Livia stood and turned her little sister around by her shoulders and gave her a soft little push away. Iona stumbled forward and then whirled around. She stared up at Livia not with anger but disarming sincerity.

"I am not weak like you think I am," she said, her voice trembling. "I...I don't want to be off having fun while you're alone. I... I won't g-go." She folded her arms in front of her chest.

Livia was still reeling from her confrontation with the Nemesai. *She had seen such ugliness in his soul*... She saw something far different now in Iona's soft, brown eyes. The contrast was so utterly profound that it took her breath away. For one brief instant, it seemed that she could gaze into the little girl's very soul. There was such kindness there... Iona possessed a boundless love for everyone around her—even the cow. Livia had dismissed this quality as childish naiveté that was sure to dwindle away in the quiet misery of beatings and forced servitude, but she had been wrong. Nothing in the world could ever make Iona cruel. Nothing would ever fill her with hate. That was a kind of strength all its own, and it was good and beautiful, and it was exactly what Livia desperately needed to see at that moment.

Slowly, Livia pulled her paper out of her pocket and pressed it against the wall with one hand while with the other she drew her pencil and wrote:

Why do you want to help me?

"Because I love you," Iona said.

The words washed over Livia, and she was staggered by their power. She felt moisture begin to build in her eyes, and she looked away, blinking. Where had this sweet little puppy of a girl come from?

"Please let me help you," Iona said in a voice that was surprisingly firm, coming from her.

Slowly, Livia's hand moved to the door, and with a strange numbness, she pulled it open. It seemed Iona could face what was on the other side and not lose any part of herself, and it would be a blessing to have someone to help.

Before they passed in, Livia raised her paper once more and wrote:

You will follow all of my instructions.

"Of course!" Iona said, beaming. They walked back into the room together to do what needed to be done.

CHAPTER 14: THE FEMALE STARBORN

We cast more condemnations upon Cassian Asango than any other figure in history, and rightly so. His evil can never be wiped from human history. Still, others bear some portions of the blame as well. The other starborn of Asango's generation could have banded together and stopped him, but instead they allowed his heresy to go unchecked, and the human race shall forever pay the price.

—Bishop Arodias of the Anti-Cassonian Church

The boy actually seemed nervous, which was something Somar had never seen in him before. Cassian drew in quick breaths in his small chair and stared at the mottled wooden wall of their tiny cabin compartment with a focused intensity, his hands sometimes twitching. These moments of agitation were interposed by flashes of serene calm and even humor as if at some unknown joke. They were about to meet the only female starborn alive.

The two of them had been at sea for eight days together. Cassian had chartered a vessel from traders who had already been headed in the general direction of their notorious destination. The crew—most of whom were superstitious and uneducated—had kept their distance from the fierce-eyed living miracle who was daring to visit the great dragon. Even when drunk, not one of the burly men had dared to say more than three words at a time to Cassian.

Somar wondered if his pupil had even noticed, distracted as he was.

"She is the one most like me," Cassian said very abruptly. His eyes remained fixed on the cabin wall, yet Somar somehow knew without question that the boy was aware of being watched. "Keska is not truly like me though. They all believe I am too... *extreme."* His mouth twitched into a brief smirk, and he let out a chuckle before adding: "Just the same, she is one of my favorite people in the world."

The sound of wood scraping against wood and creaking metal pervaded their small cabin. Somar had learned the noises of the ship well enough to understand this meant a docking. His assumption was confirmed by an abrupt halt to the vessel's motion, which caused Somar to stumble and press his hands against the side of his cot.

"Shall we?" Cassian said, rising. He veritably shot out the door and up the small stairway that led to the ship's deck. Somar followed behind at the slow and cautious pace of an old man. By the time he had finished burdening his poor knees with the hike up the creaky stairs, Cassian was nowhere to be seen. Somar could tell by the way that the crewmen were leaning over the edge of their craft though that his pupil was putting on some kind of show. He walked in close to the sailors and gazed at the young man, who seemed to be *floating* in the air, his feet dangling above the swaying ocean, an elated smile on his face. Cassian's arms were clasped with those of a young woman who was also hovering and grinning. Somar knew this was Keska Ethedrine, the only point of the star born outside of Denigoth's borders, and he found her a fascinating sight.

The young woman's skin was of a smooth brown tone. Her eyes were a dark bronze that shone in brilliant contrast to the whites that surrounded them. There was a quiet confidence in those eyes that matched what Somar had always observed in Cassian. She wore an exquisite white silken dress, simple in its perfect design and stitching as if to provide a clean canvass for the gleaming silver chain of emeralds that hung from her neck, and the accompanying bracelets, rings, and earrings. As the two starborn hovered above the ocean, they spun in a slow circle together, drawing the awe of everyone around them, including Somar.

The pair eventually floated down and over to the sand on the beach and fell into a conversation Somar could not quite hear. From their animated expressions, he could discern that they were thrilled to be in each other's company. What kind of relationship had the two of them had over the years, based entirely upon telepathy? He could see love in their faces for one another. It was the familiar kind of love that existed between close family members, or the very oldest and dearest of friends.

Cassian's face made a sharp turn toward the ship in the midst of his revelry, and with a grin unable to leave his face he shouted: "Have you men forgotten your duty? Finish docking the damned ship and lower the gangplank."

This shook the crew out of their collective stupor, and they immediately went about their duties, though Somar could see calm, contented smiles on most of their faces. They had just seen something wonderful—two living miracles levitating together in the air.

It took several minutes before the plank was lowered and Somar was able to step down onto the dock. When he came upon Cassian and the young lady, the two were both laughing about some private amusement. They both turned to him at once, and Keska pranced up and put her hands on his shoulders, saying: "So you are the one who intends to follow my insane brother down into the dragon's prison." She had a charming Alorian accent that rolled several of her consonants sharply while extending certain vowel sounds. "Dear man," she said, and she leaned up and kissed his left cheek and then his right.

Somar could not wholly stifle a chuckle at this, which drew a laugh from the starborn girl. "Is this your first visit to Aloria?" she said, raising an eyebrow.

"My associate climbed from the military into the upper echelons of Denigoth society," Cassian said, sounding amused. "He is used to our staunch, proper ladies who would not think to kiss their own children in public."

"Oh, there is more than one kind of lady in the empire," Somar said with a smirk. "All the same, I never dreamed I would be kissed in any manner by a woman nearly so magnificent as yourself."

The girl smiled, but he could tell she had not drawn pleasure from the remark. Like Cassian, this Keska had no taste for flattery. That was interesting. Somar had surmised more than once that the reason the boy had developed such a friendship with him was that he was the only one Cassian had in his life who would tell him he was wrong.

"I should like you both to be my guests this afternoon," Keska said. "My chefs have prepared a fine meal for the three of us."

This remark surprised Somar. "If... that is what you wish, but I would assume the two of you would desire to dine alone. I imagine you have many things to discuss that I would not begin to understand."

"You understand *death* I assume?" the young woman said, lifting a dark eyebrow.

Cassian sighed. "My dear sister wishes to enlist you as an ally in convincing me *not* to visit Promethiock."

"Indeed," Somar exhaled.

"You are my last hope," Keska said after rolling her eyes at Cassian.

"Well, I am not sure I can do much for you, my dear."

"You can listen to my arguments and form a rational opinion. That is all I ask."

"At least she is being quite upfront with you about her intentions," Cassian said. "That is not generally my sister's style."

Keska turned and gave Cassian a playful scowl. Then she whirled back to Somar and said: "Will you eat with me, sir?"

"No man could refuse such an offer," he answered, feeling slightly befuddled.

"Excellent," she said, and to his surprise, she offered him her elbow. He hesitated and then took it, considering as he did that he was taking the arm of the girl who would soon become the most illustrious woman in the world. Not even the wife of the emperor himself when she was alive had had quite the majesty of the only living female starborn. It sent a little shiver through him.

They walked together along the sand, and Keska periodically spoke as they passed large adobe structures, which she explained were storehouses for the shipyards or long-abandoned military structures. There was a silent sense of forgotten greatness about the landscape. Such was the case of most remaining kingdoms in the world. They could not contend with the unstoppable force that was the Denigoth Empire. People went about their business, sometimes gazing up in wonder at Keska and whispering to one another. There were sloping cliffs down to the waters covered by thick, bushy plants with purple flowers that produced a delightful vanilla scent that mingled with the salty sea air. The sun poured its gentle warmth down upon them all through their journey, never beating too harshly yet never far from the senses.

It did not surprise Somar that Keska did not travel with an entourage as any noblewoman in Denigoth would. She had an aura of power about her, much the way Cassian did, only it was not quite so blaringly pronounced. She was charming in a subtle, sophisticated style that Cassian was not. All the while as they walked, she said nothing of the dragon or Cassian's journey. This was a demonstration of self-control. The young woman would make her point when she deemed the time correct.

The three of them came upon a small but magnificent palace of white adobe and golden curved arches. A cluster of perhaps fifteen servants in precisely cut and sewn blue uniforms came upon the three of them, and Keska commanded them without words. She had but to meet the eyes of an attendant and he or she would quite suddenly burst into duty.

The three of them eventually moved up a curving stairway to a room several stories above the ground floor of the palace where they saw, resting between yet another small army of finely dressed servants, a long table filled with an array of food that made Somar's head swim. There was an enormous stuffed bird which Somar did not recognize, as well as a stuffed pig, a massive pot of piping hot stew with bits of red meat floating within. On another table rested clay pots filled with sautéed mushrooms and spiced vegetables, and ceramic trays with various pies and gigantic loafs of bread with pure silver cutting knives and smaller plates of creamed butter and spiced honey.

"I wonder if there is enough to feed the *three of us,*" Cassian said as he stared at the mountain of food.

"It is a trick I have learned with royal funds," Keska said with a silvery laugh. "All the excess food after our meal will be given directly to the city's orphanage."

Cassian moved over to the table and picked up a bit of bread and dipped it in one of the stews and took a quick bite. Once he had chewed and swallowed, he said: "The mention of the orphanage is meant as a subtle barb at us, or at least me." His eyes shifted to Somar's. "I am sure you know why there would be an abundance of orphans in Aloria?"

Somar did know. Denigoth conscripted soldiers quite often from their client kingdoms, and small nations had little choice but to bow to the empire's will and send their young men. During Somar's time in the military, he had seen tens of thousands of soldiers come into his ranks from Aloria and other tiny countries. Many such men, only barely trained to hold a sword before they were flung onto the battlefield, died to weaken the enemy so that seasoned and suitably equipped Denigoth soldiers could move in. This, of course, created many fatherless children with mothers who often had no means to support them. Somar understood that often such children ended up as beggars, or wards of the government in more generous places.

"The aftermath of imperial conquest," Cassian said as he picked a bit of pork from the enormous carcass. His gaze shifted to Keska's as he said: "The old man and I have discussed such things quite often."

"How nice for you both," Keska said with a prim grin. "I suppose the *conversations* you have had before making your plans to march into war have allowed you a sense of humanitarianism."

This drew a smile from Cassian. "Our discussions are chiefly about tactics and strategy, but they do become quite philosophical at times." He met his sister's eyes and said: "Do you wish me to tell you I find the waste of human life to be troubling? I do. Such things are hideous, and they denote antiquated and entirely uncreative approaches to politics and warfare." He sighed and leaned back in his chair, gesturing around the opulent room. "Tell me though, dearest sister, does your sense of moral superiority ever suffer from the knowledge that all the exquisite luxury in which you live has been made possible by *conquest* and military rule?"

Keska grinned, revealing the sparkling white top row of her teeth. "What a wonderful sense of moral absolutism you possess. Apparently, one must throw off all worldly comforts and go live in the bushes in order to disagree with *you,* mighty Cassian. Certainly, if I choose to live in the society to which I was born, then I *must* agree with any and all mass murder committed in the name of *empire.*"

Cassian chuckled. "Oh no, my dear sister, you misunderstand me." He made a sweeping gesture at her and said: "I wholeheartedly support your right to adorn yourself in jewelry and bathe in all the wealth this country showers upon you while you make a haughty show of condemning the actions taken to create and maintain such a kingdom. I am a quite strong proponent of freedom of expression, after all."

Keska let out a sharp laugh. "You feel moral superiority to me because I wear earrings?" She gave the diamonds a little flick with her finger. "I am going to be this country's next queen. I dress the part—play a role. You, Cassian, will murder your own brother to ascend to the throne."

Cassian's eyes narrowed, yet the smile did not leave his face. "I have no intention of challenging Dimitris to a duel as you all seem to suspect."

"No?" Keska said, raising an eyebrow. "Even if that were true, you know *he* will challenge *you* if you stand in his way."

Cassian's voice came out with a slight edge: "If he were to die by my hand in such a scenario, it would not be murder."

"It would be a dead body where a genius once existed, and all for your ambition."

"All for *his* ambition actually. As I said, I have no intention of challenging him."

"Hmm," Keska murmured, staring at him with narrowed eyes. A moment of silence passed between them. Then the young woman's gaze shifted very abruptly to Somar. "My apologies," she said, her face smoothing over into a serene smile. "I have waited years to speak to my dear brother Cassian in person, but that is no excuse to act as a poor host." She gestured at the chair nearest to Somar, which happened to be at the end of the table, and it slid out. "Please seat yourself."

"I thank you," Somar said. He took his seat, as did Keska and Cassian. Somar found it vaguely amusing that he seemed to be seated at the head of the table, while the two living miracles sat across from one another at the sides. He wondered if this were intentional, or if concerns over such things were meaningless to two such as they.

He pulled a piece of spiced duck from a silver platter near to him. As he did, a servant rushed over and whispered: "Tilsian wine, my lord?"

"I would not mind a goblet or two," he said. Wine seemed like an excellent idea. He could feel the female starborn's eyes on him as he bit into the meat. She was watching him, waiting for the appropriate moment to resume her denunciation of Cassian. He also became aware as the delicious food began to sate his hunger that she was attempting to gaze into his mind. He looked up at her, and her dark eyes stared back unashamed. Keska's psychic touch was unlike Cassian's. Whereas his telepathy came as a staggering force of will, Keska's was subtle, as if thousands of tiny tendrils of her mind were gently probing the wall around his thoughts, searching for the smallest crack through which to slip.

"That will not work on him," Cassian said after a sip of water from his goblet. "The old man is at least as clever as you."

"Hmm," Keska moaned, casting a dark and sultry smirk. "I had to see it for myself."

Somar let out a nervous chuckle. "Surely there are members of your court skilled in occlusion."

Keska lifted an eyebrow. "Skilled? No, not like you, dear man." Her eyes moved to Cassian. "I can see why you have grown so attached to this one. It must be fascinating to have a man around who can confound all your telepathic strength."

"I find it refreshing," Cassian said. He broke off a piece of the duck and leaned back in his chair. Just before taking a bite, he gestured to Somar and said: "You were going to attempt to turn him against me, were you not? Please, proceed." He sounded vaguely amused.

"All right," Keska replied in a soft voice. She drew in a slow breath and then said: "Your pupil, Cassian, has set out to begin a civil war. He is willing to tear the largest empire in history apart to satisfy his own anger."

Somar gazed at the young woman, and then at Cassian. The boy's face betrayed no emotion at her words. He quietly ate his duck leg, waiting for his sister to continue on. She did.

"My brother is a radical, as I am sure you know. He wishes to destroy the Nemesai, of course, because they executed his mother and father." Cassian said nothing to this, but a subtle coldness edged over his features. "He has declared war on them, but if they were his only targets, he could have exacted his revenge long ago. No, my brother sees them as only a small representation of the *real* evil in this world." Her voice became low and somber as she said: "Has he told you what is truly in his heart?" Her eyes trailed slowly over to Cassian as she said: "Has he told you how completely he despises the very gods themselves?"

Somar's stomach twisted just a little at these words, despite his many years and his battle-hardened soul. He could not help but stare at the boy. Cassian had set his food down and was gazing at a vague spot on the table, his sharp features locked in an expression of contemplation.

Keska frowned at him and said: "Cassian is willing to risk his own life and apparently *your life* to visit the greatest creature that has ever challenged the will of the gods. He believes that the ancient reptile will be his ally." She gave a slight laugh. "More than one foolish starborn has ventured down to visit Promethiock. Even those such as we are less than insects before the great dragon. He killed them—*all of them*."

"*Not all*," Cassian said with a shrug.

Keska's eyes narrowed. "Ah, my brother speaks of Kaleos, *the first starborn*." She spoke the words with dark amusement. "If the legends are to be believed, *Kaleos* was not like either of us, but held all five points of the star within himself, possessing power that even we cannot conceive. That legend of a man tried with all of his great magic to free Promethiock, but his power was *nothing* to the prison, which was created by the Gods themselves."

Somar knew this story well. He had learned it as a boy dressed in rags sitting atop a wall and gazing down at a Diaphan priest who was standing on a pedestal shouting out the story of Kaleos. Somar had grasped the great theme at the heart of the story even as a child: not even the most powerful mortal in history could challenge the will of the gods. Somar's faith had meant a great deal to him then, yet over the decades he had lost his connection to it, as many men do. Still, as the female starborn spoke, he felt some of that old flame rekindle within his soul.

"The dragon knew that if Kaleos could not free him, then no being in the world could, and it filled him with rage," Keska said. "Immortal creature that he is, Promethiock has remained trapped within his tremendous cage decade after decade, *century after century*. His hatred, and perhaps his madness have grown to levels we mortals cannot imagine." She sighed and said in a tone of sardonic amusement, "and yet my brother believes *himself* to be the one mortal to whom that the great dragon will calmly speak after over nine hundred years of solitude within a cold, dark prison of stone."

"Yes, I do," said Cassian with a touch of mirth in his voice. He had resumed feeding himself.

Keska stared at him for a brief moment, and it was evident that Cassian's cavalier attitude had an unnerving effect upon her. Still, she turned back to Somar and went on: "Has he told you what will happen when he comes into contact with the dragon—*his contingency plan*?"

Cassian sighed, "I was wondering when you would circle to this point. No, he does not know." He turned to Somar and said: "My sister speaks of a *nocus iviso*."

"*Psychic...moment*?" Somar said, translating the ancient Dhavic as best he could and feeling rather foolish.

"*Psychic event* is what we sometimes call it, though there is a certain poeticism to your translation," Cassian said. "It is the reason that thousands all over the world felt Markus Anias burn to death two hundred and thirty-six years ago."

Somar knew the name. Markus Anias was the last starborn to venture down into Promethiock's prison. There were indeed legends that those touched with magic had felt him die.

"It is a reaction," Keska said, "to an ancient reptilian mind that radiates psychic energy thousands of times greater than what my brother and I generate."

"Promethiock is a telepath?" Somar said. This surprised him.

"Yes," Keska said, "the strongest one on this plane of existence, and my brother wishes to *capitalize* on that. Once he comes into contact with the dragon, he will be able to tap into that power and reach out to every telepathic mind in the world all at once and shout his condemnations of the church."

Cassian rolled his eyes. "That part is true, yes, but *nocus iviso* is not a contingency plan. It was always an element of visiting Promethiock. How else would I prove that I did not simply take cover in a shallow cave on the island for a few hours and then *claim* to have visited the dragon?" He turned to Somar. "When I come in contact with Promethiock, every telepathic being in the world will see through my eyes for a few moments. They will hear what I hear and, to an extent, feel what I feel."

Somar blinked. He had assumed that the authenticity of their journey would be proven through some magical means far beyond his understanding, *which was in fact correct.* Still, to commune with every telepathic being in the world at once... What fraction of the human race had the gift of sorcery—perhaps one percent? How many thousands would that number? And they would be men and women of wealth and influence. Somar had never heard of a poor sorcerer. This would be something not even Bishop Cromlic would be able to suppress.

Keska sighed. "I believe we are all chosen by the power in the comet for different reasons." She turned back to Cassian, frowning. "There are many aspects to commanding magic, and my brother Cassian's great gift is that he possesses an almost absurd strength of mental will," her eyes narrowed, "All the unbending and uninhibited focus of a madman." Cassian met her stare, an amused smile touching his lips. He said nothing though, so Keska went on: "This is the reason Cassian believes he can defeat our brother Dimitris, an absolutely brilliant sorcerer in his own right. But Cassian's gifts could be applied to far greater goals than inflicting simple, ugly death. He could reach into other dimensions and invent healing spells the like of which this world has never seen. Instead, he wants to throw his life away venturing down to see an ancient reptilian monster that will almost certainly burn him to ash."

"Hmm," Cassian grunted in amusement through his nose. "Is that about all, dear sister?" He smiled at her and then to Somar. "We have been having essentially this same argument since we were fourteen. I was curious to see how the speech played out from her physical lips. I must say that she possesses a more charismatic voice than I would have guessed. I think my sister will make a fine orator when she is queen of these lands."

"*Cassian*!" Keska snapped. He turned to face her, and she said: "You are only doing this out of stubbornness and anger. I am trying to save you from a gruesome death."

"I thank you, my very dear sister," he said, and then he spread his hands, "but I refuse the salvation you offer."

"Because you think you are unstoppable!"

"No," Cassian said, his tone hardening, "because I am willing to risk my life to achieve my goals."

As the two starborn stared at one another, Somar detected a subtle crackling sound in the air, and he felt the hairs all over his body begin to stand up.

Keska snarled, "You are willing to risk the lives of hundreds of thousands on your insane beliefs."

"I am willing to take the actions necessary to *end* slavery and religious persecution in the largest nation in history. Please tell me what great contributions to the world you intend to achieve by marrying your cousin and becoming queen of this infinitesimal speck of a kingdom."

Keska pursed her lips. "You are even more arrogant in person than I ever thought!"

"And you are a *coward,*" Cassian said.

Keska shot up from her chair, and as she did, the space of table between the two of them shattered into splinters. The two stumped halves of it slammed to the stone floor, spilling down the great feast. Keska took a step toward Cassian, and he rose from his seat and stepped toward her. The servants in the room began to run and scream, some of them disappearing. Guards would appear soon, Somar knew, but that threat was nothing compared to the one at which he was staring.

Cassian leaned into his sister's face and snapped: "Why do we have this power? So, we can sit upon golden sofas and be fanned by servants?" His hands moved to Keska's shoulders, and the air around the two of them seemed to ripple and distort. What Somar could only conceive of as arm-length bolts of lightning flashed for brief instants around them. Cassian's voice came through the crackling: "Do you really have no drive at all to make this world *better?!* Who so well as we can see all the depravity, all the corruption, all the injustice? Whose *responsibility* is it if not ours to fix such things? If we do not improve the world for humanity, then what the hell *good* are we?"

Keska stared at Cassian. Her eyes were filled with anger, but there was something else as well. He had seemed to touch upon a nerve within her. That was perhaps the only reason she was hesitating, for Somar could see that the urge to attack lay very close to the surface within her.

"I love you," Cassian said in a more subdued voice. He leaned in and kissed Keska's forehead. She remained perfectly still as he did this. "I thank you for trying to stop me." He let go of her shoulders and stepped back.

After a moment, Keska shook her head and said with a small, dark chuckle, "You are *really* going to do it."

"Of course," Cassian said.

"The Nemesai will come for you anyway," she whispered, shaking her head. "You know that, don't you? Promethiock is not a god."

"He is close enough. If I have his blessing, the other bodies of the church will have grounds not to support my excommunication."

One of Keska's dark eyebrows rose. "That is your plan? You think you can stand up to Bishop Cromlic and his army of tattooed zealots as long as the Onkai are not with them?"

"The Nemesai are not an *army,*" Cassian said. "The *Onkai* are a military force of brave, disciplined soldiers who fight against horrors more powerful than themselves, but the Nemesai are just a pack of bullies who beat and torture frightened peasants."

"They are still tremendously dangerous."

Cassian shrugged and said with a relaxed smile: "So am I."

Keska drew in a slow breath, staring at her brother, and then exhaled: "You are the greatest fool I have ever known."

"We shall both find out soon enough," Cassian said with a sigh. He reached down to his belt and retrieved a small leather sack that clinked as he gripped it, which he tossed to Keska. She caught it by way of freezing it in the air just in front of her open palm. "For the orphans who will be without this wonderful dinner because of my arrogance," he said.

Keska's expression softened ever so slightly at these words. Then she gave a little sigh, and her eyes shifted to the door. "My men do not like assaults upon me."

Cassian turned his head in time to see an enormous, dark-skinned man in bronze armor dash at him, a long sword in his hand aimed to pierce Cassian's heart. The boy calmly raised his hand, and all the great soldier's momentum came to a smooth halt an arm's length from his chest. The swordsman was frozen in mid-stride. From the look of shock and confusion on his face and the heaving of his shoulders in contrast to his otherwise statue-still form, it seemed that Cassian was allowing him to do nothing more than breathe.

"Your men love you very much," Cassian said back over his shoulder as he eyed the soldier. "This one is willing to fight *me* for your sake. He came up here to die without hesitation to protect you." Cassian flashed the soldier a friendly smile and said: "Please relax, my brave friend. She is in no danger from me." He waved his hand, and the man slumped to his knees, looking confused and a little awestruck. Cassian turned from him and faced Keska. "This kind of loyalty doesn't come cheaply. He loves you, as so many on this island love you. You are a great leader, Keska." He drew in a slow breath, his young face shifting in a serious expression as he said: "If I *win*—become emperor—I want you to come help me shape the future."

"What do you mean?" she said, her eyes narrowing yet her right eyebrow rising.

"You, Telemachus, and I could do it together. As you said a moment ago, the power chooses each of us for a different reason. You both possess strengths I do not. I would listen to you."

"You do not listen to *anyone*, Cassian," said Keska, though Somar could see in her eyes that she was intrigued.

"I *always* consider what you have to say, dear sister, and I always will." Cassian glanced at the soldier and gave the man a little wink, and then he turned to Somar and said: "I believe it is time you and I go."

"Ah... yes," Somar said, rising uneasily from his chair.

Cassian turned back to his sister then and said: "If the dragon does kill me, you should challenge Dimitris for the throne. I think you would make a better ruler than he, and you are the only one other than myself that I think could defeat him."

Keska smirked at this. "Denigoth would never accept a female ruler."

Cassian laughed, "Why, because of *tradition*? To hell with that! They have never seen *you*, Keska Ethedrine." He gave a small bow and then turned toward the door. His eyes moved to those of the soldier once more, and he tipped his head toward the man and then left the room, with Somar following closely behind.

CHAPTER 15: LIFE AMONG THE HUMANS

Racism, slavery, and religious persecution are all symptoms of the same disease. These things can only exist in a society with a large enough combination of people who refuse to reason, cannot reason, or are not allowed to reason. As a powerful telepath, I can attest that the vast majority of the human race are good people who genuinely want to do the right thing most of the time. Yet a general attitude of goodness is not enough to build an evolved society. The "right thing" can become muddled in the complexities of the world, and only those with intelligence and courage can find it.

—Excerpt from "A Modern Empire," by Cassian Asango

Kota slowly lowered his training sword and gave the cup before him a gentle tap. He began every day with three hundred strikes, and today Gretis had instructed him to keep one leg lifted above the ground for the first hundred and fifty and then switch. Kota had been using this particular cup for over three weeks. The exercise had become so easy that he had trouble imagining he would ever break it. Over the last two moons since his training began, the muscles in his arms and wrists had swollen and grown hard like corded steel.

Kota was lifting the blade for the two hundred and seventy-first swing when he heard the faintest disturbance in the grass behind him. He whirled around with his sword, but it was too late. The tip of Gretis's blunted blade poked sharply into his arm.

"Too slow," she whispered.

Kota grunted and pulled away. Gretis never struck hard enough to render him incapable of training, but he would have a fresh little bruise to match the last four she had given him that week.

"At least you are not hesitating as much," she said.

Kota nodded silently. The sneak attacks were one of his least favorite aspects of his new life. Gretis might come from anywhere at any time and hit him. She was the most silent thing in the world it seemed. Not even his shamalak ears could detect her movements most of the time. Yet somehow, she expected him to develop the capacity to defend himself against her shadowy thrusts from behind.

Gretis raised her blade, indicating that she was to come again, but instead of launching into an attack she said: "Things are going well at the school, I understand. Your training is progressing adequately with me as well. I suppose that means there is only one step left to solidifying your place here."

Kota swallowed, keeping his weapon ready. It was Gretis's style to attack in mid-conversation. He suspected that she had chosen this particular subject to unnerve him. Gretis knew he was worried about his parents' approval of his spending ten or more years away from the tribe to train with a mysterious human woman. There was also *possibly* a measure of shame in returning home before finding his spirit, but he supposed that least of the concerns his parents would have. Kota was dreading asking their permission – especially his mother's.

"I would like to accompany you on the journey," Gretis said, remaining poised for attack.

This brought the hint of a smile to Kota's mouth. He imagined returning to his tribe with the astonishing woman.

Meeting her might do a great deal to convince his parents. "When you want to go?"

"You decide, young warrior," she said, and he felt her eyes burning into him. The way she spoke the words made him think this was another of her tests. Gretis was aware of his fear, he knew.

"Three days," he said.

She lifted an eyebrow. "Why three days?"

"Best to go sooner than later I guess," he said, keeping his grip on his weapon. "But we should wait 'till after storm."

Gretis gazed up in amusement and said: "Storm? There is not a cloud in the sky."

"It coming," Kota said softly, digging the claws into the soil. "I can smell it on the wind."

She gave the tiniest of chuckles and then moved. Her attack came so fast that Kota barely had time to whip his own weapon out to meet it in the air. Their two swords clashed, and Kota danced back, using the claws on his toes to steady his footing in the grass. He gazed at Gretis's shoulders, her arms, and her legs as she had taught him to do, scanning for the slightest indication of what might come next. Their morning sparring sessions were an intense game of concentration. Gretis held back the tremendous speed and strength she possessed just enough so that he had the slightest chance to parry her. Kota had long since abandoned hope of landing a strike of his own.

"A villager asked me the other day if you sleep in the trees," Gretis said, dancing to the left.

"You should tell him I just found one I like," Kota said, keeping his eyes on her movements.

"For all we know, the man was asking so he would know where to find you to put an arrow in your side." She sprang forward suddenly with a thrust to his stomach.

Kota managed to snap his body backward and whip his blade sideways, but he was a hair too slow, and Gretis's sword gave his left elbow a glancing slash. He lowered his sword and wrung out his arm. As he did this, Gretis leaned forward and said: "Throw your body into the opposite direction of your sword. A little more to the right and I would have missed." She raised her sword. "Here, I will make the same attack again." Kota had only an instant to return to his fighting stance before her thrust came. This time he jerked his body hard to the right and managed to avoid her weapon, but the violent movement cost him his footing, and he stumbled and had to lower his sword hand to the ground to catch himself. As he did this, Gretis's weapon poked him in the center of his chest.

"Sloppy footwork," she said. She lowered her training sword and said: "I think we need to work your legs a little harder. Go and fetch us some water."

Kota swallowed in defeat and said: "Yes, ma'am." He walked over to the entrance to her house, set his training sword carefully against the wall, and picked up the pole and twin water buckets that lay below the front window. Setting the buckets a little way apart, he slipped the pole through the two handles and made sure they caught in the notches at the ends. Then he picked the thin piece of wood up and laid it across his shoulders behind his neck. Carefully balancing the weight, he stepped forward and dropped to a kneeling position, just barely keeping his right knee from touching the ground. Then he rose and stepped forward into another, this time holding his left knee just above the ground. In this fashion, he slowly made his way the eighty or so paces to Lady Gretis's well.

"Fill them to the top," she shouted from far behind.

"Yes, ma'am," Kota cried back. He set his two buckets down and then took the much larger pail tied to the well's crank and dropped it splashing into the murky blackness below. When Kota judged it was full, he turned the wooden handle and slowly drew the heavy pail up. It took only a moment to fill the smaller buckets, but Kota groaned as he slipped the pole back through them and lifted the now quite heavy twin masses up and again set them across his shoulders. His legs trembled under the strain as he made his way through the slow, kneeling march back to Gretis's home. Despite the agony, Kota moved very carefully. If he spilled a single drop, Lady Gretis would make him begin the task over from her door.

"All right, I think you've earned your morning break," the woman said when he finally set the buckets down. "Go take your lessons with Master Bendick. I want you back here at noon."

"Yes, ma'am," Kota said. He darted into her small house and retrieved his thin stack of papyrus papers. They contained all of the writing and arithmetic he and Gretis had worked on the night before. Tucking them under his arm, he shut the door and then dug the claws in his toes into the grass and broke into a hard run. His body seemed to be growing faster and stronger every day. The wind whipped at his face and made his loose clothing flap against his skin. The muscles in his feet and legs worked in practiced unison to keep every step smooth and quiet even in a run. Gretis expected him to develop stealth along with everything else.

He was just barely panting when he came upon the town square where the people were going about their business. Only a few of them stopped to stare at his arrival. By and large, the village had grown used to its shamalak resident. The whispers of him being dangerous had become fewer and fewer, though he still heard them. More often though, he caught debates about whether shamalak were the result of humans breeding with wolves or great forest cats, and whether he could possibly be as intelligent as the human students in the temple. Kota was in his second week of tutelage from the notorious Master Bendick, and most of the town, from what his ears could decipher, did not approve.

He walked briskly through the crowd to the temple, but before he approached the doors, he turned to the right and thrust his hands up to the small lion-faced fountainhead and let the water trickling from its mouth drizzle over his hands. It fascinated him to no end that the temple had a system of what they called 'aqueducts' drawing water from the mountains behind. Kota washed his hands thoroughly and then splashed a little water on his face. Humans valued cleanliness, particularly in the Onkai temple, and he was their guest.

The guards said nothing to Kota when he approached but opened the doors. As soon as he stepped inside though, he heard a voice he recognized say: "Oh look, the vermin is here."

Kota gazed down the hall of weapons and armor to see a tall boy named Leander standing amidst a large group of other young humans. Leander was fourteen winters by Kota's best guess and had yet to earn his tattoos.

"Good morning, Leander," Kota said in an even voice. He forced himself not to react. Gretis had instructed him to refrain from any displays of anger—the Sansrit Path required a firm commitment to patience and compassion above all things. Kota moved to walk past the snickering boys. Just as he came within a few paces, Leander leaped into his path. Kota drew in a breath, awaiting the inevitable attempt to insult him.

"*Koota*, is it?" the boy said, the mocking tone in his voice utterly obvious. Kota tensed. He guessed something incredibly crude would escape the boy's lips next, and he was correct. Leander leaned in with a vicious smirk and said: "Do try not to *shit* on the floor, would you, doggy?" The surrounding boys burst out laughing.

Kota forced himself to look past the crude young man and take in a slow breath, holding back his irritation. At that moment, he noticed a tall young Onkai who had earned his apotheosis tattoos standing perfectly still down the hall. This soldier looked as though he had been walking by but then abruptly halted. He was blinking, an incredulous look on his heavily marked face. Suddenly this Onkai spun to face Kota and Leander, and his voice came out booming: "Try not to *shit* on the *floor?* What a thing to say!"

Leander's eyes went a little wide, and he whirled around to see the speaker. The teenage soldier moved a little closer, and Kota recognized him as Glavius, the student Gretis trained a few afternoons a week. Leander evidently recognized him as well, for he said in a suddenly nervous voice: "H-hello, Glavius."

Glavius looked at Leander and then at Kota, and when he did, there was a hint of a smile. The two of them had spoken very little. Their training was entirely separate from one another's, though Gretis had instructed Kota to observe here and there. Always in the lessons, Glavius had seemed nervous or frustrated, but here among the students and other soldiers, he appeared relaxed and confident.

"His name is *KOTA*!" Glavius said, shouting the last word with an abruptness that made Leander jump. The young soldier lifted an eyebrow. "You asked his name, didn't you?"

"I... uh..." Leander muttered. Kota listened to the boy's heart. It was pounding wildly in his chest.

Glavius's glare softened, and his expression shifted into a kindly smile, though there was still something distinctively dangerous in his eyes. "What's your name, initiate?" he said.

"Uh... Leander, s-sir," Leander said.

"Leander?" Glavius said as he strode up. He put his hands on Leander's shoulders and leaned in close to the boy's face and said: "Well, *Leander*, are you somehow not aware that Kota is a *guest* in our temple?"

"I was just...making a joke," Leander said.

"A *joke*?" Glavius said. His smile grew so wide that it displayed nearly every tooth in his mouth. "You called him a dog and told him not to *shit* on the floor as a friendly *joke* – this guest in our temple who *saved* the *life* of one of our captains?" Glavius was glaring in a way that made even Kota nervous. "Oh, Leander," he whispered, and he leaned in still closer. Leander's breathing became quite rapid. With an expression of mock sympathy, Glavius said: "I worry about your future here." He slid an arm around Leander's shoulder and gently turned him so that they were both facing Kota. "Our shamalak here tore out the eyes of a kothla demon. He risked his life to help our brothers—*your* brothers. If you have a shred of integrity in here," he gave Leander's chest a little pat in the place where Kota knew the heart was located, "then you will *apologize* to our guest wholeheartedly."

Leander's face was pale. Glavius had not harmed or even overtly threatened him, but apparently, he did not need to. Leander looked at Kota and said: "I . . . apologize for my comment."

"There," Glavius said, patting Leander on the back. "Doesn't it feel better to conduct yourself like a gentleman?" He stared at the boy, his eyes narrowing as he said: "You look troubled. If I didn't know better, I would say that you were *afraid,* and that would make you a sniveling little coward who's only *brave* when he's picking on someone smaller and weaker." Glavius laughed: "But you and I know that's not the case! You just got carried away, and you have apologized for it, like a *man*."

Glavius stepped away from Leander, moving toward Kota. In a loud voice, he said: "If none of the other students have said it to you, let me welcome you to our temple." He made a bow that seemed exaggerated. Kota looked around the room. Leander still looked uncomfortable, but the scorn was gone from the eyes of the other boys. One of them even met his gaze and said: "Sorry I laughed just now."

"Thank you," Kota said. In truth, it did not trouble his pride to have a protector.

Glavius rose and said: "Where are you going, Kota?"

"To Master Bendick's classroom."

"Poor bastard," Glavius chuckled. "Why don't I walk with you?' He moved next to Kota and put a hand on his back. Kota nodded, and the two of them moved down the hall through the students. They walked in silence until they turned down a hallway toward the lecture rooms, which had already emptied out from the normal students' morning classes. When the two of them were alone, Glavius said in a quiet voice: "You should really stand up for yourself more. I've seen you fence with Gretis. I'd say you stand a pretty decent chance of walloping that imbecile even if he *is* bigger and older."

"Gretis tell me that is not Sansrit way," Kota said, then he corrected himself by reflex: "is not *the* Sansrit way."

"How absurdly frustrating," Glavius said, rolling his eyes.

"It more than that," Kota said. "People here think I am *beast.* If I fight a human boy because of...*words,* people think I beast even more."

"Huh," Glavius grunted, stroking his chin. "That's a fair point. Alright then, why don't you and I make a pact?" He leaned in a little closer and spoke in a whisper: "I'll make sure none of the boys give you trouble like that again, and *you* keep it to yourself how easily and how often that woman knocks me on my ass."

"Alright," Kota said. He could not help but smile.

Glavius grinned back, but the muscles in his neck contracted as if he were pretending to be nervous. "I suppose we'll all have to get used to that smile o' yours. You look like you're getting ready to tear into my throat with those fangs."

"Oh," Kota said. Feeling embarrassed, he closed his mouth.

"No, don't be ashamed!" Glavius said, clapping him on the arm. "We're all training to be great soldiers here. I think we can learn to face a little boy with a few sharp teeth."

"Alright," Kota said, feeling reassured.

They arrived at the thick wooden door to Master Bendick's classroom. Glavius sighed and put a hand on Kota's shoulder. "Good luck in there. Don't let Bendick treat you like anything less than you are." The side of Glavius's mouth curved upward as he added: "And please do me a favor: don't *actually* shit on the floor in our temple or you'll make me look like an idiot."

From the way Glavius said the words, Kota knew they were not meant to insult him but were a joke from someone who liked him. "I try very hard," he said.

"That's all I ask," Glavius said, and he spun smoothly on his heels and strode back down the hall. Kota watched him go, feeling elated. From what he knew, Glavius was the most impressive with a blade of any student in the temple, even if Gretis did trounce him on a regular basis. Having such an Onkai on his side could make his life among the other students much smoother, but more than that, Kota found that he liked the cocky young man. It felt good to gain a new friend.

This happiness was stifled the instant he creaked open the door to the lecture hall. Master Bendick's voice came out in a gruff snarl: "YOU'RE LATE!"

Kota swallowed and stepped inside the room. "I sorry," he said as he gazed at the elderly man hunched over behind his enormous wooden desk. Master Bendick possessed no tattoos and was quite old and noticeably feeble. Still, he somehow managed to inspire fear in the temple's students, and even in many of the older soldiers who had seen battle. Kota had learned that Bendick was not a member of the Onkai Order, but a Lucinian monk. From what Kota knew, the Lucinians were an entirely separate order of men who were responsible for gathering, organizing, and teaching others the vast knowledge the church possessed. Darius had told Kota that *Old Bendick* could read and speak seventeen languages and could quote perfectly any passage from the Enumis, the grand tome that housed the holy scriptures of the church.

"You are to be here exactly at the hour of ten," Bendick snapped. He hobbled around his desk, legs shuffling under the heavy cloth of his gray robe. "You are ten minutes late! There is a sundial in the courtyard to help you keep track of the time if you are confused."

"I... I no understand how to read sundial," Kota said. He was too intimidated to ask the old man how *he* knew the precise time, given that the sundial was outside, and the lecture hall had no windows.

Bendick sighed, rolling his eyes. They had yellowed with age nearly as much as the man's teeth. "I suppose we shall have to cover that today." He gestured to the small table nearest his desk and said: "Take your seat and lay out your work."

Kota obeyed, moving through the rows of tables and taking the same seat he had the last few class sessions. Bendick reached out a veiny hand and snatched up his papers. The elderly human eyed the writing practice first, grunting inscrutably as he often did. Bendick had assigned Kota to write out every letter of the Tethric alphabet one hundred times, and Kota had taken great pains to be exact with every curve and angle. The monk was silent when he read through the arithmetic but only scratched at his thin, beardless chin. The mathematics lessons had come far easier to Kota than reading and writing, partially because his grandfather had taught him the basic human symbols and names for numbers, but mostly because his people used math for many things, and Kota had learned many of the same concepts from his tribal elders.

Finally, Master Bendick let out a low sigh and said: "It seems perhaps shamalak are not such dimwitted creatures as the texts suggest. Your handwriting is...*adequate*. As for sums though, I do not see a single error."

"Adding numbers? Oh yes, that very easy for me. I finish quickly."

"Really?" Bendick said, raising a thin eyebrow. "What is two hundred and seventy-eight plus nine hundred and forty-three?"

Kota gazed up and to the right as he often did when solving math problems. In his mind he added the ones places and then carried over to the tens, added again and came over to the hundreds. Within three of what humans referred to as 'seconds,' he had his answer: "One thousand two hundred and twenty-one."

"Hmm," Bendick grunted, eyeing him closely. "Fairly quick. You were telling me that your people have a system of math and calendars?"

"Oh, yes, sir," Kota said. "My father teach me about calendar when I very young. We no have paper like humans, but we make scratches in clay..." he searched his mind for the correct word, "*s-squares* we make."

"Interesting," Bendick said, stroking his chin again. The old man gazed up at the ceiling. "You know it's strange? Most of the truly great swordsmen I have seen over the years have displayed a high aptitude for mathematics to one extent or another." Bendick scowled at Kota very abruptly and said: "Why are you smiling? This only means I will be pushing you all the harder!"

"To learn more?" Kota said.

"Yes."

"I very happy to learn more."

"Then I shall have to provide you with a level of mathematics that is *not very easy,* boy. I assure you we can go as far as is necessary once the groundwork has been properly laid. I should like to see how you handle geometric and trigonometric equations."

"Yes, I want to try," Kota said.

This drew another inscrutable grunt from the old man. "I will have to write a paper on you for the archives." He fumbled with the pages Kota had given him, returning to the writing, which he eyed as he said: "I believe I shall have you write *me* many papers on your culture once we have developed your literacy and your grammar and syntactical skill to a sufficient degree." Bendick reached into a pocket in his robes and retrieved a piece of what the humans called *'chalk.'* He moved next to Kota and bent down and wrote three neatly scripted letters on the desk's wooden surface. "Read this word," he said.

Kota frowned at the white letters. He hesitated, then said very slowly: "H-h-hat." He looked up at Master Bendick, and the old monk nodded. Kota frowned again. "What is *hat*?"

The edges of Bendick's lips trembled upward for an instant as if a smile were trying to appear in his features, but his stern muscles battled against it and won. He answered then in a detached voice: "A *hat* is something humans wear on their heads."

"Oh. Is it helmet?"

"No. A hat doesn't protect the head from swords and arrows. It simply keeps it warm and dry."

"Like hood?" "Yes, a bit like that," Bendick said, sounding irritated. He took a slow breath through his thin nostrils and exhaled: "I believe teaching you to read may prove especially difficult even if you *are* somewhat clever. Most of the scrolls and books I have for you to practice on are about *human culture,* and that is something of which I think you have very little understanding." He narrowed his eyes and said: "Do you even understand what I just said to you?"

"I... I think so," Kota said. "Humans write about human things."

"Stated with wonderful simplicity," Bendick said. "Yes, your education will be more difficult than that of the other boys here because you know so much less than they do. It is not your fault, but the fact still remains." He gestured to the left wall where hundreds of leather-bound books and many more hundreds of scrolls were stacked upon shelves. "All this human knowledge will be incredibly difficult for you to take in."

Kota's eyes traveled up and down the stacks. He had seen Gretis reading from human books here and there in the mornings. A single one contained tens of thousands of words. The thought of reading many of the great tomes was intimidating to him, but he looked up at Bendick and said: "My father teach me not to give up just because something not easy."

"Hmm," Bendick grunted.

Kota drew in a breath and said: "I no give up if you no give up."

"I *will not* give up if you *will not* give up," Bendick muttered. "Your conditional statement is missing its auxiliary verbs in both its premise and conclusion. Still, are you certain that is your stance?" Without waiting for an answer, the old monk walked behind his desk and retrieved a long, thin stick that he promptly snapped down on his desk with surprising force. He looked at Kota then as if expecting him to shrink or flinch. Kota remained still. He had seen far more violent things than a stick hitting a desk. After a moment, the old man sighed: "If the other boys have not warned you, I am a firm believer that stern discipline is an important element of a young man's education. If you are late again, you will receive a lashing. If your use of language does not improve, you will receive a lashing. If I find your efforts to be lazy in nature at any point, you will receive a lashing. Are you sure you still wish to continue?"

"Yes, and if those is—*are* the reasons for *r-receiving* a l-lashing, then I think I never get one."

"I think I *will* never get one," Bendick said, but there was the vaguest hint of a smile on his face. "Very well, *Kota*, let us move forward." The old monk set down his stick and picked up a small cloth that was just a little damp and slapped it down on Kota's table. He used it to wipe away the chalk letters he had written, and then he blew against the desk for a few seconds, set down his cloth, and picked up his chalk and wrote again.

Kota peered down, this time at a word containing four letters. He tried again to sound out the word. It felt good to challenge his mind in this new way. He imagined being able to finish an entire book one day and mastering all the skills Gretis had to teach. Kota was willing to do all the hard work in the world to become the man he saw in that vision. All of this was a gift, and he felt sure he was the luckiest shamalak that had ever lived.

CHAPTER 16: THE ISLAND OF DEATH

According to the Enumis, the gods brought a fiery emerald comet forth from the cosmos to imbue their most loyal and obedient children, the elves, with magic, so that they might vanquish demons and bring the world to glorious order. This never came to pass. Promethiock, the greatest of the ancient dragons, decided to use his titanic power to alter the comet. He chose mortal men, whose passionate hearts were most like his own, as the recipients. For this, the gods gathered all their strength and imprisoned him within an island of cosmic stone. He resides there, century after century, and we, the beneficiaries of his gift, can do nothing to free him.

—Dracus Mobius, Starborn of the 11th Generation, First Bishop of the Onkai Order

The smell of musky salt invaded Somar's nostrils anew as the ship beneath him rocked to the ocean's machinations. He sat near the edge of the bow opposite Cassian, a table between the two of them upon which rested a cornerstone board. The game should have been impossible to play upon a rocking ship, but the many carved stone pieces were held precisely in place by Cassian's will. Somar was trying to focus on his next several moves. It was an excellent distraction to how sick he felt after so many days at sea.

"Shield," Cassian said, and Somar watched as one of the small shields in the corner of the board floated over to Cassian's centurion and lodged itself within the finely carved hooks.

Somar swallowed back his queasiness, trying to gauge the boy's attack pattern. Cassian was proving to be a very aggressive player. He had moved a good deal of his army out of its square to the center of the board early. With only the two of them playing on opposite corners, two additional corners were free for the taking on either side between them. Two-person games were the quickest in that respect, though Somar preferred when three or four people were playing. Strategies became far more complicated when more minds were involved.

He picked up his berserker and killed one of Cassian's peasants, then ricocheted it into Cassian's empress with its second attack.

"Ugh!" Cassian grunted as Somar swept away his most valuable piece.

"You are doing quite well for your third game," Somar said, and this was true. Somar was considered to be one of the finest players in the empire. He had taught many of his soldiers the game over the years. It took most individuals twenty or so games before the intricacies of the board and its pieces were fully grasped. Already though, Cassian was using impressive attacks involving multiple pieces. "You are just a bit reckless for a beginner."

"We are going to have to abandon this game," Cassian said with a shrug. "No reason not to experiment a bit."

Somar gazed across the bow of the ship to the continuously flashing point off in the morning mist. It had grown considerably on the horizon since he last looked, which was simultaneously thrilling and terrifying. "How many people do you suppose have set foot on that island?"

"Officially the number is forty-one in the last millennia, but unofficially, I have no idea. Allegedly, a few sorcerers have managed it here and there."

The mist cleared just enough for Somar to catch view of a bolt of lightning. It appeared, took shape, and vanished in a fraction of time too small to grasp, yet Somar did register that there was nearly no trace of thunder to accompany the flash. Sailors called this the 'silent storm.' It had been raging for close to a thousand years without pause, fixed entirely on the island.

Cassian laughed: "You're not growing frightened, are you?" He was enjoying himself a little too much.

"Certainly not *growing,*" Somar muttered. He gazed over at the ship's captain, an exceptionally tall man in extravagant but haggard clothing who was gawking at the lightning along with several of his men. The sailors' tanned faces showed varying degrees of anxiety. They were the sane ones, Somar thought. It was only he and the boy who had been consumed by madness.

"You seem to be losing focus on the game," Cassian said. Somar turned in time to see Cassian's centurion make a smooth leap up from the board and whisk over the berserker to land inside Somar's square, lining up flawlessly for a direct attack on the Emperor piece. The centurion was backed by Cassian's berserker, and as Somar saw this, he realized that the boy's seeming blunder had been a feint to scatter Somar's defensive pieces. He had indeed been distracted by the terrors of incineration and death that loomed ahead, and his young pupil was about to take the game.

"This is as far as we go!" the captain said very sharply from behind.

Cassian stood abruptly and looked at the dark mass far off in the distance. "You said you would take me within a league," he said, not sounding particularly angry. If Somar could see the fear in the men's eyes, Cassian could surely feel it. There were centuries of tales about ships disappearing when they drew too close to Veskethia, or as it was more commonly referred to, *'Dragon's Isle.'*

The captain looked into Cassian's eyes and said: "Please, my lord, I—"

"All right, all right," the boy said. "Lower the boat." He gestured to the cornerstone board and said: "And would you please have our board and pieces neatly stowed in our compartment?"

"Yes, of course, sir," the tall man said. He turned to his men and began issuing orders.

"Are you ready?" Cassian said to Somar.

"Not really," Somar sighed, rising up. The two of them walked to the rowboat that hung from the side of the ship by a pair of rust-covered pulleys on the ends of thick wooden poles. Somar noticed as he awkwardly climbed into the swaying vessel that there was a pair of wooden chests in the back. Curious, he reached out and pulled at one of the side handles after taking his seat, and from the lightness of the thing, he guessed it was empty.

"Are we bringing something back with us?"

"Of course we are," Cassian said. "Veskethia holds practically the most valuable substance in the world. It would be quite foolish not to gather some of it."

Somar gave a little nod. He had not thought of that, though it seemed incredibly obvious now. Dragon's tears—the small blue flowers that siphoned little bits of the titan's power—were indeed the rarest and most valuable commodity known to man. It was said that only the starborn could gather them, and here Somar sat with one, being lowered into the ocean. Among other things, the petals were the chief substance in the ink that granted the Onkai their legendary strength. How many foolish men who were not starborn had died attempting to attain the glowing flower buds from that lethal island?

The boat hit the water, and the ropes attached to its ends immediately unhooked themselves. Then the craft lurched forward, driven by an invisible force. Cassian sat perfectly still with his eyes closed. Had Somar assumed they would be rowing? He questioned the sharpness of his mind as he had many times over the past several days. In the military, he had often succeeded by his ability to quickly assess situations and make intelligent decisions, and in the Imperial Senate, he had been renowned for his wit. Here though, with the young starborn, with the Norn and prophecies, with questions of the afterlife and a trip to visit the ancient dragon who had done battle with the gods themselves, he felt like a doddering old fool. Why was his presence even necessary on this venture? What did the boy really want from him? *A friend? A father?*

The boat whisked over the water so quickly that it threw up little sprays on both sides. They passed unflinchingly through the mist toward the ominous black mass that lit up every few seconds with near blinding flashes of lightning. The storm, Somar observed as they came nearer, was not entirely silent. Each bolt tore down with a hissing crackle. The sound was unnerving, but when Somar looked at Cassian, he saw that the boy was sitting calmly.

Eventually, they passed through the outer layer of mist, and they could see the island for what it was: a body of black, jagged rock the size of a large city. Massive spires of inky stone curved upward into ghastly spears that stretched many times higher than the towers in the imperial citadel. Somar watched one such bolt streak along the island's surface, and an angry puff of steam and smoke rose up out of its wake. There was no apparent beach upon which they might dock. Waves smacked against rough black stone.

"How are you going to get us there?" Somar shouted through the cacophony around them.

"I have it under control!" Cassian shouted back without opening his eyes. His hair was soaking wet. The mist had grown so thick that every breath seemed a drink of water. "Please do not distract me or I might kill us—well, *you* at least."

"Yes-s-s," Somar muttered to himself. He reached out and gripped the edges of the boat. They were beginning to toss and turn in the waves, which were growing more violent by the second. The lightning flared brighter and brighter, sometimes with two or three bolts striking down in the span of a second. Somar shut his eyes, yet he saw the light through his eyelids and heard the terrible hiss of destructive force. There seemed no escape from this violence. Then, very suddenly, the tossing of the boat ceased. Somar opened his eyes and gasped. The tiny vessel had risen above the water. They were *floating* above it in a smooth glide toward the storm.

"Gods!" Somar gasped as they passed above the ever-darkening waves. The air grew dimmer by the second between the lightning bursts. The deep gray clouds above the island blotted out the sun almost completely.

"Try not to have a heart attack," Cassian said. *The little son of a bitch was actually smiling.* Then Cassian began to chant words that Somar did not recognize.

The boat passed over the last of the water and began to rise over the inky black rock. Lightning struck the ground around them and Somar instinctively looked up. Almost the instant he did, a screeching bolt struck down directly at him, and he let out a terrified cry, yet his body did not erupt into flame as he expected. Instead, he beheld the perhaps most incredible image his eyes had ever taken in. For an instant, he, Cassian, and the boat were wreathed in brilliant white light. Lightning cascaded around them in a glowing sphere, and Somar thought he could see hundreds of spider webs of electricity curling all around them. Then the image vanished, and they were unharmed.

"If you are curious, I am using the Daksha shield," Cassian shouted. "It is one of the legendary spells invented by the first starborn." He still seemed to be enjoying himself thoroughly. Another blast of lightning struck down, and again it cascaded around them in a terrifying and utterly magnificent corona of light.

The boat floated smoothly through the air for another moment as Somar gazed at the chaotic surface of jutting stone, scaling hills, and deep crevasses below. The landscape gave the impression of a particularly violent section of ocean frozen into a hard, inky mass. As they moved forward, he began to notice caves everywhere that emitted a soft blue glow. Eventually, they glided into the mouth of one of these caves, and Somar saw that inside there were hundreds of deep blue points of light that burned in the darkness. *Dragon's tears*! A long row of them showed that the cave was actually quite cavernous and sloped downward. Cassian finally ended his chanting as they passed under the protective vault of the cave ceiling, and the boat lowered gently onto the stone floor.

"Are you all right, old man?" Cassian said.

"Dandy," Somar grunted. He wiped a bit of water from his eyes with his sleeve and then, gazing at the boy in the soft blue light of the impossibly phosphorescent flowers around them, he said: "Are we safe in here?"

"From the lightning at least," Cassian replied with a little shrug.

Somar reached out and touched one of the little blue flowers that seemed almost to be dripping down from thick black vines that grew directly out of the rock. It shimmered brighter at his touch, and he felt a wonderful tingling throughout his body. "Amazing," he whispered.

"Everything here is amazing," Cassian said, his eyes shut again, his face holding an expression of wonder. "I wish you could feel it. The magic—it is flowing all around, vast and primal." The boy reached and touched one of the flower petals. "Imagine, these probably came from little bits of moss or bacteria that collected in the stone. *Promethiock's magic* changed them—made them evolve into this." Cassian gazed down to the stone floor beneath them both. "I can feel him down there—the creature who could traverse the cosmos and battle the gods themselves to a standstill. Could you and I ever imagine being what he is?"

"He may very well kill us for all the respect we bear him," said Somar.

Cassian smirked. "Yes, that is true. I have long accepted the possibility that my foolhardy actions would bring me to a premature death."

Somar laughed. He found the boy's bravado delightful. "That is all very well and good, but what about me?"

"Well, you are a very old man, and death will come for you soon anyhow. At least this way you get to see this world's greatest sight before you pass on."

"Hah!" Somar laughed, though Cassian's words concerned him. He was beginning to understand the boy more and more. Cassian had a tendency to use humor to anesthetize himself against his own emotions, and, as Somar gazed into his pupil's almost crazed eyes, he knew that the boy was afraid of the creature they were seeking.

Cassian gestured toward the back of a cave, which indeed sloped downward as Somar had seen, and said: "All tunnels in this island lead to the same place. Shall we?"

"Why not," Somar sighed. The two of them began their descent to their likely deaths. The air grew unnaturally warm only a short way in, and the scent of sulfur became nearly overwhelming. The path was not too steep, and the blue flowers were everywhere, illuminating all the little grooves and juts in the rock. Perhaps seven or eight minutes into the hike, when the downward path began to curve and the hiss of the lightning behind faded away, Somar became aware of a low and rhythmic sound that vibrated throughout the stone—a sound which was becoming distinctive enough to recognize as breathing.

"Can you tell how much farther?" Somar said, his heart thumping harder than it had in years.

"Not much." Cassian's voice was dry and mechanical.

"Does the creature know we are here?"

"He knew we were coming before we left my castle." Cassian turned his head to face Somar and added: "I can sense his intelligence. It is something beyond my comprehension." He spoke with a deep and profound respect—even awe. "Also," Cassian shut his eyes and smiled, revealing his perfect teeth, "the *psychic moment,* as you called it, has begun." Then the boy's eyes opened, and there seemed almost to be a glow in them.

Cassian's voice took on a strange, echoing resonance as he said: "Greetings, my fellow sorcerers and sorceresses, and hello to you as well, Bishop Cromlic, you *disgusting murderer*."

Somar swallowed. The young man did not mince words, but then why would he? He was either about to die or become untouchable. Still, Somar doubted that anyone in the whole world save the emperor himself would dare to speak to Bishop Cromlic in such a way, especially with thousands of witnesses. The bishop was the least of their worries though. They were both moving toward something infinitely more dangerous. The slow descent was surreal—every sense heightened. Only one human had ever encountered the great dragon and lived.

"He is just ahead," Cassian finally whispered. He moved down a final bend in the tunnel and came to a massive subterranean opening. The boy stepped into the entryway first and turned to face something, and then he froze, his eyes going wide.

The first thing Somar saw as he stumbled into the cavern was an enormous reptilian hand resting on a stone, illuminated by the same blue light that had guided their way down. He let out an involuntary gasp. The black, hooked claws upon each of the scaly fingers was longer than a man. The elongated hand looked as though it could defeat an army of ogres with a simple flick of the mighty wrist that controlled it. As Somar's gaze traveled up, he saw a tremendous limb of gray scales and muscle that seemed capable of any feat of strength imaginable. He felt sweat trickle off his skin and blinked and his vision pulled back to the bat-like wings, each one of which could blot out the sun for a small village, then to the long, whip-like tail with long, bony spikes. Finally, he saw the creature's face. The titanic head was turned toward them. Eyes like two blazing suns glared out, bathing them both in yellow light. Everything Somar had ever seen in his life was dwarfed by this creature. It could annihilate anything on the face of the world.

The great dragon made a sudden leap, spreading its terrible wings out and gliding across the cave in smooth, liquid motion to where they stood. It dropped to a perch on the rough floor with an impact that shook the ground. Somar involuntarily took several steps backward. When he gazed at Cassian, he noted that the boy had not moved, though his hands were in fists at his sides and they were shaking just a little.

"Hello, Great One," Cassian shouted, his voice surprisingly even.

There was a very long pause where the creature cast its burning stare directly at the boy—a moment where Somar's heart flooded with raw, animalistic fear. *Was this all a mistake?* Could the beast even respond to words after centuries of solitary imprisonment? The answer came abruptly from all around: <Cassian Asango.> The dragon's voice was like thunder formed into syllables. Its mouth had not moved as it spoke, though the blazing glow in its eyes seemed to shift with the sound.

"I answer your summons," Cassian said, his voice sharp—almost challenging. The fierce Cassian that lay underneath—the boy who spit in the face of the gods—had emerged.

The dragon spoke again in its cataclysmic voice: <You seek my blessing. If you can master your fear, little mortal, then step forward.>

Cassian seemed to stiffen at these words, and then he took a step toward the monster and spoke in a voice that sounded almost angry: "I am not afraid of you."

"You speak a lie, young starborn," the dragon hissed, and its serpentine mouth twisted delicately at the edges. "There is remarkably little fear in you, given your circumstances, but you are afraid."

"Fine then, I am afraid," Cassian said, his voice becoming fiercer, "but I will not cower—not even before *you,* Promethiock!" He marched closer, never taking his eyes off the face of the beast. "Will you give me your blessing?" he shouted. "Am I worthy?"

Promethiock's jaw opened to reveal a cage of ghastly teeth through which immense puffs of white flame escaped. Though Somar was at least a hundred paces away, he felt the heat sting his skin as if he were leaning too close to a bonfire.

<Perhaps you are the one for whom I have been waiting,> the dragon's voice boomed independently of his fire-laced mouth. <I offer you the same challenge I gave those who came before: step forward and face my flame, *starborn!*> More white fire splashed out through from the creature's throat.

Cassian was breathing hard. The flames had to be causing him pain. He was only a dozen paces away from the dragon's mouth. In a voice that rose above the inferno, Cassian said: "What is it? What will it do to me?"

<This is the fire of my heart. It will burn away your mind and destroy you if you are weak, but if you are strong enough—if you have a soul like my own—it will purify you.> The dragon leaned its head closer, and its psychic voice hissed: <I will unleash it upon you even if you beg me not to do so, for you have *dared* to tread upon my domain. Still, I give you the same advice I have given your brethren who have come before: face the flame with courage. If you do not, it will burn everything you are to nothing.>

"I see," Cassian said, his voice hard. He hesitated for a brief instant, then drew in a breath and then tilted his head up so that he was staring directly into the blazing eyes and shouted: "Do your worst, dragon!"

Somar thought he saw a grin play across the reptilian face just before an explosion of white fire leaped from within its throat. The flare seemed more brilliant than the sun, but Somar could not look away. He knew he was seeing something religiously profound.

The boy was engulfed in an instant. Somar was still far away, yet the radiating heat tore into him. It seemed to be...*searing at his fear*. It was as if that emotion itself were a limb held forcibly out into flame. He stumbled and had to catch himself against the uneven rock wall, gasping. Amidst the roar of the inferno, he could hear Cassian's screams.

Promethiock's mouth closed, bringing the spew of fire to a halt, yet the place where Cassian had been standing continued to burn like a freshly lit torch. Very abruptly, the dragon turned toward Somar. As the old man stared up into blazing yellow eyes, he heard the creature's voice seep into his thoughts: <He is going to prevail I think, Somar Dojinko.> Then the monster drew closer.

It bent down over Somar, the massive jaws coming to a sharp halt little more than an arm's length away. Immediately, Somar felt the creature's alien telepathic mind rip through every one of his mental walls. <Old soldier,> the dragon whispered into his brain.

Somar could not speak. All he managed to do was tremble as the jaws that could reduce him to gnarled meat in a single bite moved closer.

<The boy has passed my test,> Promethiock's voice thrummed. Somar gazed at the spot of blazing white in the cave. He could see Cassian's vague form within it, standing. The screams had stopped.

Despite his fear, some part of Somar's mind grasped the magnitude of this moment. *Cassian had survived Promethiock's fire!* No human in all of history could make such a claim. His mettle had been tested by the most ancient and powerful being on the mortal plane, and he had passed.

<Before Asango regains himself, I must give you a warning, human,> the dragon said. The brilliance of its yellow eyes intensified. <You will tell no one of what I am about to reveal. Swear it from the pit of your soul, or I will kill you.>

Teeth chattering, Somar managed to rasp: "I swear."

The reptilian mouth drew back, and the dragon whispered: <Forces beyond even *me* conspire around Cassian Asango. Some are of the highest order of what you conceive of as 'good,' yet others are evil beyond anything you can imagine. If Asango achieves his destiny, he will stand at the center of the final battle between these sides, and for one moment, the fate of all mortal life will rest in his hands.> The hot breath whisked back Somar's hair as the creature continued: <You have caught glimpses of the darkness residing in the boy's heart. If that darkness overtakes him, he will doom this world—perhaps even destroy it.>

Somar's gasped. He looked over at the young man. The flames were beginning to fade. The dragon's voice continued on: <Before any of this may come to pass, a moment will occur when his enemies overcome him, and he will face death. You will have the power to save your pupil, but for him to live, your life must be sacrificed. Were I in your place, I might let him die and rid the world of his threat, but then I am not a tiny mortal, and I wish very much to see what this starborn will do to disrupt the order of divinity and damnation.> There was then a low thunderous rumble of laughter from the dragon that echoed in Somar's skull.

The conflagration around Cassian dissipated into nothingness, and just as abruptly as the dragon had turned its attention to Somar, it turned back to the young starborn. Cassian's skin, his hair, and even his clothing were entirely unburned. He stood, blinking eyes that blazed a fierce yellow like the dragon's, and he began to laugh.

<I offer you congratulations, mortal,> the dragon croaked.

"I thank you, ancient one," Cassian said in a soft whisper that tore through the air nigh as loud as Promethiock's psychic voice. "You have shown me the truth of myself."

The boy's eyes, still glowing, narrowed. "To all of you who have shared this moment with me, I invite you to help me create a better world. I *will* become emperor of Denigoth. I *will* end slavery and educate the masses and feed the starving and unify the human race. Whoever you are—*all of you*—you know these things are right. Do not stand against them, and do *not* stand against *me!*" The boy paused for a brief moment, perhaps letting his words sink into the untold tens of thousands who had been forced to observe this moment. "And to you, *Bishop Cromlic*, the man who executed my own mother because she would not cower, I offer you the following terms: remove your vile bullies from the cities of this great nation, rescind the *laws* you have enacted in your desperate bid for power, return your order to what it rightfully should be under ancient church law, and step down as bishop. Do this and I will leave you in peace, much as it sickens me. If you do not, *I am coming*!"

The last words sent a shiver down Somar's spine. The boy had just leveled a direct ultimatum to one of the most dangerous men in the world.

The serpentine lips of the dragon drew back once more at these words.

The boy gazed up at the dragon and the yellow blaze in his eyes finally began to diminish, yet none of the confidence left his voice as he said: "I thank you, Ancient One."

The dragon made a small gesture with one of his clawed fingers, and a deep blue oval shape the size of a small child lifted up from a far distant corner of the cave and whisked through the air to where Cassian stood. It came to a smooth stop just in front of his chest.

Cassian's eyes were wide as he reached out and touched the enormous egg. "I—I am deeply honored," he said, emotion ringing in his chalky voice.

Somar gazed at the blue mass. *A pure-blooded dragon!* No one had seen one in perhaps seven or eight hundred years. The creature that would hatch from the egg hovering before Cassian would be a being of terrible strength and magic. With such a companion at his side, the Nemesai could scream condemnation of Cassian all they wanted, and the boy would still be sacrosanct. Promethiock had never bestowed one of his spawn on a mortal before. This was a historic moment.

Cassian held out his hands and the egg floated into them. He was covered in sweat and he seemed to be overwhelmed with elation. "This is a gift beyond anything I ever imagined receiving, but why throw your last offspring into danger? Do you not wish to keep it safe?"

A low, rumbling laugh escaped the mighty creature: "Dragons are not *kept safe*! We are the oldest and most lethal of warriors on this plane of existence! I have been forced to watch the world change slowly for a millennium without being able to influence it. I wish my last child to be part of its destiny, and I see the currents of fate swirling around you, Cassian Asango, like a hurricane.>

The boy grinned up at the colossal dragon. "You are exactly as I imagined you to be, Great One. I can never repay you for this." He stroked the egg.

Cassian nodded and walked back toward the tunnel with the dragon's egg held close to his chest. Somar followed in stupefied silence, Promethiock's words ringing in his mind. *Cassian may doom or even destroy the world.* He continued his silence the entire way back to the boat. Someday, he would face a choice on whether to save his pupil's life or let the boy die.

"Beautiful little thing, is it not?" Cassian said, holding up the egg as they came to the boat. It shimmered in the blue glow of the cave, reflecting the light from different angles like a diamond. He placed the egg carefully down in the boat's center and whispered: "This shell is harder than dwarf-forged steel, but the creature within will rip through it with ease. I can it feel right now. The little thing has slept for hundreds of years, but it is awakening... *for me.*" He drew in a slow breath and then gestured to the two chests that Somar had entirely forgotten about. They both flipped open.

"Would you care to pick some flowers, old man? After all that has just happened, I prefer to take a few moments and do this task with my simple, mortal hands."

"Oh, o-of course," Somar muttered. He swallowed, then said: "Are you all right?"

"Yes," Cassian whispered. He turned and looked at Somar and said: "Thank you for coming with me." There was a glimmer of simple humanity that shined through his eyes, which had lost the majority of their yellow glow now.

"Of course," Somar said again. He walked over and took hold of one of the blue flowers between his fingers. "I—I just pull them free?"

"Yes, they will not hurt you," Cassian said. He already had a handful of the little things still glowing in his palm.

"You're going to give these to the Onkai?" Somar asked as he plucked the flower free and felt it tingle in his fingers.

"One chest is for them; one for me."

Somar cocked his head. "Why would you need so much?"

Cassian gave a devilish little chuckle. "For my army."

CHAPTER 17: THE POWERLESS

"Many people think I wish to destroy the church. This is untrue of course. Religion is fundamental to most citizens of this empire, and I have no desire to take it from them. What I intend to shatter is the grotesque power assumed by a small faction of bullies who have manipulated a handful of obscure passages in the Enumis to justify torturing, murdering, and extorting their fellow human beings in the name of 'protecting our souls.' These men tell us what we are allowed to think at the point of a sword.

"I say that religion is a personal choice. I say that human beings are born with intelligent free will, and that the policing of our thoughts is an insult to what we are. So long as humanity submits to the authority the Nemesai have assumed over us, we are all slaves."

—Excerpt from "A Modern Empire," by Cassian Asango

"I'm so jealous of you!" Iona said in a playful tone. The adorable little girl was prancing around the kitchen as Livia fried eggs over the wood-fire stove.

Livia smiled at Iona and made a fist with the tip of her thumb poking through between her index and middle fingers, and the young girl nodded and reached for a handful of freshly chopped onions. Iona was picking up on Livia's various hand signals with surprising ease, which was nice.

"Are you going to stop in Valantus?" Iona said as she handed Livia the onions.

"We might," Hervin answered from the kitchen table, running his stubby fingers over his chin. "Last time Livia and I visited there, we brought back a handful of dwarf-made oil lamps that sold out in a week. Remember those, Livy?"

Livia turned around to exchange a knowing grin with Hervin. She was feeling quite excited about their annual summer journey to the capital city. The weather had been excellent this year, with fair winds so there would be ample trade ships to fill the markets in Denigoth with exotic goods from the small island nations in the Promethian Sea. Rumor had it that Keska Ethedrine, the recently announced female starborn in Aloria, had negotiated a reopening of trade with one of the dwarf clans across the ocean. This meant that shipments of vaunted dwarven machinery might be available at the trade fair.

Livia and Hervin would travel south along the coast together as they had for more than a decade now, taking turns driving the wagon so that each of them could lie on the blankets in back and read during the day. Some nights would be spent at festive roadside inns, and others would be around a fire in a forest clearing under the stars. They would have weeks away from Lady Sondal, and while there was always some danger when traveling, it was worth it to spend every moment of every day treated like a beloved daughter instead of a slave. Livia felt happy and free on the road. This year though, her excitement was tainted with a touch of guilt. While she went off, Iona would be left alone with the cow. Who would stop the horrible woman from drunkenly abusing the little girl?

As Livia served Hervin his breakfast, he glanced up at her and said: "What do we still need to do to close the shop?" Livia sighed, narrowing her eyes at him, which caused the short, round man to fidget in his seat. He hesitated, then said: "Yes, I...lost the list. I'm sorry."

Livia rolled her eyes. It had taken her near to an hour to write the list of tasks that needed to be done to close the business down for the month. Hervin—sweet man that he might be—was maddeningly absent-minded at times and given to losing things. It did not bother Livia too much this time though. The list had taken her so long the first time because she had had to figure out so many details. Everything was in her memory now, including what they had already done, and she was sure she could generate a second list within a few minutes. This was too good a day to grumble.

She cast Hervin a smile, which relaxed him, and then picked up a heavily tarnished bronze fork and began to dig into her own eggs, when a jolt of searing pain erupted in her skull. It was sudden and immense, emanating from the center of her forehead and wrapping around. She jerked back in her chair, shutting her eyes and clenching from the sheer magnitude of white-hot agony.

"LIVIA!" Hervin's voice shouted from somewhere off in the distance. His words were almost lost in a cacophony of strange, nonsensical sounds coming from all around her. She struggled to open her eyes so that she could communicate with him, but as her lids slid apart, she did not see her master, nor Iona, but the face of a massive, reptilian creature with blazing yellow eyes. Livia flinched away from this beast and blinked, and suddenly she was in the kitchen with Hervin and Iona again, falling back in her chair.

"LIVIA!" she heard Iona shriek, and the little girl darted in from behind and desperately gripped the back of the seat, managing to just barely catch it before Livia's head could slam into the floor. That image left her vision in an instant and was replaced once again with the face of the enormous reptile. The monster was speaking to her—*no, not to her*—

Livia had no idea how she knew that, but she did. The voice, a low and garbled rumble amidst the renewed pain of her vision, was almost impossible to decipher, yet she caught a few words here and there. *'Starborn'* and *'Asango' were among them.* The vision went on for a moment or two of incomprehensible sounds, and the reptile opened its ghastly jaws. White fire leaped from its throat, and, for a visceral instant, the pain Livia felt was magnified a thousand fold. Then her vision went black.

"Can you hear me!" she heard Hervin's voice cry. Comprehension of the words came slowly. Livia felt her eyes bob slowly open and she saw him bent over her, an intensely worried look on his round face. Iona was there too, gaping. "Are you all right, my dear?"

Livia blinked several times. Her head was swimming. She had no idea what had just happened. Her whole body throbbed with a vague pain. It hurt to sit up, but she tried and was rewarded with a wave of dizziness.

"What happened?" Iona said.

Livia drew in a breath. Instinctively her hand moved to the pocket in her dress where she kept her charcoal pencil and paper, but the simple gesture made her feel nauseous. She slumped, and her hand fell limp on her thigh.

"Y-you should lie down," Hervin said. He was trembling.

Livia frowned, concentrating and pushing the dizziness away so that she could shake her head. *Hervin needed her help with the shop.*

"I can figure things out closing up," he said. "Iona will help me. You get some rest."

Livia shook her head again, but Hervin ignored her and said: "Let's get her to bed." He and Iona each slid a hand under her armpits and helped her up to her feet. Livia turned to him to protest, but he said: "I insist." His voice was uncharacteristically assertive, and she was still feeling dizzy and disoriented. Thus, she ended up allowing the two of them to lead her back to the tiny room where her cot was and lay her down.

Perhaps half an hour passed in relative silence, with Livia alone on her small cot trying to unravel the vision that had passed through her mind. Most of what she had seen and heard and even felt was incomprehensible to her, yet she had the sense that she had been witnessing something that was actually happening elsewhere. It had been too real and visceral to be a dream... *and yet...telepathic visions were for sorcerers...* Perhaps she had eaten something that had given her a mild hallucination.

"IONA!" the cow's voice bellowed through the adobe walls. "I NEED YOU!"

Livia tensed at the horrid woman's voice. Since her new 'sister' had come to the home, she had largely escaped attending the cow and her endless needs. Sighing, Livia rose bitterly from her bed, finding her dizziness had largely disappeared as she walked to Lady Sondal's bedroom.

"YOU?!" the cow snarled from her mess of sheets, blinking at Livia. "Where is Iona?" The disgusting woman's form was splayed open-armed across a bed of white sheets in the center of the small room. Her head was propped up by several feather pillows, and she was glaring with blood-shot eyes filled with the venom that came only after nights of especially hard drinking.

Livia used her fingers and thumbs to make the shape of a square. Lady Sondal blinked at the gesture. Livia had well over a hundred hand signals she had developed with Hervin over the years to communicate various things, but the cow only understood a few. This was one of them. The square represented Hervin's store.

"BAH!" the cow grunted. "Why the hell am I stuck with *you* this morning?" Livia just stared at her. There was no point in attempting to write an explanation, since the idiot woman could not read. After an awkward silence, Lady

Sondal said: "Well, I want Iona back here. Go and fetch her, but before you do, I need water."

Livia gave her a terse nod and walked into the kitchen. She swiftly grabbed the ceramic urn from off of the table and carried it to the bucket of water Iona had brought in earlier. As her fingers gripped the handle, her mind flashed for an instant back to the blazing yellow eyes of the dragon. She drew in a slow breath, trying to banish the strange daydream from her mind. *Why had it been so real?*

"HURRY UP!" the cow's voice snarled through the walls. "IONA WOULD HAVE ALREADY BROUGHT IT TO ME!"

Livia shook her head, suppressing the hatred she felt for the woman. She finished filling the urn and walked briskly back to the bedroom.

"You STUPID little mute!" the cow hissed. "How DARE you keep me waiting! I should whip you!"

Livia stifled the urge to roll her eyes, knowing the reaction it might provoke. Still, she felt reasonably safe as she gazed at the limp, confused mass before her. The lazy bitch would not likely make it to her feet anytime soon, let alone find the energy for a beating. Livia did not envy poor little Iona for having to remain here while she and Hervin were away.

The 'high-born' lady immediately snatched up the urn and guzzled down the contents, spilling a great deal down her face into the expensive feather pillows. When she had swallowed the last drop, she immediately thrust the empty container back at Livia and said in a low voice: "More."

Livia sighed and took the urn. She turned and walked back down the hall, ignoring the cow's slurred shout of: "Don't you look at ME that way, you crippled little slut!"

As she refilled the container, her ears picked up a low male voice from among an ocean of noises on the street outside the window: "So the starborn actually visited the great dragon?"

Livia inadvertently released the contents of her hands mid-pour, and they fell down to the clay-tile floor. The bucket bounced, but the urn shattered.

"What the hell did you break?!" the cow's voice boomed through the walls, but Livia scarcely registered the words. She was leaning out toward the window, trying to listen further.

"I heard it was the crazy one—Asango," a male voice said with a nervous laugh.

Livia craned her neck to hear more. She grabbed a nearby wooden broom without thinking about it and proceeded to grip the thing so hard that the grooves in the wood dug into her skin.

"I heard he *became* a dragon," a young-sounding male voice said.

"How could anyone become a dragon?" a high pitched female voice said.

"I heard he killed Promethiock," yet another woman's voice said.

"LIVIA!" the cow shouted. "Where the *HELL* is my *WATER*?!"

"Hurry up and get to the town square!" a voice down the street shouted.

"Why?" a confused girlish voice said.

"Dathrose is going to explain everything!" an impatient voice answered.

Livia's eyes widened. Dathrose, the city's most prominent sorcerer, often explained significant events surrounding magic, demons, and starborn to the people. This was in part because he was the most educated citizen in matters of the arcane, but also because he was a renowned telepath, and this allowed him at times to acquire information far more quickly than anyone else in the town. Had he witnessed Cassian Asango's encounter in his mind's eye? What did it mean then that Livia had spent the last hour seeing flashes of the rendezvous herself? Her heart began to race within her chest.

"I'm going to BEAT YOU with Hervin's WALKING STICK!" the cow snarled. "GET ME MY WATER!"

Livia turned her head slowly in the direction of the hideous woman and then glanced at the door. This was important—possibly more important than any other moment in her life. *What if she had the gift of sorcery?* The thought was almost overwhelming. All her dreams of being more than a mute slave might suddenly and unexpectedly be right in front of her. *And the wretched cow was bellowing and threatening her over water that she could easily get for herself!*

Clenching her jaw, Livia snatched a second urn from the pantry and filled it briskly from the water bucket, spilling a great deal as she did. Then she whipped out of the kitchen, through the thin hallway, and charged into the cow's room. The look on her face must have been unusually intense, for the cow flinched ever so slightly when she saw her and offered no immediate threat or insult.

Livia thrust the container into the puffy hands and once again used her fingers and thumbs to make the shape of a square, indicating that she intended to leave to the store. Livia knew she was being aggressive, but she could not help it, and she hoped that the cow wished to be rid of her as desperately as she wished to leave.

""Yes, go, you little *tart*!" Lady Sondal snarled, "but I *demand* that you send Iona back here immediately."

Livia managed not to roll her eyes as she spun on her heels and rushed from the room. Seconds later, she was out in the street, whisking over the stone pavers in the road toward the town square. There was a sizable crowd moving in the same direction as she, though it was not so large that she could not weave through it. Livia's lithe, sixteen-year-old form danced about with single-minded determination, her thoughts alive with possibility. Even if she possessed only the most basic degree of the sorcerer's gift, it could be enough to elevate her out of slavery. Spellcraft was the most profitable talent a human could possess, and there was also the prospect of being a telepath. If such a gift were buried somewhere within her, she might be able to hone it through training to the point that she could use it to communicate with others. After so many painful years of silence, could she really have a voice?

Livia arrived at the town square - a broad expanse between several clusters of buildings - and she managed to find an open place amongst the peasants in a circle around Dathrose, who was already delivering his explanation, shouting and gesturing widely.

"—and Asango stepped forward to meet the great dragon's gaze!" Dathrose smirked after speaking the words. He was an older man, still handsome, with olive skin and an oiled beard of black and silver. He was wearing expensive robes of deep gray fabric, and a finely polished silver chain hung from his neck, at the center of which was a thumb-sized emerald orb. The wizened sorcerer had a deep, throaty voice that could reach quite far, and he was the type who utterly loved speaking to a crowd, Livia knew. The man was turning slowly about as he spoke, making sure he met the gazes of as many spectators as he could.

"Promethiock stared down at the starborn, the dragon's eyes like two blazing suns, and he said: *'If you have the courage, Starborn, come and meet my flame!'*" Livia's breathing quickened. The old sorcerer had understood what was being said between the dragon and the starborn. She had barely caught two words, but then that was likely because he was an experienced magical adept and she... *perhaps only possessed a latent talent?* Livia might ask him about this later when she approached him. For the moment, she listened in fascination as he went on: "The dragon drew back its scaly head, and white fire like that of the heavens spilled out, engulfing Asango, and—"

"I felt it!" a boy shouted from the crowd. Livia, along with everyone else present, turned to see a boy named Quentis step forward from the crowd, his eyes wide with excitement. Quentis was eleven or so and was the son of the local blacksmith. His young face was smeared with soot, which contrasted with his wide, fervently excited blue eyes. "I saw it—everything you're saying—the dragon—I saw its fire come! I swear it by the gods!"

Dathrose grinned at the boy. "Did you?"

Quentis lost some of his confidence under the sorcerer's stare and gazed away, but managed to say: "Y-yes, sir... I felt the heat and... everything went white for a moment—and I heard the words too—everything you're describing. I...I heard the starborn's voice!" Livia's eyes widened. *The boy had heard the words?* Why hadn't she? He was younger than she was, and she knew him well enough to know he was not a particularly bright child.

"He's telling the truth!" Barnock, the boy's father, shouted, coming up and putting an enormous, sooty hand on his son's shoulder. "Quentis started shouting about the dragon a short while ago. We—we didn't know what to make of it until someone told us of your vision." The blacksmith swallowed, looking at Dathrose uncertainly. Barnock was the largest man in town, a towering figure of physical strength who spent his days forging weapons and armor in his shop, yet he looked as humble as a nervous child as he said: "W-what does that mean?"

"It *means* you have a very special boy," said Dathrose, spreading his arms. Livia's heart leaped at these words, and she felt herself begin to tremble. Dathrose walked toward Quentis and said: "You shall have to come and see me later today in my laboratory, so we may speak of this, young man." Quentis swallowed and nodded. There was a look of wonder in his eyes. Dathrose returned his gaze to the crowd. "Before I go on, did anyone *else* experience this holy event?"

Livia drew in a sharp breath. She started to raise her hand but stiffened almost immediately. *It was too much...*Exciting as this all was, she was still Livia, the mute slave. She gazed around at the crowd, which was growing by the minute. These people sniggered about her, she knew. Livia was the strange cripple—the girl who was too stubborn or stupid to form words. And then there were the rumors—she had heard them whispered from time to time when people did not know she was near—about Hervin's 'pretty' slave girl who was so good at negotiating the best prices from tradesmen for him... of how she *managed* such things without the ability to speak. No... she would not make herself a spectacle before all these people. She would wait.

Dathrose's gaze swept the crowd for a moment, and then he laughed: "Well, I suppose the boy is more than enough of a discovery for one day." He cleared his throat and then bellowed: "Where was I?"

"The dragon breathed fire at Asango!" a boy about Livia's age shouted. The people were hungry for more of the story. Livia could see it in their eyes—she could almost *feel it.*

"Ah yes," Dathrose said with a chuckle. "Asango was engulfed in the flame of the great dragon. He screamed out—for I do not think we can say that *any* mortal has endured more pain than that at one time—but he *refused* to let it kill him! It was astonishing the way he clung to life."

"But when it was done, he was laughing!" Quentis shouted, evidently unable to restrain himself.

Livia nearly flinched. *The boy remembered everything so clearly.* Her vision had been a confusing mess of pain and only a few seconds of it had been enough to render her unconscious. What did that mean? She swallowed dryly as the hope that had been burning within her began to dwindle.

Did she really have the sorcerer's gift, or was that idea ridiculous? Even if she did possess it...was she somehow crippled in sorcery the way she was with speech?

Livia swallowed and listened with the rest of the crowd through Dathrose's dramatic recounting of the story, though she had difficulty paying attention to the words. Her mind kept drifting to what it all meant...*What was she?* Who was she? Livia had never known the identity of her parents. Why was her experience so different from that of Dathrose and even the boy? She did not know enough about the nuances of magic to answer such a question, but perhaps the town sorcerer would...

As these ideas raced through Livia's mind, she noticed the first of the dark figures. Large men in black leather armor were moving through the crowd, brushing and even shoving people aside. She turned and looked at one of them, and a sickly feeling passed through her when she saw the set of Nemesai tattoos on a pale, angry face. Livia glanced at Dathrose, who was waving his arms and describing some ultimatum the starborn had leveled at the Nemesai bishop. The old sorcerer had not yet seemed to notice the latest additions to his crowd.

"He actually called Bishop Cromlic a *disgusting murderer*—in front of me and every other human with the telepathic gift, he called the bishop's actions illegal and—"

"THAT'S ENOUGH!" a voice a fierce voice shouted. Livia flinched as she saw the speaker stepping forward from the crowd. It was the Nemesai who had tortured the homosexual man. Livia recalled the moment when she had stared into his eyes and seen the cruelty inside...*the memory.*

Dathrose stared at the Nemesai in an expression that was somewhere between annoyance and fear. He hesitated, then said: "Pardon me, but I believe—"

"I do NOT pardon you!" the Nemesai leader said. His soldiers were spread around the inner ring of spectators, and the townspeople were giving them a wide berth. Livia saw that at least five of them had loaded crossbows that were not directly aimed at Dathrose but held with the arrow points in his general direction. She evidently was not the only one to notice this, for Quentis and his father stepped nervously away from the sorcerer.

"You are spreading the blasphemy of the known heretic, Cassian Asango," the Nemesai spat. "You are preaching *sinful* disrespect of the holy authority of our church to these poor people." The muscles around the man's temples tightened, and he added in a voice filled with threat: "This is heresy, and it stops now! You will come with us."

Dathrose's features hardened. He drew in a breath and said in a loud, defiant voice: "*Pardon Me,* but I am relating a meeting with *The Great Dragon,* whom the church has deemed to be a holy figure." He gazed around at the men with crossbows, daring to meet each of their eyes. "Let us not make *trouble* for one another over this miracle." He raised his right palm and his fingers spread and curled upward. With a whisper of something inaudible, thin streaks of what appeared to be tiny bolts of green lightning crackled around a translucent sphere of green light the size of a grapefruit above his fist.

Livia's breathing quickened. How powerful a sorcerer was Dathrose? She knew little about the metrics of arcane power, but she understood that Dathrose was a renowned hero in the second demon war, and he had brought death to many of the soldiers of hell. It was said that unlike swordsmen and other manner of warriors, sorcerers only increased in ability as they aged.

"You would *dare* threaten us?" the Nemesai snarled.

Dathrose said in a dry, cautious voice: "I make no threats. I only seek to remind you that the gods have graced me with a gift, and it is my duty to convey to my fellow man what that gift shows me."

"You are spreading *lies!*" the Nemesai snarled.

"I speak no lies!" Dathrose shouted, almost trembling. "You would know that if the gods had seen fit to bless you with the sorcerer's gift, but they did not, did they?" There was the faintest touch of mock in his voice. Livia knew why. Unlike the other bodies of the church, the Nemesai had remarkably few sorcerers within their ranks. Some believed this to be because the activities of the Nemesai were deplorable to those with telepathic empathy. It was an extremely dangerous thing to point out to a member of the order, even by implication.

The Nemesai leader stared hard at the sorcerer for a moment, and then he stepped forward and said in a more even voice: "Take care, old man. My authority comes from the gods, and if you choose to stand against us, you not only risk damnation, but you stand against our entire order." He gestured around to his men, some of whom had drawn swords, others of whom had raised and aimed their crossbows. "How many arrows do you think your magic can stop? How many of us do you think you can kill before we cut you down?" The Nemesai's eyes narrowed as he added: "Even if you *could* stop all of us—which you *can't*—our order *does* have sorcerers of incredible power within its ranks. Bishop Cromlic himself will likely come after you, with hundreds of soldiers at his back, and nothing and no one in this world will be able to keep you from the consequence of your sin. So, I will say it once more, you doddering old fool, relinquish whatever spell you have *dared* to brandish against the holy soldiers of the church, cease this blasphemy, and come with us." He took another step forward and snarled: "I will not warn you again, sinner!"

Dathrose hesitated. Sweat dripped down his dark features. It was extremely perilous to defy the Nemesai, but it was nearly as terrifying a fate to surrender to their interrogations. Livia gazed around, looking stupidly for any kind of help. Her eyes fell on the High Mother Alcmene, who stood in her white robes with a few of her Vestilite sisters off to the side. Even her ordinarily stern features were filled with worry. She and Dathrose were good friends. Livia gaped at the old woman, searching for any sign that she would help, but there was no confidence or hope in her features. *There was only dread.*

Dathrose's arm shook as he closed his outstretched hand and the spell he had been forming dissipated away. The sorcerer swallowed and said: "I...I meant no insult to the church. I was only relating the truth of what I saw. The... he sorcerers within your order will confirm that when you send word to them."

"We'll see," the Nemesai said. He made a gesture with his right hand and said back over his shoulder: "Take him." Two large soldiers with dark tattoos on their faces darted forward to Dathrose's sides, each taking an arm rather roughly. When they had the sorcerer, their leader gestured toward two other men and said: "Take the boy as well."

"WHAT?!" Barnock said, pulling his son toward him.

"NO!" Dathrose shouted. "The boy did nothing wrong. It was all me!"

"*We* will judge the truth of those words," the leader said. With his men flanking him, he stepped toward Quentis, whose face had gone white. The small child was cringing against his father's leg. The Nemesai gazed at him for a moment, and then up at the father. "It would be a terrible mistake to defy the church. Release your child."

Livia felt her fists tremble as her fingernails dug into her palms. Never had she felt such fear and anger at once. She glanced again at Alcmene. The High Mother was gazing down, her features contorted in anguish. *She was not going to do a damned thing!* Livia's gaze shifted back to Barnock.

Tears had begun to fall down his face. "P-please, my son did nothing wrong!"

"I sincerely hope you are correct," the Nemesai said. "It is my duty, by the will of the *gods,* to find out." He made a quick gesture, and his men stepped past him, each taking hold of one of the boy's arms.

"NO!" the father shouted, and he grabbed the wrist of one of the holy soldiers. The Nemesai leader, who was significantly smaller than Barnock, shoved the towering man with one hand. Under the brunt of magically enhanced strength, the blacksmith sailed a half dozen paces backward through the air and came to a sharp skid on his back over the dirt and paver stones.

"S-stop this!" Dathrose shouted, and he tore his arms free of his captors' grip and started to rasp something Livia did not understand, but one of the Nemesai soldiers next to him drew a dagger and knocked him in the back of the head with the handle. The sorcerer fell limply back into the arms of his captors.

"Let's go," the leader said.

Without further word, the Nemesai men dragged the terrified boy and the unconscious sorcerer away. The townspeople stood staring, and Livia saw fear in all of their faces, but also anger here and there. She understood what they felt. Her eyes fell on Barnock. The enormous man had rolled onto his knees and was sobbing into his hands.

It was all too much. Livia turned and fled the town square, tears running down her face. *Why were such things allowed to happen?* She hoped that Cassian Asango would come and slaughter the whole lot of these wretched men who took sobbing children from their fathers. She hated them from the pit of her soul, but there was nothing in the world a slave like her could do.

When she stumbled into the shop, Hervin looked up and said: "Livia, are you feeling bet—Oh!" His face contorted when he saw her face. "A-are you ill?" he exclaimed. "D-don't worry, I'll take you to the Vestilites—I'll take you to see Dathrose if I have to!"

The words brought a fresh swell of tears to Livia's eyes. She brushed them away and moved to the counter and drew out her paper and pencil. With a trembling hand she wrote:

I am not well, but I will be fine.

She hesitated, then added:

Take Iona south. Not me.

Hervin read the words, then looked at her and said: "Why? What's wrong?"

Livia gazed down. How could she begin to communicate everything that had just happened and everything that she was feeling? She drew in a slow breath and scribbled:

Please take Iona. I want her to go and see the country with you. You can leave now. I will close the shop. Please just go.

Hervin stared at the paper and said in an increasingly worried voice: "What's wrong? Why are you—" He stopped short when he met her eyes. The two of them were very close, and whatever he read in her face seemed to be enough to settle the matter. After a moment he muttered: "A-all right...I'll take her."

Livia nodded and watched him walk to Iona and begin speaking quietly. Livia met the girl's excited, confused eyes for a brief moment, and then she slipped back into the accounting room of the store and sank into the chair where she spent many an hour working Hervin's ledger. There would be hell to pay later for not sending Iona to the cow, but Livia did not care. It was a comfort to know that the sweet little girl would be camping tonight, away from all of this wickedness.

Hervin was a good man. His kindness had always been the one part of Livia's life that made it possible for her to feel happy and secure, but just now she felt nothing but despair. The world was an ugly place. There was no safety for those who did not have the power to protect themselves, and who in the world had less power than a mute slave-girl—one who had been foolish enough to believe for a moment that a headache and a few unintelligible flashes were enough to make her life better?

CHAPTER 18: BISHOP CROMLIC

I hear so much talk of sin. What is sin? Holy men tend to break the concept down into a discrete set of rules. Within this line of logic, the very ideas of good and evil amount to either being within the boundaries supposedly drawn for us by the Gods or being outside of them. I can state, as a telepath, that evil is far more nuanced and individualized than that. It can burn quite comfortably in the hearts of men who make it their holy business to punish others, in their cruelty, and their hypocrisy.

—Excerpt from the journal of Keska Ethedrine, Starborn of the 19th Generation

Arkas stared across the long oak table into the dark brown eyes of Bishop Cromlic, the head of the Nemesai Order and probably the most feared human being alive other than his own father. The room in which they sat was a dim, undecorated rectangle of wood and stone in the upper levels of the Central Nemesai Temple. Arkas had ridden most of the previous day and all of the night to reach this place, having set off within an hour of witnessing Cassian's encounter with the Great Dragon. His body was tired, but his mind was alive with excitement...and fear. Cassian, the one whom the Norn had proclaimed was destined to kill him in a duel, had faced Promethiock's fire and lived, but he had also directly challenged the authority of the holy man before him. It was an opportunity.

Bishop Cromlic looked remarkably cold for one who had suffered such an insult. The gaunt, wizened figure stared at Arkas in silence from his seat. He was clothed in simple dark robes, adorned only by a silver chain, at the end of which was a small, gleaming scythe. There was a reserved confidence about the man that was almost intimidating. Cromlic was considered to be the greatest sorcerer alive who was *not* a starborn, which made him the superior to nearly any human, but not to Arkas.

“Well?” the bishop said in a low rumble, staring across the table.

"Cassian threatened you," Arkas said, unable to completely conceal the emotion in his throat.

"Yes," Cromlic said. His heavily creased face betrayed nothing of what he was thinking. Arkas felt a tinge of frustration at this. When he reached out with his telepathy to the bishop, he hit a solid wall of mental will the likes of which only a Starborn should possess.

"Word will spread soon, and many will believe that *Cassian Asango* is entirely above the authority of the Nemesai," Arkas continued. He took some small delight in the way the muscles around the bishop's eyes twitched at the words.

"Asango will be dealt with," Cromlic said.

"I certainly hope so. If that kind of brazen sin is allowed to go unpunished, people will lose all respect for your holy authority."

Cromlic stared at Arkas for a moment, his brow constricted in a harsh expression. Finally, he said: "Asango is a heretic, but I have heard many...*unpleasant* rumors about you as well, my prince."

"What of them?" Arkas said with a shrug. "Surely you have no desire to quibble about a few minor indiscretions of a starborn who is seeking to become your ally."

Again, Cromlic did not speak for a moment. He peered at Arkas, as if taking his measure. "I am not a *politician,* my boy," he said, speaking the term as if it were an ugly thing. "I am a servant of divinity, and I have dedicated my entire life to the great god Balthar and his holy justice."

"Yes, and I have nothing but the deepest respect for your work. You keep the masses humble and obedient. In my eyes, this empire should do nothing to hinder your holy authority. In fact, I believe you should play an even larger role than you do at present."

The bishop raised a graying eyebrow at this. "What do you mean by that?"

"Before I answer you, did you bring what I asked?"

"I...*brought* it, but I am not at all certain I will give it to you," the old man said.

Arkas felt himself grin. Politics was such a wonderful game! Whatever this *holy man* claimed, he was most certainly a politician. "Excellent. Then I should be happy to discuss the role of the Nemesai Order if perhaps *I* were to become emperor."

Cromlic's eyes narrowed. "Your starborn brother, Dimitris, has my support for the throne, but I think you know that."

"I do," Arkas said in as smooth a tone as he could manage. "I know that you have been using your considerable wealth and influence to bring in tutors from all over the world to instruct Dimitris in terrible ancient spells so he might kill Cassian Asango in a duel." Arkas leaned forward a little and added: "But my brother Cassian just stood up to *Promethiock's fire.* You and I both know that a battle between sorcerers comes down to more than arcane knowledge." He smiled as he added: "I am here to offer you a contingency plan, should mighty Dimitris fail—one that I believe you will find most intriguing."

The bishop drew in a slow breath, showing nothing in his expression as he then exhaled: "Make your offer then."

Arkas cleared his throat and began: "First, let me explain my vision to you. I dream of a significantly more *unified* empire. The local lords, as I see it, have far too much individual authority. They employ their own guards and militia and enforce Imperial Law as *they* see fit. Many of them fail to instill the kind of *respect* for the throne that I would demand in my regime." Arkas extended a hand toward the bishop, palm up and said: "I am sure you yourself have faced frustration at the sort of behavior that is allowed to run rampant in some parts of this empire."

Cromlic frowned. "Yes, there is a great deal of *sin* that manages to escape punishment entirely." His tone carried a hint of accusation.

Arkas let out a sigh as he said: "And your order does not have the *power* to control it. In the southern reaches of this continent, the people *laugh* at the authority of the Nemesai. Some of them even worship other gods!" The muscles in the bishop's jaws clenched ever so lightly, and Arkas felt a little thrill of triumph. Cromlic looked as though he were about to speak, but Arkas spoke again: "I believe the problem is entirely too much separation between church and state. Why should we have *city guards* enforcing laws? They are not holy men! Most of them are sinners themselves! Do they make certain that the local citizens are attending worship and tithing to the church? Do they police the moral decency of the people?" He let out a dark laugh. "Do they shut down the local brothels? No, of course they do not, because most of them are regular customers. Is *that* order? I do not believe it is. Do *you*?"

He could see a hint of intrigue in the bishop's cold eyes. "What do you propose?"

Arkas grinned. "I propose expanding the role of the Nemesai to its logical extent. Your order in its entirety is what—seven or eight hundred men? Think what you could accomplish with *thousands—tens of thousands!* What if you had a temple in every city and village in the empire, and it was staffed year-round with men who could enforce theocratic law? There would not even be a need for city guards or militia." Arkas paused for dramatic effect, letting his words sink in, and then he said in a soft voice: "I am not even certain there would be a need for local lords."

The bishop drew in a sharp breath. He could no longer conceal his excitement. "You would have the Nemesai running the cities themselves?"

"Why not?" Arkas said with a shrug. "Why should there be any distinction between the laws of this government and the laws handed down by the gods? It is all one in my mind."

"The *cost* of what you are proposing would be... *enormous.*"

Arkas met the bishop's gaze. He had chosen his words very carefully for this moment. "You and I would need to act with subtlety and in concert with each other. I would propose a slow increase in your presence throughout the empire over several years. It is only logical that the more inquisitors you have, the more sinners you might be able to discover and mete with holy justice. You would, of course, seize all property of such men and women as you do currently. As emperor I would gradually increase your legal powers, slowly making militia less and less relevant. Part of this approach would obviously entail that a portion of local taxes be directed toward your order and thus away from the local lords. It would be small at first, but gradually larger and larger. Within five or six years, the wealth and power of the aristocracy would be significantly diminished. At that point..." he paused, glancing into Cromlic's predatory eyes, "your order would begin using its theocratic jurisdiction to pass judgment on the governing lords. If you found their rule or their persons to be fraught with sin...well, the only righteous course of action would be to strip them of their undeserved authority and assume the mantle yourselves."

Cromlic stroked his long beard slowly, gazing at the center of the table between them. Arkas watched him in silence, doing his best to conceal the excitement coursing through his muscles. This was a crucial rung in his climb to the throne, one that could offer him a great deal of protection from Asango until the second part of the Norn's prophecy came to pass.

"Your proposals are quite interesting," Cromlic said in a flat voice, "but even if both Dimitris *and* Cassian are dead, I doubt your father would grant you the throne. There is still Telemachus Vale."

Arkas laughed: "The *peasant* starborn? He's a coward! He refuses even to contend for the throne!"

Cromlic frowned. "Telemachus Vale has refused thus far because he will not stand against either of his brothers. If *you* were about to ascend to power, he might behave quite differently. Telemachus is not a coward. He is perhaps a bit too soft-hearted—too ruled by compassion to make an ideal emperor, but he would most assuredly fight for what he believes to be right. That is one quality I have come to respect in starborn—even in Cassian Asango. None of them are cowards," his eyes narrowed as he added: "none except *you,* Arkas Adronicus."

Arkas felt his heart sink into his stomach at these words. Anger and panic welled up in him in equal measure, and all he could think to say was: "What do you mean?"

"What do I *mean*?" Cromlic said, his eyebrows rising. He let out a dark chuckle. "You are utterly terrified of Asango."

"W-what?" Arkas said with the most relaxed laugh he could manage. *Had this mere sorcerer actually penetrated the walls around his starborn mind?*

The bishop rose from his seat and walked toward Arkas in a slow amble. "You could challenge Asango at any time to a duel, but instead you come in here and offer me more power than any religious official has ever held in history in hopes that I will kill him for you. It is disgustingly obvious you do not believe a single word you are saying about the church and the laws of the gods. However," he put his hands on the table, "you had enough faith in our religion to visit the Norn, did you not?"

Arkas tensed. "I..."

"You visited *her*; not the other way around, which means that you asked three questions." He glared and said: "Nearly all men who are allowed to visit the Norn ask one question in particular—certainly all the cowards ask it. So, tell me, young starborn, are you fated to die by the hand of Cassian Asango?" Arkas involuntarily fidgeted for half a second, and Cromlic said: "Yes, I thought so." He looked Arkas up and down and said with an amused smile: "*A coward.*"

Arkas began to tremble with anger. He rose and shouted: "Y-you think you can mock me?"

"*There it is,*" the Bishop sighed. He leaned into Arkas's personal sphere and whispered: "The little prince who cannot remain calm when his expectations are not met. You live in a simple, superficial world, boy. Vulgar and full of sin as Cassian Asango is, he possesses courage and grit. What do *you* have, young Arkas? You reek of desperation—*of fear.* I have seen thousands of men like you in my cells—sniveling little schemers who try to *talk* themselves out of danger." Arkas started to speak, but the Bishop hissed: "You are *correct* to fear Asango, of course. Even if I gave you access to every forbidden spell the human race has ever concocted, that young man would rip you apart in seconds."

Cassian will challenge you to a duel. You will lose. The Norn's words echoed in Arkas's mind, filling him with a sickening shiver. He stared at this bishop. The man had dissected his motives in minutes. Would he discover everything else?

"Sit down, boy," the bishop said in a softer voice.

Arkas was fraught with nerves. He gazed at the chair and then at the bishop and muttered: "N-no, I—"

"*Sit down,*" Cromlic said. He did not shout the words, but there was a hard edge to the man's voice that somehow cut into Arkas's thoughts, and the prince found himself obediently taking his seat. Cromlic watched him, drumming his fingers on the rough wood for a moment before he said: "You are an interesting case, Arkas Adronicus. I find myself not wholly knowing what to do with you." The bishop gazed up at the stone ceiling and sighed: "You are correct that there is a fair degree of danger of Asango killing Dimitris if the two of them are allowed to duel. It is vastly preferable that the heretic dies before that can happen." Cromlic shifted his gaze back to Arkas as if appraising him. "Still, to rule this empire... Telemachus or even the female might well be preferable to you."

Arkas twitched. "If you were to kill Cassian, both of them would become your enemies."

"Neither one of them would ever openly stand against an arm of the church. That is one of several things you fail to understand." Cromlic scowled. "I saw that little smirk on your face when I said I was not a politician. What I meant by those words is that I do not need to scrape and scheme to hold onto my power. It comes from a *god,* and thus no *man* will ever take it from me. Your father understands this, as does Dimitris, as should *you,* but I do not believe you have respect for such things. This troubles me a great deal." He leaned forward over Arkas and said in a soft, threatening voice: "I am tempted to arrest you for that alone."

Arkas's heart began to thunder in his chest as he said: "Y-you wouldn't dare! My father—"

"I have shared this entire interaction with your father, you foolish boy." Cromlic tapped the temple of his right eye, the gesture obviously denoting telepathy. "He grows tired of your idiocy."

A sickening feeling passed through Arkas. *His father...* He gazed down, feeling his hands tremble on the table.

"Poor boy," Cromlic said in a voice utterly devoid of sympathy. "It is such a shame what you are. I suppose...in *some* ways, that is not even your fault." Something about the way the bishop said the words made Arkas look up. The grizzled man cast him the faintest smirk, baring yellow teeth, and went on: "Oh yes, my boy, I know *all* about you, and your father...after what he has just seen, has consented to allow me to finally tell you the truth."

Arkas looked up slowly. "What truth?"

The bishop sighed. "Have you never wondered why the other starborn dismiss and even despise you?"

Arkas clenched his jaw. All of this was unreal. In the course of this single conversation, it seemed that all of his plans were unraveling, and somehow there was more. "Tell me."

"Tell you? No, this must be seen." The bishop lifted his right arm slowly, extending a rough-skinned hand out through the heavy cloth sleeve. "I offer your psychic mind a memory—a sixteen-year-old memory that will explain *a great many things.*"

Arkas stared at the outstretched hand. It loomed in the air, daring him. Every instinct told him that what the bishop was offering him would be horrible, and yet what more was there to lose? He found that he wanted more than anything at that moment to finally know *why* Cassian and Dimitris and the others had always hated him. His muscles coiled in hesitation, and then he reached out.

For a brief moment, he saw and felt nothing, and then he was standing within a large stone chamber looking at his father—a *younger* version of his father whose smoother features were bathed in moonlight that shined down through an opening in the ceiling. The man looked grim—even frightened, and then Arkas saw the small baby wrapped in silk, still and quiet in Emperor Tacitus's hands.

"We can still call this off," Arkas said not of his own volition, in a voice far deeper than his. It was the voice of Bishop Cromlic, and he sounded terrified. Arkas gazed nervously toward an altar upon which sat what appeared to be a large stone box covered in runes. *There was something inside of that box.* "I—I fear what the gods will do to you when—"

"I have no time for your fears," Tacitus said in a tone that sent terror through the bishop, and through Arkas. Then the Emperor swallowed and added: "It troubles me as well, *more than you know,* but...a sacrifice is required. I do what needs to be done." And then Tacitus began to chant, and Cromlic hesitantly commenced to chant with him. Arkas recognized the names of a few of the spectral entities that rose up from the ether, but there were others that were utterly alien. He saw the translucent forms rise—entities of strange and terrifying shape and power. They began to whip back and forth from child in his father's hands and the concealed contents of the stone box.

Time slowed within the memory as Arkas began to comprehend what they were doing, and as the baby—*the infant version of himself*—began to scream. He understood what was atop the altar... and what he truly was, and the realization sparked such revulsion that he drew back from the memory into his own mind. A split second later he was sitting back in the church screaming: "OH GODS!!"

"Yes-s-s-s," the bishop said in a cold voice.

Arkas felt dizzy. He swooned in his seat, cold sweat dripping down his face, and then he leaned to the side and vomited the contents of his stomach on to the stone floor in a great heave.

"I see you understand," Cromlic said. "Take a moment to reflect on it before you speak again."

Arkas took several moments, his mind sifting back through hundreds of memories. He understood...*finally*...why his father had grown to hate him. He knew why the other starborn had shunned him from the continuous telepathic conversation they had been carrying on since they had ascended together into their power. Their contempt for him had come on almost immediately. *But how had they known?* Was it something in his aura that they could detect? No one else had ever figured it out... at least Arkas did not think so... He felt as afraid as he had when the Norn had told him Cassian was going to kill him—more so even because the two fears built upon one another. They all hated him. *It was not fair! None of it was his fault!* And yet... he was an abomination.

"I am sure you can imagine what would happen if the truth ever came out," Cromlic said.

"My life would be ruined," Arkas whispered, sweat still dripping down his face.

"Far worse than that, I think. The people would call for your head. It would, in fact, be *my duty* to kill you."

Arkas sat trembling, finding it difficult to speak, but eventually he managed to rasp out: "Y-you wouldn't d-dare speak of it. My father would kill you!"

"I believe we have been speaking of the world *after* your father is gone. Yes, you have his protection now. Even *Cassian* respects the emperor enough to keep silent. But as long as you live, the ugly truth will always be there, waiting to be...*uncovered*." The threat in Cromlic's voice was unmistakable.

"W-what do you want?" Arkas whispered. He gazed at the bishop as his heart pounded against the walls of his chest. Nothing and no one had ever made him feel so powerless except his own father. He hated Cromlic from the pit of his soul, but he feared the man even more.

"I *want* only to serve the gods by battling the horrid sins of our people," Cromlic said with a sigh. "I am a very old man though, and I have learned in my time that, once in a great while, a... *concession* must be made for the sake of the greater mission. Perhaps—and I stress the word *perhaps*—you are one such concession. Perhaps your unholy life could serve the greater good, though it will not be on your terms."

"You... you would work with me, knowing what I am?" Arkas whispered. His heart surged just a little. Perhaps there was still some hope.

"The sin is done. We may find a way to move forward from it." Cromlic's eyes narrowed into a dangerous glare as he said: "The first step in that path is that you will cease all scheming and demonstrate complete obedience to my authority."

Obedience! The word made Arkas want to kill the man. Instead, he lowered his head and whispered: "I... I understand, your holiness."

"Good," the bishop said, and there was a touch of smugness in his tone. "Now tell me, what were the other two questions you asked the Norn, and what did she tell you?"

Arkas felt his stomach twist anew at this question. If he answered it honestly, the last advantage—his great hope—would belong to this old man. Experienced liar that he was, Arkas knew hesitation only drew suspicion, and so, as the wheels lurched to motion in his mind, he began speaking, biding his time by laying out first what was true: "I asked her how I could influence my father to choose me for emperor. She said...*I couldn't.*"

"I see," Cromlic muttered as if this were no surprise to him. "What else?"

Arkas continued to stare down so that his face could betray nothing. All his hopes for the future were dependent on the next words he would speak, and whether they were believed. "I asked her how I could become emperor. She told me that my only chance at the throne was an alliance with you."

"Hmm," the bishop grunted. He sounded intrigued. Arkas swallowed. The lie was suited to the man's vanity. It put the fate of the empire in his hands. Cromlic gazed at Arkas for a moment, and then said: "Rise."

"Yes, sir," Arkas said, keeping his eyes lowered in his most subservient expression.

The bishop moved closer to him and stared. Cromlic was a little taller than Arkas, and an imposing figure. "You will henceforth display complete devotion to the gods. You will attend every religious ceremony that takes place in the capital, and you will study the Enumis until you can quote the scriptures by memory. You will curb *all* of your crude *behavior* immediately, and from this day forward, you will kneel before me once a week without fail and confess all of your sins. Do all of this, and *perhaps* I will decide that your life is worth something to my holy cause."

"I... I agree," Arkas said. It felt disgusting to speak the words, but there was no other choice.

"Good," the bishop said through gritted teeth. "Now that we have that out of the way, we should begin making plans. You are going to help me kill Cassian Asango."

Arkas swallowed. This, at least, was a powerful step in the right direction. "How?"

Cromlic frowned. "We are going to go to his village, arrest him, conduct an interrogation, and then cut his head off."

The side of Arkas's mouth twitched. Executing a living miracle was technically illegal under church law. Such an action could only be taken if a conclave of the five bishops was held, and at least three votes were cast to excommunicate Asango, but Arkas could see that Cromlic had been pushed beyond such concerns.

"Wipe that damned grin off your face," Cromlic snapped. "Asango challenged the authority of this order in front of the entire empire. He was already going to die for that. You did not *manipulate* me into anything." The bishop leaned in closer to Arkas and said: "Do not *dare* to forget who is the master of whom. Is that clear?"

"Y-yes, your holiness," Arkas whispered, the words were acid in his throat.

The bishop's features softened, and he put a veiny hand on Arkas's head. "Remove the sullenness from your eyes as well," he said. The words were a command, and Arkas found himself obeying, lifting his head and gazing at the man with an expression of pure humility. "I will help you, my boy. No one has *ever* helped you, I think. Your father has always treated you as a spoiled, incompetent prince, and the rest of the empire has followed his lead. With my guidance, you may finally learn to be a man."

"Yes, your holiness," Arkas whispered. He evinced complete sincerity, which was terribly easy, given how frightened he was. If bowing and scraping to this man was the cost of the throne, then so be it. Arkas decided it did not matter. The day would come when the Norn's prophecy would be fulfilled, and he would have the weapon. Then he would have the power to kill anyone who stood against him, and everyone who knew about his birth. *That* was a secret this mighty Bishop did *not* know.

"Good," Cromlic said. He withdrew his hand and stepped back. "Now, you asked me for a small supply of dragon's tears." He withdrew a miniature, finely sculpted metallic chest from a pocket in his robe and opened it. Inside rested ten of the brilliantly glowing blue petals – enough to diffuse into sufficient ink to mark five men with apotheosis tattoos, or, in Arkas's case, two men and one extremely large half-ogre. "Whatever do you wish them for?" Cromlic asked.

"Bodyguards," Arkas lied.

"I assume your father's legendary craith soldiers could protect you from nearly any conceivable threat."

"They could, but my father expects me to take care of myself." This at least was true.

"I see," Cromlic grunted, looking thoughtful. He placed the tiny chest down on the table in front of Arkas. "The power of the dragon is normally reserved for those in service to the gods, but...I suppose in recognition of our new *understanding,* a small exception can be made."

"Thank you, your holiness," Arkas said. He held up his hand and extended a tiny fraction of his magic, taking hold of the container and willing it to slide toward him. It felt good to remind himself that, despite how afraid he was, he still possessed all the powers of a starborn.

Cromlic gave the vaguest hint of a smile. "Let us go to the altar. You can kneel and give your first confession."

"Yes, of course," Arkas muttered. The bishop turned and walked toward the door, and the prince rose and moved to follow him. In silent anger, he prepared to lick the repulsive man's boots.

CHAPTER 19: ENEMIES IN THE DARKNESS

It was twenty-four years before Asango's birth that Emperor Tacitus finally defeated Daibok and brought the horrible Second Demon War to a close. Rather than kill the Demon King, Tacitus forced him to withdraw his forces and agree to a pact. From that day forward, none of the demon lords dared to set foot within the Denigoth Empire. The Onkai slowly rebuilt their forces and only had to deal with lesser creatures of hell that remained in the wild. This ushered in the most glorious era of prosperity and expansion our people had ever seen. Humanity grew bold and inventive and looked toward the future.
The younger of them had never experienced the fear that the generation before knew: that their entire race could be wiped from the face of the world...

—Octithorin, Grand Historian
of the Denigoth Empire

Gretis watched the fascinating shamalak boy sniff at the ground. He was on hands and knees, and the claws on his fingers were out, their tips resting against the dirt. The sun was beginning to disappear behind the treetops, and the light had dwindled significantly. Gretis knew that this meant little to Kota's shamalak eyes, but her own vision could not adjust nearly so well. Still, she was a Sansrit Master, and she could feel every rock and impression in the dirt around her, as well as the heartbeat of the boy in front of her and all the tiny movements of his musculature.

Kota had begged her to let him travel without a shirt, and Gretis had thought this a fair request given that he was seeking out his own people. As she looked at him now in the dimming light, her gaze moved over all the tiny scars on his golden brown skin. They were claw-marks, she knew. Like many of the shamalak boys Gretis had observed, Kota had participated in a great deal of play-fighting with fang and claw. Gretis had difficulty imagining Kota slashing at another person, despite the tremendous talent he was beginning to display as a swordsman. The boy was so warm and kind that it seemed impossible that he could inflict wounds on others. At the same time, she knew that for the shamalak, who lived in the dangerous wild lands, the ability to fight was a crucial element of survival. Kota had only been working to sharpen the skills of his friends, and they his.

"Shamalak I think here a day before," he said suddenly. Then he shook his head and reworded his sentence: "I...*believe that* shamalak was here *yesterday.*"

"Nearly perfect," Gretis said with a nod. "Shamalak *were* here if you are using *'shamalak'* in the plural." Immediately she saw the confusion on his face and added: "*Plural* means more than one."

"Mhh," Kota grunted, and she did not think he fully grasped what she was saying, but he was obviously trying very hard, and this pleased her.

"Can you tell the difference between humans and shamalak just by scent?"

"No," Kota said with a shrug, "not unless I know the scent of someone already, but..." he gazed at the ground, "tracks of humans have the smell of leather because your kind always wears boots or—" he strained for the word, "*s-sandals.* Tracks of shamalak is only sweat and skin. Easier to find. Easier to follow."

"Really? Can you decipher anything else?"

Kota nodded. "They are hunters."

"How do you know?"

"I guess. There is five scents. All smell like adult. All smell like male. Not enough men to make war party. Shamalak usually hunt in groups this size, especially this close to humans."

"Hmm," Gretis muttered. She was impressed both with Kota's senses and his ability to make logical inferences from them. "How far off do you think they are?"

Kota took a slow sniff, moving his nose over the ground and then said: "They not catch anything yet when they leave this trail, else I would smell blood." He peered at several impressions in the soil and added: "They were moving slowly. I think at least one was on hands and feet, following a scent." He took yet another quick sniff at the ground and added: "Whatever it was, the scent was old when they were following it, because it cold now. If they found the animal, it...*p-p-probably* took at least half a day."

"Can you find them?"

Kota smiled just a little. "Yes. If they kill animal, they stop to skin it and eat before they bring meat to tribe. If they still hunting, they not far away, I think. One way or other, I can track them."

Gretis smiled. "Lead on, young warrior."

Kota grinned and returned his attention to the trail. He moved over the ground with remarkable agility on his hands and feet in a manner that made the muscles in Gretis's back ache vicariously. She knew enough about the shamalak people to understand that not all of them inherited the full breadth of preternatural traits that set them apart from the human race. Whether this was from dilution of bloodlines due to crossbreeding with humans over the years, Gretis did not know, but many of Kota's people were born without superb senses of smell, or the ability to extend claws or hear as well as any animal in the forest. Kota possessed the full gamut of his people's gifts, and each one to its highest degree. He was what his people referred to as 'anatheral,' which meant *'one who is pure.'*

Kota had led them for the better part of an hour before Gretis felt a deep and sudden tremble in her spirit. It caused her to stumble, and she had to catch herself against the side of a tree as an involuntary gasp escaped her throat. Kota whirled around, his silver eyes filling with concern as he said: "Are you alright?"

Gretis blinked. She was not all right at all. There was something terribly foul nearby—*something evil.* It had been many years since she had felt the presence of a truly powerful demon, but the sensation was unmistakable. She gazed slowly about, her fingers locking around the handle of the sword at her belt, every muscle in her body coiling for attack.

"Are you alright?" Kota said again. Gretis glanced at him, and as her eyes met his, she felt a pang of fear. *This demon was after him!* Somehow, it had discovered what Kota was. She could feel the monstrous creature lurking around far behind the two of them and wondered if it already knew where they were. She was such a fool to bring Kota away from the safety of the Onkai temple! Out here he was defenseless. Gretis could sense the corrupt energy— it was more than that of some simple demonic soldier or scout. There was immense, terrible power. It was stronger than anything she had ever faced—strong enough perhaps to go right through her and kill her student.

"Kota," she whispered, and she stiffened as she said the word. The demon—*and probably its servants*— were very near, and if Kota caught their scent, he would be overtaken with an irresistible urge to attack. If that happened, he would die. Through some small stroke of luck, the trail they were following would lead him in a different direction than the creatures. "I would like you to go ahead of me," she said in a voice of forced calm.

"I thought you were coming," Kota said, his eyebrows knitting together.

"I have other business to attend to," she said, willing her face into a serene expression. She called upon all of her training to slow her heartbeat and suppress the fear that might leak out through her scent or her movements in ways Kota's acute senses might detect. If the young warrior perceived danger, he would want to stay and fight at her side. "You must move forward. I shall find you later." There was no time to think of a lie. Her senses were aligning more and more to the threat. As if to finalize this interaction, she turned from Kota and began to walk away from him, saying in a smooth but authoritative voice: "Go."

She sensed him hesitate behind her, and then obediently turn and lower his head to the ground once more. Gretis took what little relief she could from that. Night had fallen, and the forest around her was a chaotic tangle of brush, roots, and tree limbs all in darkness. Kota's superlative eyes would guide him, but Gretis needed to call upon her spirit—her *animus*—to form a mental picture of the world around her. When she had moved far enough away from the boy, she focused its power and began to whip over the ground at a pace quicker than a horse at full gallop. Her body moved with agile precision, her animus accounting perfectly for every low tree branch and tiny shift in the terrain and compensating with smooth dodges and sidesteps. She traversed in silence, as a Sansrit Master should.

It took perhaps fifteen minutes to trace the foul emanations back to their source, though Gretis could not be certain of time. Stray thoughts cleared from her mind, leaving room for a visceral sense of the immediate. *A fight to the death lay ahead.*

She sensed the first of her enemies as she drew near an expansive clearing in the forest. Her mind was focused on the foul emanations that pulsed from them, and so she was not prepared for what she saw when she whipped around the last tree.

Two hulking figures stood with revolting smiles across their blood-soaked maws. Their faces vaguely resembled those of bulls, though thinner and more streamlined, with jagged black horns jutting out from their skulls. They both turned as Gretis appeared, their blood-red eyes fixing upon her. They were the size and vaguely the shape of heavily-muscled men, with leather armor strapped to most of their bodies that was covered in fresh, wet blood. These unholy things had been in the middle of eating. One of them had a piece of meat in his hand that Gretis recognized with sickening revulsion to be the lower half of a human arm. Her eyes flicked immediately to the ground where she saw several bodies in front of the demons' hooved feet, dismembered and ripped open. There were two horses, one man, one woman, and...*a child...*

Gretis drew in a shrill gasp as her mind absorbed the horror before her. She stared at the pair of vile creatures and trembled at what had been done to this poor family.

One of the demons began making deep, guttural noises, almost seeming to belch words in an incomprehensible language. His thin, black lips contorting into a toothy smirk, and then he pulled a small double bladed ax from behind his belt. In a sudden blur of unnatural speed, he sent the weapon flying at Gretis. It whipped through the air toward her chest, hard and fast enough cleave entirely through her meager human flesh and bone. All of this happened in a fraction of time too short for her conscious mind to register. It was not, however, too fast for the animus within her.

Gretis felt her left arm whip up. Her hand closed around the handle of the weapon mid-spin in a precise, clean catch, stopping it dead in the air. Power coalesced through her limb, keeping her bones and connective tissue from snapping under the sharp impact.

For the briefest moment, she had the satisfaction of seeing the blood-red-eyes of the demons widen in shock. Then her animus began to pulse uncontrollably. It *hated* these creatures. It wanted to kill them, and she saw no reason not to surrender to its will.

Gretis felt her fingers twist the ax in her left hand and then her arm drew back, muscles coiling for the throw. Half a second later the blade of the weapon buried itself deep in its owner's skull with such inertia that he was knocked into a backward tumble. Gretis was on the second demon before the first hit the ground. The thing managed to fumble its sword from its belt and parry her first slash, but the effort knocked it off balance, and before it could recover, Gretis lunged forward and thrust her blade into its stomach. Channeling spiritual energy into her weapon, she pierced through the armor and unnaturally tough skin. The demon let out a guttural scream as chunks of its innards seeped out through the newly opened holes in its body. Gretis did not hesitate. She yanked her weapon free and delivered an upward slash, taking the demon's sword arm off at the elbow. As it screamed out, Gretis hacked its other limb off just below the shoulder and then she raised her leg and rammed the bottom of her boot into the thing's chest, sending it back into the trunk of a tree. She darted forward before her victim could bounce and ran her weapon through its chest, pouring more energy into the blade so that it pierced through breastplate and bone, and sank deep into the tree behind.

Gretis took a moment to pant as she stared at the horrid monster. It snarled and writhed against the trunk. Inky black blood was spurting from its two stumped arms and from its torso, yet she knew the unholy thing was not near to death.

Its body could regenerate the entirety of its missing flesh—probably within a few hours. There were very few ways to end the life of a demon such as the one before her, but Gretis knew them.

Slowly, she knelt down and drew the dagger she kept concealed within her right boot and brought it up under the demon's throat. It watched her do this with cold hatred, hissing through gnarled teeth.

"Do you understand this language?" she said in a cold voice. The blood red eyes narrowed. *It understood.* "I think you know what I am. You should realize then that in *my hands,* this small blade is enough to separate your head from your body."

The demon bore its pointed teeth at her. "You are Sansrit," it said in croaking voice that made her skin crawl. "I did not anticipate your speed. Had I been ready, you would be dead, *bitch!*"

Gretis pressed the blade of her dagger a little deeper into the soft, furry throat. "Why are you in Denigoth?" she said.

The demon cast her a grin filled with cruelty. "Why would I tell you? Are you going to *spare my life*?"

"No, but I will let you grow both your arms back and put a sword in your hand. That is my offer: a fair fight before I kill you."

The creature's eyes narrowed, and it stared at her, considering. Demons, Gretis knew, had no real loyalty to one another. The monster in front of her had been a human once, but he had willingly sacrificed his soul for this unnatural life. He was no longer capable of love, friendship, or any other emotion that extended beyond his base desires.

"Swear it on the blood of Nataka," the demon finally said.

Gretis's jaw clenched. This creature knew precisely what to demand of her. *What else did it know of the secrets of her ancient art, and how?* But there was no time to worry about such things.

"I swear upon Nataka's blood that *if* you tell me the truth, and I am able to confirm it, I will allow you a fair fight."

"*Confirm it?*" the creature laughed. "My master will cut you to pieces if you go near him."

Gretis cut a little into the soft throat. The demon winced, and dark blood leaked out as she said: "Then we *do not* have a deal?"

"FINE!" the demon snarled. "I'll tell you! It does not matter! You do not have the power to stop us!"

"Why are you here?" Gretis said.

Glaring at her, it said: "We are hunting a child!"

Gretis felt her heartbeat accelerate into a mad frenzy. *They really were hunting Kota!* Her muscles constricted, holding back raw panic. "What child?"

"I do not know its name," the demon grunted through its teeth. "A mortal child—one that will grow to become our kind's greatest enemy if it isn't killed. That is what he told us."

Gretis yanked her sword from the demon's torso and flung the creature onto its stomach. "WHERE IS YOUR MASTER!" she screamed, unable to control her fury at all. *They would NOT kill Kota!*

Coughing, the demon gestured with its snout and grunted: "That way!"

Gretis's grip tightened on the hilt of her weapon so hard that the metal squealed. *Her animus was on fire.* It wanted to slaughter the creature at her feet, but she remembered her oath and instead plunged her weapon through the thing's back into the place where she knew its black heart to be. The demon let out a horrid scream, convulsed several times, and then went limp on the ground. It could heal even from that, *but not quickly.*

Gretis took a few steps away and knelt down on the ground then. *She had expended so much energy...* This had been necessary, but she knew that she needed more to have any chance at all against the Archdemon that commanded these creatures. Gretis let her fingers press gently into the rough grass beneath her, the hot sweat from her hands mingling with the icy dampness below. She willed what was left of her animus's power to reach out and find the infinitesimal spiritual energy of the grass. It was there—*a tiny charge of beautiful and natural life*—and she used it to link to the other plants around her. The bushes held a little more than the grass, but not so much as the trees, some of which were far older than Gretis herself. Without words, she begged them to lend her some of their power, and, slowly, they did. New energy entered her body, along with new strength, *but it was not enough...*

Gretis reached deeper. She knew to fight an Archdemon at all, she needed to draw from the immense corona—the heart of the world itself. Using what she had just acquired, Gretis reached out to that great spindle. All life was connected, her master had taught her so many years ago, and all natural life held spiritual essence. She could feel the enormity of that primal power coursing all through the world—a vast ocean. She reached to the swirling sea. There was no language with which to communicate with it, but it could respond to feeling—*to need.* She opened her heart, laying her desperation bare. *Help me!* Her very soul screamed out.

Gretis felt a sensation of profound warmth as the great corona acknowledged her plea, and then power raced up into her so fast it threatened to tear her body apart. Before she knew what she was doing, she was on her feet and the cold night air was whipping at her face as her body whipped forward toward her enemy. The perfect clarity of this mortal battle washed away her sins and illusions. It brought back flashes of her life before she had taken the name Gretis—when she had been known as *Princess Angretta.*

Suddenly her animus—extending far beyond the limits of her sight—carried back an image of the enemy that lurked through the next cluster of trees. It was a creature of far grander power than the ones she had just faced, a titanic mass of unnatural muscle that stood at least twice her height. Without thinking, Gretis drew a concealed dagger from her left sleeve and sent it spinning through the brush toward the thing's neck. Almost instantly though, her senses registered a powerful hand snap up and catch the projectile in midair. She caught a mental image of fingers far thicker than her own closing around the thin handle.

Gretis dashed around the last trees and suddenly beheld a true creature of nightmare. She nearly flinched as she saw him. The Archdemon had the mass of perhaps four or five grizzly bears. Like the lesser members of his brood, he possessed a pair of black horns, though his were far longer and thicker. His face was covered in slick black fur, and his eyes, which gazed at her in the darkness, glowed a blazing red.

"You thought to kill me with a *knife*?" the monster said in a horribly deep voice, the black lips grinning to reveal fangs the size of fingers. He unclenched his enormous left hand, and her dagger fell away to the forest floor. Then the Archdemon took a step toward her on hooved feet, and his silver breastplate glinted in the moonlight. The metal was ancient and full of nicks, but at its center was a deep gash. As Gretis saw this, she knew who the creature was, and it filled her with new fear.

"You are a Sansrit Master," the Demon Lord Rakathon said in an amused voice. He was not afraid of her at all. *Why would he be?* Rakathon had singlehandedly butchered an entire platoon of Onkai in the Second Demon War and was rumored to have done far worse in the first. He held the shaft of his legendary sword in his right hand. It was as long as a man and probably weighed more than Gretis did, but he held the weapon as if it were light as a twig.

Her own sword raised, Gretis took a step closer to the brute, and he mirrored her with an immediate bound of his enormous legs. *She was about to die*! There was a chance she could take Rakathon with her, but it was a very small one. Still, she had to try.

"I see," Rakathon hissed, his face still smirking. "You are *the protector*." The notion seemed to amuse him. "Tell me, are you the only one I need to kill to get to her?"

Her? Gretis stiffened as the unexpected word sliced into her thoughts. *Was the demon confused?* He sounded so certain—in fact, he seemed drunk upon his own confidence. She scarcely had time to ponder the mystery before the enormous blade lurched toward her in a sudden downward slash. Gretis's sacred animus moved through her, bringing her own sword up and infusing the steel with a portion of its energy. The demon's attack came as an explosion of power. Her feet sank up to the ankles in the hardened dirt below. It took every shred of strength she had not to buckle under the first blow, yet she had only an instant to recover before the second came.

Her right wrist snapped her sword up to intercept the attack while her left hand moved up the flat of the blade to brace it at the top. Rakathon's massive weapon rammed into hers in a lateral strike with so much force behind it that the impact sent her sailing through the air. Gretis's back hit the side of a tree hard enough to crack the trunk, and she bounced off it, shrieking in pain. As she panted on her knees, some part of her comprehended the fact that if she had forced a hair less power into her weapon, the Archdemon would have sliced through it and split her in half. The vast swell of energy the spirits had lent her had been diminished far more than she would have believed in the span of a few seconds, while Rakathon had likely only begun to show his strength. As if to prove this, he pulled something shining and circular from behind his back and sent it whipping through the air at her.

Gretis recognized the projectile as a *chakram,* an ancient weapon that was something like a wheel of blade all around. She had never heard of one so large and heavy. The ring of dark metal sliced through the brush and stray tree branches between the two of them like they were cobweb. Gretis's mind went blank as her animus made the decision on its own to spring up and backward, sending more of its ever-diminishing power into her legs. Her leap carried her over the chakram an instant before it hit the tree trunk behind hard enough to split the trunk with a terrible crunch.

Time slowed as Gretis reached the apex of her leap, and her thoughts resumed. The Archdemon was glaring up at her, and as she glared back, her left hand moved to the small dagger she always kept concealed behind the nape of her neck. The ancient spirit within her carried out her intention, feeling out the distance to Rakathon's skull, taking aim, and then snapping her arm forward in a precise throw. In less than half a second, the dagger buried itself up to the hilt in the monster's left eye. Gretis felt a little thrill as Rakathon let loose a thunderous scream of pain. His left hand jerked up to its blood-spurting-socket while his right limb thrashed the enormous blade wildly in a half-blind flurry.

Gretis landed in near perfect silence on the ground some thirty paces away from her opponent. She could not entirely suppress the smirk that threatened to overtake her face. *She had managed to injure Rakathon!*

"I'll hack you shreds!" the Archdemon snarled. He let out a guttural roar that made the ground tremble beneath her feet.

Gretis whipped away, darting between and around tree-limbs. She knew she had only seconds to analyze her situation before the beast regained its focus. Her chances of killing a demon lord were something akin to a house cat's odds at killing a mountain lion. The reserves of preternatural strength within her flesh were draining by the second. When they were spent, she would be little more than an injured human in the forest with a simple steel sword. *And she still did not even understand what was going on.* Rakathon seemed to be after a girl. *What girl?* What had summoned this ancient monster into Denigoth? He had only brought a small contingent of soldiers with him, which meant... *what?* She had no idea.

"You do not even know what the girl is!" Gretis shouted back through the brush at her opponent in the vague hope that this might elicit an illuminating response.

The Demon Lord gave a snarling chuckle. "You think *you* do?" She could just barely see him through the plants and darkness. Rakathon still had one meaty hand over his eye. He slashed out with his sword and split at least five tree trunks in half, causing their upper sections to fall in a mess of leaves and branches around him. "Come and fight me, *witch*! It has been more than three centuries since I have killed one of your kind!"

He broke into a sudden charge, and his colossal mass began to simply snap and uproot trees in front of it. As Gretis watched the onslaught, she knew she could evade no longer.

She sprang up on top of a boulder nearly as large as Rakathon himself and stared as he came. Something akin to madness overtook her as she shouted: "How's the eye, imbecile?" She flashed him a fierce smile and dropped behind the large rock into a crouch.

Her mind had formulated a very simple, if desperate plan. She shared her intentions with her animus in simple images it could understand, and then she surrendered entirely to it. If her movements were not perfect in the next instant, Rakathon's blade would slash her to pieces, and even if they were... *No, there was no room for doubt!* Gretis stilled all thought and readied herself.

Rakathon shoved the heavy boulder to the side with a bat of his left hand. He had his sword raised, having evidently expected Gretis to continue her retreat or cringe in terror when he uncovered her hiding place. Gretis did neither. She dashed at her opponent and dove between his legs. Rakathon stabbed down immediately, and she sensed the massive blade stab deep into the soil just behind her as she rolled under him. Her body came back up into a kneel just behind Rakathon, and she thrust her sword backward, stabbing into the center of the demon's left thigh. Gretis felt her blade slice deep into the dense flesh where it met the steel-hard bone within and snapped it.

Rakathon let out a deafening roar and dropped onto his hands. Gretis rose to scamper away, but her well of power was running quite dry, and her movements had slowed considerably. She had only just started to run when her animus alerted her to the enormous hoof coming in from behind. It took half a heartbeat to realize she would not be able to dodge. Her animus let out one last flicker of power within her as it focused all it had left into the point of impact in her spine. Then the monstrous leg struck her. Gretis heard it before she felt anything: a crunching sound like a blacksmith's hammer shattering a rock. She felt herself being thrown forward and the cold night air began to whisk like water against her face. It was perhaps her mind separating from her body that allowed her to take in every detail of the ground rushing by beneath, and the tree trunk that drew closer and closer until her right shoulder struck into it. Then there was a thumping sound, and the world spun as she bounced off onto the ground and rolled. She ended as a limp mass on her stomach, scarcely having the strength to shut her eyes as her forehead pressed into dirt and dead leaves.

Gretis lay there for a moment taking in shallow, rasping breaths. Her body felt as though it were on fire from within, and the sensation was so immense and engulfing that she could not decipher what injuries she had suffered. No part of her flesh would respond to her mental commands. All she could do was lie in the dirt and listen to the sounds of the forest, and the snarling breathing of the Archdemon.

At some point, Gretis heard her enemy rise. He hissed as he walked toward her, but he *walked!* Gretis felt a massive hand roll her onto her back, and she gazed up to see Rakathon staring down at her. His eye had already regenerated into a smooth, red orb that once again glowed in the darkness. He knelt down, wincing as he put weight on his leg, and rumbled: "No human has *ever* given me a fight like that!"

Gretis managed to wheeze out: "Come...closer, I'll...take your....other eye." She did not know why she said the words save that nothing else came to mind.

The Demon Lord moved his right hand to her throat and took hold. He did not squeeze, but they both knew he could crush her neck with ease. Instead, Rakathon leaned in closer so that she could feel his hot, sulfur breath on her face. "In just a moment, I'm going to rip your head off this weak, human body, but it does not have to be that way." He cast her a ghastly smile and hissed: "A warrior like you has value." He leaned into her right ear and whispered: "If you willingly drink my blood, all your wounds will heal within moments, and you will be even *stronger* than you are now." He cast her a wild grin. "You could live *forever*, powerful and fierce... *and beautiful*."

Gretis gazed into the revolting face for a brief moment, and then spat at it. Rakathon snarled in irritation and rose, lifting her off the ground. She felt his fingers squeeze just hard enough to make it impossible to breathe.

With his free hand, the Demon Lord wiped away her spittle, while Gretis choked. "You are ready to die like a warrior," he sighed through gritted teeth. "I think I shall take that away from you." With a smirk of slick fur, he said: "You have *failed,* witch. I am going to rip the girl limb from body and then come back here with her head. It will be the last thing you see before you die." He flung Gretis back, and her limp, half-dead body turned in the air and dropped into a violent roll over the rough ground. She came to a stop with her head turned in the direction of the Demon Lord.

Rakathon spread his great arms, and black flesh erupted from two points on his back, growing and spreading into bat-like wings near the size of ship-sails. The Archdemon cast her a quick look and then brought his wings down in a tremendous flap that threw up so much air at Gretis that she was nearly rolled over once more. As she squinted to keep the dust from her eyes, her enemy shot up into the sky, sword in hand.

A biting fear rumbled through Gretis. As the Demon Lord had said, she had failed. He was moving to kill someone—a female it seemed. Gretis had no idea who it was except that she was a child. Perhaps he would rip some poor young girl to shreds and then realize, through whatever mechanism had guided him, that his target was still alive. Then he would move on to Kota. If that happened, Gretis could not stop him.

She could still feel Rakathon as he flew away. The Demon Lord was not soaring in a straight line but was moving about slowly. This told Gretis that he had not yet deciphered the precise location of his prey. It also told her that he did not fear being seen, or at least that killing this girl was more important to him than hiding from humans, which was troubling. The presence of a demon lord within the borders of Denigoth might be enough to trigger a third demon war. None of their kind had dared such trespass since Tacitus, the starborn emperor, had defeated the

Demon King in battle and forced an armistice. If Rakathon were indeed after Kota, then this was an understandable risk, but if he genuinely was after some human girl, *then what did that make her?*

There was so much Gretis did not understand. The ancient prophecy had been vague and ambiguous on many details. Still, this was not the time for contemplation. The enemy had come!

Rasping for breath, Gretis drew her hands along the dirt until they were parallel with her shoulders. Pain screamed through her with every tiny movement, but she found she could move. She laid her hands flat on the ground and pushed.

"HAHH!" she shrieked as she made it up onto her knees. Evidently, her animus had been able to hold her spine together, for she could still command her legs. She stood, gasping as she straightened. The pain in her back was so intense that her vision began to blacken. Gretis ignored it, shutting her eyes and connecting with her animus. Depleted as it had been, it was already starting to regain its power. She could feel that primal force within her wanting to push forward, and this helped her face the agony.

When Gretis had steadied herself, her eyes fixed on the sword she had dropped on the forest floor. Rakathon had not even bothered to take it or destroy it. *Why would he?* The Archdemon could come back and kill her with ease. He could probably track as well as a shamalak and was the kind who would enjoy hunting down a victim. There was no use in going to Kota then. She could never get him far enough away before Rakathon slaughtered them both. Instead, she bent down and picked up the weapon, her arm exploding in new pain as she did. Perhaps there was still something she might do...*something*.

Gretis slid the sword back into its scabbard at her waist and then fixed her mind on the demon's location. He was quite easy to track now that she had come into contact with him. Rakathon's body emitted immense waves of corrupted energy. She followed that power, willing her body to dash over the forest floor with as much stealth as it could manage. Within several minutes of whipping over the terrain, she caught pace with the creature, and she looked up and saw his great wings blotting out sections of stars. Rakathon floated along, turning here and there, either not noticing her presence or not caring. Again, it jarred her how unconcerned he seemed to be with being spotted. If he did not care about sparking another war, did that mean that the demons were already planning on wide-scale battle?

She and the archdemon moved in relative silence together for the better part of an hour, Gretis limping along while her horrid opponent bobbed and weaved in the night sky, his blazing red eyes continually shifting about. Then, from nowhere, the great monster made a sharp jerk in the air and started to descend very quickly toward something.

Gretis sprang forward. She had recovered a fair degree of her spiritual power, and she forced it through her injured body, trying to match the speed of the Demon Lord as he dove.

She came suddenly to a clearing, where a wagon and two horses rested near a pair of figures camping in blankets on the ground next to the remains of a fire. Rakathon was diving straight toward one of the campers, his massive sword drawn back. The victim was quite small—smaller than Kota. It was a child, Gretis saw as she came closer, a young girl with brown hair. Horror filled the Sansrit Master, and she pushed her body harder, willing her animus's power into her legs so fiercely that her feet tore into the ground, ripping up sprays of dirt and roots behind her, yet even as she did this, she knew it was not fast enough.

"NOO!" Gretis shrieked in horror as Rakathon dropped at the blanketed mass.

The girl sat up very suddenly, her eyes opening to reveal orbs of blazing white fire. Gretis felt a swell of power unlike anything she had ever encountered. The child's hands rose as the Demon Lord's blade came at her. Nearly blinding white energy erupted from her tiny form, and Rakathon was engulfed in it. Gretis saw his dark outline within, massive at first, then reduced to something like a skeleton, and then nothing. The light abated as quickly as it had come, and the girl fell back limp upon her blankets.

"IONA!" a roundish man shouted, shooting up from his own bedding on the ground. He scurried over to the child and put his hands on her shoulders. He was not troubled by the remains of Rakathon...*because there were no remains*...The young girl had obliterated the Demon Lord from existence! "My dear!" the man shouted, shaking her. "What was that sound? I thought I saw a light! Are you alright?"

Gretis watched from the shadows of the forest, utterly in awe. The child did not move at first. It took a few seconds for her to even let out a moan. Finally, she murmured: "W-what? What's wrong?" She slumped in his hands and sighed: "I'm so...tired."

Gretis blinked stupidly. No mortal could do what that girl had just done to an archdemon like Rakathon. Not even an elder starborn at the height of his skill possessed such power. The round man shook his head and muttered: "I must have been dreaming—I thought I saw... light." He had no idea it seemed, and unless the child was pretending, neither did she.

<Leave them alone,> Gretis heard a soft voice whisper in her mind. She whirled, but there was nothing behind her.

"Who?" Gretis whispered, gazing about. Her animus could detect nothing.

<Move away from them, and we shall talk,> the voice whispered. It did not sound malevolent.

"I... all right," Gretis whispered, not knowing what else to do. A feeling of utter bewilderment had set over her. She ambled through the forest back in the direction from which she had come.

<Thank you,> the voice whispered.

"Who are you?" Gretis rasped.

<A guide,> the voice answered, and it was suddenly very close. Gretis spun to see a very tall figure shrouded in a black cloak, and she flinched. Her animus could detect nothing of what she was seeing. It was as if the being were not real. Gretis lifted her sword, feeling uneasy. The cloaked figure gazed down at the weapon and let out something that sounded like a soft chuckle. <Neither one of us may harm the other, my dear.>

"You are...the Norn?" Gretis blurted without thinking.

<That is one of the names by which I am known to this world now.> The figure was perfectly still except for a strange billowing of its cloak that did not correspond to any wind. <I am allowed to appear to you this one time, to help you understand.>

Gretis swallowed. She could not begin to make sense of what had happened over the last few minutes. The Norn stood in silence while she slowly processed her thoughts. Finally, she looked up and said: "Who is that girl?"

<She is...*perhaps* the most important being in the whole of the world right now.>

Looking back in the direction of the child through the trees, Gretis murmured: "Is she a starborn?"

<No,> the Norn whispered. <She is no sorcerer, and what you just witnessed was not magic.>

Gretis trembled. "What is she?"

<Much as I should like to tell you, or her for that matter, I cannot.>

Gretis's mind flashed to the girl's face. She thought she could remember a thin blue mark going down the girl's cheek. "She is a slave, isn't she?" Gretis muttered. She gazed up into the blackness under the hood. "Why is she a slave?! A child like that should be protected—should be *worshipped!*"

<She is exactly where she is meant to be, and what she is meant to be.>

"No!"

<Yes.> The Norn's voice was soft and patient, even kindly. <You may do nothing to help her. If you try, you will bring only disaster. Your destiny lies with the boy—to instruct him and guide him to where we all need him to go.>

Gretis's heart nearly leaped out of her throat as she thought of Kota. "Then he truly is... he is the child of your prophecy?"

<You already know he is, and all that entails. Kota will face enemies even stronger than the one you just fought. If our side is to have any hope of prevailing, you must prepare him.>

Gretis remembered the moment she had gazed inside of Kota and felt the spirit deep within him. "He has *so much strength,*" she whispered. "If I fail—if *he* fails... he will become as dangerous as the demon lord I just watched die."

<Far worse, I am afraid.>

Gretis began to pant. "Then you offer me no assurance that he can master the force inside him?"

<None at all. His fate depends upon you, and upon himself.>

Emotion welled up in Gretis. "Why was I chosen? Surely there are better candidates. I am a wretched fool who has already failed profoundly as a teacher!"

<You are what Kota needs. He loves you already, and that love may hold the beast in check where nothing else can.>

Gretis felt tears leak down her cheeks. "Please, I am too weak—too damaged. Let another, more worthy than I take up this cause."

<There is no other. Only you can take Kota where he needs to go.>

She wanted to fall to the ground. The weight placed upon her was crushing.

<You were chosen for good reason,> the Norn's soft, psychic voice whispered. Two shrouded limbs moved to Gretis's shoulders. There was no sensation of physical touch, yet there came a strange feeling of warmth that spread slowly through Gretis's body. It was profoundly serene, and it reminded her of the clarity that her deepest meditations provided. <You were *meant* to see the girl tonight, and the demon as well.>

"Why?" Gretis whispered, but she knew the answer. She had needed to know what was coming—to understand the full scope of things. For all of her mastery of the Sansrit path, she had done little more than annoy the archdemon, and Rakathon was not even considered the strongest of Daibok's servants. From what Gretis understood, he was as nothing compared to the demon king himself. She looked up into the silent, shrouded face of the Norn and said: "What is Kota destined to face?""

<Apocalypse,> the Norn whispered.

Gretis drew in a slow breath, as the awesome scope of the single word bore down on her. After a brief moment, a thought struck like lightning within her mind. "Asango!" she hissed. "If Kota is the reincarnation—"

<Yes-s-s,> the Norn's psychic mind whispered.

Gretis stared up into the blackness under the hood and said: "Cassian Asango must be killed!"

<Do you think you could?> The Norn sounded half amused.

"Even starborn can die," Gretis said, as her hand edged to her sword.

<True, but this one is...*quite resourceful,*> her immaterial limbs dropped away from Gretis's shoulders and the

warmth they had been radiating died immediately. <Anyhow, he is not your concern any more than the girl.>

Gretis glared up. "You expect me not to act when I know that a sixteen-year-old boy may very well destroy all life in this world one day? Why did you even give the prophecy to the Sansrit in the first place?"

<My prophecy was not for the Sansrit.>

"Then who the hell was it for?"

<One individual. Over two thousand years ago I told him his future. He chose to write it down and pass it on to the humans to whom he taught his art, hoping that when he was finally born once again unto the world, the knowledge would fall to his hands.>

"Reincarnation?" Gretis whispered, her eyes widening. She hesitated before giving voice to an unbelievable notion: "Then Kota is—"

<The one who *created* the Sansrit Path,> the Norn said with the hint of a chuckle. <Not wholly of course. He has his own mind and soul, but what you call the '*animus*' of the legendary being your master taught you about has indeed taken up residence in the shamalak child.>

"Gods!"

The Norn moved a little closer, seeming to float over the ground rather than step. <I have revealed far more to you of the past than I have done for any mortal in many centuries. I do this out of respect for your predecessor, and because you must face the challenge before you with open eyes.>

Gretis paused for a brief moment. Her many wounds were throbbing in the cool night air. She gazed down at her sword hand and saw spider-webbing patterns of dried blood. "Tell me the future," she whispered.

The Norn seemed to rise, or perhaps stretch up from the ground, and her voice grew louder within Gretis's mind: <Kota's fate is bound with that of the starborn. Neither can fulfill his destiny without the other.>

"Is it Kota's destiny to kill Cassian?"

<Perhaps. The reverse is at least as likely, but other possibilities exist as well.>

"*Possibilities*!?" Gretis grunted. "You're the *Norn!* Can you not provide me with more clarity?"

<No,> the Ancient One answered in a grim whisper. <You cannot imagine the scale of forces at play. We stand before the final battle between gods and demons for dominion over this world. If I showed you the darker potentialities I have glimpsed of the future, they would drive you mad!> The Norn leaned in closer and hissed: <Whether you train him or not, the enemy *will* come for him one day. He is inextricably linked to the final battle for this world.>

Gretis blinked at the intangible creature before her. The weight of the words pressed down upon her heart. The Norn, perhaps reading through Gretis's thoughts, whispered: <There is enormous consequence to what you know. For this, I am so very sorry.>

Gretis's mind flashed to the image of the young girl destroying an ancient demon lord without even understanding what she was doing. In a dry whisper, she said: "There is hope though?"

<There is *always* hope,> the Norn said, and her ethereal voice radiated a strength that reminded Gretis of who she was—who she had chosen to become long ago.

Kota... She thought of the wonderful young man. The ancient spirit had chosen its host quite well. "I... will do what I can."

<Believe in him and believe in yourself.> The words came out in a rumble and then, very suddenly, the Norn was no more.

For a long time, Gretis stood still, gazing out into the night. The oracle's words throbbed in her mind. She thought of the small slave girl over and over, and *the white light.* What was that power if not magic? *The prophecy she had inherited was incomplete...*

CHAPTER 20: A CLANDESTINE MEETING

In the early years, Cassian Asango had few allies. Slaves and other downtrodden souls spoke of him with hope, but he was primarily despised within the upper echelons of the empire. Men of power feared the changes he threatened to make. Religious men reviled his blasphemy. Only the wisest of men truly understood his potential, and they feared him most of all.

—Bishop Arodias of the Anti-Cassonian Church

Somar sipped at his goblet of ale and tried not to stare at the doorway to the Dragon's Tooth Tavern as a smooth-skinned young man close to Cassian's age walked in. Somar had been waiting for hours for this moment, and now that it had come, his nerves were stirring. The boy's crystal blue eyes gazed out from under his hood immediately, scanning the room until they fell on Somar. As they did, he gave a little grin and began making his way through the crowd.

The tavern, which lay at the furthest northern edge of Cassian's lands, had quite a few customers this evening, more than a few of whom were significantly drunk. A musician was playing a fast tune on his lute and singing a melody about a lady, her lover, and her angry father armed with a pitchfork. Men and women were stomping their feet and clapping hands to the lively rhythm. The young man was forced to weave through the patrons, which he did with awkward, clumsy movements that were almost comical. In the span of perhaps thirty paces, he bumped into five different people, giving each one a quick, smiling apology before setting forth again. None of them seemed to recognize him as the living miracle that he was, but then who would except those who had been in his region of the empire?

The youth finally maneuvered to the table where Somar had seated himself and leaned forward across it as he said: "I know your face!" He held out his hand, then muttered: "Oh, wait," and lifted both hands to draw back his hood, revealing astonishingly handsome features. He extended his hand outward again, flashing a smile of perfect white teeth.

Somar took the young Starborn's hand and shook it, saying: "It is my esteemed pleasure to meet you, Tel—"

"Hold off on using names for just a moment," the boy said, his eyes widening. He waved his hand around and whispered several words that sounded like gibberish, and Somar felt the tiniest tingle under his skin that he had come to associate with a starborn working magic. "There we are," said the boy, grinning. "We may speak freely now. No one will overhear." He flashed his bright smile once more and said: "As I am sure you have ascertained, I am Telemachus Vale, Starborn of the Nineteenth Generation and all that."

"Somar Dojinko," said Somar, smiling at the boy's seeming good humor. "I am but a simple tutor nowadays." He glanced back at the entrance and said: "Did you travel all the way here alone?"

"No," Telemachus muttered, rolling his eyes. "A half dozen of my *bodyguards* are just outside. The Obsidian Guild has grown extremely...*protective* of me, but I managed to convince them that I could walk in here *all by myself*."

"I see," Somar said, continuing to eye the doorway. Despite the Obsidian Guild's attempts at a clandestine existence, they were widely recognized to be the largest and most influential sorcerer's organization in the known world.

They produced and sold enchanted objects and contracted out spell casting services to kings, bishops, wealthy nobles, and even the Emperor himself. It was no surprise that they had inducted one of the new generation of starborn into their ranks. The guild had maintained a starborn leader since its original formation three hundred years before by the infamous Novinia Sorn, a female starborn who invented a position of great power for herself when none were available to her. This tradition had only been broken by the second demon war, when all points of the star but the emperor himself had been slain. Somar wondered what the guild had promised this Telemachus Vale.

The boy sat down and gestured toward the tavern musicians, who had taken up a fast-paced song about a sailor pursuing a farmer's gorgeous young wife, which was surprisingly beautiful for its relatively crude and graphic lyrics.

"So that is what you coastal folk like as music," Telemachus said.

Somar smiled. "I have not been one of the *coastal folk* for very long, but yes, Lord Cassian makes virtually no attempt to censor music here. I have noticed they tend to play quite differently than in the capital."

"Indeed," Telemachus laughed, leaning to the side in his chair to look closer at one of the minstrels. "He is playing that baccoi so fast! Look at him work the strings! Such clever finger work!"

"Do you play?" Somar asked, watching the boy's gaping blue eyes.

"That much depends on how you define *play*," Telemachus sighed. "I can produce the basic notes, but once a piece grows a bit more complicated than that my *playing* starts to sound like a dying cat." He straightened in his chair, returning his attention on Somar. "Thank you for meeting me."

"A humble man such as myself does not refuse a meeting with a Starborn."

"Oh, you needn't fear any of us," Telemachus said with a soft laugh that sounded almost nervous. "I do not even think Dimitris would dare give you trouble. You have become quite important to our brother, Cassian."

"Have I?" Somar muttered, feeling a little taken aback.

"Certainly. He speaks of you often—well, *speak* is a clumsy word for it. I have seen you here and there through his eyes. He has shared a few memories of your lessons with me. Quite fascinating stuff, I must say." Telemachus flashed his white teeth once again in a grin. "He truly respects you, which is quite rare for him, but it is more than that."

"Oh?"

The young man leaned back in his chair and looked up at the ceiling. "Has my brother ever told you he had an uncle who tried to assume control of the Asango fief after his parents died?" Somar shook his head, and Telemachus shrugged. "We were all just beginning to see through each other's eyes back then—Cassian and I more than the others because we happened to live so close together. My brother's uncle—Davin I think his name was—tried to take the role of a second father to Cassian, but my dear brother was not *interested* in a second father, or in anyone telling him what to do. He threw the poor man out of his castle and declared himself Lord at eleven years old, and, to everyone's surprise, the Emperor actually let it stand. Since then, Cassian has not really listened to anyone... until *you*, Somar Dojinko."

Somar pressed his fingers together in a steeple and studied his opponent's eyes as he had so many times in the Senate. "I suspect we are rapidly moving to the subject of this meeting."

Telemachus stared at him for a brief moment, then muttered: "Gods, I really cannot catch even a sliver of thought from you. How amazing. I suppose I need to ask plainly then. Did you tell Cassian you were coming here to speak to me?"

"No, but that is no promise that I will not once we are finished here."

"I see. Did he suspect anything?"

"Your brother's mind is rather occupied at the moment," Somar said, and this was true. The dragon egg had hatched within a few days of leaving the island, just as Cassian had promised. A reptilian beast had come crawling onto the deck of a boat filled with terrified sailors. Cassian had immediately fallen in love with the little monster and spent every moment of free time he could with it. He had named it 'Titus,' which somehow seemed to fit the creature, whose scaly skin was a beautiful speckle of gray, black, and white as if made of living granite. When Somar had set out for this journey, Cassian had been playing a game he had invented for his pet. He would send fist-sized rocks soaring high into the air with his magic, and the dragon would shoot up on its reptilian wings and shatter them to dust with bursts of mystic white flame, which seemed more like lightning than fire. At two weeks old, the dragon already understood several dozen commands. It was a highly intelligent and terrifyingly powerful little creature, and, as Promethiock had promised, it seemed to be utterly loyal to Cassian.

As Somar thought on this, a barmaid scampered up to Telemachus, her face, which showed her to be at least ten years older than the young man, was glowing with excitement. She leaned in very close to him and said in a sultry voice. "Good evening, my lord." She had, of course, assumed he was noble, with his fine clothes and his almost ridiculously handsome features. Somar watched with amusement as Telemachus actually blushed a little under her attention. "May I fetch you something?" she whispered, her soft tone full of suggestion.

"Mutton and water, please," he said in a forcibly even voice.

With a little giggle, the barmaid said: "Right away, my lord."

Somar took a quick moment to assess Telemachus Vale. It was interesting to meet yet another starborn —a child who wielded the kind of power Cassian did. This one was considerably different from both Cassian and Keska. He did not seem to possess the same degree of confidence or force of will that they did. He was friendly, unassuming, and at least a little insecure. Was this because, unlike the others, he had been born to peasants, or was it merely part of his nature? Whatever the case, Somar decided he liked this Telemachus, yet he understood why the young man had abdicated his claim to the throne. He lacked the ruthless drive needed to compete with his brothers.

Deciding to take a direct path, Somar said: "Why did you ask me to meet you?"

"Because I want you to stop Cassian."

Somar raised an eyebrow, though he was not particularly surprised. "Actually, I have been hired to do quite the opposite," he said. He noticed as he spoke that much of the humor had vanished from the starborn's face.

"You know that Cassian is a radical, do you not? Has he shared all of his ideas with you?"

Somar suppressed an urge to sigh. This was remarkably similar to the conversation Keska had had with him a month before. In a patient voice, he replied: "Cassian has shared some ideas. I know he seeks progress for the empire, and I trust him to bring about that progress intelligently, else I would not be helping him."

"All of us believe in *progress*," Telemachus said, his pale blue eyes staring into Somar's with an eerie sobriety. "It is impossible to possess the degree of telepathy we do and not be acutely aware of the injustices that happen every day. But

Cassian wants to tear the empire apart, and he *will*. You have to know that."

Somar's mind flashed for an instant to the moment Promethiock's blazing eyes had turned to his deep within the stone prison. *He may doom the entire world,* the Great Dragon had said of Cassian. Had Somar gone a full hour since that day without thinking of those words and wondering how dangerous his pupil truly was?

"I know that is what many are afraid will happen," Somar said, concealing his thoughts and keeping his face calm and impassive. "It seems that you would have Dimitris as emperor?"

"Nigh everyone would have Dimitris as emperor."

"Everyone at the *top* of the social ladder."

"Yes, and everyone who wants to live in obedience to the gods."

"Really?" Somar said with a small laugh. "I would not so easily dismiss the blessing of Promethiock."

"Yes-s-s-s-s," Telemachus said, rolling his eyes. "Even I did not think Cassian was crazy enough to try a stunt like that. I am sure he will be pleased to know the church is in quite an uproar."

"I can imagine so," Somar muttered. He found it a tad distasteful that Telemachus had referred to the journey that had changed his life as a 'stunt.' "Are you part of that uproar, young man?"

Telemachus sighed. "Promethiock has been a kind of symbol for hundreds of years. We worship him for the enormous gift he gave us, but we also understand that his imprisonment is a lesson that not even the most powerful creature in the world can stand up to the will of the gods. He is—"

Telemachus stopped as the barmaid returned with a steaming plate of mutton and a goblet of water. She placed them in front of him and said: "Here you are, my dear. Please let me know if there is anything *else* I can do for you." She gave him a little wink.

Again, Telemachus's features showed uneasiness under the woman's lustful gaze. "Just now I need to speak with my friend, but thank you." He reached under his cloak and drew out a gleaming golden coin, which he tossed up to the girl. Her eyes went wide as she caught it, as did Somar's.

"I—I don't know if we can make change for this, my lord," she said, staring at the gold piece in her hand.

"Keep it, but please do your best to see that my friend and I are not disturbed."

"Of c-course," she said, scarcely able to speak. She clutched the coin in her hands and wandered off.

"That was generous of you," Somar said. The golden docknar Telemachus had given the girl was worth a hundred meals.

"That woman has four children at home, all from different fathers," the young man muttered, staring after the woman. Then his eyes shifted back to Somar's, and again they grew severe. "Listen, I understand why Cassian despises the Nemesai. *Anyone* would feel the way he does after what they did to him. The order is disgustingly drunk with power at the moment." His eyes narrowed a bit as he added: "Your generation handed them *far* too much authority in the second demon war. But their reign will diminish gradually on its own. The people will not long tolerate—"

"Will Dimitris outlaw religious persecution?" Somar said.

"Dimitris will restrict their ability to confiscate money and property from the *sinners* they accuse. The practice will die away quickly when it ceases to be profitable."

"Do you think so?" Somar said with a dark chuckle. "I am not a telepath, and even I understand the hearts of men better than *that.* Some *live* to judge and punish others, and, anyhow, if Dimitris only limits legal confiscation, do you not think the noble inquisitors will simply resort to extorting bribes from people who are terrified of torture?"

Telemachus frowned. "I do not like what the Nemesai do, but we are speaking of a matter of ancient theocratic law, and such things matter very dearly to the people. If you challenge the church directly, you create a potential civil war. Thousands—maybe *hundreds of thousands* will die. What cost does the human race have to pay for Cassian to avenge his parents?" Telemachus let out a sigh of exasperation and added: "His stance on slaves is quite similar. I want to see slavery end, and it is already dying away naturally, *and peacefully*. In a few hundred years it will be gone, but at this moment, slaves harvest three-fourths of this empire's food. Cassian—"

"Will plunge Denigoth into famine when he frees the field workers," Somar said, cutting the boy off. "Yes, Cassian and I debate such things often. Perhaps you are unaware I spent over a decade in the Senate and know something about how this empire operates, or perhaps you believe your brother is far less intelligent than you. He is not, I assure you."

Telemachus stared down at his food, looking quite flustered. "It is not only the politics. You have never met Dimitris. He trains every day to kill Cassian. I am sure you have witnessed your pupil burn through sorcery instructors left and right."

"Yes," said Somar, mentally noting that in the last handful of months Cassian had gone through six tutors from various corners of the empire and beyond. He devoured their knowledge and abilities with an ease and speed that had filled Somar with confidence he was the ultimate starborn. Yet the tone in Telemachus' voice cast doubt to this notion.

"Dimitris and his people snatch up nearly every one of those teachers and track everything he or she taught Cassian. They sit in a room once a month and try to chart out every spell Cassian knows and how best to overcome each of them."

"Have you shared this information with Cassian?"

"Yes," said Telemachus, his voice soft and despondent. "My brother shrugs it off. He believes—truly I do not know *what* he believes, but the knowledge does not deter him at all."

"No, it wouldn't," Somar said, a slight smile coming across his face. That was the very quality that had drawn him to Asango. Every starborn in history had had power, but Cassian had tenacity.

"I am seeking your help as a last resort. I do not wish to see my brothers kill each other." Telemachus's face held more than a little desperation. This was the real reason he had come. Somar eyed the young man, assessing everything he had observed and assembling it into a cohesive picture. The young man had a soft heart. He was the kind and gentle sort who could never truly reconcile the killing of another human being.

Somar smiled. "You are a good friend, but you cannot stop Cassian, and neither can I. He will succeed or die trying. That is why Dimitris fears him so much that he spends countless hours plotting how to defeat him. Do you think Cassian loses so much sleep on Dimitris?"

"No, he does not," Telemachus whispered. "His own life and the fate of our people hang directly in the balance of a confrontation between the two of them, and my brother loses no sleep at all." He sounded frustrated as he spoke.

"That is not quite true, but close enough I would say. This is what bothers you. You think Cassian is impossibly arrogant."

"Is he not?"

I do not know." Somar chuckled. "All great men have a touch of arrogance, I believe."

"How romantic you make it sound," Telemachus murmured, his tone growing bitter as slumped in his chair. "People will die if Cassian ever sits on the throne."

"I am sure they will," Somar said, allowing his voice to rise a touch, "though I think not in anywhere near the great numbers you imagine. Still, this is not some friendly game we are speaking about. This is an *empire*!"

In a delicate voice, Telemachus said: "I think your mind may be a little too trapped in Denigoth's violent past."

Somar blinked. "*Violent past,*" he said with a sigh. He took in a slow breath, relaxing as best he could before continuing. "I was your age when what we now refer to as the second demon war began. People were being killed left and right. When I joined the army, I saw brave men die fighting things you cannot imagine, my boy. We watched in horror as our great starborn fell one-by-one—the older generation and the new—and most believed that it was only a matter of time before the human race was nothing more than a memory. Yet we fought anyhow, driven on by desperation and the stubborn refusal to surrender to extinction. I rose up through the ranks, and I sent boys younger than you to their deaths because that was what needed to be done to keep the rest of our people alive. When that hell was finally over, Emperor Tacitus himself promoted me to the rank of general, even though I was the bastard son of a prostitute. He sent me out to conquer lands for him, and I did it. I commanded legions to conquer and destroy kingdoms that had existed for hundreds of years. I led the imperial army because it made me rich, and because I was better at it than anyone else. Many hundreds died by my command and my ruthless, efficient tactics, and the whole time I knew that I was no longer fighting to defend my people. I was a conqueror." Somar leaned across the table and stared hard into the boy's eyes. "Can you imagine what I told myself for all those years—how I justified all of it?"

Telemachus did not answer. He simply stared back in bewilderment.

"I respected what Denigoth was," Somar said. "Hundreds of small, competing tribes and kingdoms spread out across the continent meant endless war and pillaging. A great empire was the only means to true and lasting peace." Somar gestured toward the young man and said: "You are fifteen or sixteen years old, and I dare say you have never seen an invading army coming over the hills to take everything you have—to rape your mother and your sisters, and kill you, your father, and brothers if you show the slightest hint of defiance. That was the world into which I was born, and it is gone now." Somar made sweeping gestures with both hands and said: "You live in this time of peace and order because men like me and men like Tacitus had the heart to do what was needed to create it."

Telemachus swallowed, fidgeting in his seat. In a sharp, quiet voice, he said: "Now you have that peace you were seeking. Why are you willing to support more war?"

"Because I want to see it *mean* something!" Somar grunted. "Because I see the faces of those I killed and ordered killed every night! It is a hell I hope a gentle soul like you never needs to face." He furrowed his brow at the young starborn. "I helped build this empire, and I want it to be better than it is. It damned well *should* be better! Denigoth has a responsibility to all the great kings and brave men it slaughtered to become something worth all that bloodshed."

"So you want more death to atone for your sins," Telemachus said.

"You misunderstand me, boy," Somar sighed. "I am not ashamed of *anything* I did for this empire. I believe in Denigoth because I have lived the alternative, and it is a thousand times worse." He shook his head at the frowning starborn and said: "I don't know if you can appreciate this sentiment, but with all my heart, I want the government for which I sacrificed all of my innocence to be the beautiful thing I know it has the capacity to be." He gave a dark laugh as he added: "I think I believed for nearly a full hour that I could bring that reality into being when I joined the Senate. I quickly came to learn the truth: my glorious empire is rotting from the inside. I have witnessed the contempt and apathy the ruling class have for the dirty, uneducated masses beneath them. It shocked me when I came to see it—*me,* a man who had spent well over three decades in the business of killing!

"This nation is headed directly down the path toward revolution. That is the *real danger,* my boy. It may not come under Tacitus's reign, for the people love him far too much for delivering them from Daibok's demon legions, but the infection has taken root, and it is festering. The *progress* your Dimitris will offer shall not be enough to keep pace with the anger of the men who will one day realize that they are only being taxed and starved and worked to death by their own consent. *Then* people will die!"

Telemachus took a slow breath, considering these words. He had lost some of his certitude, Somar could see. "And...you believe Cassian is the answer to all of this?"

"I watched a sixteen-year-old boy stand up to the fire of the great dragon," Somar replied. "That force of will, combined with a fiercely intelligent mind and all the powers of a starborn..." He smiled at Telemachus and said: "I have never met your Dimitris, but I do not believe he stands much of a chance against Cassian, nor does the Senate, nor anyone else." Somar exhaled slowly and whispered: "Your brother has made me believe it is possible. That arrogant little bastard brought purpose into my life when I believed it was gone forever from me."

"What about the church?" Telemachus muttered as he fiddled with his food. Already, he seemed defeated.

"As you said, *my* generation handed the Nemesai far too much power. We felt we had no choice at the time, given how effective they were at sniffing out Daibok's agents, but that era is long over." Somar shrugged. "A fairly simple fact about human beings is that we do not *like* to live in fear. Denigoth is far readier to be rid of its moral police than you seem to guess."

"I cannot convince you then," Telemachus said, raising his eyes to meet Somar's. It was not a question.

"No," Somar said plainly. "I will do everything I can to help Cassian reach the throne." His heart swelled as he spoke the words. He had needed to have this conversation, for Promethiock's warning had lingered long in his thoughts. *The boy might doom the world.* There could be no more terrible threat, and yet Somar found he had the audacity to believe in Cassian in the face of it. Someday, if the dragon's words proved correct, he would hold the boy's life in his hands, and he could make a choice then. Until that moment came though, Somar could work to shape Cassian into a just and honorable man. He could think of no higher goal for which to dedicate the rest of his life.

Telemachus forced an uneasy smile across his handsome features and said: "I suppose that is that." His features softened by degrees over the next several moments, as if he were letting go of the matter. After a long silence, he looked up with a pleasant expression and said: "Before you go, please, would you tell me what it was like to stand before Promethiock?"

Somar laughed. "I should love to."

CHAPTER 21: THE BEAST WITHIN

Why did I like the shamalak boy so much? He was not afraid that I could see into his thoughts. Nearly everyone I meet fears me for that. They are terrified of what I will see of course, but Kota was not. He had an inner strength in him that was wholly different from my own. I could sense it immediately, and it fascinated me. I think I should like to see him again. The eleven-year-old 'lesser creature' who tore the eyes out of a demon...

—Excerpt from the personal journal of Cassian Asango

Kota peered at the faint footprint in the dirt as his nose slowly drew in the scent. The sun had long since passed from the sky, and the moon was only a sliver in the night. Still, Kota's silver eyes retrieved every detail from the terrain. A shamalak foot with five hooked claws had made the impression. He recognized the familiar shape, much like the ones his own feet made, only larger. Tiny nuances of the odor told him it came from a male—one who had been sweating as he walked.

Kota crawled over the dirt and leaves, being careful to move in silence. The scent of the older shamalak grew stronger, and it was met with the those of others. Kota shut his eyes and let the tickling sensations in his nose tell him a story. There were four men—no, five. They had tracked a dear and killed it perhaps an hour ago. Kota could almost taste the metallic scent of dried blood from the drops that had spilled about as they carried off the carcass. He moved forward in a hunched manner as the smells became more distinct until he could rise and follow them on two feet. Kota's blood burned hot with the thrill of tracking, but he knew better than to come upon five seasoned hunters at a threatening pace. Instead, he moved at a slow gait, his hands purposely kept away from his dagger.

Eventually, the scents grew so thick that he knew he was within a few hundred paces of his quarry. With nerves standing on edge, he drew in a slow breath from the chill night air, then howled aloud up into the sky.

To any human, his howl was indistinguishable to that of a wolf, but, to the ears of other shamalak, it was something far more distinct. There were forty-one such howls his people used to talk with one another over distances. His pitch and the timing of shifts communicated that he was a friend seeking a meeting. After a moment of silence, an answering howl came. It was long and slow, followed by three much shorter cries. Kota recognized the response: *'Come in peace.'*

Slowly, Kota navigated through brush and trees under the moonlight until he caught a whiff of smoke in the air, and his ears detected the crackle of burning wood. A few moments later, he saw the orange-yellow glow of fire filtering through a wall of brush. It was then that he heard a rustling of leaves. Kota became still, holding up his hands in front of him.

"Who comes?" a deep, male voice shouted in the shamalak tongue, laced with the sharp accent of the Dentha tribe.

"I am Kota of the Nakawa," Kota answered in his native language. "I come in friendship."

Very slowly, a sizable figure of bronze skin and taut muscle emerged from the shadows. Kota gazed at the warrior. His hair was a deep black, as was the fur on his pointed ears. With a dagger gripped loosely in his right hand, the hunter stared at Kota with silver shamalak eyes that glinted in the moonlight.

"Hello, little one," the figure said. He cast a quick glance around and then said: "You are alone?"

"I have been on my spirit walk," Kota replied.

The hunter looked him up and down, then smiled, and he slipped his dagger back into its sheath on his waist. He held up an open hand, seeming to signal those behind him that there was no danger.

"I had heard that the Nakawa still sometimes send their children on spirit walks," the hunter said with a chuckle. "As you may know, we Dentha gave up the practice a generation ago. Too many dangerous humans poking about in our territory, looking for slaves." He took a step toward Kota and said: "It is good to see a Nakawa. You are welcome to share our food and our fire—*if* your *spirit walk* allows such things of course."

"It is allowed," Kota said. He moved toward the hunter, and as he did, he saw other figures emerge from the shadows. The members of this group all looked to be around twenty in age. All were clothed only in leather pants and had the builds of those who ran and climbed and fought on a regular basis. While Kota enjoyed interacting with humans, he had found that most outside the Onkai temple were of fairly poor physical condition by shamalak standards. He had supposed this was because their lives were so much safer and easier, and because they ate such rich food in abundance.

"My name is Vishri," said the one who had first emerged. He gestured to the others, introducing them as "Tama, Cochet, Kuruk, and Taza." These hunters regarded Kota with the same friendly smiles as Vishri. Kota thought he understood this. They were away from their tribe and near to humans. It was reassuring to them to meet another of their kind, especially an unthreatening boy. The Nakawa and Dentha tribes had long been allies and had arranged many marriages between one another so as to be connected by bloodlines.

"It is an honor to meet all of you," Kota said.

The one named Cochet sniffed in Kota's direction and said: "You stink of humans, little brother."

He smiled at Cochet and then at the others. "I have a story to tell. That is why I sought you all out. I need to get word back to my tribe."

Vishri raised a dark eyebrow at Kota. "Nothing like a good story around a campfire." He gestured toward the glow through the brush and said: "Why don't we go and get warm."

Kota followed the hunters back to their campfire where they gave him a juicy cut of roasted deer leg to eat. He filled his belly before he began his tale, taking some small measure of joy in the anticipation of the silver eyes upon him. Finally, when he was finished, he stood in front of the flames and told the group first about meeting Cassian in the woods and then of his interactions with the Onkai. Almost immediately, the hunters were spellbound. He saw eyes widen and muscles tense as he told them about the Kothla, and about how he drove Cassian's magical dagger into the creature's neck. He drew that blade from a hidden sheath under his pant-leg and let them see its brilliant blue glow, which out-shined even the fire. Though the five hunters could easily overpower him and take the enchanted thing, Kota trusted them not to do so. He could tell they were good men, and his story was filling their minds with wonder and respect. He even allowed them to pass the weapon around for inspection.

The men listened in rapt attention as he described the way Gretis could fight. He told them about life at the temple and learning to read and write, and about the friends he was making all the time. Most passionately though, he described his apprenticeship to Lady Gretis, of how she was teaching him to fight and to view the world in new ways. When he finally finished speaking, there was an awed silence for several moments. Kota let the men digest his story before he said: "I am going to stay with Gretis and learn everything she has to teach me. I think that is my spirit walk."

"I think maybe you are right, Kota," Vishri said. Kota noted that the man had not called him 'little brother' this time. It seemed his tale had elevated him from the status of a child.

"Whatever the case, I want my parents to know that I am alive and that I love them, but I think this is something I must do."

"I will find them and tell them myself," said Vishri. "I give you my word."

"Thank you," said Kota. He sat back down before the fire for a time, relaxing with his shamalak brethren as they asked him about human society. They wanted to know about marriage customs, weapons, buildings, money, the notorious Onkai, and many other things of which they had heard. Kota did his best to answer, enjoying being the teacher for once rather than the student. The way knowledge passed from him to these men slowly made him realize just how much he had learned in the short time since meeting Cassian that fateful evening.

Kota did not finish his discussion until deep into the night. When the moon had begun its decent in the direction Gretis had taught him was called 'east,' he finally rose. "I must return to my teacher now."

"I envy you your incredible life, Kota," Vishri said with a warm smile. "How long do you believe you will be gone?"

"Ten seasons," Kota said. This answer caused several pairs of silver eyes to widen. He quickly added: "I shall try to visit when I can, but—" he paused for an instant before saying, "my heart tells me this is where I belong."

"I understand," said Vishri in a soft vice. Then he chuckled: "At least I *think* I do. You are the first one of our people I have ever heard of to learn such secrets." He gave Kota a wry smile and added: "Among my own tribe, at least, I think your name shall become legend. I will do my best to tell your tale as you have told it to me."

"Thank you, mighty hunter," Kota said, speaking in a tone of sincere respect, "and thank all of you for sharing your food." He met the eyes of each man and nodded, and then he moved away from the group, walking in silence back the way he came. His heart felt lighter.

Kota supposed his mother might be troubled for a time over this decision, but his father would understand. On countless nights, the two of them had stared up at the stars and talked of other peoples. Kota's father was filled with a sense of wonder about the world and a desire to learn and explore, and Kota reasoned that he was honoring the part of the man's heart that they shared.

"You told your tale quite beautifully," a soft voice said from behind in Tethric.

Kota whirled to see Gretis a few paces back from him, and he noticed immediately that the dark clothing she wore had been ripped in places. The woman regarded him with a calm expression, her body perfectly still. No one else he knew in the world could have snuck up on him like this. His ears had detected nothing, and even now as he sniffed at the air, he only caught the faintest trace of her scent.

"How long you watching me?" he said, returning to his clumsy command of the human tongue.

"Perhaps an hour," Gretis said. She moved to his side and motioned for him to continue his walk. Kota obeyed, and they fell into step with one another. After a few moments, she said: "I thought you were going to go all the way back to your tribe."

"It better this way," Kota said.

"Is it? Your parents might not wish you to stay among the treacherous human people. They might desire that their son spend his youth with them. Is that why you are content to send your message through others? Are you afraid to face them?"

The muscles in Kota's throat tightened. He calmed himself before answering: "My spirit walk is my own, as is my life. I am of age."

Gretis cocked her head toward him as they walked. "Even the adult shamalak I have known show great respect to their parents' wishes. Is it different in the Nakawa tribe?"

"I *do* show respect," Kota said. He stopped walking and turned to face her, and she halted as well, meeting his gaze. "My father would support my choice. I know he would because I know his heart. My mother might try to stop me because she too afraid. My parents would fight, and my father would win because he the man. My mother would become very—how you say—*bitter.* It easier for them both if they don't have to see me leave their tent—to have me come home only to leave again."

Gretis stared at him for a long moment, her face as still as a statue. Finally, she said: "And what if your father commanded you to return to the tribe?"

"I would go."

"Mhh," she grunted. "And you are *absolutely certain* he would wish you to live amongst humans and learn my deadly art?"

"Yes," Kota said, and a smile touched his face. Her question had dared him to look within himself, and he felt confident in his answer. This allowed him to meet Gretis's cold, human stare, and, as he did, he guessed at what was within her heart. "Was you hoping I would change my mind when I see my people?"

"Hoping?" she said with a small, sharp laugh. "Oh, my dear young warrior, if only you understood." She turned and began to walk again, whispering: "Come." Kota fell into step with her once more, and he noticed that she was not taking him in the direction of the Onkai temple.

"Where are we going?" Kota said.

Gretis gave no answer but marched him across the wet grass and fallen leaves. Kota noted that she moved with remarkable grace over the uneven terrain, dancing over and sidestepping roots and stones without ever seeming to gaze down. "I swore to myself I would never take another apprentice," she said abruptly, in a voice tinged with nerves. "Until I met you, I had not *dreamed* I would break that oath."

Kota thought of her notorious first apprentice. Gretis's son, Soulic, was a murderer whom no one seemed able to catch. She had yet to share anything about Soulic, or the nature of her mysterious power for that matter. Kota thought it disrespectful to ask about such things, yet a question formed in his mind that he needed to speak: "Why you offer me choice to train with you?"

"I am trapped," Gretis said in a low voice. She gazed at him, and Kota felt her eyes travel up and down his form. "I fear for you, young warrior."

Kota considered Darius's warning about Soulic: *"He went insane."* He considered his words carefully before asking: "Do you think I strong enough to go through your training?"

"Strong enough?" Gretis exhaled, and then she gave an uneasy laugh. Her gaze shifted up into the trees, and she whispered: "There are many kinds of strength in this world, Kota. The part of you I am afraid of is very, *very* strong."

Kota blinked. He did not understand what Gretis was talking about, though he dared to make a guess: "Do you mean that part of me that made me attack the demon?"

This drew a smile from the woman, though her eyes only seemed to grow more troubled. "Tell me, Kota, do you feel that part of yourself stir when you are angry?"

"What you mean?" he said, feeling confused.

"I know a few of the children in the temple have been cruel, and I am sure your excellent hearing has deciphered many whispers from the people in the town about you. Do you feel the beast that lies within you begin to snarl and rage in such moments? Do your claws and teeth begin to extend when something angers you? Tell me truly. I shall not judge you."

Kota frowned, gazing down at the dried leaves beneath him as he considered her questions. The beast that lay within him had only made itself known twice. Once was during the battle in the forgotten city, and then the other time when Gretis had taken his hands in hers and somehow drawn it out. It had nothing to do with the frustrations of daily life. "I not feel it stir when I angry," he said finally.

Gretis breathed in slowly and then said in a soft voice that sounded almost kind: "I do not think I have ever seen you angry."

"Nothing to be angry about."

She let out a sharp laugh at this. "You live your life surrounded by people who look down on you for what you are. That does not frustrate you?"

Kota drew in a slow breath through his nose. "It not make me happy, but other people not decide who I am. I do. I choose to be here. I choose to work hard. I want to learn to read and write, and to be your—" he paused, struggling for the word, *"apprentice."* He looked up into Gretis's eyes. "No shamalak I ever heard of get such a chance to have a teacher like you. That much more important to me than silly whispers here and there that I am half wolf."

"Still, the constant disrespect must be trying. I am not altogether kind to you either. Every day I work you into a gasping mess of sweat and pain. It would be entirely normal to feel resentment at that—it would be *human* actually."

"I not a human," Kota said with a grin. He gazed up at his teacher to share the humor, but he found only coldness in her eyes. He swallowed then and said: "The hard work not bother me too much. I like it. I happy to work even twice as hard if I can learn to fight like you."

"And why do you wish to learn to fight like me?"

Kota gazed out into the shadows of the forest, seeing them dance as the soft spring air blew the bushes and tree branches in the moonlight. "Because I saw a real demon," he said, and the grimness in his voice was surprising even to him. "I know creatures like that exist now. I also know that very brave men—the bravest I have ever known—fight and bleed and die to keep them away. If Onkai not fight to keep these lands safe, I think my tribe be killed off a long time ago. I want to help the Onkai if I can. This is very important to me."

"Indeed," said Gretis. From the tone of her voice, Kota guessed that his answer pleased her.

They walked in silence for a time, Gretis leading the way through the trees. It was then that Kota began to notice things about her that troubled him. There was a sharpness that appeared in her step every so often, as though she were in great pain. Her breathing was uneven and full of faint hisses. She leaned to the left side ever so slightly. He thought back to the moment they had separated in the woods. Gretis had been fine then, he was sure of it.

"Is you—*are* you all right?" he said.

Gretis did not answer but kept on in her uneven walk. Kota sniffed quietly at the air around her. She had masked her human scent with salves that blended with the smells of the forest—a practice she often undertook when sneaking up on him—except that underneath this, Kota thought he could detect the trace of blood.

"Do you truly wish to face demons?" Gretis said quite suddenly in a hard voice.

"I—yes," Kota said.

"Very well then. Give me your weapons."

Kota swallowed, but then drew the crystal blade Cassian had given him and handed it to his teacher and then reached down and took his other knife from his ankle and surrendered it as well. Gretis slipped the weapons into a concealed pocket within her coat.

Kota felt himself began to tremble. Gretis's icy expression made the hair all over his body stand up. He walked on with her, knowing somehow that she would not reveal what was coming to him even if he begged her. They had gone another few minutes when he heard a rustling up ahead. It was the sound of furious movement and loud, strangely guttural breathing.

"I am sorry for what must be done now," Gretis said as the two of them came around a large cluster of bushes.

Kota suddenly saw a large figure obscured in shadow against a tree some forty or fifty paces away. The first thing he noticed about it was the pair of horns—large and long and curved. The creature's body was a mountain of bulging muscle, and it was thrashing with all that strength. Kota peered and saw that there was rope wound many times around the demon, holding it to the tree—a cord of woven plant fibers like the ones Gretis had been teaching him to make. He had only a few seconds to process what had likely happed: his teacher had somehow found and captured a demon and then carefully kept Kota downwind of the thing while leading him to it so that the scent would not draw out the beast within him. The stench found its way to him now. It was a foul stink of sweat and death and something unspeakably horrible, and it made Kota's blood burn in his veins.

He blinked as his thoughts faded away. The hooked claws on his fingers began to grow and his muscles tightened. He heard his own breathing loud and rapid as his lips drew back, revealing his teeth to the air. Kota let out a snarl of fury and charged at the unnatural monster, but the instant he sprang, a figure moved in a blur between himself and his prey. He glared at her—a human woman.

"Kota!" she said in a sharp voice.

The name sounded vaguely familiar, but he could not place it, and anyhow he had no time for words. The stink of the demon grew stronger in the air, and he renewed his charge, moving to dance around the woman. She responded so fast that he scarcely registered anything before her hand struck his chest. He was shoved back so hard that he tumbled backward onto the ground.

"Can you understand me?" the human said.

Kota rose in a snarl. What was this woman trying to say to him? *Why was she in his path?* He lunged again, this time trying to dodge to the right. Instantly, he felt a hand close around his arm and a foot sweep underneath him. The world spun, and suddenly he was on his chest in the dirt with his right wrist twisted up behind his back.

Kota struggled against this force bearing down on him, but the woman's grip was unbelievable. *How could any human be so strong?*

"Calm down," he heard her say. He could not remember what the syllables meant, but the sternness in her voice was plain enough. He felt fingers close around the back of his neck, and then there was a soft repetition of words that made even less sense to him than those she had already said. All the while, the demon snarled off in the distance. *It needed to be put to death.* Kota's blood screamed for this.

He began to feel a warmth pass into him from the woman's palm. It was subtle at first, but then it grew. His trembling muscles started to relax, and his breathing slowed.

"There we are," the woman whispered. "Can you understand me now?"

Kota clenched his teeth, but he managed to piece together what the words meant, and he answered in a snarl: "*Un-der-stand.*" The hand holding his wrist let go, and he rolled over and glared up at the human woman.

"You must control yourself," she said.

He gazed around her to the demon. The wretched thing was tied to a tree. He felt an overwhelming drive to tear into it with his claws. *It needed to die!* Killing it was his duty. Every fiber of his being cried out for this.

The human knelt down in front of him, and her dark eyes caught his. "You wish to attack that creature," she whispered.

"YES!" Kota hissed through his fangs.

"I will continue to block your path to it."

"NO!" Kota grunted, and he sprang up onto his haunches.

"Yes," the woman replied. "You cannot pass by me. I am far stronger and faster than you." She reached into a pocket in her right boot and drew out a small knife, which she placed on the ground in front of her. Then she stared hard into his eyes and said: "If you wish to get to that creature, you must kill me."

Kota's breathing quickened at this. "No!" he grunted. "You move!"

"I will not," she said in the same calm voice. "If you wish to pass me, you must draw that weapon and slice into my throat." She lifted her chin, exposing the soft skin of her neck. "Go ahead. I will not stop you."

Kota stared at her, and then his eyes traveled down to the knife. All he had to do was draw it and cut. The putrid demon behind her was growling. *It had to die!* His right hand fidgeted, edging for the dagger, but then hesitated. He did not want to kill this woman.

"Y-you move," he said again.

"I will *not* move, save to knock you back," she whispered. "I am your obstacle. You must decide what you will do to me."

Kota began to tremble. It was only good and right that he kill the demon. *Why could this human not understand that?* "You m-move... p-please."

"I will not. You must choose. Would you take my life to get at that monster? Decide what is *right,* young warrior."

Behind her, the demon snarled in a croaking voice: "Cut her throat! Then come and face me, you filthy little shamalak!" It laughed: "I can feel your hatred! My kind will sweep through these lands and slaughter every last one of you mongrels! COME!"

Kota's hand was only a short distance from the dagger, and the demon's words were grating in his mind. *Would this foolish woman really make him kill her?* He did not want that. She did not need to die. Yet he could not get to his prey without cutting her throat... He *had* to kill the demon... This thought passed through his mind as his hand moved closer and closer to the weapon, but when his fingers touched the handle, he froze. *'Young warrior,'* she had called him. It sounded familiar. Everything about the woman seemed familiar.

Kota's heart thundered in his chest. Two pieces of who he was were battling one another. *It hurt.* There was a terrible chaos in his mind, and then one side prevailed. Slowly, he drew his hand away from the dagger and bowed his head. Letting the demon continue to draw breath was agonizing, but he would not slice this woman's throat. Kota dug the claws of his fingers into the ground, shaking in frustration.

"I am very proud of you," the woman said in a quiet voice. She rose to her feet and moved in the direction of the demon, stooping along the way to snatch up a black-silver sword from the ground. Without turning to look at Kota, she said: "The part of you that wishes to kill this creature is primal and violent, but it is *not* wrong. Demons *are* to be destroyed!"

She moved her weapon in a sudden downward slash that sliced cleanly through the rope binding her prisoner. The thing let out a vicious growl and lunged for her, claws moving to rend her neck and face. Gretis made a quick horizontal slice that cut into the bull-like face across the snout. The demon jerked back, clutching its maw and roaring with fury. "Here," she said, and she tossed the sword to her enemy. It drew a bloody hand away from its wound and caught the weapon by the handle, and Gretis dropped smoothly into what some part of Kota's mind recognized as the Din-Sul stance, her sword poised for attack.

"I'll gut you, wretch!" the demon snarled, shaking with rage. "Then I'll make you watch as I hack up the boy!"

Gretis gave no visible reaction to these words but remained still, eyes focused. The demon lunged toward her, raising its sword and bringing it down in a leaping strike. Her blade snapped up and knocked his weapon to the left with a fierce clang that made every muscle in Kota's body convulse. The demon's leap was brought to a halt mid-air, and as its hooved feet touched the ground, Gretis's left hand plunged a small dagger into its right shoulder that Kota had not even seen her draw. The monstrous figure staggered back, clutching at the new wound.

"This creature knows *nothing* of compassion," Gretis said in a hard voice. She kept her eyes on her enemy, but Kota knew her words were meant for him. "Demons do not truly suffer when you hurt them. One must possess a *soul* in order to know agony." She parried a slash meant to take her head off with the flat of her weapon, and sparks flew up in the air as metal scraped metal. She circled the creature, weapon raised as she continued to speak: "This *thing* has a mind, but it is a cruel, twisted machine, driven only to feed its base desires and remake the world in its own horrid image."

The demon tore the dagger from its shoulder and slashed wildly out with its sword. Gretis's blade snapped up and knocked away the blow. A second strike came and then a third. She stood her ground, beating away the lethal slashes as if they were of no more concern to her than a small child swinging a stick.

"If you allow such a monster to live," she said between parries, "it *will* commit murder. That is its nature." She dodged back suddenly from a lateral slash and then sprang forward again, stabbing through the demon's black armor into where Kota guessed its heart to be. The monster convulsed in pain, and Gretis yanked her sword back in a spray of dark blood. She wasted no time but cut again into the armor, this time slicing the creature's stomach open. As it fell forward, clutching at the enormous gash in its flesh, Gretis slipped behind, lithe and silent. Her blade moved too fast for Kota to perceive, and the horned head and the hulking body fell to the ground as two separate pieces, each leaking thick, syrupy blood that shined unnaturally in the moonlight.

The rage suddenly left Kota, and he became himself again. For a long moment, he stared at the bloody mess that had been a demon and at his human teacher, completely speechless. Then his eyes shifted to the knife on the ground a few paces away.

"No..." he whispered, his limbs beginning to tremble. Unlike the first time the beast had taken him over, he could remember everything, and he recalled reaching for the dagger and considering whether to cut Gretis's throat. "I... p-part of me was ready to kill you."

She stared at him for a moment, and then said in a remarkably calm voice for one who had just fought and killed a demon: "Yet you ultimately triumphed over the urge. I needed to see you do that."

Kota drew his hands from the soil and rose. He stared at the mess of blood and gore that had been the demon's body. "I am afraid," he said. "What is inside of me?"

"Something very ancient and very, *very* dangerous," Gretis said. "You have only touched upon the tiniest sliver of its power."

"Is... is it evil?" Kota whispered. He was shaking.

"No," Gretis said. She slid her weapon back into its scabbard and moved to him, and she placed her hands on his shoulders and whispered in a soft voice: "Is a wolf *evil* when it kills a deer? It has no concept of such things, but simply acts according to its primal instincts."

Kota swallowed, rolling these words in his mind. "Tell me what it is. Please."

Gretis drew in a slow breath and then exhaled, seeming to consider her words. "Kota, because you are destined to face a burden greater than any I have ever borne, I believe I must reveal some small measure of the secrets of the Sansrit path to you. Then you can make a choice—a more *informed* choice than I have allowed you to make thus far."

Kota felt his heart flutter in his chest. Blinking at Gretis, he managed to utter in a dry voice: "Please tell me."

She nodded. "What lies within you is a creature far older than human beings, or even elves. It was once a beast of enormous power from a race whose sole purpose for existing was to hunt and kill the primal demons of this world." Gretis hesitated, staring into his eyes, and then whispered: "There are so many things I should like to tell you, but what you need to understand here and now is that *you* were chosen to be this creature's host, and for that I am sorry."

"What you mean?" he whispered.

Her voice became ashen, "Something...*terrible* is coming to this world, Kota. It may even be here already. Whatever that evil is, it is powerful enough to draw the force inside you back into this world. There may be more like you—I do not know—but *you,* Kota... the creature burning inside you is known to the followers of the Sansrit path. Only one mortal in history has ever been able to contain it."

Kota stared at his teacher. This moment felt like a dream to him. His imagination was flashing in many directions, trying to visualize and make sense of the vague words. One thought bubbled above the others and escaped his lips in a troubled voice: "What if I no can *contain* it?"

Gretis hesitated, then said: "I believe you were chosen because you *can,* Kota. The creature has been with you since you were born. It is *not* your enemy. It is a profound part of the person you are and shall be until you die." She gave him a smile that seemed filled with both affection and pain. "I am willing to dedicate the rest of my life to helping you, my dear boy. But I will not lie to you. If you *cannot* control the beast, it will take you over. You will become far too dangerous to be allowed to live." Her eyes lifted and met his. "I will be forced to kill you...*or die trying.*"

Kota and Gretis stared at one another, and neither of them spoke for a long time. Kota sat perched upon the soil trying to weigh all that Gretis had said to him, and she knelt in front of him, waiting patiently for him to speak. Finally, he gazed into her eyes and said: "Why this creature here? What is the evil you just talk about?"

"I know very little of it," Gretis said, and he detected a note of fear in her voice. "I think about it all the time, trying to assign specific meaning to a prophecy spoken in vague terms more than two thousand years ago. I believe though—" she drew in a frustrated breath, "it is not my role to understand. My purpose is only to help you reach your potential." Her voice hardened, "But I will not do that—gods themselves be damned—unless it is what you choose!"

Kota gazed down and thought upon these words for a long time. Again, Gretis waited patiently until he spoke: "I can help the people of this world against...whatever this danger is, if I strong enough?"

"Yes," Gretis whispered.

"And you think I is—*am* strong enough?"

Gretis smiled at him, and a tear rolled from her right eye. "If only you could see yourself as I see you, *dear young warrior*. Yes, I believe if anyone I have *ever* known could wield all of that savage power and never harm an innocent soul, it would be you."

The faith in Gretis's eyes made Kota's heart swell. "I will not fail you," he whispered. The words came from the deepest depths of his soul.

"Then you choose to move forward... *with me*."

"I do," he said in a grim voice.

"Gods save us both," Gretis exhaled. She reached under her vest and drew out a small glass phial which held a milky white liquid inside. Delicately, she drew the thumb-sized cork away and Kota's nostrils immediately detected a stinging scent of something like a mixture of mushrooms, garlic, and incredibly concentrated alcohol. "Someday, I shall teach you how to draw out the hidden essence of the living things of this world in ways not even the starborn can accomplish. For this night though, I simply need you to drink this."

"What is it?"

"You must trust me."

Kota hesitated only for an instant, then said: "I do trust you." He took the tiny bottle from her and drank the fluid in one draught. It burned his throat, but almost immediately after swallowing, he felt a profoundly warm sensation overtake his senses. Suddenly, Kota's mind and body were lost to an indefinable happiness, and he slumped forward, letting out a laugh.

"Kota," he heard a voice say. He looked up and saw his teacher, Lady Gretis. "I need you to forget all of what just happened—between you and I and the demon, and all we said after that—everything that happened after you separated from those hunters."

"*Forget,*" Kota repeated, blinking very slowly. He thought of the last few moments, with the demon and his teacher. He held a mental image in his mind and then willed that image to fade into nothingness. All the words and feelings slipped away into some distance recess where they would be burned from his memory forever. He gazed up at the stars after that, feeling a strange but pleasant haze. He could not quite recall where he was, or how he had gotten there.

"Kota!" he heard a voice shout, and fingers snapped in front of his face, making him jump.

"What?" he said, looking up at Lady Gretis. He shook his head, feeling confused. "What happened?"

"You went to sleep on the forest floor," his teacher said.

"I did?" he grunted. He looked at his arms and legs and saw bits of leaves and smears of dirt on his arms and legs. "Oh, I very sorry."

"It is all right, young warrior. Tell me, did you find your people?"

Kota's mind was groggy from the nap he could not quite remember taking, but as he searched back through his most recent memories, he saw himself speaking to a group of shamalak. "Yes," he murmured. "I find my people. They will bring word to my mother and father."

"Good," she said, smiling at him. "I suppose that matter is finally settled then. Shall we return then?"

"I... yes," Kota said. There was something it seemed he was forgetting, but every time he tried to grasp for it, it slipped through his fingers like dry sand. He supposed it must have been some element of his dream. "I am ready."

"Good," Gretis said. She turned and began to walk. Kota stared at her. Was she moving like an injured creature? No, of course not! What could possibly harm her?

CHAPTER 22: THE POWER OF A STARBORN

Before us, no generation of starborn had ascended to their abilities before the age of twenty-five. We were all eleven years old when we felt magic and psychic awareness so intense that they called us living miracles. Many have posed theories as to why we ascended so much younger than any before us, but there was no great celestial event, nor divine intervention. It was Cassian who was responsible. His anger and his despair shattered the barrier between our young, immature minds and what we were. We did not know it then, but it was a sign of things to come.

—Keska Ethedrine,
Starborn of the 19th Generation

Sweat dripped down Arkas's face as he crouched in the shadows between two peasant hovels. He was suppressing his power and holding back the psychic emanations of his mind. Asango was fewer than a hundred paces away, dismounting his horse. It was terrifying to be this close to the mad heretic, and yet there was also an underlying thrill.

It was late in the afternoon. Most of Asango's peasants were moving about their business, unaware that the son of the emperor was disguised in a tattered cloak in their midst. More than a few of them had gathered around the woman Arkas had subtly brought to harm. Maris was her name, a widow of middling age who worked in the local butcher's shop to feed her children. Arkas could feel her continued horror as blood leaked out from where he had caused her cleaver to come down on her fingers. She would be dead in a few moments without Cassian's help, leaving her two children orphans.

<Stay calm,> he heard Cromlic's psychic voice in his mind. <If he detects you, we are not yet close enough to attack. Be ready to defend yourself.>

Arkas dug his fingers into his palms. He dared not answer the bishop. A single stray thought could lead to a fight to the death with the person the Norn had revealed was destined to kill him. If all went according to plan over the next few minutes though, the threat of Cassian Asango would be no more.

They had lain an excellent trap. As Arkas had told Cromlic, Cassian could not resist helping a dying mother. That was his absurd weakness. Asango had faced the fire of Promethiock himself, yet the soft place in his heart after the death of his own mother had made him rush out without taking any precautions, just to save the life of a filthy peasant. He had to know that the Nemesai could make an attempt on his life at any time for his unbelievably brazen declarations.

Arkas watched as Cassian ran in through the shop doors to the woman. The heretic's mind was a psychic fortress, and yet Arkas sensed shadows of fear in his brother starborn...*for a lowly peasant*! That was excellent. Cassian was distracted, as Arkas had hoped he would be—too distracted to sense the two hundred Nemesai soldiers encroaching into his village on all sides.

Asango rush to the dying woman, power already burning forth from his hands before he gripped her arm. Arkas's senses picked up the action in flashes. Cassian inspected the thumb and fingers that had been sliced away and then carefully pressed the first of them back into its bloody stump. "I promise you, you will be fine," his voice rang out through the window.

Nemesai soldiers were moving in on all sides of the town, and they began throwing off the brown cloaks they had used for disguise. It had been an extremely slow and tedious process moving scores of tattooed soldiers through the countryside at different routes, carefully avoiding Cassian's *many* spies. The bishop had made this bold and arguably illegal move faster than Arkas had suspected, but it was in response to critical new information: Asango had managed to acquire a pure-blooded dragon! No one knew how quickly dragons grew and matured, but the threat existed that one day the creature could become as dangerous as its master. The heretic could not be allowed to gain such power.

Arkas sensed the subtle swell of magical energy as his brother slowed the peasant woman's heartbeat, limiting the flow of blood through her many exposed arteries as he began to apply his healing spells. *Cassian was a genius,* Arkas was forced to admit as he felt the elegant application of magic. It was remarkable to perceive—a level of precision with infinitesimal energies that began to reattach necrotic tissue to living flesh and repair damage that Arkas knew he could never replicate.

After a few tense moments, the inner wave of Cromlic's force moved close enough that Arkas sensed a ripple of tension from Cassian's mind. At that moment, feeling his victory at hand, he could not resist a telepathic taunt:

Asango went absolutely still for several seconds, and then, to Arkas's shock, his attention returned to the injured woman, and he renewed his healing spells. As this occurred, a telepathic response came thundering back from Cassian's mind: <You injured one of my subjects, little prince. There will be retribution.>

<Retribution?> Arkas transmitted with a telepathic snarl. <Poor fool. You are beaten.>

<We shall see,> Cassian responded as he sealed a collection of arteries within the stump of the woman's

forefinger, which would save her life, but likely meant that her fingers could never be reattached. Then Cassian's voice moved from the psychic plain to that of the physical, and his voice came from every direction at once through an awesome display of sorcery Arkas could not decipher: "MY PEOPLE, THE NEMESAI HAVE COME TO ARREST ME. I NEED YOU TO FLEE THE STREETS SO THAT I MAY DO BATTLE WITH THEM UNENCUMBERED."

Arkas felt a delicious wave of hysteria erupt from all around him. People immediately began to dash about in a wild frenzy. Many tried to run for the street ways leading out of the town, but their paths were blocked by walls of armed Nemesai soldiers.

<I am sorry, but I am afraid this entire village will face inquiry after you are apprehended,> Cromlic's telepathic voice interjected. <Your ungodly influence must be fully expunged from this world.>

Scores of tattooed soldiers marched into the town square. They organized quickly, blocking all possible routes of escape. The cowering peasants retreated to the homes and shops about, huddling together in fear. Cromlic had assembled the force well. There were twenty-eight men with heavy crossbows, one hundred and sixty-five men with blades and shields, and twelve of the most skilled sorcerers in the order. By contrast, Cassian did not have a single soldier at his disposal. Arkas smiled. *Everything had gone perfectly.*

The Bishop moved to the center of the street, flanked by his sorcerers, and he glared at the shop in which Cassian was still hunched over the injured woman. "There is no escape, Asango! If you try to fight or run, you will be cut down in seconds. Surrender. I place you under arrest in the name of the gods!"

"YOU DO NOT HAVE THE AUTHORITY TO ARREST ME!" Cassian's voice answered immediately, thundering through the air with unbelievable volume. Some of the soldiers glanced stupidly about, unable to comprehend how the words seemed to come from every direction. "I am a point of the star. My conduct may only be judged by a conclave of all five bishops. Your actions here are illegal, and *you know it.*"

Cromlic gritted his teeth and shouted: "When you refused a holy prophecy from our beloved Norn, you stood in direct defiance of the Gods! You have forfeited all the holy protections of your birthright!"

"Your childish logic is no more impressive here than it would be before the other heads of the church," Cassian snapped. "You have grown far too drunk with power, Cromlic, and you have now stepped fully outside the very laws you claim to uphold. I offer a single warning to you and every man here: any violence against me or my people *will be answered.*"

Arkas felt the Nemesai around him quake in apprehension, and his own anxiety rose. *No! Cassian would not manipulate his way out of death!* Arkas ran to Cromlic and snapped: "He is trying to convince everyone here he has the upper hand. It's a delay tactic. He's telepathically marshaling his forces back at his castle. We cannot give him time to do that." Arkas glanced around at the cowering people. "His weakness is his need to protect these idiot peasants. Use it!"

Cromlic said nothing to this, but the muscles around his eyes twitched, and then he drew in a breath and shouted: "My men will NOT be cowed be the desperate threats of a cornered heretic! You face the Nemesai Order, *boy!* You will surrender now, or we will consider you and *every one* of your subjects an enemy of the holy church, and we will summarily put the lot of them to death while you HIDE!" The bishop clenched his jaw, seething. "I will spare these people only if you surrender now!"

Arkas sensed a flicker of something resembling frustration from his brother. Magic began to swirl around Cassian in a furious torrent.

H-he's going to fight," Arkas panted.

To his surprise though, Cassian appeared in the doorway of the butcher shop, arms lowered. With cold eyes, he gazed around at the Nemesai force, his stare lingering briefly on Arkas, and then he locked eyes with Cromlic and began to walk forward. Arkas gaped in shock. He had expected to provoke his mad brother into foolhardy action, *but outright surrender?* The swell of magic was gone, Cassian having evidently willed it away. *Was he really going to give himself over to torture and death to save a group of filthy peasants?*

Almost trembling with excitement, Cromlic made a series of directive gestures to his men, and scores of Nemesai soldiers stepped cautiously in around Asango, their blades out, leaving him a narrow path to their bishop. Not one of them moved to grab Cassian though. *Even now, they were afraid of him.* A few of the archers had taken the initiative of climbing up upon the sturdier rooftops in the small village where they now knelt, slowly sweeping their aim in time with the heretic starborn as he walked.

<Have your most dangerous spell at the ready, but do not cast it unless I give the order,> Cromlic telepathically whispered to Arkas, and very likely the other sorcerers around him.

"Deth Eskathian Hess," Arkas hissed. Each of the three words pulled a spectral entity from the ether. They formed at the gloved palm of his right hand, congealing together into a cloudy mass of deep blue that began to swirl. "Deth" was an entity of wind and motion, while "Eskathian" was gas and flame. "Hess" was supposedly a spectral of hell. The instant he called its name, it enveloped and overwhelmed the other two, absorbing their essence and transmuting all three forces into a black storm of death and destruction. The spell *wanted* to kill Cassian. Indeed, it subtly shifted and expanded with the pulsing of Arkas's hatred.

"Lord Asango," Cromlic said, his voice a strange mixture of nerves and cruel delight. "Your surrender comes far more easily than I ever would have imagined." The bishop straightened his aging body and raised his voice so that it would carry quite far: "It is a shame that *fear* must be used to bring prideful sinners back into the grace of the gods. Tell me, starborn of the nineteenth generation, do you have anything to say for your audacious blasphemy before this holy army begins its inquisition?"

"No," said Cassian in an equally loud voice, staring into the bishop's eyes. "I believe I have made myself extremely clear already."

Cromlic bared yellowed teeth at these words, and Arkas sensed fury rise up in the man. "Are you looking for a quick death, boy? You will not provoke me into that. I am—"

"You are a depraved, miserable craven who hates his fellow man," Cassian said in a sharp voice that stupefied the bishop. He gazed around, daring to meet the eyes of his killers. "So are many of you—sniveling little children. I can see the moments in your past. You were bullied by others—beaten by your fathers—rejected and despised by people from whom you wanted *love*! You felt weak, and now you think that making others feel as weak makes you *MEN*, but you are nothing but *deplorable COWARDS!* " As he said these words, *no one attacked*. Arkas could feel it—a tiny miracle of sorts that would only last a few precious seconds—Cassian had shocked these men into silence.

Cromlic broke the quiet: "Enough, *sinner*!" He raised his right hand and reached deep into the ether, whispering names that Arkas did not know. Dozens of immensely powerful spectrals answered his call, manifesting and combining together. The resulting spell was like nothing Arkas had ever seen. Within a fiercely glowing mass of translucent blue haze, thousands upon thousands of tiny particles began to explode against one another continuously, releasing focused bursts of heat that Arkas perceived to be several hundred times hotter than a roaring fire. Nervously, he edged back, letting the construct of magic in his own hand dissipate as he realized what the bishop had summoned. It was the *Vekthross Zall*, one of the thirteen legendary spells of destruction said to have been invented by the first starborn.

Such were forbidden spellcraft, withheld from the world of sorcery because their terrible energies were too difficult to control. Many men had died trying to summon the power Cromlic held under his will. *Some of them had even been starborn...*

"Kneel, Boy, *or I will take a limb off!"* Cromlic snarled.

Arkas began to tremble with delight. No matter how much skill Cassian might possess, he could never throw up a defense in time to protect himself from such an awesome attack from so close.

For a moment, Cassian stared into Cromlic's eyes as the crackling construct bathed his face in blue light even under the glare of the sun. Then an almost drunken smile came over his face. "It takes every shred of mental strength you have to hold that spell together." His green eyes blazed with excitement. "Your walls are slipping apart, *Great Bishop!* I can see deep into your hideous mind!" Cassian began to laugh, and he gazed about at the army that surrounded him, shouting: "Did you know that this holy man, who has so aggressively punished homosexuals, has lain with—"

"ENOUGH!!" Cromlic screamed, and he hurled his spell directly into Cassian's chest. Arkas's heart flinched back as the near blinding eruption of magic struck. It ripped into Cassian, meeting no more resistance than if he were made of air, and then...Arkas gaped in incomprehension as the thundering spell came out through his brother's back, *leaving no mark at all!* Cassian stood unharmed—not even a singe in his clothing—as the deathly construct continued to sail through the air until it struck a Nemesai soldier in the shoulder who had been standing behind him. The man screamed as his left arm was incinerated off his body in an explosion of smoke and charred flesh. A half second later the spell collided with the next victim in its path, this time taking a soldier of the order in the center of the chest. It burned through his breastplate, flesh, and organs, and was through and on to its next victim before the poor bastard could even cry out. Arkas blinked, trying to register what was happening. By the time his mind wrapped itself around the only possible answer, Cromlic's spell had cut a path through more than *ten* Nemesai, all of whom had fallen to the ground either dying or dead.

"*H-he's an Illusion*!" Arkas screamed. He glared about, scanning the town for the real Cassian with both his eyes and his magic. *Was he still in the shop with the widow? No...no trace of him remained there!*

Cassian's image vanished suddenly and reappeared directly behind Cromlic, whose eyes had gone wide. "You could not see it," the phantom said in a sharp voice. "I scarcely believed my projection would make it more than ten steps before you realized. Do people truly believe you are on the level of a *starborn*?" The image vanished, and then a loud shriek tore through the air. All eyes turned to see an archer at the outer edge of the assembly of soldiers lift up off the ground. Arkas could sense invisible tendrils of magic around the man—*Cassian's power*. The hovering Nemesai let out several panicked screams as his body lifted higher and higher, and then he was suddenly hurled backward toward the wall of a small house. He slammed hard against it with one final cry and then bounced off to the ground where he ceased to move.

A second shriek came immediately from the opposite side of the army. Arkas turned his head in time to see another crossbow-wielding man sail into a wall and crash fully through it in a spray of wooden shrapnel. Swells of fear rose up in the minds of Nemesai all around at this seemingly invisible enemy.

"W-where is he?!" Cromlic shouted, glaring frantically about as Arkas had just done.

"I am *here*, you fool!" Cassian shouted.

Both Arkas and Cromlic whirled around to see Cassian standing in the middle of the street, his right arm raised, a brilliant yellow spell of some sort swirling above his palm.

"KILL HIM!" Cromlic screamed.

The bishop need not have given the order. Bolts and daggers were already flying. Many of them were clumsy, nervous shots, but two arrows struck Asango directly in the chest, and his eyes went wide with shock. *Only...they were not Cassian's eyes.* The illusion vanished and a Nemesai soldier stood in its place, gazing stupidly down at the arrow ends protruding from him. He fell forward, a crossbow dropping from his hands.

Almost immediately after, a snapping sound came from the right, and nearly everyone whirled in time to see the crossbow of an archer atop a house rip apart so violently that it knocked the man down through the thatched roof. Arkas blinked. *How was Cassian willing magic around so fast and in so many directions? Just how strong was he?*

Cromlic screamed: "He's using the damned elvin talisman from the reports! Don't rely on your eyes. Asango can probably disguise himself as anyone or anything! We have to find the focal point of his magic!"

Arkas shut his eyes and felt around for any kind of swell of power within the village, but his senses quickly encountered a vast field with no center and no discernible source. Somehow, Cassian was able to make himself an innocuous droplet of water within the interconnected rivers of magic he was conducting about. Arkas's father had said more than once that Cassian had the most exceptional mental command over raw magic of the new generation, *but this seemed impossible!*

"He could be anywhere!" Arkas whispered, opening his eyes and looking all around the village.

Another archer lifted up from amidst his comrades and flew backward, this one striking the side of a wagon hard enough to knock the thing on its side.

Asango is attacking archers! Arkas sensed the thought, though it did not come from his own mind. Dozens of men were reaching this conclusion at once. A soldier holding a crossbow in the street threw his weapon onto the ground hard enough to snap it and then raised his hands in a desperate gesture of surrender. Almost immediately, several more archers followed his example.

"WHAT?!" Cromlic screamed, glaring in disbelief. "DO not COWER! You are men of the CHURCH!"

Yet another rooftop soldier's crossbow exploded in a spray of splinters so furious that it sent him tumbling over the side of his perch. He let out a scream as he fell that was stopped abruptly when he hit the ground. A sense of panic began to set in among the troops, and at least ten more archers threw down their weapons.

"THE NEXT MAN WHO THROWS DOWN HIS WEAPON WILL FACE TORTURE!!" Cromlic shouted. His face had gone red, veins around his eyes standing up under his skin.

Arkas stared around at the fear on the tattooed faces all around him. Cassian's abilities were so much greater than Arkas had ever imagined them to be. *Were the others this strong?* Had his father's spell left the aura of magic within him mangled and weak? *What had the procedure done to his mind?*

Arkas shook his head suddenly. *No!* He had the same power Cassian did! He was a living miracle but was not enslaved to the weaknesses of sentiment like the others. His eyes scanned the battlefield with renewed focus, and they fell upon a small figure crouched and trembling inside of a broken, empty barrel in an alley. It was a boy who might have been five or six years old. The child was terrified, helpless. *He was perfect!*

Arkas dashed toward his new target. From behind, he heard Cromlic shout: "Don't run away, you little coward!" but he ignored the words. When he came within a few paces, he focused all of his Starborn power. The boy let out a cry as tendrils of magic ensnared his small body. Arkas yanked him from his hiding place and held him suspended in the air, squeezing hard enough so that the little rat could scarcely breathe.

<Asango!> he psychically shouted.<If you attack another Nemesai, I will crush this boy!?>

The random attacks throughout the village ceased instantly. Cromlic stared at Arkas with eyes that slowly filled with comprehension, and then a smile of approval flashed across his wizened features. Somehow, despite Arkas's hatred for the man, this made him swell with pride.

Cassian's image appeared very suddenly before Arkas, glaring. "Why are you doing this?" *it* said in a cold voice.

Arkas could not resist a smirk. "The only thing you need to understand is that if you don't surrender, this boy will only be the first to die."

"We both know I can shatter your life with a few sentences. Release the child, or I will reveal what you really are to all the hundreds here."

Arkas tightened the tendrils of magic around the boy, and the projection of Cassian's face clenched its jaw. This filled Arkas with a surge of confidence, and he could not help chuckling. "Threaten me again, brother, and I snap this little peasant's neck with a thought. *You know I will.*"

"Excellent work, Arkas!" Cromlic said, walking up from behind. He moved into the view of Cassian's image, an excited smile on his face. Gazing at it, he said: "Do these people to whom you have spread your blasphemy matter so much to you?" The bishop let out a chuckle. "Yes, I suppose they must be the only *family* you have left."

Something dangerous flashed in Cassian's eyes, and the currents of magic flowing all around the village grew suddenly more intense and electrified. Cromlic turned to Arkas and said: "You may kill the corrupted child if you like." He gestured around to the peasant homes and said: "We have an abundance of sinners to take hostage." The bishop's eyes shifted to Cassian's image again, and he said: "I still have well over a hundred armed soldiers. How much more power do you think you can throw around? Are you growing tired yet? How far will you go to protect these sinners?" He turned to the handful of sorcerers still standing at the center of the army.

"Kill the woman Asango was healing!" he shouted.

The eyes of Cassian's phantom went wide, and then it vanished. Arkas turned and watched in anticipation as Cromlic's twelve sorcerers moved toward the house. Several dozen armed men flanked them.

<Tear away the wall!> Cromlic commanded through the psychic plain. <I want him to *see her*. Do not kill the wretch until I give the order>.

The twelve men took action. Working in unison, they began to will raw telekinetic magic into the front wall of the building. Their power ripped it away in great chunks, sending them crashing into the adjacent structures. The thatched ceiling of the shop began to collapse in, but sorcerers whisked it away in a spray of straw and wood. Perhaps intoxicated by the destruction they were wreaking, they tore apart the sidewalls, and then the furniture. The poor woman had taken refuge behind a small counter, which the men ripped away. She was on her knees shrieking in terror, her face so pale it was almost green. Whether that was purely from fear or some combination therein with the blood loss Arkas had caused her was difficult to determine, but whatever the case, the pathetic wretch seemed to lack the ability to run or even stand.

<Use *Enthreka,* all of you at once,> Cromlic's telepathic voice hissed.

Still holding the boy with his magic, Arkas watched the twelve men begin spell-casting. *Enthreka* was a magical construct that mimicked lightning in a storm. Searing electrical energy crackled around and between the sorcerers, their conjurations connecting with one another, combining and multiplying each other's power. This was why Cromlic had chosen this particular spell. *If Cassian wanted to save the woman, he would have to stop all that destructive force at once.*

Arkas watched eagerly and detected a sudden shift in the energy in front of the Nemesai sorcerers. He saw something like a moving blur—nearly invisible but not quite—*something in the shape of a running figure.* The blur moved between the Nemesai and the woman an instant before their spell was unleashed, and then there was a near-blinding flash of light.

"GYAAHHHHHH!" Cassian screamed as the full brunt of twelve arcane lightning spells struck him at once. He took it all—enough kill a pack of ogres. Arkas grinned, his mind beginning to spin with elation. He watched the electrical energy rip through his brother's body, yet he blinked once the maelstrom ended. *Somehow, Cassian was still standing!*

The heretic was panting. Sections of his clothing had been burned away. Thin trails of smoke lifted off scorched patches of his skin and even from his hair. The detail that stood out past the others though, was the golden amulet that hung from his neck. It was emitting tiny golden sparks, and Cassian was staring down at it, eyes gaping. The flashes continued for a second or two and then died away, and a little puff of black smoke burst out of the thing.

"That was your elvin trinket, wasn't it?" Cromlic cried, a half-mad grin on his face. "No more illusions, boy." Then he telepathically commanded:

The Nemesai sorcerers began to gather magic and shout arcane names. For half an instant, Cassian stared at them, and then his hands suddenly rose. A massive spray of dirt shot up through the street stones all around. Within the blink of an eye, Cassian and his twelve opponents were enveloped in a cloud of dust so thick that not even their outlines could be seen. Within this chaos, a battle commenced.

Sounds like thunder crackled through the air, and within the haze of dirt, Arkas saw flashes of white and yellow and green. It was impossible at first to discern how the fight was going within that chaos, but then the screams began. These lasted only a few brief seconds, and then, along with the flaring of spells, they came to an end. For several heartbeats, Arkas stared into the cloud, not understanding what had happened, and then he noticed that the dust was not dissipating into the wind as it should. *Cassian was still in control!*

His brother's voice boomed suddenly from all corners of the city: "YOU THINK YOU CAN COME INTO MY VILLAGE AND THREATEN MY PEOPLE?!"

The closest Nemesai swordsman to the cloud cried out as his legs were yanked out from under him. "NO!" he shrieked, "NO! GODS!" His flailing body was pulled into the murky brown swell and all sound from him disappeared.

Arkas felt raw terror pulse through every remaining soldier in the village. There was a strange, morbid fascination in seeing more than a few men take nervous steps away from the cloud. Arkas knew, as Cromlic surely knew, that Cassian was nearing the end of his strength. The power that burned within that sustained haze of dust was a pathetic wheeze compared to the inferno displayed at the beginning of the battle. If only a quarter of the Nemesai rushed Cassian now, they could likely cut him down before he could kill a single one of them, *but they did not know that.* His theatrics had terrified them. Some of the men on the outer edges of the force were actually slipping timidly away from their comrades.

<You were *marvelous,* brother,> Arkas whispered through the psychic plane, <but we both know you are finally out of power.>

<Why not come and finish me off then?> Cassian snarled back. <If you managed to kill me, people might actually take you seriously. Come! I dare you!>

Asango will challenge you to a duel. You will lose. The words played again in Arkas's mind, and he felt a shameful swell of cowardice in the pit of his stomach. Even now, with the battle all but won, he was afraid of Cassian. How he hated his brother for that!

"THE TIME HAS COME FOR THE HERETIC TO DIE!" Cromlic screamed. He stood a few dozen paces from Cassian's dust cloud, glaring with a crazed, predatory look.

Arkas felt himself relax. The bishop would kill Cassian now, and this would all be over. He shifted his gaze to the child he still held within the grip of his magic. The filthy urchin was rasping, his young face pale and full of dread. <Cassian,> Arkas transmitted, <as a parting gift to you, I am going to tear this boy's body apart. I want his screams to be the last thing you hear before you die.>

Arkas focused his energy. Only a dozen paces away, Cromlic was organizing his troops for the kill. The moment was surreal and perfect. Arkas smirked at his young victim, knowing that Cassian was watching as he said: "Goodbye, you disgusting little—" he paused as he noticed a shadow appear on the ground between himself and the child. It was a very peculiar silhouette. At first, he thought it was that of a large bird, but the wings were far too...*bat-like.* The shadow quickly grew darker and sharper, and Arkas's Starborn senses suddenly detected something of incredible primal power moving toward him.

Without thinking, he released the boy and whirled to hold up his hand and form a protective barrier. His eyes fixed upon a blurred gray shape perhaps the size of a wolf with two blazing yellow eyes. It opened a ghastly mouth of fangs and let out an ear-splitting shriek. Arkas knew suddenly what it was, and pure terror ripped through him so completely that his concentration snapped. His magic faltered only for an instant, but that was all it took. *Cassian's Dragon* bit into his outstretched hand. He felt its teeth tear through sinew and bone, and then there was a sharp yank of its scaly neck. Arkas screamed louder than he ever had before as the dragon flapped free from him, taking a third of his hand with it as it returned to the air.

He collapsed to the ground and rolled about wildly, hugging what remained of his right hand to his chest. Blood was spurting from places where fingers had been. The pain was unbelievable. *Gods, no!*

He might have rolled on the ground whimpering for a long time, but when heard the dragon's terrible roar, fear made him blink through tears and look up. Cassian's pet was darting about through the air. Its silver reptilian wings—seemingly too small to carry the weight of its muscular body—somehow enabled it to make incredibly sharp and abrupt shifts in its direction. One of the few men who still retained a crossbow took aim at it and fired from the street, but the dragon dodged up and to the left almost the instant the weapon fired. It darted far and away, yet half a heartbeat later it came shrieking back through the air. The soldier managed the beginnings of a cry before a ball of white fire the size of a melon shot from the dragon's maw and struck him in the chest. The poor man was sent skidding backward over dirt as smoke hissed out of a newly formed crater in his torso.

Arkas suddenly realized why Cassian had been eliminating the archers. The epiphany came as he watched the wretched serpent descend upon the last man wielding a crossbow on the battlefield. It dropped to a perch on his shoulders, digging the claws of its hind legs into his flesh as it bit down on his throat and wrenched out a bloody chunk. Arkas reeled in frustration. Nothing on the battlefield could attack the damned dragon now except Cromlic and himself. *Clever Cassian!*

Arkas shut his eyes and whispered the incantation of the most potent healing spell he knew. He felt spectrals manifest and rise around his mangled tissue. Slowly, through processes too minute and precise for him to understand, they decreased the flow of his blood and caused the torn skin to fold in and knit around the gaping wound the dragon had left. The pain receded slowly. When it was finally manageable, Arkas dared to lift his hand so he could see it, and when he let out a shriek of horror. There was nothing left save his thumb and its two closest fingers. All else had been torn away by the beast's teeth, and he could *never* get it back!

The Prince might have sobbed if he were not in the midst of battle. Instead, his feverish vigor twisted toward vengeance. Still lightheaded from blood loss, he forced himself to rise and run through the panicking soldiers to Cromlic. He found the bishop glaring back and forth between the cloud around Cassian and the dragon, seemingly unsure where to hurl his magic. Cromlic seemed to have reached the obvious conclusion that if he focused entirely on one, the other would attack him.

"You have to kill Asango before he regains any of his strength," Arkas hissed through gritted teeth. "I'll keep the lizard off your back!"

Cromlic gave a fierce nod and turned his attention back to Cassian. The instant he did though, the dragon dropped from the sky, diving down into the cloud of dust to its master. The brown haze began to dissipate then, and within a few seconds, Cassian and his pet could be seen at the center, standing side by side.

"All right, Your Holiness," Cassian's voice boomed from all around as he glared directly at the bishop, "Show me the might of the Nemesai Order! Come and take me, if you have the courage!"

Cromlic hesitated. He could perhaps feel the raw fear in his men as Arkas could. It seemed that less than half of them remained. This was logically more than enough to rush the weakened starborn even with the addition of the dragon, yet the Nemesai soldiers were not moving forward. It was glaringly apparent at that moment that Cromlic's men, for all their enhanced strength and speed, were *not* soldiers. Face to face with dangerous opponents, their fervor for divine justice did not seem to be enough to drive them forward.

"FIRE!" a deep voice cried from behind.

Arkas sensed a flurry of motion behind him, and he turned in time to see dozens of arrows hit the ground just behind the feet of the outer row of Nemesai soldiers. Shocked, he lifted his gaze and saw archers all along the eastern side of the village—*not Nemesai men, but soldiers wearing Cassian's colors!* Several clusters of men with bow and arrow stood in tight formations between fully armored soldiers with blade and shield, but there were also men with crossbows planted on top of houses and aiming out of open windows. Arkas reeled in disbelief at what he was seeing. Cassian's soldiers had not merely rushed in. They were positioned in tight, military formation, and they had surrounded the Nemesai and were poised to fill the holy men with arrows from any side.

An old man stood at the eastern edge of the town square issuing commands. He was wearing the gleaming silver armor and flowing red cape of an imperial general. Arkas stared in disbelief at the man. Whoever it was, he had managed to file these soldiers into the village and station them in near silence while Asango and the dragon kept everyone's eyes pointed away. Arkas turned back to Cassian. There was just the vaguest trace of a smirk on the son of a bitch's face.

"SOMAR DOJINKO!" Cromlic shouted, glaring at the old man. "YOU DARE TO ACT AGAINST THE NEMESAI? YOU WILL STAND DOWN IMME—"

"He is acting under my orders," Cassian's voice thundered from every direction in magic-amplified resonance, easily drowning out the bishop's voice. "As I have already pointed out, this attempt to arrest me is a violation of theocratic law. I was quite clear that I would defend myself." Cassian shifted his gaze away from Cromlic and swept the invading force with his eyes as he said: "Nemesai force, you are defeated. Throw down your weapons, or my men will kill you."

The entire holy army stood in tense hesitation. Arkas saw wide eyes and pale faces gazing about. Their minds were overcome with confusion and disbelief. The Nemesai army had never before faced an enemy that could actually defeat them. This deathly silence went on for several tense heartbeats, and then at least ten men dropped weapons to the ground.

"Don't listen to him!" Cromlic screamed. He glared at the silver armored man. "None of his soldiers will *Dare* attack men of the church!" He whirled on Cassian and cried: "The heretic is out of strength! The time has come to rid this world of his corruption!" Cromlic summoned his magic then.

Arkas stepped back as the bishop conjured the Vekthross Zall spell once more. The blue cloud of destructive power rippled into existence, larger than before. Cromlic had thrown every shred of magic he had left into it. Arkas's heart began to pump very fast. *Could the bishop really do it?*

"Stop, Cromlic!" a deep-throated cry came from behind. The words had come from Cassian's commander, Dojinko. The wizened man had a dozen archers aiming at the Bishop. "If you attack Cassian—" His threat abruptly cut off mid-sentence, his eyes fixing on something.

Arkas turned and saw Cassian holding his right hand up, seeming to motion for his commander to stop. The heretic's eyes were locked on Cromlic though, and they shined with hatred. "If you believe you can kill me, Your Holiness, then do so." He lowered his hands, seeming not to attempt a counter-spell—no protective barrier of any kind.

Cromlic glared back at the young man, red-faced, and then he screamed: "AS YOU WISH, INFIDEL!" He hurled his attack. As the blue cloud flew across the twenty paces between them, Cassian remained perfectly still, and yet...*the spell began to slow.* Arkas watched in confusion as it drew to a hissing stop in the air.

Cassian's eyes were fixed upon the deadly construct, a look of furious concentration on his face. The translucent mass shook violently in the air, crackling and sparking, and Arkas saw bits of blood drip from Cassian's nose, from his eyes, and even his ears. *Was this even possible?!*

Arkas's felt his heart drop into his stomach as the Vekthross Zall ceased its gyrations, and began to glide away from Asango, back in the direction of the Bishop. Cassian was using the Bishop's own magic against him! The degree of will and focus to achieve something like that—on a sorcerer as powerful and experienced as Cromlic no less—*No one in the world had that kind of mental strength!*

"WHAT?!" The Bishop screamed, and he waved his hand at his conjuration. The hissing mass gave no reaction. *It belonged to Cassian now.*

Asango began to walk toward Cromlic, blood still dripping down his face. The Vekthross Zall moved with him. *It was growing!*

The bishop's face filled with horror. Arkas could sense that there was nigh a shred of power left within the old man. He began to tremble as the blue cloud floated toward him, and then to step backward with creaking legs.

"I believe I told you men to throw down your weapons," Cassian's voice hissed from every direction as he glanced around at the remaining Nemesai. "Do as I command! NOW!" Every tattooed soldier still holding a sword threw it down. Cassian turned his attention back to their leader. "Whatever shall we do now, *Bishop Cromlic*?" he said, drawing closer. There was murder in his voice. "Do you wish to run away now, Holy Man?" Cassian's dragon lunged a little ahead of him and snarled up at the nearest Nemesai men, who cringed away.

"Y-you wouldn't *d-dare kill me!"* The Bishop screamed just before he stumbled back onto the ground.

"Once again your thoughts are leaking out, Cromlic," Cassian's magically augmented voice tore through the air. "I sense *tremendous* fear! Should a bishop of the church not face death with more composure?"

The cloud of destruction floated up to Cromlic and reshaped itself smoothly into a dome around him—one that allowed no means of escape.

Now truly panicked, the bishop shrieked: "S-stop this! You cannot—" the dome tightened abruptly, shifting into a form-fitting, almost coffin-like field of glowing death around him. Its edges bit into the soil and paver stones, searing chunks of rock into burning orange chunks of shrapnel that struck Cromlic in the face and all over his body. He let out a terrified scream: "NO! PLEASE! DO NOT DO THIS!"

"If I let you go, you will come after my servants," Cassian whispered.

"NO!" the bishop shouted. "I pardon them! I swear it!"

"Swear by your god that neither you nor any of your men will ever return to my territory!"

"I swear it by the name of Balthar!" Cromlic screamed, "the Nemesai will never return to your lands!"

"I will not ask you to pardon me, for such a request would indirectly validate that you have any authority over me at all," Cassian said in a subdued voice, "but I thank you for your oath." He made a flicking gesture with his right hand, and the spell vanished into vapor. Cromlic stared up with gaping eyes.

"You seem confused," Cassian said in an icy voice. "I shall not kill you this day." He leaned into the bishop's face and whispered: "You have no idea how badly I wish to do so, you disgusting cancer of a man, but that is not the correct move at this moment. It serves my ends far better to do nothing and let your utterly staggering failure this day speak for itself."

Cassian's words left the bishop speechless. Arkas was bewildered as well, and yet in the back of his mind, comprehension slowly began to dawn. The heretic was correct that this failure would speak for itself. Cromlic had overstepped the bounds of his authority to attempt to arrest a living miracle, but that fact might have ultimately been swept aside by the complicated politics of religion, *if had he succeeded.* In overreaching his authority *and* failing though, the Bishop had made himself a spectacle of foolishness before the whole empire. The people would speak of this for decades—perhaps even centuries.

Cassian was probably handling the situation in the best possible way, politically speaking. If he were to imprison or kill a bishop of the church, he might bring about the wrath of every pious soul in the empire—even from those who might otherwise side against the Nemesai. Defeating Cromlic and then letting him go made Cassian clearly both more capable than Cromlic and far more magnanimous. It was an incredibly cold and calculating move—one that required Asango to let the man who ordered his parents' execution walk free.

After a long moment of stupefied silence, Cromlic jerked to his feet. He was shaking with rage as he snarled: "You—you stand there so disgustingly proud! You have *murdered* holy men, Asango, and you will be excommunicated and hunted down by the Nemesai, the Onkai, and the Emperor himself!"

Cassian stared at the bishop, the hatred within him under tight control as he said in a calm voice: "I have not killed a single person in this entire battle." He gestured back to the sorcerers who still lay on the ground. "I have *severely and irreparably injured* quite a few, but no one is dead by my hand." Cassian reached down and stroked under his dragon's neck. "Titus here did, in fact, kill two of your men, but I am afraid dragons do not fall under the purview of your theocratic authority. And anyhow, I should think that his actions are the least of your concern. After all, Your Holiness, you killed seven of your own men in an act of extraordinary idiocy." Cromlic glared up and took seething breaths through his yellow, crooked teeth. Cassian sighed and added: "I must thank you though for teaching me the Vekthross Zall. Your order has held the secret of that spell for what, three hundred years?"

"And you, *Prince Arkas,*" Cassian said, turning his head and meeting Arkas's eyes. "You caused one of my people to lose two of her fingers." Asango cast a brief look at Arkas's own mangled hand, and, just for an instant, a grin touched his face. "I would like you to compensate her for that injury. I believe your fine horse, the ruby ring on your left hand, the gold chain around your neck, and your royal oath in front of all these men to send her an additional fifty-thousand desseks will do."

Arkas's mouth opened. That was more than his yearly royal stipend. "F-for a *peasant*! Are you—"

"You will do this, my prince, or you and I shall fight to the death right here," Cassian said, and from the look in his eyes, it was clear he meant it.

Arkas felt the blood leave his face. Undoubtedly Asango was out of power now, and yet Arkas's hands began to tremble, and he rasped almost without thinking: "I... I would, of c-course, be happy to make amends."

"Good," Cassian said. "Leave the trinkets I mentioned with my men." He stared at him a moment longer, and then he turned away and walked in the direction of his soldiers, his dragon scraping along the ground next to him. Without looking back, he said: "That will be all, gentlemen. Be out of my town within half an hour. None of you have my permission to pick up your weapons."

"ASANGO!" Bishop Cromlic snarled, finally finding his voice again. His face had gone several shades darker, and the veins around his eyes were standing up. Arkas could sense that something like madness had overtaken the man's mind. "You are a hideous stain upon the legacy of the starborn, and I am certain that is because you are a bastard, *whore* that your mother was!"

Cassian froze mid-stride, and several of the paver stones around his feet cracked as if struck by pickaxes. All those around Cassian—*even his dragon*—edged away from him.

A furious grin came across Cromlic's face. "The slut confessed to every manner of adultery behind your supposed father's back before I cut her throat!" The bishop's shivering cowardice was gone. The shame—the disgrace of what Cassian had managed to do to him seemed to have pushed him past all sense of self-preservation.

The heretic turned slowly around, and Arkas took a nervous step away from the bishop. Magic was beginning to pulse from Cassian once more, regenerating at a rate Arkas would have thought impossible. The muscles around his eyes twitching, he hissed: "Cease your lies, holy man, or *I will silence you.*"

The bishop's smile only grew as he went on: "She offered herself to me before the end, but then she did the same to every man in the building."

Cromlic intended to die! Arkas watched in disbelief as the bishop drew back his hand and began to chant. His magic had not returned to the degree Cassian's had, but a fist-sized orb of green energy still started to form in right palm.

"No," Cassian whispered, and he made a quick, sweeping gesture. His magic moved through the air like a blade, slicing through the bishop's spell, which vanished into a puff of emerald mist. Cromlic gazed at his hand, a stupefied expression on his face. His glare returned to Asango though as the starborn stepped in front of him.

Yes! Arkas's thought as he backed away from the duel. *Kill him, you stupid bastard!* If Cassian were to murder the bishop now, all his accomplishments would be undone. He would become the enemy of both church and state, hunted to the ends of the world.

"I thought you had destroyed my very soul once," Cassian said. He stepped up to Cromlic, and more paver stones cracked around his feet. "I thought I would simply die." His right hand snapped up to Cromlic's throat as he rasped: "Yet I did *not* die!"

Cassian did not squeeze—his grip on the bishop's neck actually seemed quite soft—yet Cromlic's eyes went so wide that they looked as though they would burst out from their sockets. The old man began to pant wildly.

"Cassian!" a deep, oaky voice called from behind, and the old man in imperial armor who had been commanding Asango's guard—Somar Dojinko, Cromlic had called him—clamored up, his armor scraping against itself at the joints. When he was near enough, he wheezed: "You...cannot kill this man."

"I assure you I can," Cassian said, his voice laced with cold fury.

The bishop let out a shriek. His body had gone rigid, and from the way his eyes gawked up at the sky leaking tears, it seemed that he was held in some incomprehensible agony.

A silvery gauntleted hand clapped down on Cassian's wrist, and the heretic starborn turned and glared at Dojinko. The old man stared back, unblinking. "Are you going to be weak and simple now?" he said in a gravelly voice. "If you kill a bishop of the church, you will never sit the throne. You will never accomplish *any* of your goals." Dojinko edged closer still, holding Asango's gaze and hissing through his teeth: "Are you the man who can lead this great empire, or are you just some simpering child with too much power? Decide now! If you fail in this moment, you fail completely."

Cassian remained perfectly still for a long moment, still holding Cromlic with his power, and then finally he said in a quiet voice: "Thank you, my friend." He and the old soldier shared a nod, and then Dojinko withdrew his gauntleted hand.

Cassian returned his attention to Cromlic. "I shall not kill you, but I will never again tolerate your slurs of my parents."

The bishop's head jerked back suddenly, and he let out a shrill gasp. Arkas could not decipher exactly what Cassian was doing save that it was some kind of telepathic attack.

Perhaps a moment passed where the only sound in the immediate vicinity were Cromlic's shrieks. The Nemesai soldiers tensed here and there, but not one of them made a move to save his bishop

When the heretic finally drew his hand away, Cromlic stared up at him with a dumbfounded expression, tears flowing from his eyes. Cassian looked back at him and whispered: "And now *you* shall know true fear, Your Holiness."

Cromlic swallowed. He seemed to be in a state of wild confusion. Arkas could read the edges of his thoughts. The bishop knew that Cassian had done something to his mind, but he could not decipher what it was, and not knowing terrified him. He turned to Arkas, his eyes wide and questioning, but Arkas could not begin to unravel the machinations of Cassian's telepathy.

"You shall walk whatever time you have left in this world upon a tightrope just over a pit of spears," Cassian said. He bent over Cromlic. "The next time you speak of my parents – even in the vaguest sense – a massive aneurism shall trigger in your brain. I *suspect* it will kill you outright, though it may leave you alive in some twisted state, paralyzed perhaps...blinded, or mayhap it will turn you into a slurring imbecile." Cassian shrugged, "Neither of us has any means to know until it happens."

Asango's eyes narrowed then, and he went very still. For a few heartbeats, scarcely a sound could be heard in the village as all waited to see what the young man would say or do next. Then a slight grin touched his lips, and he refocused on Cromlic and said: "I have a message for you, good Bishop."

Arkas saw it then—a shifting of Cassian's brilliant green eyes to ones much darker. His smooth skin seemed to shimmer in the sunlight, refracting into wrinkles and creases that were there but were not. Angles of an entirely different face appeared, then vanished, then appeared again, and Arkas recoiled in horror as his mind stitched the pieces together into a cohesive image.

<It seems you have made quite a mess of this operation,> the oaky, rumbling tone of his father—Emperor Tacitus—came through Cassian's mouth. His dark eyes were fixed upon Cromlic in an expression of disapproval.

"Y-y-your g-grace?" the Bishop stuttered, gaping up at the phantom. He looked as stupefied as Arkas felt.

<I must admire young Asango's restraint,> the apparition said in a voice that hissed across the psychic plane. <The things you said about his mother... I quite thought he would kill you.> The shimmering silhouette turned its head to gaze about the battlefield, and Cassian's neck moved with it in perfect synchronicity, *as if they were one being*. <This is indeed quite a mess,> the deep voice sighed, and the dark eyes shifted to Arkas for a brief moment. <Some might even say a *disgrace*.>

Arkas felt more horror in that moment perhaps than when the dragon had taken his fingers. *His father had seen everything* – not only his failure, but his cowardice before Asango's threats.

"I was..." Cromlic muttered, blinking at the translucent image, "I was within my rights to come here. Even now the boy—"

<Oh, come off it,> the Emperor said, frowning down at Cromlic. <*The boy* has beaten you quite soundly, despite the fact that you had over two hundred men at your disposal, the element of surprise, and...> once again the visage fixed on Arkas in an expression of disgust, <another *starborn* in your retinue.> The Emperor turned back to Cromlic. <I have tolerated quite enough disruption to my empire.>

The Bishop gave no response, though Arkas could feel anxiety seeping off the man in waves. There could be no twisting of the truth now. Not even Cromlic would dare give an account that would contradict the Emperor's.

Tacitus's eyes swept the village. <I think it is time for you and your men to return to your temple. You gave your word you would leave after all, and Lord Asango and I have matters to discuss.>

Arkas rose slowly, his body numb. Sweat dripped into his eyes as he backed away from his father's image. For just an instant, Asango glared at him from within the glowing features, a look of lethal anger in those dark green eyes. *Now they were enemies...* Arkas turned away, feeling his limbs tremble. Had this been the Norn's plan all along? In her infallible omniscience, had she whispered the words to steer him down precisely this course? Perhaps there never would have been a duel between Cassian and himself, but now that he had done all of this... Arkas turned away, overcome suddenly with such cold terror that his eyes began to leak. He bowed his head and fell into step with the retreating Nemesai, sobbing under his breath: “Oh gods, please don’t let him kill me!”

CHAPTER 23:
A CHANCE ENCOUNTER

We think of prophecy as a gift—a light to shine our way through the darkness of time. In my experience, it has proven to be a very small light, and one that is maddeningly fixed and cannot be moved to illuminate the parts that would seem most necessary to know. Uncertainty is perhaps the cost of free will. Thus, in the end, we must strike a balance between doing as we are told and what our hearts tell us is correct.

—Taken from the unfinished memoir of Lady Gretis

Gretis knocked softly on the small wooden door of the tradesman's home. It was late in the afternoon, and she hoped this little town's legendary mute master of the suture was available. Gretis despised going to another for help, but her battle with Rakathon had left her with several deep gashes in her back that she could not reach herself, and they would become infected if not treated quickly. Her animus, for all its power, could do nothing at the moment to repair the damage done by the Archdemon.

Gretis thought on these things as her senses aligned to thin, delicate feet moving slowly toward the door from the other side. The door creaked open to reveal a beautifully sculpted face, the top of which was framed by a tied back mane of blond hair. For an instant, Gretis stared at the girl. *This was a slave?* The perfection of her bone structure, her tall and thin build, and the intelligent gaze of her blue eyes all bespoke of the highest aristocratic breeding. Still, the slave tattoo traveling down from her cheek to her neck was unmistakable. Perhaps this was a descendent of some great house—even a royal family—of some small nation laid waste to by the armies of Denigoth. Gretis knew all too well such things could happen.

"You are Livia?" Gretis finally said, remembering that the unfortunate child could not speak.

Livia nodded. There was a quiet pain behind her eyes as she stared forward.

Gretis smiled at the lovely girl. "The Vestilite sisters tell me you are without equal with a needle and catgut. I have several wounds in urgent need of sewing. If you can spare the time, I can pay quite well."

"Who is at the door?" a low, and tired sounding feminine voice bellowed from behind Livia.

"A wounded soul directed here by the Vestilite sisters in need of your slave's stitching talent," Gretis said aloud, knowing that Livia could not answer. The sisters had warned her about the crass, often drunken woman to whom this girl was saddled.

"The Vestilites?" the grating voice barked. "Yes, of course. Livia, you *fool*! Don't keep the poor woman waiting at the door."

The muscles around Livia's eyes tensed slightly, but she opened the door the rest of the way and made a smooth, inviting gesture into the house.

"I thank you," Gretis said.

Livia led Gretis into the heart of the home and gestured to a small sofa. Nodding, Gretis moved to it and sat. Livia stepped in front of her and drew out a neatly folded piece of parchment from a pocket and unfolded it to reveal a single question that stood amidst dozens of mostly erased markings. She held it up so Gretis could see the beautiful handwriting, which read:

Can you read?

"I can," Gretis said, marveling at the exchange.

This seemed to bring some small sense of peace to Livia's sullen features. She pressed her paper against the wall of her home, drew out a charcoal pencil, and began writing. After a moment, she held up the new sentences:

My stitching is free. I will go and get my things.

Gretis watched the slave disappear down a narrow hallway. There was something so intriguing about this *Livia* that went beyond her unusual condition. It was enough to draw Gretis's mind away from the throbbing pain that pervaded her body. Some part of her wished that Kota were here to meet this girl, but he could not be allowed to learn of her injuries of course. She had carefully concealed the scent of her open wounds with potions, but she was aware he had been noticing the subtle changes in her posture and voice from the pains she was suffering. Gretis had left him to sleep in the forest while she took this trip to the village along the road "*to purchase supplies.*"

The scent of alcohol permeated the air as Livia reemerged from the hallway holding a small clay bowl and cloth in one hand and a handful of catgut and a needle in the other. She carefully set these down on the table in front of the sofa and then looked up at Gretis.

"The wounds I need sewn are on my back," Gretis said, guessing what the girl wanted to know and trying to prevent her from needing to write. Livia's eyes narrowed in an expression of scrutiny. Gretis thought she knew why and said: "I fell against some jagged rocks."

Wounds on the back that required stitching, Gretis knew, usually came from victims of a whipping. It was not uncommon for a woman to go to the local Vestilite temple for healing after being flogged by her husband, which was entirely allowed in most parts of the empire. Whip-marks specifically upon the back though were more likely the result of trouble with the Nemesai Order, and that could mean "follow up" visits upon a sinner at any moment. Gretis could understand why this would make Livia uncomfortable.

She sat down on the couch facing opposite the girl and lifted her form-fitting black tunic up high enough to reveal the area of damage, and as she did, she felt the tiniest hiss come from the girl. Rakathon had kicked her so hard that parts of her skin had burst, while other sections were horribly bruised. Gretis's animus sense pulsed out and around Livia and carried information back, creating a perfect mental image of a horrified expression.

"It was a very long fall," Gretis said, keeping her voice calm.

Livia turned away, took out her paper, and began to write. After a moment, she held the sheet in front of Gretis's eyes. It read:

I have poppy tears for the pain.

"I have already taken some," Gretis lied. It was forbidden for followers of the Sansrit to consume anything that could dull their concentration. Without a sober, guiding mind, the animus that burned within her was a lethal force incapable of judgment or self-control. Thus, it was Gretis's bitter duty to bear the full pain of her injuries.

Livia gave a nod and then dipped her cloth into the bowl of astringent and gestured toward Gretis's back with a questioning expression.

"Yes, please begin," Gretis said.

The girl leaned in and began to wipe at the wounds, and Gretis was immediately impressed at her incredibly light, yet precise touch. Livia let the alcohol do most of the work for her, as she should, and only made quick, delicate dabs here and there. It was dexterous, precise work that would sterilize without inflaming the already severely damaged tissue.

Gretis shut her eyes and remained perfectly still, concentrating and relegating the tiny stabs of pain from her wounds into a distant corner of her mind. When the girl finished cleaning, she picked up her catgut and curved needle and began the process of stitching open wounds shut. Livia's work in this was elegant—better than Gretis could have done herself even. Gretis followed every tiny movement in fascination, and so she was acutely aware when the girl froze, her eyes suddenly fixing upon the bracelet on Gretis's left wrist.

"Do you recognize this symbol?" she said, raising her wrist, suddenly feeling too intrigued to hide the fact that she could perceive the girl without looking at her. She sensed Livia look up at the back of her head, the young girl's heart beginning to thump in her chest.

"It is all right," Gretis said in her most soothing voice. She turned slowly around, lifting her wrist and displaying the sculpted Dhavic character of man and spirit enjoined. "There are probably only two or three hundred people in the entire world who could recognize this symbol, but you know it, I can tell." She allowed herself a smile as she met Livia's gaze and said: "To confirm your suspicions, yes, I am a Sansrit Master."

Livia's eyes widened, and she fidgeted awkwardly and then bowed her head. Gretis let out a soft chuckle and reached out and touched the girl's chin, gently lifting her face. "Please relax, my dear. You have nothing whatsoever to fear from me, I swear it. I would like to ask you though how you learned the symbol of my art."

Livia hesitated, then drew out her paper and pencil again and put them on the table in front of the sofa so Gretis could see her write:

I saw it in Toklius's Eastern Histories, I think.

"Toklius's works are written in the scholar's language if I remember correctly. Can you read Dhavic?" Livia nodded. "Fluently?" Livia nodded again.

Gretis smiled at her. "That is quite an academic accomplishment for someone outside of a religious order, let alone a slave. May I ask, did you have a life before you belonged to this family?"

Livia gazed down and shook her head in the negative.

"How did you learn then?"

Again, Livia used her paper to communicate:

The Vestilite sisters taught me a little. My master sometimes trades in ancient texts, and I used some of them to teach myself the rest.

"Goodness," Gretis laughed, gazing at the girl. Through her animus, she perceived every muscle fiber in Livia's body, the beat of her heart, and the temperature of her skin. The child was being entirely honest.

Just then Gretis sensed movement from behind and turned to see an enormous woman come huffing into the room, her hair a disheveled mess of red-dyed tangles, her face a smeared mosaic of thickly applied makeup. The woman's body was enveloped by a white, silk nightgown covered in stains.

This hefty figure looked Gretis up and down for a moment, her eyes rather obviously fixing on the pieces of jewelry that Gretis wore. Then she smiled and said: "You must be a noblewoman, like *me.*" She emphasized the last word by placing a hand on her chest and speaking with the reverence one might use toward an elder starborn or a god.

"I am highborn, yes," Gretis said, keeping her voice neutral. She immediately disliked this woman. "I am afraid though that my family has many enemies, and I cannot give my surname. You may know me as Lady Gretis."

"Lady Gretis," the woman repeated with a nod. She moved into her kitchen and retrieved a clay urn, which she uncorked and moved to her lips. The glaze on the woman's eyes as she drank suggested the liquid was wine. When she finished, she said: "I am Merith Sondal, but I come from the house of Akilion. You may have heard of my grandfather, the great Senator Markus Akilion."

"I regret I have not," Gretis said.

This drew the faintest expression of irritation from this Merith Sondal, who muttered: "Well, perhaps your family has not risen quite so high as the imperial senate. No matter." She turned then and glared at Livia and said: "All the same, you should be honored to serve one of the nobility." Her gazed returned to Gretis as she added: "I am afraid this sullen little harlot thinks at times that she is too good to take orders from her betters."

"Indeed," Gretis said, and she found herself edging a little in between Livia and this horrible woman. She could sense Livia's muscles tightening at the embarrassing exchange. "I find I am quite impressed with her work."

"At least she is able to do *some* things right," the woman said with a sigh. "Truly though, she doesn't hold a candle to Iona, my favorite slave."

Gretis drew in a sharp breath at this name, her mind flashing to the moment she had watched a young girl obliterate an archdemon in an explosion of white light. *Could it be the same child?* She looked at Livia, who was staring down at the floor, and then returned her gaze to the lady of the house and said in the most even voice she could manage: "Where is this Iona?"

"Off with my husband," the woman said with a sigh. "They are traveling North on business."

"Just the two of them?" Gretis said, feeling her heart quicken.

"Yes," the woman grunted after another long sip from the urn. "He did not *ask me* if he could leave with my favorite slave. He just *took her* and went, and I was left to attempt to decipher what had happened from this useless mute." She gestured at Livia.

"I am sorry," Gretis said, staring at the crude woman. She felt a powerful urge to take Livia from this place. Perhaps she could purchase the brilliant young girl, or abscond with her, or just hack this *Lady Sondal* into several pieces as her animus seemed to wish. But this was a delicate matter, requiring thought.

"We of the nobility must bear our burdens with dignity," Lady Sondal said with a nod as if to herself, and then she turned and began to walk back toward her bedroom.

"Yes, of course," Gretis said as she watched the repulsive creature disappear down the hallway. She turned back to Livia, who was blinking at the wall, her face marked with resigned anger. "I am so very sorry," she said quietly.

Livia gazed up at her, and there was perhaps some vague relief or even excitement that someone—*anyone* understood what she was going through. After a moment, she picked up her needle and catgut and somehow managed to communicate entirely through her eyes the phrase: *Should I resume?*

"Yes, please," Gretis said. She turned away and offered up her injured backside once again. As Livia returned to her clever stitch-work, Gretis's mind rolled different pieces of information around. *This was not a coincidence.* If she had been *meant* to see Iona destroy the archdemon, then, logically, the same strings of fate were playing a role here. *But why?* The Norn had told her that Iona was not her concern. There had been no hint of any role to play in the child's destiny, even tangentially.

Gretis considered Livia's strange inability to speak. Surely if it were due to damage to her vocal chords, the girl could still manage to whisper, but she seemed unable to use language in any form other than writing. Was it due to magic of some kind? A curse? Gretis had traveled to many corners of the world and witnessed all manner of afflictions of the arcane, but never had she seen anything like this. *But it could not be a coincidence.* Livia's condition and Iona's unbelievable power had to be connected somehow.

Gretis clenched her jaw. *What was she supposed to do?* She might well be the only mortal in the whole world that understood what Iona was—or at least had *some understanding.* The little girl in the forest was of enormous importance to the fate of the world, and as Gretis looked within herself, she found she believed Livia was as well. It seemed wrong to leave the two of them to the mercy of their vulgar mistress, and yet Gretis had already expressed concern over Iona being a slave to the Norn herself, and the oracle had answered: "*She is exactly where she is meant to be.*" Still, there had to be a reason Gretis had been guided to this particular home to this particular girl. There was no clue she could see that shed light on that purpose, save who she was—the connection she had to both these children.

"I was a slave for a time," Gretis finally said as the girl finished the final stitch. The words caught Livia by surprise, and Gretis sensed her go still. "I was not born into it as you were but was *taken* after my family's kingdom fell to the unstoppable Denigoth military. I came to belong to a high ranking officer and he...*used me* as crude men use women." Livia slowly edged around Gretis so she could meet her eyes, an expression of concern on her beautifully sculpted face.

"It was the worst time of my life," Gretis whispered, gazing into the girl's crystal blue eyes. "The rest of my family was put to death, and I was left alone to a fate more horrible than any I had ever imagined. I thought I would die from despair." She reached out and took Livia's hand and said: "But someone rescued me—an incredible person who saw something in me I never would have dreamed was there."

She cast Livia a kind smile and said: "I do not know you, my dear, and perhaps I am wrong, but I sense in you both the desire and *the capability* of rising above your status. I wish to tell you that it *is* possible, even for a slave girl."

Livia stared at her, bewildered by the words. Gretis cast a quick look down the hall to make sure the lady of the house was still in her room, and then she reached down and untied her coin sack from her belt, retrieved a few silver pieces for her journey home, and then held the rest out. In a soft voice, she said: "I *must* insist on paying you for your fine stitch work on my back. Please accept this."

Livia hesitated, staring at Gretis, and then she slowly reached out and took the bag. When she undid its opening and looked inside her eyes went wide, and she drew in a gasp.

"There should be roughly four thousand desseks in there," Gretis said.

Livia began to breathe very quickly as she stared down at the silver and gold in her hands. Gretis put a hand on her arm and whispered: "That should be enough to purchase your freedom and perhaps that of another slave, with still a fair bit left over." She watched the child go still at these words, a look of uncertainty flashing on her face. Gretis felt nervous herself at what she was doing, afraid she was interfering with destiny as the Norn had admonished her not to do, but her heart told her this was right. "I am certain a girl as clever as you has hiding places. I suggest you tuck this money away and think carefully. You are quite young, and many paths may yet open up to you—perhaps avenues you never imagined. The money will be a resource for you if and when you need it."

Livia continued to stare into the pouch for a long moment, and then she carefully placed it on the floor to the side of the sofa in a place the woman of the house would not likely see if she sauntered out. Then she took her pen and paper and wrote a single word, which she held up for Gretis to see:

Why?

"Because I know what it is to feel powerless," Gretis said. "Because I see a touch of myself in you." She smiled and added: "We slave girls must look out for one another, and I have acquired a fair amount of wealth for myself and can easily afford to do this." She rose slowly and pulled her tunic down her newly stitched backside and then added: "And please know that you have a friend and ally in the North. I have made my home just outside the Northern Onkai temple, and I invite you to call upon me if you ever find yourself in my corner of the empire."

Gretis could see exhilaration in the mute girl's eyes, and she watched as Livia went to her paper and began to write with a trembling hand. When she finished, she held the sheet up, and it read:

I do not know how to thank you. I can scarcely believe your kindness.

The girl looked as though she were about to cry, which almost pained Gretis. It would be a far more logical thing to buy Livia and free her then and there. Such a large sum of money in the hands of a mute slave could bring suspicion. But that level of interference would definitely be going too far—*if she had not gone too far already...*

Gretis steeled herself, banishing the uncertainty from her mind. The gods or fate or some other force had brought her to this girl, and she could not have walked away doing nothing. Gretis had faith that this Livia would be shrewd enough to use the money correctly. That was what the universe seemed to be demanding of her in all of this: *faith.*

"The money is only a fraction of the kindness that was once given to me when I had a need," Gretis said. She drew in a slow breath, wondering how much more she dare say. If any of her assumptions about Livia were correct, the girl would face enormous danger someday. "One more thing," she finally said in a soft voice. "If you are ever in trouble and Onkai soldiers are near, write them one of your notes explaining that you are a friend of the Blade Witch. Every member of the order knows me, and any will give you aid if you invoke my name, including even the Bishop himself." Livia blinked at these words, and Gretis leaned in and whispered: "Remember, Lady Gretis, the Blade Witch."

The girl drew in a breath and returned to her paper, writing four words, which she held up:

I shall never forget.

Gretis smiled. "Good." She gave her tunic a final straightening and then said. "It was very nice to meet you, Livia. I hope we shall reencounter one another someday."

The mute girl cast a gorgeous smile, her crystal eyes welling with hope and profound gratitude. Gretis nodded and then turned back toward the door, her stomach fluttering. *So much depth and intelligence in a slave...*it was a great wrong, and it made Gretis wish to side with the Asango boy and all of his radical plans for the empire, despite what she feared he might become.

As she reached for the door, her mind sifted through the impressions her animus had carried back from the slave behind her. It had not detected a latent aura of one with the sorcerer's gift, nor any other swell of power that Gretis had thought to find—*not at first.* But now she finally felt something small and distant. There was a tiny flicker in the darkness that shined for less than a second. *What was it?* Some sleeping power within the girl? Something broken? It was not like the awe-inspiring force that burned within the other slave—it was not like anything Gretis had ever felt.

She shook her head and stepped out of the small home. *These were things she was not meant to know.*

CHAPTER 24: THE ELF AND THE STARBORN

How many innocent souls died because Cassian Asango could not accept the world as it was? He thought he knew better than the long-established traditions and social customs of his entire race. He thought he knew better than our Gods!

—Bishop Arodias of the Anti-Cassonian Church

"We are being watched," Thalice said in a quiet voice as she ran her fingers through the grass beneath her. She was lying back against it, feeling the tickling warmth in the morning sun.

"I know," Cassian said, his hands behind his head as he stared aimlessly at the drifting clouds. "I can feel your people's enchantments all around us. Many soldiers stand ready to kill me right now."

Thalice could not help sitting up and glancing around. Even to her elven eyes, they were alone on the edge of a quiet meadow surrounded by nothing more than trees and mountainside. "Have you developed the capacity to feel other elves like you can me?"

"I cannot feel anyone like I feel you," he said.

A smiled touched Thalice's face almost involuntarily, *as if she were a human girl.* "You make my people...uneasy. You are a mystery to them. No one in my palace can comprehend why you have come here without a military escort and allowed yourself to be surrounded."

"Human emotion," he sighed. "I needed to see you."

She swallowed. "Why?"

"I came close to death, and I thought of you," he said.

Thalice blushed a little as she laughed: "And so after coming close to dying, you decided to illegally trespass onto the lands of a people who owe you no mercy?" She heard the dark edge to her voice. This was *his* sardonic humor taken root within her mind because he was near. "Do you not fear them?"

"No," Cassian said with a callous shrug, "but they should fear me."

Thalice sensed an edging nearer from all directions. Dozens of elite soldiers awaited the order to kill. "Your life could end right now," she whispered, not meaning it as a threat so much as a warning.

"I doubt it," Cassian sighed, still gazing at the clouds. "Elves are patient and calculating; not given over to acts of impulsive violence even for the sake of pride. They will, of course, remember that I have the last of Promethiock's children bonded to me." Cassian's tone shifted, becoming like steel the way human voices could. *He was speaking to her kingdom now rather than her.* "Dragons are creatures of fierce loyalty and long memory. Titus is a fledgling now, but in six or seven hundred years he may be strong enough to come here and tear your lovely palace to pieces, and then hunt down every elf on the continent—perhaps even in the whole world."

Thalice could sense ripples of trepidation among her people at his words. Unlike them though, she did not fear the wild starborn, and she said: "Such lovely words you come to share with me. What other threats shall you level before our visit is done?" *Again, she sounded like him...*

Cassian chuckled and relaxed back down onto the grass. "Tell them to turn their minds away and let us be."

"Is that a demand?" Thalice said.

"It is a request for courtesy," he muttered, rolling his green eyes, "and I shall take offense if it is not granted. They may interpret that as they will."

Hundreds of elves were acutely observing through the open conduits of Thalice's eyes and ears. There was hesitation among them for a long moment, and then, one-by-one, their psychic minds drew away from hers.

"It seems you have frightened them," Thalice whispered.

"I apologize for my brutish tactics."

"Is that an apology to my people, or only to me?"

"Only to you," he said with a slow breath. "Your people are no longer listening."

"You find amusement in exerting pressure upon beings hundreds of years older than yourself."

"I strive hard to rise above such pettiness," Cassian said, his tone seeming to convey he had not entirely succeeded at this and felt a touch of shame. This was part of his duality, she knew from their interchange of memory. His brazen side caused him guilt, and yet he was in love with it.

"The soldiers remain near, my Cassian," Thalice said with vague nod in the direction of the palace guards, if only to playfully remind him he had not fully won.

"Our relationship is not without complication," he said.

"No, it is not," she said gently. "We have this time together, as you desired. What do you wish to discuss?"

"Everything," he said. "Have you unraveled all the nuances of the human world from my memories?"

Thalice frowned. "No, not yet. So much of what you gave me is strange—alien even. I have yet to decipher the vast majority of it, and yet I possess all of your mind, as you have all of me."

"I think it shall take my feeble human intellect a decade at least to analyze all your elven memories," he chuckled, "yet I believe my task is far simpler than yours. So much of what I gained is calm and logical. What you took from me must have been utter chaos by comparison."

Beautiful chaos, Thalice thought, but did not say. She felt trepidation at the idea of defining what she and Cassian had shared. It had changed her to such a degree that she was virtually an aberration among her own people, but telling Cassian of this would only fill him with guilt. Thus, she turned the conversation to more tangible matters: "Tell me of your defeat of the Nemesai."

"Hmm," Cassian grunted, blinking and shifting his thoughts. "I overcame their incompetent attack." He did not sound particularly proud. "Cromlic is humiliated, but not ultimately beaten yet. Still, the defeat was extremely valuable. So much of the Nemesai Order's power comes from the perception that they are invincible acolytes of divine justice. I demonstrated to the world they are not."

Thalice could feel the depths of Cassian's anger as he spoke. This victory had done little to slake it. *No elf could ever hate as a human could.*

"What did the Emperor have to say to you?" she said after a moment.

Cassian let out a low sigh and resumed gazing up at the clouds. "Tacitus had warnings for me."

"What were his warnings?" Thalice whispered.

"That I must face the natural consequences of my actions."

She frowned. Cassian's mind was there, but she could not pull pieces of thought from it to clarify the meaning of his cryptic words as she might with another elf. There was less comprehensibility to their connection, and yet so much more emotion, and what she felt in Cassian seemed to be grim resignation.

<What might be the *natural consequences* of your actions?> she transmitted.

Cassian telepathically responded in kind: <My own execution, for one.>

<Your emperor would have let you come to harm?>

<It was my series of decisions to provoke the Nemesai that led them to come for me. If I were unable to protect myself from the obvious repercussions of those choices, I would not be worthy to sit the throne of Denigoth.>

"So, he would have let them cut your head off?" Thalice said, returning to verbal speech.

"Most likely, yes."

"How barbaric," Thalice whispered.

This brought a dark smile to Cassian's lips. "This not a friendly contest. The Denigoth Empire governs more than eighty percent of the human race. Its ruler *must* be competent. Too many lives are at stake for it to be otherwise."

Thalice blinked. So much of his world still seemed incomprehensible to her elvin sensibilities. "Your own people consider you to be a 'living miracle.' To put your life at risk seems absurd."

"It is a test of my character—*my resolve*," Cassian said. "The empire is infinitely more important than even the life of a starborn, and so it should be."

"Still, your contest seems so brutal and...*primitive*."

"Do you look down on us?"

"I suppose I do," she said.

Cassian chuckled. "Elves are so wonderfully honest."

Thalice returned his smile, knowing that her Cassian possessed what his people called 'thick skin' to the highest degree. "Deception is not a part of our culture as it is yours."

"We can be very dishonest, yes, but there is more than one kind of integrity, my dearest," Cassian said with a sigh. "You may scoff all you like at our militaristic ways, but it was *we* who fought Daibok and his vast army of demons when they came, while your people crouched in their hidden cities."

Thalice felt a touch of bristle inside her stomach—like Cassian's sense of humor, she was feeling his human combativeness. "We are not your keepers. Elves are beings of peace who live in harmony with nature and strive to expand knowledge, while humans consume every resource they lay eyes upon so they can reproduce and spread over the land as no creature has before. You made *yourselves* into the most significant target in the world."

"You are correct," Cassian said, "you are *not* our keepers, and so we must keep ourselves. Our strength is in our numbers, and our defenses are in the great cities we construct and the metals we pull from the world to forge weapons. In all your condemnations, you might keep in mind that humanity accomplished something the elves could not in four thousand years: *We defeated the legions of hell.*" He exhaled up at the sky: "Twice actually."

Thalice narrowed her eyes. This was dangerous territory. Cassian knew the history of her people as no human should ever understand it. Their connection had granted him *all* of her memories. He knew the location of every elven city in the world, he could speak and read their language, and he had as strong an understanding of their resources as she did. That made him a threat to the elves, particularly given the fact that he might well become the next Emperor of Denigoth. Their two races were ultimately competitors who could easily come to war someday. That was why many in her kingdom called for his death. Cassian surely suspected this, and yet he lay back so relaxed, for the Great Dragon had burned away all his fear.

"You should be careful with that pride," Thalice said in a quiet voice. "Daibok's armies were only able to swell to their great numbers because so many of *your people* were willing to damn their souls in exchange for eternal life."

"Yes, we can be quite ugly creatures sometimes," Cassian sighed.

"*You* are not ugly," Thalice whispered, and she slid her hand across the grass to his. The rough, mortal fingers felt so warm and live.

"I think about you often," he said, his voice changing. "Do you think of me?"

Every minute of every day, she thought, but only answered: "I worry for you." It felt strange to hold back, as a human girl might. Images of her Cassian's death sometimes passed through her mind, filling her with anxiety. She clutched his hand tighter. To be without him in the world felt horrifying.

"Is it even possible to win the contest now?" she asked. "Would your people accept a ruler who essentially placed a death curse on a bishop of the church?"

"Of course they would," Cassian said. "Cromlic is one of the most feared and despised men in the world, and I made him look a fool. Many will be grateful to see the mighty Nemesai knocked off their pedestal." His voice lowered as he added: "And anyhow, he called my mother a whore. I was only defending her honor. Even Emperor Tacitus found my actions acceptable."

Thalice weighed these words. She still did not understand humans well, and perhaps never would. "Why did Tacitus appear at the end of the battle? Was it to stop you from killing Bishop Cromlic? Would he still have spoken if you had lost?"

"To the second question, I do not know, but I doubt it," Cassian murmured, glancing up at the clouds again. "As for my killing the Bishop, I had already decided not to take the action, and I believe *that* is why Tacitus appeared. I had passed a test, and my Emperor rewarded me...or perhaps it was simply of no more use to him to have the Nemesai on the attack. A balance must be struck, after all, between putting a potential heir to the throne through trials and keeping peace in the empire." Cassian drew in what sounded like a troubled breath then and whispered: "When all of it was over though, Tacitus did give me a single command."

Thalice felt a strange tingle spring up through her from where her hand was clasped with Cassian's. Before she even processed what was happening, his psychic tendril slipped into her mind. "Forgive me," he said in a soft voice as she felt it happen: *he obliterated a memory from her brain*.

Thalice drew her hand back with a sharp gasp, staring at her mortal companion. "What did you do?" she whispered.

Cassian looked at her, his face cold and sober. "You took an incredibly dangerous state secret from me in our exchange—one that I was forbidden to reveal to anyone."

She stared down at her hand, still feeling his touch upon it. "This meeting was a trap," she said.

"I had to do it," Cassian replied, and there was neither pride nor remorse in his voice. "Tacitus would kill you for knowing what you did—it is a secret that could unravel the empire itself. I promised him I would take it from you. This was the only way to save your life."

Thalice swallowed, edging back. "What did you take?" Even as she asked the question, she sifted through the network of her memories. Within the tens of thousands of moments both of her life and his, there seemed to be an empty void where something that had been very important—something very troubling to Cassian—had been. She blinked, tracing the edges of this black hole and muttered: "It was about one of the other starborn: Arkas Adronicus."

"Such an ordered mind you possess," Cassian said, breaking his gaze with her and leaning back onto the grass with his hands clasped together behind his head.

"Why did you not simply ask me?" she said, narrowing her eyes.

"Informing you ahead of time I was going to remove a piece of information from your memory would cause you to think very hard about said information. It would create dozens of new associations in your mind, making my task much more difficult, as well as dangerous to you."

"How did you know I did not write it down or share it with some of my people?"

"I know you." Thalice stared at him. *Of course, she had not shared anything of their association, nor written down a single word.* What they had shared was more intimate than anything she ever had, or likely ever would experience again. It was private and sacred to her. It was also something that no one among her cold and logical people could ever understand.

"I know you as well, Cassian," she said, hearing the anger in her voice. She lay back down on the grass next to him, though she did not take his hand this time. It was not ultimately surprising that he would do such a thing. For all his great passion, Cassian had a cold, even ruthless side to his nature. He would do what he believed to be necessary, *whatever it was,* even if she hated him for it. And yet he probably knew, as she did, that she could never hate him. After a moment, Thalice said in a bitter voice: "Am I safe then?"

"I believe so," he said.

She rolled her eyes. "And are *you* safe? I assume from what you've said that if Bishop Cromlic succeeds in convincing the other bishops to agree to your execution, your Emperor will do nothing to stop it."

"Your assumption is likely correct, but Cromlic cannot win such a vote. He knows this as well as I, else he would have held a conclave instead of rushing into his illegal attack on me."

Once again, Cassian's memories proved too nebulous within her to provide a clear and easy understanding of his assertion, so she said: "Please explain."

The young human sighed: "What does Cromlic have? Only one order is with him: the Diaphans."

"Your priests class," Thalice said, the association coming immediately, and then she frowned. "But I thought the Lucinians—"

"It is slightly confusing," Cassian sighed. "The Lucinians educate, and the Diaphans preach. The chief difference is that Lucinian monks share knowledge of mathematics, language, science, and academic study of the Holy Enumis, while Diaphan Priests manipulate people with emotionally driven speeches designed to frighten them into sheepish obedience and giving large donations to the church."

"Such a cynical summation," Thalice sighed. "I wonder why they are against you."

"Not all of them are bad," Cassian said with a shrug. "In all truth, quite a few are honest men who feel a calling to faith." He smirked. "However, their bishop is specifically against me because I have dared to write, among other things, about the wide-spread practice of faking faith miracles with actors planted amongst crowds of peasants to be called up and *healed.*"

"I see," Thalice said. "That is two votes for your execution then."

Cassian sat up a little straighter. "So, what do I have?" He held up one finger and said: "The Vestilite Order supports me because I spend a great deal of time and money doing what they do: healing the sick and feeding the poor, and because they have been fundamentally against what the Nemesai have become for decades." He extended a second finger. "The scholarly Lucinians are also in disagreement with the actions of the Nemesai, and their Bishop has become obsessed with my visit to Promethiock. He has already sent three letters begging me to let his monks study my dragon." His two fingers wiggled. "Those orders are extremely valuable to me, but Cromlic could probably bully the both of them to his side if not for my dear friend, Bishop Otho, of the Onkai." Cassian chuckled up into the clouds as he said: "Cromlic is about as intimidating to him as a yappy dog is to a grizzly bear."

"That seems tenuous," Thalice said. "If Cromlic were desperate enough, he could have one of the other bishops assassinated, could he not? Then he could work to have the man replaced with someone on his side."

Cassian rolled his head sideways on the grass toward her and said: "There are *rules*. The Emperor would never tolerate such a disruption to the order of his empire, and Cromlic could not carry out the assassination of a bishop under the nose of an elder starborn."

"Yet your *Emperor* tolerates Cromlic's attempts to quietly assassinate you."

"Yes, since I was eleven," Cassian said with a shrug. "I believe he sees it as another test of my resourcefulness. I see it as simply another element in the equation of my path to the throne, and certainly not the one that troubles me most."

Thalice locked eyes with Cassian. "You mean something *actually* troubles you?"

He flashed her a bewildering grin and said: "So strange to see scorn on your elven face. How long shall you despise me?"

"Centuries," she hissed back, though she found herself oddly unable to resist returning the smile. Cassian extended his right hand toward her, offering it, palm up. Thalice hesitated, but then took it, and the instant she did there was a dizzying increase in the flow of his wild human emotions.

"You give me peace," Cassian said in a low, breathy voice, his eyes shut. "*Nothing* gives me peace."

"Answer my question," she almost panted, "What troubles you the most?"

"My brother," he whispered, "*my equal*, Dimitris."

Thalice blinked. She had impressions of Cassian's one great rival. The two of them had never met in person, but they knew each other well. They continually studied one another's capacity and accomplishments. There was respect between them, though it was grudging.

"Cromlic asked Dimitris to come and help with my arrest," Cassian said. "If my brother had agreed, I would be dead right now or in chains." He let out a low sigh. "Dimitris did not warn me, but he did not come either."

"What do you discern from that?"

"From that and so many other things, my brother desires to defeat me honestly." Cassian blinked several times, staring down at the grass as he whispered: "I will almost certainly have to kill him to ever sit the throne...unless he kills me first."

"Which outcome do you fear more?" Her grip on his hand tightened. "You have never taken human life before, and you do not have to. You know this. You can abandon this deadly game before it consumes your soul and—"

"Do you really think I am going to abandon anything?" he muttered.

"No," she said in a tone of irritation, "you are far too stubborn and too self-righteous."

"Agreed," Cassian exhaled, "though I sense you have more to say. Please hold nothing back, my dear."

She scowled at him, frustrated by his amusement. "Despite your intelligence and empathy, you can be unbelievably single-minded, and choose to be most of the time. You possess an almost manic faith, but it is directed at *yourself* rather than the gods."

"I am what I need to be," he whispered. "Faith is an incredibly potent mental tool that allows one to overcome fear and misery, and self-doubt—it empowers the mind to think through nigh impossible obstacles." He looked deep into her eyes as he added: "But you are *wrong*. My faith is not only in myself but in my people. I walk in the dreams of hundreds every time I close my eyes. I see all the untapped genius—the unrecognized moral strength that exists within the vast multitudes that await deliverance from their antiquated and illogical bondage. I love them, and I am going to tear my empire's ugly hierarchical system to shreds and empower the so called *peasants* and *slaves* to become what I know they can be."

Thalice stared at him for a moment, then said in a quiet voice: "I know you love your people, but you are different than when we met. Your heart—your *mind*—I do not understand what Promethiock did to you, but I can see the change, and it frightens me."

He leaned in so close to her face that she felt the heat of his mortal breath on her skin. "The dragon's fire made me pure," he whispered. "For all his determination, the boy I was before might not have been strong enough to keep his head when surrounded by hundreds of Nemesai, but I think I can face *anything* now. No matter what lies in my path—no matter how many are against me and how powerful they are—I will believe in myself and keep fighting. That is the truth I found in my heart as the flame burned into everything I was."

Cassian leaned back and gazed at the sky once again. *He truly thought he could take on the world.* What would she do now that she was so inextricably linked to this wonderful, half-mad human? Being near him made her happier than anything else in the world, yet in the deepest recesses of her soul, she felt a growing sense that her Cassian was doomed, and he would doom her with him...

End of Book I

DEDICATION:

This book is dedicated to my wife, Angelique, who has been more supportive of my writing than I ever had any right to expect. Her focused, positive thinking and near superhuman resourcefulness have been the fuel that has allowed this train to finally leave the station. She is my partner, my best friend, my most important reader, and the one who kicks me in the ass when I get stuck, and for that I shall forever be in her debt.

ACKNOWLEDGMENTS

Editor – Angelique Russell
Editor – Stephen Parolini
Proof Reader – Kristina H Russell

Wattpad Proof Readers who have provided me with invaluable help, mentioned here as I have known them, in their usernames:
“Ectheldir”
“DragonKingCole”
“Writing-new-worlds”
“Finish-your-book”
“SkyAngel_”
"TheGybberishGod"
“Alainson8”
“Disneymedley”
“Joshua _Timi”
“Jhatka”
“Steenee”
“Jaderock101”
“WillPische”
“Ame84”
“Darthschrik”
“JimmyRichardson9”

Thank you so much for your feedback and encouragement. This has been a wild ride, and it was good to have all of you with me on the way.

AUTHOR'S SOCIAL MEDIA

Website: www.dragontoothpress.com/Authors

Twitter: @AuthorRussell

Facebook: Search "Age of Asango" to join the fan group

42597682R00209

Made in the USA
Middletown, DE
15 April 2019